MY ONE MONTH MARRIAGE

SHARI LOW

Boldwood

First published in Great Britain in 2020 by Boldwood Books Ltd.

Copyright © Shari Low, 2020

Cover Design by Lexie Sims

The moral right of Shari Low to be identified as the author of this work has been asserted in accordance with the Copyright, Designs and Patents Act 1988.

Every effort has been made to obtain the necessary permissions with reference to copyright material, both illustrative and quoted. We apologise for any omissions in this respect and will be pleased to make the appropriate acknowledgements in any future edition.

A CIP catalogue record for this book is available from the British Library.

Paperback ISBN 978-1-83889-199-2

Ebook ISBN 978-1-83889-201-2

Kindle ISBN 978-1-83889-200-5

Audio CD ISBN 978-1-83889-250-0

MP3 CD ISBN 978-1-83889-687-4

Digital audio download ISBN 978-1-83889-198-5

Boldwood Books Ltd
23 Bowerdean Street
London SW6 3TN
www.boldwoodbooks.com

This book is dedicated to my aunt, Liz Murphy Le Comber, an incredible woman of strength, substance, wisdom and talent who will always be the yin to my yang.
To Rachel and Eleanor Le Comber, who are just all kinds of awesome. I adore you both.
To the memory of my uncle, Dr Steve Le Comber, who will forever be the missing link in our family and our Trivial Pursuit team.

And as always, to my menfolk, J, C & B... Everything, always. X

YOU ARE CORDIALLY INVITED TO MEET THE BRIDE AND GROOM'S FAMILY AND FRIENDS...

The Bride – Zoe Danton, 33 – strong, driven partner in the cutting-edge marketing company, The B Agency, still tender after being dumped by the love of her life.

Tom Butler, 31 – Zoe's business partner (present tense) and the man who broke her heart (past tense).

Chrissie Harrison, 31 – Tom's childhood sweetheart and mother of his twelve year old son, Ben.

Roger Kemp 44 – hotel chain owner and client of The B Agency. Married to Felice, 26, a model who last smiled sometime in the nineties.

Sister of the Bride - Verity Danton, 34 – an exercise-obsessed primary school teacher who works with kids and doesn't even pretend to like grown-ups.

Ned Merton, 32 – Verity's colleague, friend and the object of her affections. She just hasn't told him yet.

Sister of the Bride – Yvie Danton, 31 – the youngest sister, a nurse on the geriatric ward of Glasgow Central Hospital, funny, kind, caring and the best friend that everyone should have in times of fun and crisis.

Charge Nurse Kay Gorman, 35 – Yvie's best mate in and out of work. A single parent, raising her son, Chester, 6.

Dr Seth McGonigle, 38 – socially awkward and perfectly formed orthopaedic surgeon, married to the head of cardiology.

Carlo Moretti, 30 – Yvie's friend and waiter in the whole Danton family's favourite Italian restaurant, owned by his father, Gino.

Sister of the Bride – Marina Danton-Smythe, 35 – the eldest sister, a wealthy helicopter mum who runs her family's lives with military precision.

Graham Smythe, 35 – Marina's husband of thirteen years, a wealthy banker, who has somewhere along the years changed from being her dashing Alpha male to a workaholic bore.

Oscar and Annabelle Danton-Smythe, 12 – Marina's phone-obsessed twins.

Mother of the Bride - Marge Danton Walton Morrison, 53. Now on her third husband, Derek, 55, and it already looks like he's going to have as much marital success as their father, Will (divorced in 1999), and Marge's second husband, Gregor (divorced 2008).

Father of the Bride - Will Danton – Marge's first husband and father of the Danton sisters.

1

I'm in one of those unofficial clubs that no one really wants to be in. You know, like the 'Association of People Who Got Jilted at The Altar'. Or 'The Secret Society of Dumplings Who Let Online Scammers Empty Their Bank Account Because They Believed They Had A Long-Lost Uncle Who Left Them Millions In His Will.'

In this case, I'm Zoe Danton, the latest fully paid up member of the 'Collective Of Fools Who Had Marriages That Lasted For Less Time Than A Four-Part Mini-Series.'

A month. Thirty days to be precise.

It's not even as if I have the folly of youth as an excuse. Thirty-three years on this planet is long enough to learn some vital life lessons. For healthy oral hygiene, always floss morning and night. If it sounds too good to be true, then it probably is. If you get caught in a riptide, swim parallel to the shore. Pot pourri has no purpose. And if you're getting married, ensure that it'll last longer than the flowers you carried up the aisle.

Otherwise, you'll be me, the idiot who is sitting on her

wide plank, oak floor, consumed by fear that the local newspaper will use my story as a human-interest feature, surrounded by gifts that I need to return. Except the cocktail shaker. That one's already open and in use.

'Do you feel like an idiot?' Verity asks, handing me a drink that's so pink it could very well be radioactive. She was the first member of the Sister Emergency Service to respond to my text and rush over to my city centre Glasgow flat. I hope she kicked the bin bags containing the last of my short-lived husband's things on the way in to our marital home. Actually 'marital home' is a stretch. It's my flat, a one bedroom waterfront apartment in an eighties block on the city side of the Clyde, and even though he's lived with me for the last year or so, I realise now that it always felt like he was just visiting. Maybe that should have been a hint. So, to answer Verity's question, did I feel like an idiot?

'No,' I lie, only to be met with her raised eyebrow of cynicism. I capitulate like an eight year old caught spray-painting the school toilet walls. 'Okay, of course I do. I mean, even Kim Kardashian's shortest marriage lasted seventy-two days. It's a sad day when I make worse life choices than a reality show star who built her career on the size of her arse.'

I take a sip of... 'What is this?' I ask, when my taste buds throw their hands up, at a loss as to what they are faced with.

Verity shakes her head, her deep red ponytail swinging as she does so. Even on a Sunday morning, in the midst of this traumatic episode in our family's history, she still looks great. My elder sister has been on this earth for fourteen months longer than me and something happened in those fourteen months that gave her a level of physical superiority that the rest of us could only aspire to. She's one of those women who has visible cheekbones and naturally fiery, thick long red hair, so you could pretty much put her through a car wash and she'd come out the other end, sweep her hair up in a messy bun and look fabulous. Even more annoying, she has absolutely no awareness of this. Her appearance and personality are the complete opposite of each other. On the outside, fierce, bold, striking. On the inside, restrained and the most conservative of us all. Now she is shrugging. 'No idea. I just put a bit of everything in the fridge into the cocktail shaker. There's gin, cream, raspberry juice, pineapple—'

'I don't have pineapple juice,' I interrupt.

Verity doesn't break stride. 'Crushed pineapple from a tin... you'll find it lurking at the bottom of the glass. Vitamin C has so many benefits...'

'Will it prevent me marrying dickheads in the future?'

She glides right over that. 'No, but it does help with the absorption of iron, decreasing blood pressure, combatting heart disease and...' Off she goes into full education mode. This is what happens when one of your three sisters is a primary school teacher. Not only is she relentlessly organised and can calm a class of stroppy eight year olds with some kind of Jedi mind trick, but she has a remarkable memory for facts and an absolutely pitch-perfect technique for delivering them.

Unfortunately, in this case, her pupil has zoned out. What does it matter what is in there? As long as it contains alcohol that will reduce my feelings of general crapness by even one degree, I'm game.

There's a crash at the door.

'What have I missed?' Yvie wails as she enters the room, balancing several plastic bags and a tray giving off a distinctly 'lasagne' aroma on her forearms.

I swallow a slither of pineapple. 'Just some rampant self-pity, wails of regret and general pathetic wallowing.'

My younger sister nods thoughtfully. 'All just as expected then. Will lasagne help? Jean, one of the cleaners on the ward, made it. She says it's her ancient, traditional family recipe, but she's from Paisley, has no Italian ancestors and has never been further than Great Yarmouth on her holidays, so I have my doubts. In saying that, I'm starting the diet tomorrow, so no point letting this go to waste.'

Dropping the bags on the floor, she wanders out in the direction of the kitchen clutching the lasagne, the stiff blue trousers of her nursing uniform rustling as she goes. The youngest of the four of us, Yvie is a nurse on a geriatric ward at Glasgow Central Hospital. When I'm in my dotage, there's no one else I want to look after me. Although, I'm hoping that she'll tend to my every need on the fourteenth deck of a cruise ship floating around the Caribbean, rather than in an aging Victorian building on the edge of the city centre with a bird's-eye view of the nearby motorway. Still, she loves her job and nursing is what she has always wanted to do. Even when we were kids, she got an undeniable thrill when one of us needed emergency first aid.

I hear the sound of the oven door banging shut, before she re-enters with a glass of radiation pink. 'I took some of this from the cocktail shaker,' she informs us. 'It looks suspiciously like something I'd prescribe for acid reflux. Right, what's the latest? Married anyone else since I saw you yesterday? Divorced yet? Engaged again?'

I refuse to rise to her innocent-faced sarcasm, instead going for dry threats and indignation. 'If you carry on like that, I'm going in to work.'

'It's Sunday,' Verity points out, always one to insert facts into the equation.

'And I hate to point out that your job was at the root of this whole debacle in the first place,' Yvie adds, following it up with, 'Jesus, my bra straps are killing me. Did I mention I'm going back on the diet tomorrow?'

'You did. Is it the same one as last week? And the week before?' Verity teases.

'Not sure, but right now I'm hoping I lose nine and a half stone of smug older sister,' Yvie fires back. She takes no cheek from anyone and I love her for it.

'I thought you were embracing your curves?' I enquire, confused.

'That was last week. This week, I want to book a holiday, wear a bikini and I've realised that to feel good about that I'll need to lose the equivalent of a small dinghy in weight in a month and a half. Starting right after that lasagne.'

I don't argue. Only a fool would get in between Yvie and her ever changing body-confidence issues.

'Anyway, I preferred it when we were revelling in your disaster of a life,' she tells me. 'Where were we?'

'Where were we?' It's like an echo, only said in a voice that is sharper than the other three in my living room. Marina, only her head and neck visible round the side of the door, is the oldest of the four of us and the designated grown-up. She's the kind of woman who makes lists, has a pension plan and who knows the difference between a vintage bottle of plonk and something off the shelf at Lidl.

'Yvie has just pointed out that my job was to blame for all this.'

'Yes, well, she's not wrong. At least at the start. Although, to be fair, you did take an unfortunate situation, handle it

badly, then let it descend into a complete roaring balls-up,'
Marina concurs before her head and shoulders disappear
and I hear the sound of her clicking heels fading as she heads
down the hall to the kitchen. I'd bet my last pound that she is
carrying a bag containing sushi and hummus – she considers
healthy food to be the only option, even in a crisis.

Yvie gestures to the door. 'See? Even her Highness agrees.
I finally feel validated as an adult.'

I ignore the playful barb. Successfully negotiating life
with three sisters is fifty per cent love, thirty per cent toler-
ance and twenty per cent dodging the ever-changing
dynamics between us.

Especially, in this case, as they both have a point. My job,
first as sales director, then latterly as partner of Glasgow
marketing company, The B Agency, definitely contributed to
my current situation. If I hadn't worked there, I wouldn't have
met Tom. I wouldn't have fallen in love. He wouldn't have
broken my heart. And then I wouldn't have gone on to screw
up my life so colossally that I'm now contemplating eating
dodgy lasagne while wondering what I am going to tell my
mother when I return her generous wedding gift of a lavish,
smoked glass beaded chandelier. Granted, it is lovely – in a
blingy, wear sunglasses because it's so bright it could cause
eye damage, kind of way. But the fact that I live in a flat with
low ceilings transforms it from an ostentatious decorative
statement to a concussion risk.

But back to the point. Yvie and Marina are right. If I
worked anywhere else – the Civil Service, Top Shop, NASA –
then none of this would have happened.

And to quote everyone in the entire history of the world
who ever messed up, I just wish I could go back in time and
change so many things.

In fact, right now I'd settle for just understanding what has happened to my life because there are still so many questions. So many uncertainties.

My phone buzzes and I stretch over a ceramic planter in the shape of a pair of wellies (from Auntie Geraldine – she has a picture of Alan Titchmarsh on her kitchen wall) to retrieve it from the table beside the sofa.

Marina's heels click into the room and in my peripheral vision I can see that she slides elegantly into the armchair by the window, plate of sushi in hand.

The name at the top of the notification makes my anxiety soar. Roger Kemp. Sadly, no relation to anyone who was ever a member of Spandau Ballet. Or that slightly scary bloke who played Grant Mitchell in *EastEnders* and now makes documentaries about criminal gangs and serial killers.

With a shaking thumb, I swipe open the message.

Roger Kemp is a friend and client, the director of a hotel chain that employs our agency for all its marketing needs. After the proverbial hit the fan, I'd asked him for a favour. A slightly underhand, confidentiality-breaching, possibly borderline-illegal favour. With a bit of luck, the bloke that makes the documentaries about true crime won't find out about it.

I'd asked Roger to check on who paid for a room in one of his hotels last weekend, on the night that my husband broke his vows only thirty days after making them. You know, that fairly insignificant one about being faithful in good times and bad. You see, I know it wasn't my husband because he'd put his credit cards in my handbag that evening, so it must have been someone else. The other woman.

The thought forces me to take another swig of the unidentifiable pink cocktail.

Anyway, the favour I'd requested of Roger would mean asking someone in his financial team to pull up the credit card records and sharing the sordid details with me.

Now I stare in disbelief at the answer, typed right there on the screen of my phone.

This didn't come from me and I'm sorry – the name on the credit card was Ms Danton.

Fuck. Fuck. Fuck.

One for each of the three of my sisters. And yes, I'm aware that I'm not yet in possession of the facts, but right now, I don't feel like being balanced and reasonable.

The idle chit-chat in the room stops as each of my sisters, Marina, Yvie and Verity, spot my expression and realise that something is very, very, wrong.

Marina, always direct in any situation, is the first to react.

'Oh God, what now? What is it?'

Without even realising what I'm doing, my gaze goes from one of them to another as I speak.

'I just need to know...' I say, my voice low as I struggle not to choke on the words. 'Which one of you slept with my husband?'

2

ZOE – EIGHTEEN MONTHS BEFORE

Princes Square, a gorgeous shopping centre on one of the busiest streets in Glasgow, had always been Zoe's favourite place for a pre-festive lunch. On the Friday before the chunky bloke in the red suit and beard was scheduled to arrive, and despite a mighty hangover from the annual work's Santa Shindig the evening before, she knew – just absolutely knew – that this was going to be her best Christmas ever. Oh yes, it was all going so well. She'd worked her arse off to become sales director at The B Agency, an up-and-coming marketing company that was based in uber-cool city centre offices. She was madly in love with Tom, one of the two founding partners, and the most thoroughly decent, not to mention cute and sexy guy she'd ever known. Life was great. Actually, it was spectacular. That afternoon, as Tom and Zoe rose in the glass lift of the upmarket, luxury shopping and dining emporium, climbing the height of a beautiful, cone-shaped, ice-white tree that soared from the ground to the fourth floor of the stunning atrium, she was positively oozing happiness.

Mistake. Huge. Mistake.

She'd barely sat down in one of her favourite restaurants when she sensed that something wasn't quite right with the love of her life. Not to come across as gushy nor needy – because she was neither – but she truly felt that's what he was, and for the first time ever she was in a relationship with someone she could actually envisage a future with. They'd been best friends and work colleagues for years, a couple for six months and there was a gift-wrapped key to her home under her tree with his name on it.

'Looking handsome today, Mr Butler,' she told him as the waiter disappeared with their coats and their drinks order. Water for Tom, champagne for her.

Okay, so that was a bit gushy but she was awash with festive joy, so it was allowed. Unfortunately, it also threw up the first sign that something was off. Normally, he'd compliment her right back, but today he said nothing. She let it go. It was Christmas. His grandfather was unwell and in hospital. His estranged father was on his way from Australia and due to arrive later that day. The guy had things on his mind.

Oblivious to the juggernaut headed her way, she went on, 'I've said to my sister that you'll try to make it for Christmas dinner.' As always, Marina was hosting the festivities and it was being run with military precision. 'I know it'll be difficult with your grandad being ill and your family being here, but I'm hoping you'll get a chance to slip away. Or maybe you could bring your parents? I'm dying to meet them and I'll have to do it at some point, so Christmas dinner is as good a time as any. Marina always lays on far too much food anyway – I think she's doing turkey, ham and steak pie this year – so there will be loads to go round. I was going to pick up a gift for your parents this afternoon, so they won't feel left out. I want to make a good impression on your mother—'

'Stepmother,' he corrected her. His weary tone was warning number two, but she missed it again. Clearly her emotional radar was sitting in a corner, pissed on mulled wine, watching reruns of *Elf*.

Still oblivious, she went on, 'Of course, stepmother. Anyway, I was thinking we could nip to Vivienne Westwood and pick up something nice, maybe earrings, for her. And for your dad—'

'Zoe, we need to talk.'

There it was. The first line of almost every break-up speech in history, yet still she didn't register the vibe. Must have been getting to the good bit in *Elf*. 'Yes, of course, darling. You don't think you'll make it for dinner? It's fine. I understand. I really do.'

'We need to talk about us.'

This time she paused, reality finally dawning, dread swooping right in after it.

'About?'

Aw, crap. Crap. Crap. *Say you want to discuss the weather. Or the price of tinsel. Anything but—*

'I can't see you any more. I mean, outside work. In a relationship.' He was stumbling. 'I'm sorry. I hate to do this, I really do. I've had a great time with you but—'

'Who is she?'

'What?'

She took a slug of the champagne that had just been placed in front of her, resisting the urge to ask for the bottle for pain-numbing purposes. Sixty seconds ago, she couldn't see this coming, yet now she absolutely knew it was going to hurt like hell.

'Who is she? There's someone else.' On the outside, she was calm. Measured. On the inside, she was fourteen and having a bigger emotional break than when she'd discovered that Slash from Guns & Roses had got remarried to someone who wasn't her.

'I promise there isn't,' Tom vowed.

Zoe thought about it for a few seconds. Of course, there wasn't such a thing as a 'type' that cheated, but if there were, then Tom would be a founding member of the Monogamy Club. She'd never seen him so much as use someone else's milk from the office fridge. He was honest. Decent. Upstanding. So, if there wasn't someone now, then it had to be...

'But there *was*?' It had to be someone from his past. She'd always wondered why a guy like him had reached thirty and never married, settled down or even had a relationship that lasted longer than the one they were currently having. Or currently ending.

He didn't answer. Suddenly, she hated being right.

'An ex,' she charged on. 'How long ago?'

His whole body slumped in surrender. 'Twelve years ago.'

'Twelve years? But you must have been—'

'Eighteen,' he replied.

No. Come on. He was chucking her for someone he'd dated at a time in his life when he lived in student digs and survived on Pot Noodles?

'And you're seeing her again?'

'No. I haven't seen her since.'

'For God's sake, Tom, you were a kid. You can't still have real feelings for her. You're seriously dumping me for the memory of some high-school girlfriend?'

'I know it sounds crazy but—'

'There is no "but". It's completely bat-shit crazy.' She realised that sounded harsh, so she immediately ramped it down and came back a little more conciliatory. 'So, did she break your heart and leave you scarred for life?'

'No. I broke hers.'

'Oh, for fuck's sake,' she groaned. 'This is what I get for choosing a nice guy for once. I bloody knew it was a mistake. So, go on then, tell me. How did you break her heart and why did you not fix it before now?'

He sighed, as if *he* was the one having the bad day. 'It's all a bit tragic and pathetic.'

'I like tragic and pathetic,' she countered. 'I was supposed to be having lunch with my boyfriend, but he just dumped me, four days before Christmas. Right now, I'm cornering the market in tragic and pathetic.'

That tipped him over into a space where his pity for her made him relinquish and spill the whole story. The bullet points were something like boy meets girl, parents don't approve, they split up and boy moves to Australia, they lose touch, he comes back, can't find her, every day since then, he regrets what he's done. Now, nine years after he left her, he's just discovered where she is and he can't stop thinking about her.

Zoe knocked back the rest of her champagne and signalled for another. This was definitely a three-glass conversation. Four glasses, when he admitted that he now felt an irrepressible need to go and see his ex, share his feelings of regret and beg her for another chance. Zoe thought about pointing out the folly of his ways but could see it would be fighting a lost battle. He was torn up, conflicted, rattled. She had to let him go and get answers and just hope that he would come back to her.

She drained her glass. 'Then I think you need to finish it, one way or another, otherwise you're going to live a lonely life, Tom,' she said, not unkindly. 'And if she's married, with sixteen kids, and has an arse the size of Govan, give me a shout. In the meantime, I'm going to go to Vivienne Westwood for some consolation retail therapy.'

She left him with the bill, then went and shopped out her feelings. One pair of Vivienne Westwood earrings later, she didn't feel any better, so she took the only reasonable, mature path... She showed up at Verity's school at 3 p.m., just as the final bell of the term was ringing, with two bottles of Prosecco and a yule log, and she begged her to go and drown her sorrows with her. When it came to her choice of sister, she was hedging her bets. Marina would undoubtedly have the kids, and as for Yvie, with her crazy shift patterns at the hospital, there was a better than average chance she'd be working. Verity was definitely the best option, given that she had a social life of monastic levels. 'I'd rather read a book. Or wash my hair. Or rearrange my knicker drawer,' she'd say when they were teenagers and Zoe was trying to drag her out to a club. Wild social abandon and spur-of-the-moment parties had never been Verity's thing. In fifth year, she'd required at least a week's warning if any guy wanted to kiss her under the mistletoe at the school disco, and even then she'd bailed out early because she said her boob tube was giving her a friction rash under her arm. Zoe, on the other hand, would walk on heels until her feet bled, wear jeans that cut off circulation to her lower limbs and a ponytail so high and tight it gave her a migraine, for the sake of looking great and snagging some bloke she had her eye on.

True to form, Miss Danton, primary three teacher and Best Behaved Sister of the Year Nominee, didn't capitulate easily, which – admittedly – put Zoe's hackles up. It's not as if Miss Uptight had anything else planned. However, she was a chucked woman on a mission, standing in the middle of a school staffroom, surrounded by snowman pictures made out of cotton wool and buttons, and she didn't give up easily.

It took some persuading, a whole lot of pleading and a fair amount of emotional blackmail, but eventually Verity agreed.

Much, much later, Zoe would look back and think that if only Verity had said no, then she wouldn't be sending back the wedding presents.

3

VERITY – EIGHTEEN MONTHS BEFORE

'Miss Danton, the Virgin Mary's skirt is tucked into her knickers!'

Verity had never wanted a day to be over more. The nativity play was on its second run of the day and so far they'd had three sobbing sheep, a wise man who punched the innkeeper because he claimed he stole his playtime Wotsits, Joseph had dropped the baby Jesus twice and now Mary was having a wardrobe malfunction.

Thankfully, Crystal McNamee, aka The Virgin Mary, heard the comment and swiftly modified her robes.

'Thirty-five minutes,' came a voice just behind Verity's left ear, as she stood at the side of the stage, praying her class of eight year olds would nail the first verse of 'Away In A Manger'. The questionable high notes had compelled an elderly gent to take his hearing aid out at the morning performance. Probably just as well. No matter how much she'd drilled the correct words into them, a confused few were still singing that the baby Jesus had no crisps for his bed.

Behind her, she could still feel the presence of her

colleague. Was she imagining it, or could she feel his breath on the back of her neck? And should she really be contemplating how sexy that voice was when she was in close proximity to several biblical characters and the local vicar, who was sitting in the front row with the other invited guests?

'Sorry? I couldn't hear you over the sound of "Away In Manger".'

His face came within inches of hers. It wasn't an unpleasant sensation. In fact, it was the closest she'd come to an intimate encounter in longer than she chose to remember. When she'd been working with the kids on writing letters to the House of Claus, she'd been tempted to write her own.

Dear Santa, please bring me a love interest for Christmas. I've been way, way too good. And not that I want to appear too demanding, but if I can specify the aforementioned love interest, please make it Ned Merton, my fellow teacher, he of the River-Island-model looks and the husky voice. Thank you.'

Her attraction to Ned Merton had sparked on the first day she met him when he joined the school a few years before. In the last year or so, though, it had grown to almost fantasy proportions, despite the fact that she'd heard rumours that he'd dated at least three of the other teachers and one of the office secretaries. Not that the women in question had confided in Verity. She had no interest in personal chat or joining the cliques in the staffroom. She preferred to go in, do her job and leave. Anyway, none of the alleged relationships had lasted, so if the gossip was true – and it probably wasn't, given that the staffroom was worse than the playground for exaggerated tales – then all it meant was that they hadn't been right for each other. No harm in that, was there?

Now his husky voice was whispering in her ear. 'Thirty-five minutes and then we're out of here for three whole weeks. I'm counting the minutes.'

'Me too.'

That was true. But while she was fairly sure that Ned Merton was counting down to some kind of post-term revelry, she was staring down a night of gift wrapping, card writing, and perhaps – if she felt really wild – a bit of ironing and then a five mile run before bed. Alone.

'A few of us are heading out after work today. Fancy coming along? Just into town for a few beers, something to eat and a general rant about how we're overworked and underpaid.'

She shouldn't. She absolutely should not. She had things to do. Gifts to wrap. Cards to write. Trainers to pull on. And she'd rather be tied to a tree with tinsel and starved than socialise with the rest of the people she worked with. But this was Ned Merton. And she did concede that somewhere in her mind – although not in a weirdo, stalkerish way – she'd replaced the whole 'nativity' scene characters with her, him, a non-virgin birth and the inclusion of a comfy room at the Holiday Inn.

Did he feel it too?

Dear Santa, PS: Can I also have some joie de vivre and a more carefree attitude. Thank you. x

Sod it. Why not?

'Sure, that would be great.'

A general murmur in the audience distracted her from his reaction, then a giggle that escalated and spread and...

Oh, dear God. The baby Jesus had now been propped up in a corner and told to watch TV while Mary and Joseph wandered off the other side of the stage, claiming they were 'going for a snack'. You take your eye off a religious tradition for two seconds and suddenly a biblical couple are up on child-neglect charges.

Verity swooped round behind the curtain to the opposite side of the stage, ambushed Mary and Joseph and ushered them back into the spotlight, to more hilarity from the audience – which would have been highly mortifying if it weren't for catching Ned Merton's eye and being rewarded with a wink and an empathetic grin.

Half an hour later, play over, bell rung, kids dispatched, Verity boxed up the day's Christmas swag. There had been an article in the *Daily Mail* about how pupils' parents were trying to outdo each other with Christmas gifts for their little darlings' teachers, splashing out on Prada purses and Chanel perfumes. Not around here. She bundled up approximately fifteen boxes of Roses and Quality Street, five supermarket scented candles, six bottles of wine and a Body Shop gift set that had definitely been sitting in someone's bathroom cupboard since the nineties. Not that she'd become a teacher for the material rewards. Her career choice had been down to a real desire to pass on knowledge. The real desire for Ned Merton came later.

Hands full, she tapped the staffroom door with her foot and, as it swung open, she jolted, then flushed, as a grinning Ned held it for her to pass through. For a split second, her spirits soared and she was sure, for the first time, that this wasn't a one-way thing. Was he attracted to her too? Why else would he be smiling from ear to ear, why would he look so happy to see her, why would those gorgeous eyes be twinkling with merriment? It had to be...

'Zoe!' Her sister. Half leaning, half sitting on the window ledge, a bottle of wine in one hand, and a mug in the other. Going by the flush of her cheeks and her slightly swaying frame, Verity guessed it wasn't the first. 'What are you doing here?'

'I've come to take you out for a Christmas drink,' Zoe chirped, as if this was the most normal thing ever. Verity counted up in her head the number of times they'd been for a Christmas drink – or in fact, *any* post-work drink – and it amounted to precisely zero.

'But why?'

She caught Ned's flinch of surprise at her reaction and immediately reminded herself to adjust her tone, understanding that 'short and snippy' probably wasn't the usual reaction when your sister pitched up and announced she wanted to take you out.

Zoe didn't let it dissuade her from the cause. This wasn't a surprise. Zoe hadn't let anyone get in her way since she was six years old.

She held up her wrist to her face so that she could peer at her watch face.

'Because, as of, eh, two hours ago, I'm officially single and I've nominated you to be the person who comes with me to several bars, listens to me ranting and tells me he's a complete bastard who didn't deserve me anyway.'

Verity's reaction was instinctive and admittedly poorly thought through. 'It's over with Tom? You're kidding! He's so lovely!'

Zoe rolled her eyes in disgust. 'I don't think you're getting the hang of the whole "tell me he's a bastard" thing.'

'Sorry.' Verity took a short pause to think. Buggery bollocks. This was what happened when it finally looked like she might finally be jump-starting her dead love life. A sister in a crisis just pulled out the plug.

Why couldn't Zoe have got dumped on any other day?

Did it really have to be the very afternoon that Ned Merton had asked her out? Okay, so not strictly asked her out on a fully-fledged date, but that was just semantics. Now she was in a no-win situation – say yes and she blew her opportunity to get to know him, say no and she'd look like a heartless cow and he'd probably avoid her for ever more. And that lot in the manger thought they had problems.

'The thing is we were actually already planning to go out tonight and...' She flicked a glance at Ned, who immediately put his hands up.

'Don't worry about that. This is an emergency situation that clearly trumps post-term celebrations.'

Zoe's face lit up. 'No, it's perfect. A celebration sounds like a much better idea. I've got at least a week and a half for self-pity and bitter recriminations, so I'll start tomorrow instead. As long as you don't mind me tagging along with you tonight.' Her hopeful face was completely irresistible...

Except to Verity, who did her very best to resist it.

'Well, the thing is, it's just the teachers and—'

She was immediately drowned out by Ned. 'Of course we don't mind. It'll be great to have you with us. It'll stop us talking shop all night. Good plan! Right, I'm just going to grab a quick shower, then I'll be right with you.'

Off he trotted to the male locker room next door, leaving Zoe looking decidedly apologetic. 'Sorry. I feel like I've completely hijacked your night.'

'You have. But it's fine. It was just a few drinks anyway.'

'Good. So... not a date then?' There was a hint of a tease in there that Verity chose to overlook.

She shook her head. 'No, not at all.' Years of experience had taught her to keep everything to herself. The minute you told one sister that you wanted something, everyone was in on the act and they either teased you, took it from you, or added so much drama it became an ongoing mini-series. She hadn't seen her pogo stick since it mysteriously disappeared from her room in 1996 and she was fairly sure Zoe – ever the businesswoman even then – had flogged it to buy a space hopper. Of course, the acquisition of a sister's possessions had never progressed to boyfriends, but Verity wasn't up for testing the theory.

Zoe took a swig from her wine mug then grinned. 'Good. Because you know that old adage about the best way to get over someone? I think I just found the perfect candidate for my rebound guy. At least for tonight.'

Verity felt six boxes of Quality Street simultaneously begin to tremble in her arms. Seriously? It had taken years to get to the 'going out for a drink' stage with Ned Merton and Zoe wasn't swooping in and claiming him. 'Oh, I think he's erm... in a relationship with someone,' she lied. 'Look, why don't you and I just head out now. Just the two of us. We were going out with a few of the other teachers and they'll bore you to death anyway. I'll let you cry on my shoulder all night and I won't complain once.'

'As long as there's alcohol involved, I'm in. Although, Ted—'

'Ned,' Verity corrected her, bristling.

'Ned...' Another swig of wine. 'Would have been a lovely distraction. Sorry, I'm objectifying him and I know that's wrong, Miss Political Correctness 2018...'

Great. So now she was getting teased. Still, at least it beat Miss Stick Up Her Arse 2012–2018, which had been her previous moniker within the family. Why, oh why was this happening to her? Why couldn't Zoe have crashed Marina or Yvie's nights?

'But, in my defence, I just got chucked. Did I mention that?'

'You did.'

'So tonight I'm having a night off from being a grown-up. I may even objectify several members of the opposite sex, so you might want to get a pair of earmuffs on.'

Verity's teeth clamped tight to stop her biting back. It never changed. She was a grown woman. She had a professional career. She owned a house, a car and made healthy contributions to her pension. Yet, in the presence of an irritating sister, she still had occasional urges to thump her with a pillow and then go complaining to their mother about how Zoe was being a cow, trying to steal her stuff and it wasn't fair.

'I can handle it. Come on. Grab this stuff and help me out to the car.'

'As long as I can take the wine,' Zoe nodded to the box of bottles at Verity's feet. 'And I can't guarantee it'll all make it home safely.'

Verity shrugged. It would be a small price to pay to get her out of here and away from Ned Merton. And as for her crush? There was always next year. Or perhaps she could call him over the Christmas holidays. No, not a call, a text. Yep, that would be easier. She could come up with some work pretext and then maybe suggest they meet up somewhere that wouldn't be spoiled by interference by anyone else. Especially someone who came from the same womb.

She watched Zoe drain her mug, then put it down on the windowsill. She swallowed the urge to complain that it would leave a ring on the wood and insist that her sister wash it and put it on the drainer. No time. Let's go. Vacate the area. Abort Mission Ned.

They were almost at the door when it opened.

Ned's delight was obvious.

'Great, you're ready! I've texted the others and told them we won't make it. They're just down in some pub near here anyway. Thought we could head into the city, make a night of it.'

Verity's heart sank. She hated city centre bars. She hated the noise, the chaos, the prices. Total rip-off. Although, she'd have been more than happy to endure it if it was just her and Ned and a cosy corner for two. Not three.

'A man after my own heart,' Zoe was agreeing.

Damn. Now if she refused she'd look like... like... Yep, Miss Stick Up The Arse, 2012–2018.

New plan. She'd go along with it and hope that Zoe had such a head start in the vino stakes that she was in a taxi and on the way home before seven o'clock. Then she and Ned could go out for dinner, perhaps somewhere quiet, somewhere they could really talk and get to know each other better. Then she might even invite him back to her house. She kept it spotless so she never had to worry about unexpected guests. Not that she ever had any. She much preferred life to be organised in advance. That thought gave her a glimmer of hope that it might just work out after all.

'Here, let me get that,' Ned was saying now, as he took a box containing six bottles of wine from Zoe's arms. 'Verity, do you need me to grab anything else?'

Me, was her first thought, but she kept that to herself. There was plenty of time to work on that tonight. Much as she loved her sister and would give her the world, there were limits. She had been prepared to let the pogo stick go, but Ned Merton?

Heartbroken or not, her sister wasn't taking him too.

4

Yvie was hanging a large gold ball on one of the slightly threadbare tree branches, when a scene in the corner of the day room caught her eye.

'Babs, back away from the target. Take a hint, my love.'

Babs, all seventy-nine years of her, rolled her eyes, breaking her expectant stare at Cedric, who was trying his best to pretend he was reading a two day old newspaper, which he was holding up in a strategic position between their faces.

Conceding defeat, Babs pushed her Zimmer in Yvie's direction, then lowered herself into an armchair and tossed a branch of mistletoe over the shoulder of her bright red jumper emblazoned with the words 'Gangsta Wrapper'.

'Bloody useless stuff. I remember when it meant something. You could have a year-long drought, but as soon as the mistletoe came out, the lip action was on.'

'Can't be using that nowadays, Babs. You'll end up on a watch list. The Mistletoe Prowler. Armed with a small branch and a wave of nostalgia.'

Despite her malcontent with the modern world, Babs let out a cackle of laughter. 'At least it'll be more bloody interesting than this place. I'll give you next month's pension if you break me out of here.'

Yvie dangled a flashing snowman from another branch. 'Can't. I'd miss you too much. And so would Cedric. Avoiding you is giving him a real purpose to his days here. You're great for getting his activity levels up.'

Babs snorted out another cackle. That was the thing about Yvie's favourite patient; she could dish out the banter, but she loved it when someone came right back at her.

Yvie reached up to place the last reindeer on a high branch. The tree had originally been put up on the first of December, but the lovely Mr Dawson (rheumatoid arthritis, requested custard with every meal) had clipped it with his wheelchair and sent the whole thing crashing down behind him this morning. Restoring it had taken Yvie the best part of an hour after she'd finished her shift, but it was worth it. It gave the patients and their families a little bit of normality at what was invariably a difficult time.

Ward 54 was the long-term geriatric ward at Glasgow Central, and Yvie had worked there since she'd qualified eight years ago. Other friends in the profession had moved around, tried out different fields, but from the moment she'd started her rotation in geriatrics she knew it was where she belonged. Of course, this specialty brought heartbreak, nursing so many patients in the final chapters of their lives. But nothing else had come close to the enjoyment and fulfillment she got from working with people who were around long before internet and smart phones, who had stories to tell, lives to recount. And who, in the case of Babs and the many others like her, were still determined to make every day count.

'Right, Babs, that's me off for the night. I'll see you in the morning.'

'Not if I manage to escape during the night. I just need to think of a way to distract the bouncers.' With that, she gestured to the window that separated the day room from the corridor, where the senior charge nurse, Kay Gorman, was marching from one end of the ward to the other. 'There's a wumman that could haunt a hoose,' Babs said archly, her Glaswegian brogue thick with disapproval.

Yvie did her best to hide her amusement with a professional attitude. Kay was her best mate, but she conceded that she did give off a slightly stern aura. Underneath, she was pure mush though.

'I'll pass your comments on to Charge Nurse Gorman.' She couldn't keep up the formality: 'You know, in case she's looking for a new hobby. House haunting might work.'

Babs' chuckles were still ringing in her ears as she headed out into the corridor and down past the nursing station.

'What's set Babs off this time?' Kay asked, an amused glint in her eye.

'Mistletoe. Don't ask.'

'Is she still calling me a torn-faced old boot? Or was that just yesterday's slight?'

'Nope, she's got you haunting houses now.'

'Excellent. I think that means I must be growing on her. Anyway, are you still okay for tomorrow?'

'Absolutely.'

It was their only day off together all month and they'd planned shopping, eating, drinking and general Christmas merriment before Yvie clocked back on for five days straight.

Yvie always worked double shifts Christmas Eve, the 6 a.m. to noon shift on Christmas morning, then double shifts on Boxing Day and the day after to let the staff with young families – Kay included – have as much time off as possible. It suited Yvie perfectly, as it meant she got to spend Christmas morning with her patients, then make it in time to Marina's for the family lunch.

'What plans are you two hatching now then?'

Yvie felt herself jump at the sound of the voice behind her. Why? Why, bloody why did Dr Seth McGonigle have this effect on her? Just the mere appearance of him made her feel flustered and judged and she wasn't sure why. Her only theory was that her buttons were pressed by the cool, accomplished perfection of him. Not that she found him attractive. Definitely not. There was a long list of reasons why he absolutely wasn't her type. Number one, he was very much married to a very aloof, perfectly formed cardio surgeon who worked out of the fourth floor. Number two, he was a health-obsessed exercise freak who cycled to work every day and he made her self-conscious because she had forgotten to go to the gym. For approximately 654 days in a row. Number three, in the two and a half years that he'd been the consulting orthopaedic specialist on this floor, he had been all brusqueness and barely offered a single moment of friendliness. And number four...

'Not sure yet, but it involves shopping, cake and it will probably end in a karaoke bar with me murdering "Last Christmas".'

Number four – she always blurted out nonsense when she was in his presence.

Again, why, bloody why? Since the first moment he'd crossed the threshold into their ward, rubbing sanitiser into his hands as he strode purposefully towards the nursing station, he'd caused some kind of chemical reaction in her brain that proved that when intelligence was mixed with professional decorum and Seth McGonicle, the result was a mortifying explosion of verbal diarrhoea.

He took a moment to digest the karaoke comment, before he shrugged, muttered a clearly unimpressed, 'Whatever floats your boat,' and sauntered off.

Yvie's head thudded down on to the top of the nursing station, while Kay giggled.

'You tit. You're trying to impress him with Wham songs?'

'Don't say another word!' Yvie stopped her, then picked up her bag and gave Kay a doleful kiss on the cheek. 'I just don't get why he can't smile and be friendly. And I'm not trying to impress him – I was just being nice. Even so, I can't believe I said that. I'm away home to wallow in my shame and incompetence in private.'

'Are you sure you don't fancy him maybe just a little?' Kay asked, sceptically. 'Because, you know, he's cute. And fit. And smart. With only one major potential character flaw...'

'Which is?' Yvie asked, even though she really, really, didn't want to.

'He might not know the words to "Last Christmas".'

Yvie paused. 'I need a new friend,' she said archly and took off, trying not to giggle, despite Kay's laughter following her all the way down the corridor to the exit.

The car park was deserted, and so were the roads. Eight o'clock at night on the Friday before Christmas clearly wasn't prime driving time. Only twenty minutes later, she was turning the key to her flat in the Southside suburb of Busby. Yvie often thought it would be easier to move nearer to work, but then she came home, to her lovely little home overlooking the river, and all thoughts of moving evaporated.

In her bedroom, she took off her clothes and dropped them in the laundry basket, pulled on a onesie – fur leopard print – and brushed her teeth. She'd once read that brushing the teeth reprogrammed the mind and made it less likely that you'd over eat afterwards. Final rinse completed, she contemplated the fact that she still did it even though she knew it was a load of bollocks, all the way to the fridge in the kitchen.

Okay, pre-prepared salad (made the night before from a Weight Watchers recipe). Chicken breast with wholemeal rice? (Slimming World). Two chicken breasts (Keto). Or maybe she should just shut the door and stick to the intermittent fasting plan she'd decided on when she woke up that morning.

Her stomach rumbled the answer. She was tired. She'd worked a twelve hour shift and then stayed behind afterwards to redo the tree. It was the Friday before Christmas and she was at home, alone, at nine o'clock at night, while the rest of the world was getting into the festive spirit. Sod it, she deserved to be nice to herself.

The chicken and sweetcorn pizza was out of the freezer and in the oven before she could stop herself. At least the sweetcorn had to count as one of her five a day. Oh, and take that, minty fresh breath.

Two opposite waves of feeling squared up against each other in her gut. Delight and anticipation held hands on one side, knowing they were about to be comforted by the giddy delight from Chicago Town. While a knot of disappointment gathered speed as it twisted up to tornado level. Seriously? Where the hell was her willpower? Her discipline? Her self-pride?

The ticking hands of the clock above the oven door were a welcome distraction as she spotted they were counting down to ten seconds to nine, eight seconds, five seconds, three seconds, one...

Her phone rang, right on schedule. It wasn't even necessary to look at the screen.

'Hi, Mum,' she answered. 'How are you doing?'

'I'm leaving him, Yvie. I've made my mind up this time.'

Sighing, Yvie opened the fridge again, took out a bottle of Prosecco and, cradling the phone under her ear, popped the cork and poured a large glass. Again, sod it. It was empty calories, but it was worth it to get through what would undoubtedly be at least twenty minutes of her mother discussing plans to leave her husband. Poor Derek. Husband number three, and it was beginning to look like he was going to join her second husband (divorced 2008) in the Marge Danton Walton Morrison World of Past Tense.

Yvie felt her skin prickle as she thought about the first person who belonged on that list. It was twenty years this month since their father, Will Danton, had left. There in the morning, gone by nightfall, deserting them before Yvie even made it to her teenage years.

The shock of the cold wine hitting her stomach snapped her from the memory and halted the emotional train that was plummeting downwards.

Back to the call.

'Why, Mum?' She should have said, 'Why today?' or 'Why this week?' The threat was frequent and consistent, only the reasons changed.

'Because what's the point? Seriously. What. Is. The. Point?' Marge wailed.

Decision time. Make some urgent excuse and cut it short

or commit to what would undoubtedly be a long, agitated ramble, which would include several self-help quotes and at least one reference to Oprah Winfrey.

Reluctantly, but with an air of resignation, Yvie took her phone from her ear, switched it on to speaker and placed it on the counter. Only when she was braced, prepared, and had her wine back in hand, did she give the cue to open the floodgates.

'The point of what, Mum?'

'Of staying when he doesn't nourish my soul? He just wants to give up. To sail into old age. I'm fifty bloody three, not eighty-three. I need more in my life, Yvie.'

'I know you do, Mum.' Her very best sympathetic tone. Drawer open. Plate out. Another drawer. Pizza Cutter. A pang of guilt. Solution. Open fridge again. Retrieve salad and decide to only eat half the pizza, and to have salad with it. Another one of her five a day.

'You know, Oprah says we all have to live in our truth...'

Hell no. Fridge open again. Salad back in. This was a whole pizza kind of night.

The timer on the oven dinged just as her mum was winding up the conversation. 'So I'm going to suggest he comes to yoga with me in the new year. I feel it's his last chance to make an effort.'

'Good idea, Mum.' Pizza cutter in action. Six slices in seconds. Glance at the phone screen. Nineteen minutes her mum had been on for. Pretty much standard.

'Anyway, I'd better go, Yvie. I want to get some reading in before Graham Norton comes on. Keeps the mind active.'

'Okay, Mum.'

Wait for it. Here it comes.

'Right then. How are you anyway, pet?'

There it was. The question to which the only desired answer was...

'I'm fine, Mum.'

'Lovely! Right, I'll talk to you tomorrow then. Cheerio.'

Click.

Yvie carried her plate and wine glass through to the living room and plumped down on the sofa, before flicking a few buttons on the remote control. What was she in the mood for? She consulted her Sky planner and went for *Grey's Anatomy*. There was nothing in this world that couldn't be solved by an interlude with Amelia Shepherd, Meredith Grey's flawed, spiky, funny, and unpredictable sister. In her mind, they were kindred spirits – minus the alcohol addiction (Amelia's), the trail of gorgeous lovers (Amelia's), the size 8 jeans (Amelia's) and the large chicken and sweetcorn pizza (Yvie's).

The first bite of pizza had barely been taken when the phone rang again.

Verity. Sigh. Answer. She could hear what sounded like music and revelry in the background.

'Hey, lovely, what's up?' Yvie answered.

A pause. A sniff.

'Verity, are you crying?'

Another pause. Then a launch. 'No, I'm not bloody crying, I'm bloody seething. Remember Ned?'

Yvie felt her teeth clench. What now? 'Of course I remember Ned.' She had met Mr Merton when, accompanied by a reluctant Kay (bribed with a bottle of plonk and a night's babysitting into coming with her), she'd gone into Verity's school to talk to the students on career day. She'd extolled the virtues of caring for others, talked about social responsibility (right over the heads of the younger classes) and how fulfilling it could be to play a part in restoring someone to health. At the end of the final session, she'd asked how many thought that would be a cool job and got zero hands up. None. Even the Just Eat delivery guy got three students who wanted to follow in his footsteps. Verity's colleague, Ned, had joined them for impromptu consolation drinks afterwards and they'd ended up in a club until 3 a.m. It was a long story that she hadn't entirely shared with Verity, because her sister's early morning call expressing outrage that she hadn't been invited and demanding to know every detail of what had happened had left Yvie with a very definite – and sinking – feeling that her sister had feelings for Mr Merton and would not at all be happy if she were to hear the truth, the whole truth and nothing but the truth. The memory made Yvie's toes curl and her stomach lurch.

Verity was still ranting though, 'So we had plans to go out tonight, and what happens? Bloody Zoe gets dumped by Tom and she comes and gatecrashes our night.'

Yvie put her own feelings and opinions on Ned Merton to one side and focussed on what was important here.

'Zoe got dumped by Tom?' Yvie blurted. No way! They were great together. Yvie had ten quid in the sisters' sweepstake that they'd go the full distance and they'd all be in salmon pink bridesmaid's dresses by next summer.

'Er, yes,' Verity spluttered, and Yvie sensed that hadn't been the point of the call.

Christ, Zoe would be devastated.

'Poor Zoe. Is she crushed?'

'No, she's completely pissed and singing that bloody Mariah Carey Christmas song to Ned. I mean, how mortifying is that? The poor guy doesn't know where to look. You can tell he's mortally embarrassed and desperate to leave.'

Yvie immediately guessed that wasn't an entirely accurate interpretation of the situation given that a) she'd already learned that Ned definitely wasn't averse to a bit of female attention, and b) if there was a sister who was least likely to be rejected in any state, drunk or sober, it was Zoe.

Yvie stopped herself from contributing this information by taking another bite of pizza. Who needed the TV when there was the Danton family?

'So what are you going to do?'

'I'm going to put her in a taxi and insist she goes home, whether she likes it or not.'

Yvie laughed. 'Yep, good luck with that. And if it works, be sure to make an official announcement that you're the first person in history to make Zoe do something that she doesn't want to do.'

'Urgh, you always take her side,' Verity sniffed, leaving Yvie completely bewildered as to how her last statement constituted side taking. Jesus. They were all circling both sides of thirty, yet sometimes it felt like nothing had changed since the days of teenage bickering.

'Look, I'm not on anyone's side, but try not to worry about it, Ver. It's just one night. And even if she's not acting like it, you know she must be gutted about Tom. She really thought they had a future. Go easy on her. She'll need you.'

Yvie knew that would chip away the fury. Verity, for all her defensive irritation with the rest of them, and much as she'd never admit it, liked to be needed. She was the least emotional of the four, the most closed up and dismissive, but Yvie had sussed a long time ago that she also sometimes felt like the outsider of the group.

'Okay, I suppose...' The reluctant concession proved her point.

Another bite of pizza, then, 'Call me later and let me know how it goes. I'm always here.'

'I will. You know, you really need to get a life.'

And then she was gone, leaving Yvie wondering how in hell she was the one who came off that call feeling worse than when it started.

Two more things to do before she could relax. She picked up the phone and fired off a text to Zoe.

Hey… love you. X

As expected, there was no immediate answer. The phone would probably be in her bag, the sound of the incoming text drowned out by the noise of the pub.

Next, she pressed Marina's number.

'Hi,' she answered, almost immediately. One word, yet Yvie could already hear that she was stressed, tired, brittle.

'Hey, how's it going?'

'Oh, you know… usual. Not enough hours in the day.'

There was so much that Yvie could say to that. Marina was the only one of them who didn't work, yet she never had a spare minute because she filled her days micromanaging every single aspect of life. Yvie knew the answer to the next question before she asked it, but she went ahead anyway.

'I'm just checking if you need me to bring anything on Christmas Day? I mean, apart from my wit, charm and fondness for trifle.'

'No, I'm sorted, thanks.'

'Okay, well you might have to set one less place. Zoe and Tom have split up.'

'What? Oh Christ.'

'I know. She'll be devastated.'

'She will. Look, I have to go and check Annabelle and Oscar are in bed. I'll see you Christmas Day.'

Yvie really hoped that the curt dismissal was compounded by a need on Marina's part to get in touch with Zoe, although she very much doubted it. Practical help came under Marina's area of expertise, emotional support not so much.

Everyone checked on, Yvie exhaled, stretched out on the sofa and tried to force her shoulders to relax.

She was on her fifth episode in the *Grey's Anatomy* binge when her phone pinged. Zoe.

You still up? xx

Yup. You okay? xx

It's over with Tom. Long story. Can't believe it. Gutted. xx

Oh hon, I'm sorry. Want to come here? xx

Thanks, but otherwise engaged. Another long story. Hurts tho. xx

Otherwise engaged at 2 a.m.? So Verity's taxi home plan didn't work then. No surprise there, really, but Verity would be fecking furious. Why did this have to happen at this time of year when they'd all be spending so much time together over the next couple of weeks?

All I want for Christmas is a peace negotiator.

I know, darling. If you need me, just call or come over. Love you xx

Love you too, sis xx

Yvie clambered up and took her plate over to the kitchen sink, a rising wave of emotions going with her. Poor Zoe. She'd be feeling it all the more because she'd never been chucked. Zoe was their goddess, their alpha female. She'd always been the one who set out her goals and then worked her arse off to get them. She'd somehow taken the scars of their younger years and used them as building blocks for a future on her own terms. A future, she'd just been telling Yvie last week, that included Tom. She must have been completely blind-sided by the break-up.

And poor Verity. She definitely had her knickers in a twist, and the fact that it was Ned...

Another twist of emotion as a memory emerged. Regret. Mortification. Desperate to squash the thought, she went for a distraction. The tub of caramel ice cream was out of the freezer and open before she was even conscious of her actions.

Ned was a very short chapter she'd rather forget. But, of course, she couldn't share that with anyone. That wasn't how the dynamics of this family worked.

Twenty years ago, a bomb had exploded in all their lives. Since that pivotal moment, Yvie had always been there for everyone else. Always. But it wasn't a two way street. That was okay though. She didn't need to bare her soul. She was fine. Completely on top of things. And at least focusing on the others left far less time to be worrying about her own problems or regrets. Especially the one involving Ned Merton.

5

Marina hung up. Dammit. Zoe and Tom splitting up left an odd number for the Christmas lunch. She'd been planning to sit Tom next to Graham's mother. He'd always been so good-natured about listening to her mother-in-law droning on.

She called up her to-do list on her iPhone and made a note to send back his gift. Not only was he losing Zoe, but he was also losing a gorgeous cashmere V-neck in duck egg blue.

She spent the next couple of hours adjusting plans and noting everything that she needed to get done over the weekend. It was 11 p.m. when she finally went upstairs and checked in on her twelve year old twins, Oscar and Annabelle, both of whom were lying on their beds watching TV. Of course they were. Friday night was the only night that she allowed them a couple of hours off, after 9 p.m., to do whatever they liked – which mostly consisted of Annabelle watching some kind of trash TV and Oscar playing some inane game on his PlayStation. Now it was time for lights out. Annabelle had dance classes – contemporary and ballet – in the morning, Oscar had rugby, and Graham was away on business, returning on Christmas Eve, so she was on her own this weekend. Not that she minded, because she'd rather block out the rest of the world and focus on getting that to-do list sorted out.

The next three days, as with everything, went exactly how she planned. All thoughts of Zoe and Tom, or anything else for that matter, were lost as she spent her time planning, organising, decorating, cooking, preparing, cleaning and wrapping with a fervour that some might call obsessive. She preferred thorough.

All that mattered was that on the twenty-fifth of December, the setting for the family gathering was flawless.

And it was.

On Christmas Day at noon, Marina scanned their formal dining room with a critical eye. In the corner, the tree (real, of course) was glistening and tastefully decorated in silver and white. The fire was burning, with the Jo Malone candles on the mantlepiece giving off an intoxicating woody, Christmassy scent. The long walnut table carried on the colour theme, set for twelve, each place marked by a beautiful silver charger plate, ornate cutlery, exquisite, tall crackled wine glasses and cotton napkins edged with silver thread.

It could be a cover for the December edition of *House Beautiful* magazine.

'Looks good,' Graham said, as he came up behind her. 'Have you put the white wine in the fridge and uncorked the red?'

It was only the swift use of superior breathing control, perfected over years of daily yoga, that allowed her to stop herself from visibly bristling. 'Of course.'

'Great. I'll go and check on the kids. They should have finished clearing up in the lounge by now.' Off he went, his leather Burberry slippers making a faint patting noise on the American walnut floors.

Marina cast her eye across the room again. How different this was from her Christmas experience as a child. Back then, the living room would be strewn with wrapping paper, and they'd spend the whole day eating, playing and generally causing chaos. Their dad loved Christmas, so – just as with every other special occasion – he would lead the fun, creating games and making sure they all had a fantastic day, while their mum would ignore the squeals and dramas as she pottered about putting together a makeshift lunch or took a nap to recover from their Christmas morning excitement. Looking back, it was all pretty pathetic. Thank God for evolution. And John Lewis.

The doorbell cut through her thoughts, followed by stampeding thuds as Oscar and Annabelle stormed to the door to greet the visitors. The twins' hopes for toys had long since been replaced by requests for technological gadgets that would command their attention and prevent any need to physically interact with the people who were actually under the same roof. Marina had caught herself texting Annabelle to come downstairs for dinner last week and, even then, there had been a full-scale argument because her daughter had decided that the 'no phone at the dinner table' rule was 'like, seriously oppressive'. Almost as oppressive as the fact that despite allowing Annabelle to have social media access before the age of thirteen, she was required to share her passwords for Facebook, Instagram and Snapchat with her mother. According to her daughter, this was an 'invasion of privacy' that would leave her 'scarred for life'. Well, scarred for life she may be, but at least Marina could monitor everything they got up to, protect them from unwanted advances, ensure they were making the right kind of connections and check they didn't do or say something so imbecilic they'd end up a viral laughing stock who would never get into the right university because they'd been caught calling someone a repulsive fucker when they were twelve.

Nope, not on her watch.

She hadn't dedicated the last thirteen years of her life to creating the perfect home, the perfect family, and the perfect marriage...

The last thought derailed her. Hardly the perfect marriage, but there was no point in dwelling on that right now. Not when she had a perfect Christmas Day to pull off.

'Mum! Auntie Verity is here!'

Of course Verity was first. She was the only other person in this family who paid any attention to punctuality. Out in the hall, Graham was already taking Verity's coat.

'Merry Christmas!' Marina greeted her, with a kiss on each cheek.

'You look lovely!' she said, meaning it. Verity was wearing a simple red shift dress, with sleeves that reached her elbows and a hem that went to just above the knee. Classic. Stylish. Conservative. And very typically Verity.

'Isn't Zoe with you? I thought you were picking her up on the way?'

A flicker of something crossed Verity's face and Marina recognised it immediately as a subdued frown of irritation. Marina quelled an inner sigh. For God's sake. After all the effort she'd put in and already there was some kind of tension between the sisters. If they spoiled today, she'd bloody kill them.

Before she could probe, the doorbell rang again and Yvie

– still in her hospital scrubs – and Zoe boomed in, closely followed by her mum, Marge, and her husband, Derek.

'Merry Christmas,' Yvie exclaimed, setting them all off on a flurry of hugs and festive greetings. 'I'll just nip to the loo and change into something that doesn't smell of NHS cleaning fluid.'

Off she went as Derek handed over a bottle of red and Marina rewarded him with a kiss on the cheek. Marina never thought of him as a stepdad – Marge's third husband had come on the scene when she was already an adult with children of her own – but he was nice enough and he always brought decent plonk.

When Oscar had taken all the coats as he'd been primed to do (there may have been a small financial bribe involved), Marina shooed them along the hall.

'Head into the lounge for drinks and I'll be right with you. I'm just going to check on things in the kitchen.'

Graham led the visitors in the direction of the drinks trolley, playing the perfect host as always.

In the kitchen, Marina realised Verity had come in behind her. 'How can I help?'

That sent Marina's suspicions meter straight to high. Yvie helped. Zoe occasionally pitched in. Verity was far more likely to go off and get into some discussion with Graham about the property market or the dire state of the pound against international exchange rates. Marina would rather poke her eye out with a salmon fork than join in.

Now, she raised an eyebrow, as she glanced at her sister while continuing to roll the sushi starters. Not traditional Christmas fare, but she liked to introduce a bit of interest into the menu. Plus, it gave her a chance to show off the skills she'd picked up at the sushi preparation course she'd attended every day onboard their cruise around the Caribbean last summer.

'You can uncork the bottle of red that Derek brought,' she gestured to the bottle sitting on the quartz worktop next to two that were already open. The wine was a relatively safe delegation. There was no way she was trusting Verity with the sushi. 'And then you can pour me a Chardonnay. There's an open bottle in the fridge. Help yourself to whichever you prefer.'

Verity did as she was told, while Marina went back to rolling her rice on the kitchen's centre island.

'Darling, where did you put the...?' Graham paused in the doorway as he spotted the wine bottle in Verity's hand. 'Ah, great. Thank you. Verity saves the day.' He grabbed a couple of glasses and held them up to the light, checking they passed inspection. 'My parents have just arrived, darling. I said you'll be in to say hello shortly,' he told Marina. 'Mother said not to disturb you while you're preparing a masterpiece so I'll just keep them entertained. Not sure how the sushi will go down with mother though. Might want to have some Scotch Broth on standby.'

As he left, it was Verity's turn for the raised eyebrow of inquisition.

'Did you choose sushi deliberately because you knew his mother would hate it?'

Marina gasped in outrage. 'No!' Then grinned, 'Okay, maybe. I'll bet you ten quid she's bought me another bloody cookbook for my Christmas. It's like my whole life should be dedicated to her son's stomach.' She paused.

'Anyway, how many times will I have to ask you why you're pissed off with Zoe before you crack and tell me everything?'

Verity's lips pursed into a thin line of irritation as she crossed the room and pulled out a bar stool, so that she was sitting in front of where Marina was working. 'I'm not, it's just... well, okay, I am.'

'What did she do? Hang on, don't tell me... she borrowed something and forgot to give it back again? What was it this time?' Marina was trying to be interested, she really was. But a lifetime of dealing with her younger sisters and their dramas had given her a healthy resilience to bickering, and pretty strong confidence that everything blows over eventually. Their dad used to say that all the time. 'It'll pass,' he'd shrug, when one of them was raging at another. 'You're all sisters and you have to stick together,' was another of his frequent laments. 'Accept each other's faults.' 'Love each other no matter what.' All wise words. Marina wasn't sure that they managed to keep to them – especially the one about accepting each other's faults – but they did their best, especially when it really mattered.

After their dad left them, her mum would ignore the conflicts, taking herself off into another room to do yoga or some life-affirming bloody chant, leaving Marina to stop Zoe whacking Verity with the living-room lamp, or to make Verity apologise to Yvie for cutting off her Barbie's hair with the garden shears. Their teenage experiences had bonded them, but in adulthood they'd all settled into their own personalities and lives. The years had brought times of distance for some, closeness for others, and the odd bout of resentment or disagreement. Now, she could see that Verity was having an inner debate on whether or not to share the details. Of all of them, Verity was the most closed off, the most reluctant to share her problems or dramas. Uptight. Reserved. Measured. Stick up her arse. The description depended on which sister was describing her and whether it was in the heat of an argument.

Not today. Completely uncharacteristically, Verity spilled all the gory details. Marina continued to roll the sushi while she spoke. Priorities.

'Ned. You know, my colleague at school...'

'I know Ned.' Oh yes, she knew. At the last school fundraiser Verity had dragged them all to, Marina had won a dinner with the lovely Ned as a raffle prize. That reminded her – she must get in touch and sort that out. 'Easy on the eye.'

That caused an irritated pursing of the lips that had to be reversed before Verity could carry on and give a blow-by-blow account of the last day of school before the Christmas break. Marina was standing back, admiring her completed sushi plate by the time Verity got to the bit where she attempted to talk Zoe into getting a taxi home.

'She point-blank refused. Said I was spoiling her fun. *I was spoiling her fun?*' Her face was flushing as her irritation rose. 'I mean, seriously. What the hell did she think she was doing to mine?'

Marina had sympathy. She really did. Sort of. But did Verity have to choose now to have an emotional crisis when there were guests in the next room and a tray of sushi that wasn't going to keep all bloody day? Not to mention the five bird spectacle in the Aga, the vegetables and trimmings warming in the other ovens next to the fresh baked bread, and the choice of three desserts (apple crumble, Cointreau cheesecake and home-made trifle) that had to be baked, defrosted and whipped up in perfect synchronicity so that they'd all be ready at the same time. There was a schedule here and it didn't include time for Verity's drama, not if today was going to go without a hitch.

Marina pushed her hair back from her face with the back of her wrist, careful not to do anything that would replace her eau de Chanel with an eau de Sashimi.

'Okay, let me get this straight. You've got a thing for Ned...'

Verity squirmed a little at that. 'Not a thing, as such. But he's my... friend.' Being completely emotionally stilted and obsessively private about her feelings, she hadn't actually confirmed that there was a romantic attraction there, but it was easy to read between the lines. The red flush that was rising up her neck now confirmed Marina's assumption.

'Then it's simple. Tell Zoe that you like Ned and she'll back off. It sounds like it was just a bit of a drunken night and there was nothing between them anyway.'

Verity needed a bit of convincing. 'Do you think so?'

Marina really didn't have time for this.

'Yes! It's Zoe, for God's sake – she can have any guy she wants. There's no way she's going to want the one man on earth who has given you your first romantic spark since that bloke from Boyzone.'

Marina was trying to defuse the situation with a bit of teasing, but it fell flat given that it was pretty close to the truth. Verity was a year younger than her and – other than a five year relationship that ended the year after she left uni and a few romances that fizzled out after a month or two – as far as Marina knew, she'd been pretty much single for the best part of a decade. Marina reckoned it was because she had major trust issues and barriers that were almost impossible to penetrate, but then, who wouldn't in their situation? Hadn't they learned when they were teenagers that everything can change in a heartbeat, that the people you trust can be the ones who cause the most pain, that you can't count on anything in life? And those sentiments were never more prevalent for them all than at Christmas.

All four sisters had found a way to rationalise their father's absence from their life, but Verity had definitely been left with the most ongoing damage. And if she did actually feel that this guy was worth dropping her guard for, then it was a cruel irony that he was currently being nabbed by their own sister.

'Just tell her how you feel. She's just broken up with Tom and she'll still be heartbroken over him. This guy will mean nothing to her.'

'What guy means nothing to who?' Zoe and Yvie had slipped in the door without the other two hearing a thing. That's what happened when you insisted your guests took their shoes off so their heels wouldn't damage the walnut floors. Thankfully it seemed like they'd only caught the tail end of the conversation.

Marina thought fast and bluffed her way out of it. 'Oh, eh, just a friend. She hooked up with some guy on Tinder.'

'Ooooh, get you, all up to date with the dating apps,' Yvie chuckled. She was changed now, wearing a jumper with a giant, flashing Christmas tree on the front. 'Hope you're not tempted to go looking for some extramarital action.'

Marina didn't dignify that with an answer – which was a mistake, because it left the door to speculation open for Zoe to step right through.

'I can't tell you how much I hope that's true. Come to think of it, Marina, in the movies it's always the ones you suspect least who are picking up strangers for wild, random sex. I haven't been in your spare room for a while. If it's been set up as a swingers' sex dungeon, I'll be totally impressed,'

Zoe joked, using the diversion of Marina's eye roll to sneak a morsel of sashimi off the platter and into her mouth.

Not for the first time, Marina decided that the crassness of Zoe's conversation was a stark contrast to the elegance of her style. Today, her sister was stunning in her cream jersey turtle-neck and wide palazzo trousers of exactly the same shade. With her blonde hair left loose and messy, she was a cross between a gorgeous surfer chick and something out of a Dolce and Gabbana advert.

Meanwhile, Verity's neck flush made it to the roots of her hair and Marina thought how typical this was. She and Verity had always been the more mature and conservative of the sisters, standing on one side of the responsibility net, while Zoe and Yvie were dancing until midnight on the other side, caring not a jot about what anyone thought of them. Well, good for them, but they had to realise that sometimes you had to grow up and do the right thing. Even if it meant losing a bit of fun. Or staying in a situation that had long since stopped bringing you joy. Or happiness. Or excitement.

Realising that thought was way too close to home, Marina shook it off. There was no point going down that path, not today.

Instead she went for a complete change of subject. And if it delivered a reality check to her sister, well, maybe that wasn't such a bad thing.

'I'm sorry about you and Tom. I thought you two were in it for the long run.'

Zoe reacted with a sad shrug.

No jokes about Tinder and wild shagging now, Marina thought.

'Och, me too. I was completely blind-sided by it, but what can you do? I'm not going to sit around moping. Not at

Christmas. Definitely not today,' she finished, and they all understood why. No. Definitely not today.

'Are you going to try to talk him around and make it work?'

Zoe shook her head. 'Nope. It's a long story. It turns out, the teenage love of his life – her name's Chrissie and I met her yesterday...'

'You met her?' Verity said, shocked.

'Yeah. They came round to the flat. Look, Tom and I were mates long before we got together, we worked together for years and we will have to work together for a long time to come. We both want it to be cool, so he brought her round to explain everything. I'm disgusted to say she's actually lovely,' she said this with a rueful grin, 'and she has been pining for him too. They lost touch when he moved to Australia with his family when he was eighteen and... I feel I should have a drum roll for this bit.'

Yvie obliged, putting her glass of wine down and then slapping out the sound of a beating drum on the quartz worktop.

'Now that they've found each other again, he's discovered that she had a baby boy eight months after he left.'

Even Marina felt her chin drop. 'He has a son he didn't even know about? Oh, my word, that's astonishing. How does he feel about that?'

'He's delighted. Gutted that he's missed Ben's childhood, but he and Chrissie are focusing on what comes next and they both seem so happy.'

'And what about you?'

Zoe shrugged again. 'I have to accept that there's no way he's coming back now. So I pick myself up, move on and see what happens.'

On the other side of the island, Marina spotted Verity's shoulders tense and knew she had to elicit some kind of response that would assure her that Zoe wasn't actually swooping in to claim Verity's secret crush. Dear God, this was like navigating the pogo stick mystery of 1996. And she was still convinced of Zoe's guilt in that matter.

'Well, just take your time and give yourself some breathing space. The worst thing you could do is rush into something else.' There. Subtle. To the point. Sound advice. Situation defused.

Although, apparently no one passed that conclusion on to Zoe.

'Nope, I'm going along a different route,' she said, completely oblivious to Marina's flash of horror, Yvie's anxious glance at Verity, and the fact that Verity's face was now bordering on tomato. 'You know what they say about the best way to get over someone...'

Marina tried to head it off. 'Oh, for goodness sake, all that "get under someone else" stuff is nonsense.'

'Well, I'm giving it a go.'

Bollocks. Trust Zoe to make it worse by being typically ballsy and completely open.

Then, to make it worse, she added an incredulous, 'Verity, I can't believe you never snapped Ned Merton up for yourself. He's fricking gorgeous.'

See! This was what happened when a sister didn't share her feelings. Zoe had absolutely no idea that Verity had any interest in Ned whatsoever. It wasn't too late to tell her.

Marina threw a knowing stare at Verity, who immediately grasped the subliminal signal but gave a subtle but ferocious shake of the head. The message was clear. Do. Not. Say. Anything.

Well, bugger that. There was no point having unspoken tension between them, not when she'd gone to all this trouble to make today absolutely perfect. As usual, she was going to have to be the one who stepped in, cleared it all up, Zoe would ditch Ned, Verity could pursue him and all would be fine.

'The thing is, Zoe...' Marina began.

It all happened in a flash. Verity's eyes widened with fury, then her hand moved, it bumped her wine glass, the goblet fell, the red liquid splashed out and disaster struck. One plate of ornately formed sushi drenched in Merlot.

'Nooooooo!' Marina howled, furiously, adding an unspoken, 'Fuck!' Audible profanity was too uncouth, but 'fuck!' again. That was it! She was done intervening between these two. She now had much bigger issues to solve than their pathetic romantic dramas.

Fighting to regain her calm, as Yvie and Zoe frantically mopped up the mess with kitchen roll, Marina went into disaster-limitation mode. The story of her life.

'Yvie, can you grab a couple of cans of Scotch Broth out the cupboard?'

This was going to be a perfect fucking Christmas if it killed her.

6

THE GIRLS – CHRISTMAS DAY 1998

'Dad, do we have to listen to that crappy Boyzone stuff all day? I swear I'm going to put her CD player in the bin,' Marina warned.

Will Danton responded in the same way he always did when Marina was revving up to have a rant – he put his arms around his thirteen year old daughter and kissed her on the cheek.

'You won't do that because you're lovely and a lot sweeter than you pretend to be,' he teased her, the grey hair of his fringe flopping into his eyes. He always claimed that he was so grey in his early thirties because he had four daughters, but he said it with a cheeky wink that told them he wouldn't have it any other way.

Right now, though, Marina was resisting his charm. 'I'm not. I'm going to poison her food. Then she'll be too sick to care.'

Sitting at the kitchen table, her brand new CD player – her very best pressie of the day – only inches away from her,

Verity glanced up from her book, eyes narrowed. 'Try it. I dare you, cow face.'

'Hey, that's enough,' their dad intervened. 'We don't fight on Christmas Day. Save it until tomorrow and then you can fight all you like,' he added, laughing as he let Marina go and headed back into the lounge.

Verity went back to her book and Marina carried on peeling the potatoes for the Christmas dinner, just as Zoe appeared carrying a huge plastic bag.

'Right, that's the living room cleared up,' she announced, opening the back door and dumping the black plastic bag full of discarded wrapping paper she was carrying into the bin. They'd had such a brilliant morning opening presents, singing along to Christmas songs and, miracles, praise be, not one argument or bicker between them, but of course that was too good to last. Boyzone would, no doubt, be the start of a slippery slope into full scale huffs and strops.

'What else needs doing?' Zoe was asking now.

Marina eyed her suspiciously. 'Why are you being so helpful today?'

'Because it's Christmas Day!' She could see that Zoe was trying to bluff it out.

It didn't work. Marina stopped peeling again and was now holding the peeler at a threatening angle. 'And...?'

Zoe caved. 'And Dad promised me a pound if I did all the clearing up for twenty-four hours.'

Before they could get into an argument about Zoe's profiteering, Dad reappeared with a huge pile of board games, nine year old Yvie trailing behind him clutching a selection box and a Terry's chocolate orange.

'Right, Verity, get that stuff off the table. It's Monopoly time.'

Marina was the first to object. 'But, Dad, I've got the dinner to make and I can't do it with everyone in here.'

She knew she had a point. The kitchen diner in their seventies terrace house on an estate on the edge of Glasgow was tight enough, before five people, two board games, copious snacks and dinner preparations were added.

'Yeah, well, it can wait. Come on, let's go. Winner gets to choose what movies we watch tonight.'

That was all he needed to say. The minute he added some competition to proceedings, Marina, Verity and Zoe were in. Yvie just went along with it because she'd do anything that sounded like fun. Boyzone were switched off, which was some consolation for Marina, and the CD player shoved under the table to make room for the board.

They were almost set up when their mum came into the kitchen shaking her freshly painted nails.

'Do you want to play, Mum?' Zoe asked. 'There's loads of room and we'll let you be the car,' she said, holding up the tiny pewter vehicle that had been her mum's choice the last time they played.

Their mum wrinkled her nose. 'No, you're fine, darling. I've just painted my nails.'

'Come on, Marge,' their dad tried to cajole her. 'Just one game. Won't kill you.'

Maybe not, but if looks could kill, the one that their mum shot their dad right then could have stopped his heart in an instant. Marina, Verity and Zoe all noticed and pretended not to. Only Yvie was oblivious, as she shared out the contents of her selection box, putting one bar of chocolate in front of everyone.

'No, it's fine. I'll, erm... I'll look after dinner.'

They all glanced up in surprise, Marina the most shocked

of all. Mum never cooked any more, having delegated that job to the chores rota, although it almost always fell to Marina because she was the only one who actually put any effort into it. There was no choice really. If it was left to the others, they'd live on chips, sausage rolls and pizza.

'Everything is pretty much done,' Marina told her. 'The turkey is already in, and the potatoes are peeled. Just the veg and the chipolatas to do.'

'Great,' their mum chirped. 'I'll get on to that then.'

True to her word, she did. But all that was left to do took about ten minutes out of the next four hours of raucous Monopoly. For the rest of the time, Marge lay on the couch, chatting to her friends on the phone and watching her favourite programmes on TV. Marina even had to dive up from the table and take the turkey out of the oven when the timer dinged.

They didn't care though. Dad's jokes and the fun they had playing made the hours whizz by. When they eventually cleared away the board games so they could eat at the table, they even pretended to enjoy the soggy Brussels sprouts, mushy potatoes and crispy turkey. Mum had forgot about the veg and left it all too long.

It didn't matter. They ate dinner, pulled crackers, read the silly puns and laughed until their sides hurt at Dad's daft songs and impressions.

'What was your favourite present today, Dad?' Yvie had asked him as Marina served up the Viennetta for pudding.

He'd grinned that crooked way he always did and given her a hug.

'You lot,' he said, kissing the top of her head. 'We're so lucky to have each other. So yeah, you guys... And my new Brut aftershave, of course,' he joked. They'd all chipped in to buy it for him and he'd loved it. 'Family forever,' he said, raising a toast that they all matched with their glasses of Irn-Bru.

'Family forever,' the girls echoed, beaming.

Only it wasn't.

Because one person at the table already knew that this could be the last Christmas Day they would all spend together.

7

Tom leaned in the doorway of her office, his wavy brown hair pushed back from his face, in his standard uniform for dress-down Friday: black jeans, white T-shirt, black boots. His twice weekly five-a-side football sessions and morning runs kept him looking exactly the same as he had done for years.

'Is there any chance you can develop a liking for pies and completely let yourself go, just to make me feel like I had a lucky escape?' she asked him, drily.

His face cracked into a grin. To onlookers, it might look like there was some unresolved tension between them, but they both knew differently. This was their norm. Their whole relationship – brilliant as it had been until the moment his ex appeared on the scene – had been built on the foundations of love, trust, compatibility, mutual admiration, her sarcasm and his enjoyment of it.

The first week back after Christmas had been a bit awkward with lots of walking on eggshells. The second week, they'd relaxed a bit – especially when their personal feelings had to be put aside to focus on reorganising the company after Tom's founding partner took off to set up a new office in New York. Zoe had been offered a partnership in the company and stepped into his shoes. She'd lost the love of her life but achieved a huge career ambition. It was a small consolation. On the third week, they'd settled into their redefined relationship with just a few moments of uncertainty. And now, they were back on solid friendship terms, as witnessed by the full return of Zoe's dry barbs. Normal service resumed. She just had to make sure he didn't realise that she still missed him desperately and hadn't quite shut off her 'I love Tom' gene.

Grinning, he pulled a Greggs bag from behind his back. 'It's as if I could read your mind.'

'If there's a maple doughnut in there, you're forgiven for dumping me.'

'Yassss!' he punched the air, swooping the bag down on to her desk and tearing it open to reveal her favourite cake. One that came with a soft dough, a sweet topping and a pang of 'How bloody wonderful is he?'

She ignored the last ingredient.

'Forgiven. Anyway, what's up?'

'Nothing.

She eyed him suspiciously. 'It's Friday, you're in my office, you've brought a bribe. That's not "nothing".'

'Okay, I just wondered how long I need to leave it before I can ask if you're really okay and we can talk about our relationships like we used to do when we were best mates?'

Zoe sat back in her leather chair and put her feet on the desk, her black leather spiked heels landing squarely on top of the Kemp Hotel Group contract. It was up for renewal and she was going through it, making sure they'd met all their commitments before pitching for it to be extended. Roger

Kemp was a nice guy, but he had tough demands and expected them to be on top of their game at all times. That wasn't a problem for Zoe. It wasn't like she had much else going on to distract her. Unlike the bribe-bearing man in front of her.

'Depends. Are you going to tell me how Chrissie is the most wonderful woman you've ever met and you've never been happier?' she asked with the kind of eyebrow arch she could only do now that her one-time brush with Botox had worn off.

His silence and rueful shrug was her answer.

'Then I'm thinking it's going to take two doughnuts before I've eaten enough of my feelings to go along with it,' she replied, grinning as she took her first bite.

Tom laughed as he crossed the room and pulled out the chair on the other side of her desk. 'Okay, I'm doing it anyway. I need to know you're moving on and happy. It's the people-pleaser in me.'

She knew that was inherently true, so she refrained from pointing out that he hadn't bloody pleased her when he'd dumped her four days before Christmas.

'I'm happy. I'm fine,' she argued, maple icing sticking to her lips as she took another bite. 'I've tried to keep my moping over my newly single state to a respectable ten minutes a day and then I give my inner miserable cow a good talking to and get back to work.'

Tom's eyes crinkled and a bit of her melted. She'd always loved to make him laugh. Still did.

'Seeing anyone?' he asked, lifting the other doughnut for himself.

She shook her head. Finding someone else was the bottom of her list of priorities. Getting over Tom was at the top. 'I'm throwing myself into my work. I have a very demanding business partner who hides his relentlessly high expectations under a veneer of being a nice guy.'

'Sounds like a complete twat,' Tom offered, laughing again.

'Indeed, he is.'

'Anyway, back to you. What about the guy you hooked up with at Christmas? The teacher?'

Zoe took a sip of coffee this time, buying a few moments because she wasn't quite sure how to answer that.

'He's called a few times, left a few messages, but I've blanked them. I know that sounds heartless, but I decided it would be a bit of a dick move to use him to make myself feel better. It wouldn't be fair to him.' She was going for nonchalance but wasn't sure if she was hitting martyrdom instead.

'Are you crazy? If someone like you wanted to use me to get over an ex, I'd be all for it,' he joked.

As if the cosmos was listening, her phone buzzed at that moment and that familiar name popped up on the screen:

NED TEACHER BLOKE. She'd put that in her contacts when she woke up in the morning after the night that they...

Shuddering, she pulled open the curtains on the mental image. Ned had been gorgeous. Fun. But that night she had been a drunken mess. It had been all been pointless too. In her tequila-fuelled haze, she'd thought it would make her feel better. It didn't. And despite all her chat on Christmas Day about having a fling with him to get over Tom, she hadn't actually followed up on it.

Tom stretched over, saw the name flashing on the screen of her phone, then leaned back in his chair. 'Go on. Answer it.'

'Nope.'

'Why not?'

'Because...'

She stopped, realising she had nothing. Not a single viable excuse for rejecting his call. Ned was handsome. Smart. Interesting. Funny. He worked with kids, for God's sake. What was wrong with her? The answer was obvious. He just wasn't Tom. Not that she was going to say that to the man in front of her now, but, come on, of course the bruising would take a while to heal. They'd only been together for six months, but after a couple of years of friendship, which developed into so much more, she'd really thought they were both on the same path. One that ended with lifelong commitments and at least a couple of episodes of reproduction. That was a tough future to rewrite.

'Because I'd rather call him back later when I don't have an audience. Look, don't worry about me, I'm fine. I promise. I'm loving the new role and personal stuff will just have to take a back seat for a while because I want to focus on this.'

He seemed to accept that he wasn't getting anywhere and went for a change of subject. 'How's the family doing?'

Zoe thought about it for a moment. 'Marina's finally over Sushi-gate. I think. It's hard to tell, given that – much as I adore her – her happy-go-lucky face is almost exactly the same as her resting-bitch face. And Yvie, well she's just gorgeous, happy Yvie. Nothing ever gets her down. Something's going on with Verity, but I think I need to bring in CIA interrogators to get it out of her.'

'What kind of thing?' One of the many things she'd loved about Tom was that he was genuinely interested in the people he cared about. He'd always been hugely fond of her sisters and had got to know them well over the years.

'I don't know. She's just off. A bit reclusive. That's nothing new but she's even worse than usual. I've asked her to go out a few times over the last month and she always has an excuse. I'm giving up and waiting until she comes out of it on her own. Hopefully it'll be before we retire and start taking bus tours together.'

It had been genuinely puzzling to Zoe, though. She'd asked Yvie and Marina if they knew what was bugging Verity, but they didn't seem to have a clue either. Not that they'd tell her. The four sisters had had a pact since they were in their twenties, that if they were sworn to secrecy on something by another sister, they had to stick to it. Interference and gossiping never ended well.

'She'll come round. She always does. Maybe she's just got some work stuff on her mind.' He thought about it for a moment. 'Or maybe... is there any chance she likes the guy?'

'What guy?' Zoe asked, genuinely puzzled.

'Ned. The one you went out with that night.'

Zoe's reaction was instinctive. 'Noooo. No way. She's worked with him for years. If they were going to hook up, they'd have done it long ago.'

'Eh, can I point out that we worked together for years before we developed a relationship?'

'Yes, but that's because you were my boss. This is different. They're just co-workers, so there's no political stuff to get in the way.' She chewed on another chunk of doughnut while she pondered it some more. 'No, they'd definitely have got together by now if there was any kind of spark between them. Our Verity is a bit reserved that way, but she's not completely hopeless.'

Tom scrunched up the Greggs bag and tossed it in the direction of the bin. Of course, it went in first time. 'When was her last relationship?' he asked, making a gentle point.

Zoe conceded defeat. 'Okay, so she *is* a bit hopeless, but if she liked Ned, I'd know. I'm sure of it.' She filed the thought under 'ridiculous' and pushed it to the back of her mind. 'Right, be gone and let me get some work done.'

'Sure thing,' he said, stretching out of his seat. She ordered her libido to be completely unaffected by this. It did its best to comply. 'Can we go over the Kemp contract at three o'clock? I want to get away sharpish tonight. We're taking Ben out for dinner and then to a basketball game.'

His face lit up as he said it and Zoe's heart melted. He was so happy, so thrilled to discover that he was a dad, and she couldn't begrudge him that. Even if her uterus hadn't been involved in creating the situation.

As the door swung behind him, she paused, glanced around the open-plan office. There was Dex, the head of the art department, over by the kettle, whipping himself into a frenzy as he shared his plans for the weekend. He and his boyfriend, Jasper, were off to Barcelona on the last flight tonight.

Cally, the receptionist, and Sarah and Becky, the marketing managers, were all heading out straight after work to some restaurant opening. They'd invited her, but she'd declined. Now she wasn't sure why. She continued her scan of the room. Every single person had something planned for the weekend, somewhere to be, people to see, except her. She'd maybe call Yvie and see if she wanted to grab a curry, or land on Verity with a bottle of wine and beg her to stay up past ten o'clock.

Something snapped. Enough. No more moping. Time to get back out there. So, two choices. A dating app or... or... did she want to see Ned again?

Really, how many relationships that started off with a drunken one night stand ever actually worked?

It hadn't been her finest moment. Casual sex wasn't generally her thing, but it was one of those right place, right time, take her mind off Tom bloody Butler things. And it had worked. Immediately afterwards, she'd had all intentions of seeing Ned again, but somehow she'd just let it drift. Her mind went back to their one and only call on Boxing Day. They'd chatted for a while, exchanged Christmas Day stories, Zoe omitting the bit where the starter was ruined, Marina was furious, Verity was a moody cow all night, her mother and Derek had a terse argument about God knows what, and Graham's mother made a passive-aggressive comment about every single aspect of the dinner, making Zoe remove all sharp objects from Marina's vicinity. It had been tense and uncomfortable, so Zoe, Yvie and their mum had overdone the wine and ended up singing Christmas songs around Annabelle's piano. By the third rendition of 'Do They Know It's Christmas', they'd pretty much cleared the room. Marina had muttered something about 'so much for a perfect bloody Christmas' and gone off to bed.

'School doesn't start back for another week and I was thinking maybe we could make the most of it? Spend some time together?' he'd suggested at the end of the call.

Tempting. So tempting. But by then, the reality of her split with Tom had descended with a vengeance, and she didn't have the luxury of a week off – she was back to work the next day. All in all, she decided she had enough on her plate without the added complication of a prolonged one night stand. 'I appreciate you asking, I really do. But the thing is, I'd just split up with my boyfriend the day we met...' she'd explained.

'You might have mentioned that once or twice. Or sixty-seven times.'

His teasing had made her laugh, and for a moment she had almost wavered. Almost. The reality was, she needed to come to terms with losing Tom before she dived into something new.

'Yeah, I'm sorry about that. Tequila makes me repeat things,' she'd said.

'Well, when you're ready to repeat us, give me a call.' Funny. Smooth. Not helped by the fact that she could see his cute grin in her mind and the complete package made him just a little bit harder to refuse.

She'd hung up before she'd buckled. It was the right thing to do.

But now?

A month later, maybe it was time to reconsider. There was nothing to lose and a good night out to gain. Tom was right. She had to get back out there. After all, he'd very definitely moved on. She was single. Ned was single. And despite Tom's earlier question, she was 100 per cent positive that there was no way that Verity was in the least bit interested in Ned Merton, so there was no reason Zoe shouldn't have a bit of heartbreak-soothing fun.

She picked up the phone and dialled Yvie, who answered on the first ring.

Zoe cut right to the point.

'Hey, it's me. Do you think it's time for me to stop moping and get my flirt back on?'

'Abso-fucking-lutely.'

'Excellent. Good chat.' The two of them were laughing when she hung up.

Yvie was right. It was time.

Zoe picked up the phone and toyed with it, rolling it around in her hand. Then she clicked on 'recent calls' and stared at his name:

NED TEACHER BLOKE.

All she had to do was press the button.

8

'Miss Danton, Caleb just told me to fuck off!'

It took every single ounce of restraint, and the fortuitous ringing of the bell, for Verity not to say, 'Well, tell him to fuck off right back.' She loved her job, she truly did, but sometimes she had to launch a search party to find the joy in it.

It had been a long month. January was always tough. The weather had been horrendous, meaning that the kids were often stuck inside at break time and lunchtime, giving them no opportunity to run their energy off. They'd swapped the fun Christmas stuff for more concentrated learning. And it always took a while to get them back into a routine after the break. It didn't help that she pretty much wanted to tell the world to fuck off too. Of course, she wouldn't. She'd always thought swearing just demonstrated a lack of vocabulary.

As soon as the bell had cleared the room, she sank back in her chair. Another week done.

'You look knackered.'

The voice from the doorway made her spring upright and she automatically responded with a smile.

'I am. Long week. How was yours?'

Hands in pockets, tie loose, Ned leaned against the wall like a catalogue model. 'Same. We're at that final year in primary school stage where it's only a few months until they go to high school and they already think they know everything and they're too grown up to be here. I just caught one of my groups discussing how it's only a few years until they can go to Magaluf. God help us.'

That threw up a recollection in Verity's mind. Her and Zoe. Age seventeen and eighteen. A fortnight in Benidorm paid for by their Saturday jobs. All Zoe wanted to do was party all night and sleep on the beach all day. They hadn't seen one museum or place of cultural interest for a fortnight. And no, Zoe's argument that the Orgasm Bar was a place of cultural interest didn't wash with her.

Stay cool, Verity told herself. *Act nonchalant. Casual.*

Her gob didn't appear to be listening. 'Any plans for the weekend?' She'd overheard a conversation in the ladies' toilets a couple of days before that hinted he was now seeing one of the teachers in the nursery section of the school. Something about Tinder and a random hook-up, but she wasn't sure she'd picked it up right. That night she'd signed up to the app, swiped through every guy who lived in Glasgow, searching for Ned, but come up blank.

Ned shrugged. 'Nothing much. I was going to go to the gym now, but I've decided my need for a beer is far greater.'

Ah, so the hook-up story definitely couldn't have been about him or he'd probably be going off out on some random date. She'd thought it was pretty far-fetched and that had been confirmed when she'd failed to find him on the dating app. Why would a guy like Ned Merton have to use an app to get a girlfriend? She'd deleted her profile, case closed.

And now he was suggesting a drink.

Excellent.

Again, stay cool. Think this through.

Okay, so he'd spent the night with her sister. The memory of it still gave her a burning sensation in her chest. After a dinner and several hours of festive drinks in a packed bar, she'd given up and suggested they go home, only for Zoe to jump, giggling, into a taxi with Ned and off they went. Zoe had texted her the next morning to say thanks for a great night and let her know that Ned had stayed over. Thankfully it seemed like that had been a one-off. Zoe hadn't mentioned him again since the Christmas Day conversation with Marina and Yvie. Meanwhile, Ned had made a couple of casual 'How's Zoe doing?' enquiries over the last month, so they clearly weren't in contact. That had to mean they weren't into each other, otherwise, they'd have gone out again. And if they weren't into each other, then maybe there was still a chance that she didn't have to spend half her life talking herself out of her attraction to him.

'I was just thinking the very same thing.' She wasn't. She'd made plans to meet Yvie for some pasta at their favourite Italian restaurant later. Nothing a quick text wouldn't sort.

'I like your thinking. Wine bar? Head off in half an hour?'

'Sure.'

Nonchalance on the outside, internal organs doing a Mexican wave on the inside.

In the staffroom, she straightened her skirt, gave her face a quick once-over with a bit of Max Factor, unleashed her ponytail so that her flaming hair fell loose around her shoulders and added a spritz of the Dior perfume that Zoe had bought her for Christmas. Zoe always went for extravagant gifts, whereas Verity preferred something a bit more practical. The waterproof toilet bags she'd bought all her sisters would come in handy for holidays.

Ned was waiting at the front door half an hour later and they both jumped in Verity's Volvo, chatting about school politics and gossip all the way into the west end of Glasgow. Not that it was easy to concentrate on what he was saying. This was the first time they'd been alone together outside school and her senses were in thrill overload.

'There's a space,' Ned pointed out, as they turned into Byres Road, directing her to a slot right outside Oran Mor, a beautiful historic church that was now a bar and restaurant, famed for its theatrical performances. One of the most popular recurring events was called A Play, a Pie and a Pint, and featured an eclectic range of themes and talent, from the famous to the obscure. Verity had been to many of them and loved them all.

Inside, they found a booth, and Ned got the first round in, while she fired off a text to Yvie.

Something's come up. Have to cancel tonight. Sorry.

'Everything okay?' he asked, as he sat down with their drinks.

She could see two women at the next table watching him out of the corners of their eyes and no wonder. He'd changed into jeans, and he was wearing a pale grey shirt under his dark Crombie coat, his black hair short at the sides, longer on top. Verity had always thought that if she had to name a celebrity she bore any kind of resemblance to, it would be Christina Hendricks. Ned? Definitely a bit of a Ben Affleck.

'Fine!' Her voice was just a little higher than normal. 'Just, eh... asking my sister to pop in and feed my cat.'

Damn! Why did she say that? She didn't even own a bloody cat.

This is what happened when someone who had the romantic life of the last woman on earth was finally unleashed on something that came close to a date.

'Zoe?' he immediately asked.

'No, Yvie,' she blustered, kicking herself for bringing up the subject of her sisters. Tonight should be all about the two people here, sitting at this table.

"This is a bit different to our last night out,' Ned said, and she thought she could see a tiny flinch of embarrassment. And no wonder. It was probably the excess of alcohol consumed that had caused the whole debacle. Zoe had been so forward with him that night, the poor guy hadn't stood a chance. Perhaps he'd realised it was a mistake, and now, tonight, they were rectifying it. Having a do-over. And this time, it was the two who were best suited who had finally managed to get it together. Maybe it was time to forgive Zoe, now that things had worked out the way they should have done in the first place.

'Does she ever mention me?'

The chill started somewhere in the pit of her stomach and began to work its way outwards.

'Zoe?' she asked, stating the obvious.

'Yeah,' Ned said, and suddenly it was obvious. He wasn't embarrassed because he'd ended up with the wrong sister last time. He was embarrassed because he was blatantly using Verity to get information on Zoe's feelings towards him. How could she have got this so wrong? And how should she respond? What she wanted to do was get up, leave and tell him where he could stick the cucumber from her gin and tonic. But then... she had to work with him every day. Maybe she was being too hasty. Perhaps he was just trying to ascertain whether there were any residual feelings that would cause a problem if something were to develop here. Further clarification was required.

'And you're asking this because...?'

He had the decency to look even more embarrassed. 'Look, I know it's pretty pathetic, but I've texted and called to ask her out a couple of times and she's knocked me back. I get that she's just out of a relationship—'

'Tom was the love of her life,' Verity blurted, before she could stop herself. It gave her a twinge of satisfaction that the drop of his eyebrows suggested this was a bit of a blow.

'So you don't think there's any hope? She hasn't said anything at all?'

Verity made a split-second decision. Sod it. Rip the Band-Aid off. With any luck, he would go along the same train of thought as Zoe and decide that the best way to get over someone was to get together with someone else. Preferably someone who was sitting right in front of him. She didn't even stop to question why she was still interested in him despite the fact that she was very clearly second choice.

'No. Look, I'm sorry but... do you want me to be honest?'

'Yes. No. Okay, but only if you think my ego can take it.' He knocked back a slug of his Peroni, then shook out his shoulders like a boxer preparing for a fight. 'Right, on you go. I'm ready.'

Was she really going to do this?

'The thing about Zoe is, well, she's always been a bit high

maintenance when it comes to men. She likes the Master of the Universe type. You know, slick marketing guys or loaded businessmen that show up in their Porsche to collect her and who only fly first class. That's the kind of life she has always aspired to and she doesn't really settle for anything less.'

Yes, she was doing it. She was telling a huge fib to make her sister sound like a superficial, shallow cow who couldn't possibly be interested in a bloke who earned less than forty grand a year and drove a five year old Fiesta. The truth was, Zoe's boyfriend before Tom had been the plumber who'd fitted her new wetroom and the one before that had been a long-distance relationship with a skint surfing instructor she'd met in Cornwall.

Verity told herself that Zoe never had to know what she was saying. Besides, that wasn't the purpose here. The point of this was to close down the Zoe question in Ned's mind, so he could move on. Besides, if Zoe had any interest in him, she'd have acted on it, so she obviously wasn't into him at all. By nipping this in the bud, Verity was doing them both a favour, really.

He exhaled long and hard, like he was still in that boxing ring and had been dealt a blow to the solar plexus. 'Ouch. Well, if I was looking for some brutal honesty—'

'Sorry,' she blurted. Okay, she might have gone too far. She could backtrack or... 'But it's better you know so that you don't waste your time.'

The women at the next table were now doing a really crap job of pretending that they weren't trying to suss out what was going on here. By the doleful look on Ned's face, it would seem like they were having some kind of lovers' tiff and no doubt the onlookers were hoping that they'd get a chance to swoop in and console him.

Get to the back of the line, ladies. I'm way ahead of you.

Reaching across the dark wood table, she put her hand on his and spoke with a voice that oozed sympathy. At least, she hoped it did. Sympathy had never been one of her strengths. That was Yvie's job and she was damn good at it.

'I'm sorry if that's not what you wanted to hear. But look on the bright side – it's Friday night and we have beer and gin. How bad can it be?' She rounded that off with a wide smile and a squeeze of his hand. Oh, the irony. She was trying to get him to forget Zoe by saying something that came straight from the Zoe Danton book of life. Look on the bright side. Count your blessings. Let's party our way out of this. Never once had any of that come naturally to Verity. Well, maybe it was time she took a leaf out of her sister's book of positivity and enjoyment of life.

It seemed to be working. The shoulders at the next table sagged with disappointment as Ned's eyes locked on hers, then he put his hand on hers, making a three hand pile-up, leaned forward and grinned. 'You're absolutely right,' he said, casting off his cloak of 'woe is me'. He was stopped from saying anything further by a loud ring coming from right behind him.

Her mind attempted to send him subliminal messages. *Don't answer it. Don't spoil the moment. This is it. The start of something. We'd be great...*

He was leaning back again, fishing in the pockets of the jacket that was hanging on the back of his chair. Eventually, he located his phone, pulled it out and stared at the flashing name on the screen.

Don't answer it. There's no one you want to speak to right now. No one – NO ONE – is more important than what's happening here in this moment.

His mind clearly wasn't receiving the communications. He looked up, caught her eye again, then broke the gaze as he gestured to the phone he was now turning around in his hand so that she could see the name flashing up on the screen.

'It's Zoe.'

9

Yvie picked up the phone on the first ring.

Kay's weary sigh was the first thing she heard. 'Is that the family and friends' twenty-four hour helpline?'

'It certainly is. Here to solve your problems and we take payment in cheap wine. How can we help you this evening?'

'I need a team of extraction specialists to storm the building and come save me from this place. Babs has just tried to sneak Cedric out of the ward. She claims she was taking him to the canteen for a romantic dinner.'

'Oh, feck. She's almost three times my age and she has more gumption than I'll ever have. And more flexible hips too, now that she's had the op.'

Kay's chuckles made Yvie smile. Her pal didn't do that enough. Between the stress of the long hours, bringing up her six year old son, Chester, (even with her mum's help) and an ex-husband whom she claimed had the habits of a killer whale – only surfaced now and then, blew his top, then drifted off whenever he pleased – she didn't get much time for enjoying the more carefree things in life.

'Anyway, I'm free for extraction services this evening and willing to oblige.'

'Really? I was kidding. I was just calling to check in and say enjoy yourself because I thought you were meeting Verity for dinner?'

'She bombed me out. Got a better offer.'

There was silence on the other end of the phone and Yvie knew what was coming.

'Don't say it!' she warned.

'How about if I say it really fast and you can take the phone away from your ear until I'm done?'

Yvie knew that resistance was futile. Better to get it over with. 'Okay, go.' She stretched her arm, moving the phone handset at least two feet away. Nevertheless, she could still hear every word Kay was saying.

'You really need to stop letting people take the piss! Verity and Marina are grown women who can handle their own problems without calling you up every bloody night to moan. And don't get me started on your mum. Does anyone ever ask how you are? No, they bloody don't. It's time you start putting yourself first and stop allowing your whole existence to be about supporting everyone else. Oh, and you need to get a life. And have sex. End of sermon.'

Yvie returned the phone to her ear. 'Sorry about that. I just nipped to the loo,' she joked.

She could picture Kay shaking her head. This was a conversation they'd had at least once a fortnight since the beginning of time. Except, she hadn't thrown in the standard line of...

'Seriously, Yvie, come on. They think they can just snap their fingers and you'll come running every time.'

There it was. That old, familiar but admittedly true, chestnut.

There was no point even delving into this argument because Kay was absolutely correct. However, saying that she needed to stop being everyone's emotional crutch and doing it were two very different things. Besides, wasn't that what family was for? And, for the purposes of that viewpoint, she was overlooking the fact that the only person who ever reciprocated any kind of interest or care was Zoe. There were givers and takers in life. They'd all long conceded that Marina and Verity paddled in their mum's side of the gene pool, while Zoe and Yvie clearly had some kind of regressive gene that facilitated concern for others.

'I know. You're right. I'll start establishing some kind of boundaries, I promise.'

'You do?' Kay sounded genuinely surprised, probably because Yvie usually ignored her complaints about the Danton family taking advantage.

'I do. And I'll... Oh, bollocks, I need to go – Verity is on the other line.'

'Aaaaghhhhhhh...' Kay was still screaming in frustration when Yvie disconnected her.

'Hey, luvly, what's happening?' she asked, in the same soothing voice she used for a patient that was one the edge of a serious crisis.

'YOU WILL NEVER FUCKING BELIEVE THIS.'

It took Yvie a moment to compute. It was Verity's voice, but Verity – like Marina – never swore. Not ever. She said some pretentious twaddle about it showing a lack of vocabulary. Honestly, sometimes Verity treated them all like they were her pupils and only just stopped short of telling them to sit up straight and get their Janet and John books out. Thus, whatever had riled her to expletive levels had to be monumental.

'What? What's happened?'

'I'm not talking about it on the phone. Can you meet me like we'd planned?'

Kay's words rang in her ears. *They snap their fingers and you jump*. Or something like that. Guilty as charged. She should take a stand. Say no. Stick to her guns and refuse to be anyone's fallback plan. But then her eyes fell on the Weight Watchers 350-calorie lasagne that was sitting on the kitchen counter, and her mind went straight to the menu at Gino's trattoria. Bruschetta. Chicken arrabbiata. The most exquisite focaccia she'd ever tasted.

'Sure. I can be there in fifteen minutes.'

'I'll see you there.' Not even a 'thank you'. Kay was so right, but she didn't care. Who was going to be there for her sisters if she didn't rise to the task?

Microwave meal shoved back in fridge, she summoned an Uber and headed downstairs when she heard it beep its horn outside. The roads were quiet – the Friday-night rush hour long over, the taxis carrying revellers on nights out only just beginning to crawl round the 20mph zone in the city centre. Gino's was in the Merchant City, a cosmopolitan, trendy area packed with upmarket bars, restaurants and boutiques. Yvie had discovered it because it was at the end of a gorgeous street of shops and salons that she loved to go to on her day off.

Gino himself was in his seventies now but he still had the gregarious, smooth charm of someone half his age. He'd come over to Glasgow when he was fourteen to work in his uncle's ice cream shop for the summer. The week before he was due to return to his village in a remote area of Cassino, two months wages in hand, he'd met a young girl called Alice, his first and only love. They'd married fifty years ago, had three children and eventually inherited his uncle's shop. His hard graft and good business sense transformed it over time into a thriving restaurant that became one of the legendary eating establishments in this area of the city. Tonight, he welcomed her as he did all his regular customers – like she was a long-lost relative coming with news that she'd just won the lottery and was prepared to share it.

'Yvie, my darling!' he bellowed, making everyone within earshot – which included most people in his postcode area – smile. 'I thought you cancelled your table, bella, no?' Bugger. That small but pertinent detail had slipped her mind.

'I did, but we've had a change of plan. Do you still have a table free? If not, it's no problem. It's my fault for cancelling.'

'For you, I find the moon and the stars,' he promised her, with a twinkle in his eye. He gestured to his son, who had just delivered a pizza the size of a satellite dish to a nearby table. 'Carlo, show our favourite lady to her special table.'

Carlo grinned as their gazes met, both of them acknowledging the inside joke that Gino told everyone – male or female – that they were all his favourite customers, and there was absolutely nothing that made the table she was being shown to any more special than the other forty just like it.

'You'd think it would get old,' Carlo quipped, with a grin, as she sat down at a gorgeous red leather banquette, that semi-circled around a solid, aged, but utterly beautiful deep mahogany table.

'And yet, I'll take it every time. Honestly, my ego adores him,' Yvie chuckled. 'How's Suzanne? Suzette? Suz—'

'Ah, long gone,' Carlo admitted, with not too much regret,

as he took a white cloth napkin from the table and flicked it expertly on to her lap.

'Carlo! You're really going to have to come to terms with the concept of longevity, you know.'

After Gino and the chicken arrabbiata, teasing Carlo was her third favourite thing about coming here. They'd been friends for years and over that time she'd watched a string of girlfriends come and go. It was easy to see why he didn't have too many problems securing dates. In his early thirties, his omnipresent stubble, sallow skin and beautiful brooding dark eyes balanced the Roman nose and angular jawline. Add a genetic win with his father's charm gene, and it pretty much made him irresistible. Except to Yvie. She'd never even considered anything more than friendship because he was a guy that liked them dark, slim and exotic – the closest she got to exotic was necking a Turkish Delight on payday.

'How many times do I have to tell you I'm waiting for you to fall in love with me? The others are just a distraction until then.'

Ah, his father's charm struck again. They both knew that just as Gino promised that each customer was his favourite, Carlo turned on the charm to everyone he served and his declarations of affection were throwaway lines to make her smile.

'Sorry, I'm saving myself for Zac Efron. I've got such a feeling he has a thing for chunky nurses.'

Carlo's laughter was raucous, but he was prevented from continuing the conversation by a bloke a few tables away, who was beckoning him with a loud, 'Excuse me.'

Instead of using words, Carlo feigned stabbing himself through the heart, then staggered off in the direction of the customer. Yvie was glad she'd come. She needed a giggle.

And she also knew Carlo would be back shortly with a large glass of vino. He didn't even have to ask. They had an ongoing tradition where he would bring her a new wine to try every time she came. Some of them were awful, some were wonderful. A bit like her sisters, she could hear Kay saying in her head.

Talking of which, strange that Verity wasn't already here. She was sure she'd said something about already being in town.

Yvie opened the flap on her gorgeous black Ted Baker bag (a gift from Zoe, naturally) and pulled out her phone.

Shit. A text notification on the home screen and even just glancing at the first line, she could tell what was coming.

Sorry Y – another change of plan. Too bloody furious to meet. Just going home. Will call you tomorrow. PS: Hope you haven't left yet. Vx

Spirits down, blood pressure up. Damn.

Checking the time, Yvie saw the text had come in while she was in the Uber. She'd been too busy chatting to the driver to notice the screen light up and she must have accidentally flicked it to silent when she slid it into her bag.

Again, damn.

'Can I have that to go?' she asked, as Carlo returned with something of a rosé variety.

'You have been stood up?'

'I have.'

'I'll kill him,' Carlo offered, making her laugh again.

'Thanks, but that won't be necessary. It was Verity I was supposed to be meeting.'

'Okay, I'll let her live. But only because she's family.'

'I'll pass on the good... Aw!'

Her phone buzzed in her hand, startling her.

She didn't even have to look at the screen. It was her mother's standard time slot.

Carlo backed off as she put it to her ear.

'Hi, Mum,'

'It's not mum, it's me,' Marina said tersely.

Yvie's worry mechanism switched to high alert. Marina sounded stressed. But then, when was she not?

'Where are you?' Marina demanded, dispensing with any small talk.

'I'm at Gino's. I was supposed to be meeting Verity, but she's stood me up again.'

'Oh, thank God.'

Not the reaction Yvie had been expecting.

'I need to talk to you,' Marina continued.

'You want me to come over?'

'No, I'll come to you. I'll be there in about half an hour.'

The line went dead before Yvie could ask any more.

A twist of anxiety began to make her breath just a little shallower and she fought to suppress it, push it back down. What now? What fricking drama was about to befall them this time? And how was she going to sort it and keep everything on an even keel? Christ, life would have been easier if she'd taken another path. Maybe joined a United Nations peacekeeping force in a war-torn nation.

Deep breath. Try to exhale the knot in her chest. Big smile on. She could do this, but she might need a little help. She held up her wine glass. 'Carlo, keep them coming. It's going to be a long night.'

10

Marina barely heard the noise of the crunching gravel as she accelerated out of the driveway. The dual thunders of guilt and panic were blocking out all sounds, just as they were now in control of her driving, putting her on autopilot as she made her way to the restaurant.

It went without saying that the previous night had been a mistake. Perhaps her biggest one ever. And until the day she took her last breath, she'd never understand why it had happened.

There was nothing too out of the ordinary about the first few hours of the day before. As always, she'd got up at 5 a.m. to work out, then ordered an online grocery shop to be delivered at the weekend from Waitrose, answered all the emails about sports practices, social events, kids' parties and dinner invitations and checked everyone's schedules for the day. So far, so normal.

Graham regularly accused her of being a helicopter mother, but what he didn't realise was that the world demanded this level of parental input now. One of Oscar's friends had spent the summer in Beijing practising his Mandarin, another had a former professional footballer as a private sports coach, and so many of Annabelle's friends were being hothoused, there must be an orange glow over their area that could be seen from space. This was the reality of bringing up children in the post-millennial generation. The twins weren't falling behind, she'd make sure of it. Besides, he seemed to require her to organise the minutiae of his life too, so it was definitely a case of the pot calling the kettles high maintenance.

Early morning duties complete, her mind went to the day ahead. Oscar had a maths exam that she wasn't too worried about, because she'd doubled up on his tutor this week to prepare for it. Graham had an important meeting, so she'd had his favourite suit dry-cleaned. The housekeeper would be in at 9 a.m., so she'd left meticulous instructions on the extra tasks she wanted completed, then dropped a text to the florist, reminding them that she wanted only long stem lilies in her weekly delivery. Fresh flowers in the hallway were a must.

Only when all that was done, did she make three individual, nutritionally balanced breakfasts, rouse a snoring Graham with a cup of coffee and a copy of the newly delivered *Financial Times*, then wake the kids. As always, he was dressed and out of the door, newspaper under his arm, before Annabelle and Oscar even made it down for breakfast. Sometimes she wondered if he had any idea what was going on in their lives, and every time she came up with the same answer – he hadn't a clue. Their marriage had somehow evolved into an arrangement reminiscent of the 1950s – he focussed on work and financially supporting them while she took care of everything else. Although, unlike a fifties mother, she was a woman with an international business management degree who'd given up her career before it even started and who now spent her day mapping out her offspring's lives using Excel spreadsheets, Google diaries and tracking their every movement with Find My Family.

At the kitchen island, she made a quick slice of wholemeal toast with avocado for herself, then. 'Annabelle, are you ready for today? Have you done your stretches? I'll come up after breakfast and check you've packed everything you need in your bag. I've notified your teachers that you'll be off today and tomorrow. Oh, and Oscar, I've called Mr Angus about your French grade. It's clearly wrong. There's no way we're settling for a C after all the work that we did to prepare for it.'

What was the point of bringing in a French tutor for six months if the result was going to be a diabolical C? It was total nonsense. There had to be an error in the marking and she was damn well going to get it sorted. Graham had suggested letting Oscar deal with it himself, but this was too important to leave it to a twelve year old who would undoubtedly be railroaded by some incompetent teacher who was probably too busy planning his next holiday to concentrate on getting Oscar decent grades.

Urgh, she despaired. But that was a problem for later. Today there were other priorities.

Twenty minutes later, they had loaded overnight bags into her Range Rover Evoque – she'd wanted the Discovery Sport, but Graham had said they couldn't justify it, although apparently they could justify his new top-spec Jaguar – and were on the way to the first drop-off of the day.

They'd pulled up outside the private school that both he and Annabelle attended, but unlike every other morning,

Oscar was going to school but Annabelle was staying in the car.

Oscar had unclipped his seat belt and leaned forward to whisper to his sister, 'Good luck.'

Annabelle stopped biting her bottom lip for long enough to reply, 'Thanks.' She even sounded like she meant it.

Well, well, well – a whole conversational exchange without an argument. Hallelujah. She and her sisters still hadn't managed that and they were far from their pre-teenage years. Perhaps by the time the twins thirteenth birthdays rolled around in a few months, they'd be bosom buddies. She could live in hope.

'Goodbye, darling,' Marina said, as Oscar pulled the door handle. 'I've texted you reminders of everything you need to do before we get back tomorrow, but just call me if there are any problems.'

Oscar gave her something between a nod and a shrug that she took to mean 'okay, Mum' in the body language of the prepubescent male. And female for that matter. Although her children were twins, they shared very little in common except the same family, same environment, same birthday and same ability to react to most instructions with a blank stare and a shrug.

Marina blew him a kiss as he closed the door behind him.

'Are you okay there?' she'd asked her daughter, who – right on cue – shrugged and nodded her head.

Marina had steered the car out of the space, dodging streams of other 4x4s on the school run, and made their way to the M8 motorway, heading towards Edinburgh. The destination was only an hour away, but it had taken two years of work to get this far. The Caledonia Academy of Contemporary

Dance and Drama was a revered place in the world of theatre and art, a boarding school that had been the training ground for some of the nation's biggest stars. Now Annabelle was about to audition for a place and Marina could feel the anxiety rising with every passing mile. Annabelle must be feeling it too, because she'd barely spoken a word since they left the house.

'Are you okay? Are you coming down with something?' Marina had asked, the car wavering slightly as she reached over to the passenger seat to check the temperature of Annabelle's forehead.

'I'm fine,' came the sullen reply, as her daughter ducked away from her reach, swatting the air as if defending herself from an irritant.

That had made Marina even more concerned. Sure, Annabelle could be stroppy, but this was her dream, the goal she'd been working for since she'd pulled on her first leotard at four years old. A career in dance was all that she'd ever wanted and her talent had been clear from the start. Well, perhaps not right at the start, but after two years of supplementing her classes with far too bloody expensive one-on-one lessons, she'd began to rise above her peers. Everything they'd done – all the training, the shows, the competitions, the sacrifices Marina had made to facilitate Annabelle's ambitions – had been leading to this. And now Marina was getting the sullen treatment?

'Are you nervous?' Marina had probed.

Annabelle didn't even drag the gaze of her beautiful big brown eyes from the window. She'd definitely taken her looks from Marina's side of the gene pool. Thank God.

'Then what's wrong, darling? Surely you should be excited about today?'

'I am. But it's just... I'll be at boarding school for years. Don't you even care that I'll be gone?'

Marina was so shocked, she momentarily lost concentration and the car swayed again, this time the left hand wheels crossed on to the hard shoulder.

'Of course I'll miss you! Every single day! How could you even think that I wouldn't?' Astonishment mixed with irritation had made her knuckles turn white as they gripped the wheel.

'Darling, everything we've done over the years has been to support you in your dreams, and that dream has always been to go to the dance academy. If you're telling me you've changed your mind, then I'll turn this car right around and we'll go straight back home.'

Like hell we will, said the voice in her head labelled 'maternal martyrdom'. Getting Annabelle to this point had been almost a full-time job – she'd been chauffeur, costume maker, advisor, financier, agent, manager and bloody cheerleader for years and she'd done it all because she was going to make sure Annabelle reached her full potential. Didn't that girl know how lucky she was? When Marina was a kid, she'd had no support, no help. Everything she'd achieved, she'd done it on her own. In fact, it was the opposite way around. She was the one who'd taken care of her sisters, who'd made sure everyone was where they needed to be, who filled the maternal role when their mother was off on another bloody yoga retreat.

A full-scale rant was building up like a tsunami of recrimination, but she'd held it back. Now wasn't the time to escalate any kind of emotional confrontation, not when Annabelle had a group choreography and rehearsal session this afternoon and then a two hour dance audition the following morning.

She'd watched her daughter's flawless face turn to her. 'No, I do want to go,' she'd murmured, shoulders shrugging, her words saying one thing, her body language and the hesitation in her voice saying another.

It was all Marina needed to hear. Back on course. Situation normal. Puberty had a lot to answer for, she'd decided, and the best thing to do was... The thought had tailed off as it suddenly struck her that she had to call Oscar's French teacher. And then the travel agent who was planning their mid-term ski break to Gstaad. And the car needed a service. And dammit, she'd forgotten to cancel her yoga class today. Maybe if she called right now, they'd waive the twenty-four-hours' notice policy. Especially after all the money she'd poured into their Lycra pants over the years.

The rest of the journey had been spent ricocheting from one call to another, organising, sorting, firefighting. When they'd reached the hotel, there was time for a quick lunch and then a five minute drive to the school.

Marina had tried to watch the session through the window of the dance studio door, but was shooed away by a member of staff who eyed her with blatant disapproval. Afterwards, all she could get out of Annabelle was that it had been. 'Fine. And like, seriously, Mum, you need to chill. By the way, Cindy is here too and she's asking if I can stay in her room at the hotel. Can I? Please? They're on the same floor as us, but they have a suite and there's an extra bed.'

Marina's display of nonchalance was so well portrayed she could have secured herself a place at the Academy of Contemporary Dance and Drama. Cindy Holten was the other star in Annabelle's dance club, and the closest one to her in talent. Personally, Marina was sure her daughter was slightly ahead of the competition, but Cindy's mum, Geraldine, was one of those relentless stage mothers. She shouted the loudest, pushed the hardest and she'd sell her granny and her Mercedes GLC if it would further Cindy's career. It was typical that she'd booked a whole suite for just the two of them, and typical too, that she hadn't even given the slightest hint that Cindy had secured an audition.

'Honey, no. You need your sleep before tomorrow and–'

'But it means we can practice!' Her daughter had countered.

'It also means you won't get enough sleep and that's more important.'

'But, Mum! Aaargh, you never listen to me! I need to PRACTISE!'

Marina had thought about it for a moment. Compromise. 'Okay, well, you can go and practise and then come back here at nine o'clock to sleep.'

By nine o'clock, after a terse phone call from Graham complaining that he'd had to leave work to collect Oscar from chess club (welcome to my world, she wanted to say), then another one asking if she'd sorted out the travel arrangements for Gstaad (she had), three calls to Oscar, checking he had everything he needed for the next day at school, a room service club sandwich, Marina had cracked open the minibar wine and poured a much-deserved glass.

This would be worth it. It would. When Annabelle had been accepted to the school, when she'd then used that training to go on to a glittering career on the stage, it would all be worth it. She would be the best, and Marina would support and encourage her every pirouette of the way.

The phone rang at five minutes past nine and Geraldine

Holten's plummy vowels assaulted her ears. 'Marina, darling, the girls are fast asleep. They practised for a couple of hours and then just conked out. Do you want me to wake Annabelle? She looks so settled.'

Marina could feel her teeth grinding together with annoyance. Bloody typical. If she woke Annabelle now, who knows when she'd get back to sleep. She'd been outmanoeu-vered by a twelve year old and a rival mother and it stung. 'No, that's fine, Geraldine, let her sleep. Send her along in the morning when she wakes up.'

'Yes, I think that's best. Goodnight, dear.'

Marina had disconnected the call and tossed her phone on the bed with a furious sigh and a discontentment that wouldn't budge, especially after another call from Graham to remind her to order flowers for his mother's birthday. What was she – a mother and wife, or a personal assistant and skivvy?

It was just after 10 p.m. when she'd switched off some trash TV programme starring a lot of tanned people with very big white teeth and decided to pour another glass of wine, only to find that she'd somehow managed to empty the half-bottle in the minibar. Call room service or break the monotony by going down to the bar and picking one up herself?

Pulling a black cashmere cardigan over her jeans and white T-shirt, she'd slipped on her Prada trainers and headed downstairs to the opulent lounge on the ground floor. She'd come here with Graham once, before the kids, when they were still in the giddy stages of love. They'd drank cham-pagne, then headed upstairs and made love until it was daylight outside.

A shiver of something had passed through her as she

climbed on to an ivory leather bar stool. Sadness? Regret? Loss? Maybe all of the above. Sure, she had security and comfort now, but at what cost? When had her life become one long list of mundane tasks and organisation for other people? When had she become the type of person who would feel her blood pressure rising about a twelve year old's low grade or the fact that non-organic bread was delivered by mistake? When had she made everyone else the priority? When had her life stopped mattering?

The barman, the kind of twenty-five year old, square jawed, attractive guy who probably modelled part-time and was called something like... she peered at his name badge... yep, Zac, gave her a warm, well-practised, tip-earning smile.

She was about to ask for a bottle to go, when she'd had a sudden feeling of independence. How long was it since she'd sat in a bar and been a grown-up? Since she'd actually been in her own world and not stressing about everyone else's? It felt... wonderfully liberating.

'A large glass of Merlot, please.'

He'd delivered it with the kind of smile that belonged on the trash TV programme she'd been watching twenty minutes ago. Wow, he was gorgeous. And damn, what was that stirring in her lower regions that hadn't been stirred or shaken in a long, long time?

The bar was quiet, just a few people scattered around on the plush red velvet sofas, some obviously work colleagues in groups, and two other tables occupied by the kind of couples who look far too into each other to be picking up socks and discussing wedding anniversaries.

Another feeling of freedom had flushed to the outside of her skin. A thrill. A decadence. There she was, across from a gorgeous man, in a beautiful room, and not a soul knew who she was.

One glass had turned to two, then three. Zac's brilliant white smile came closer to her face as he chatted to her. Marina found herself leaning in, and not because she was struggling to hear him.

They'd talked, they'd flirted and the whole time, cells of her body that had lain dormant for way too long, pinged back to life in such numbers that they formed some kind of rebellion, storming down a path that Marina, the wife, the mother, the organiser, the supporter, hadn't been down in way too long. It transpired that she was right about the part-time modelling and wrong about the age – at twenty-eight, he was only seven years younger than her.

It was way past midnight when Marina had realised they were the only people left in the room. It was immediately sobering. This poor guy must have been humouring her because she was a paying customer, when really he wanted to finish up for the night.

'Shit, I'm sorry. You must be desperate to get out of here.'

'I am,' he said.

Bugger. She'd definitely outstayed her welcome, even if it had been fun while it lasted.

That's when it happened. She'd realised he was still staring at her, a gorgeous, sexy grin on his face.

'But only because I have a room upstairs. They provide them for the bar staff when they're going from a late shift to an early shift.'

He didn't say it, but there was no mistaking the question written across his beautiful face. No. This was ridiculous. She couldn't. Wouldn't...

Something Zoe had said at Christmas came back to her, a

glib comment about Marina being the least likely of them all to pick up a stranger in a bar. That was enough to stage the final charge of the rebellion.

She'd picked up her glass, and the cashmere cardigan that had been discarded over the back of her bar chair, and said – oh, the mortification of the memory – 'I think I'd like to see that.'

Now, twenty hours later, only the sound of her tyres crunching to a halt outside Gino's restaurant stopped the replay of the previous night. Thank God. If it had kept going, she'd have relived going up to his room, feeling the most delicious thrill as he undressed her, and then many hours of the kind of ferocious, intoxicating, orgasmic sex that had been stuck somewhere in her distant memory. She'd also have relived a frantic return to her room that morning, a guilt-soaked shower, the return of Annabelle – clearly shocked that her mother didn't even chide her for the obvious stunt of manipulation the night before – and then a whole day spent in an emotional pendulum that swung between shock and panic, with just a brief pause at happiness when Annabelle was awarded a place at the school for the following year.

Right now, unbelievably, given that it had been their focus for years, that was the least important thing on her mind.

Yvie was so busy chatting to Carlo, she didn't even register her until she slipped into the seat across from her and stretched across Yvie's bowl of penne to give her a hug. Carlo went off in search of a Diet Coke, pretending not to be shocked that she wasn't ordering her usual Merlot.

'You rescued me!' Yvie exclaimed, her beaming expression warm as ever. She really was one of those people who radiated happiness. Marina felt a tug of jealousy – how great it would be to feel that carefree and content. 'Verity stood me up – twice actually – and I was facing a night of looking like Nobby No Mates, comfort-eating my pasta.'

Marina took a deep breath, completely unaccustomed to a situation which – for once – she had absolutely no control over.

'Actually, I need you to rescue me,' she said, watching as Yvie's face remodelled to reflect her confusion. Marina couldn't recall when she'd ever asked any of her siblings for anything.

Yvie put her fork down. 'Really? Okay, shoot. You know I'll do whatever you need.'

'Erm. So. Well...' The words were stuck in her windpipe until she performed the exasperated, panicked equivalent of a self-Heimlich and blurted them out.

'I need you to get me the morning-after pill.'

11

It is like one of those scenes in a sci-fi movie where some galactic evil force has attacked the good guys' spaceship with a super-weapon that freezes them in time. All three of my sisters are absolutely still, staring at me, jaws dropped, eyes wide with questions.

As always, it is Marina who lays her sushi on the coffee table and cuts to the point first.

'What the hell are you talking about? Is this some kind of joke?'

Right now, there is nothing I am wishing for more. 'The room that Ned was... was...' *Come on, say it*, I tell myself. '... Shagging someone else in, was paid for with a credit card in the name of Ms Dalton. I don't understand. The obvious explanation is that...' I stop. Unable to say it again. We don't get on all the time. We have our differences. God knows, we drive each other nuts sometimes. But I honestly can't believe that one of them would do this to me. My brain, however, is zipping ahead of me, coming up with odds, and probabilities, and suggestions and, eeeew, get that mental image out of my mind.

The fact remains that there are only four options for a credit card in that name and one of them is mine. And I know exactly where my credit card was that night, and it was nowhere near the room in which my husband was energetically abandoning the concept of monogamy.

If this were a dodgy Hollywood detective show, they'd look at who had the strongest motive. That one is easy. One of my sisters definitely comes up as suspect number one on that list. Although, I just wish I'd known that from the start, instead of finding out when the damage was already done...

12

'Good morning, gorgeous,' Ned murmured, as his body wrapped around Zoe's, his hand settling on her naked stomach, warm from the heat of her thick white duvet. 'You look deep in thought there. Hope it's about me.'

She was glad the blackout blinds were keeping her face in shadow, so he wouldn't see the glimmer of panic, before she made a quick recovery with, 'Nope, I was thinking about Brad Pitt. He's been calling me three times a day. Won't take the hint.'

Ned nuzzled sleepily into the concave of her neck. 'I don't blame him.'

Holding her breath, Zoe stayed perfectly still, hoping he'd go back to sleep. He'd got into a routine of staying over at her flat after they'd been out at the weekends and he liked to make love when they woke up in the morning. It was usually Zoe's favourite part of the day, but not today.

Today, on Easter Sunday, her mind was consumed with Tom. They'd been supposed to fly out this morning on a two week all-inclusive break to Mauritius, a holiday that was booked last November, a month before his ex, Chrissie, came back and reclaimed his heart. Instead, they'd cancelled the trip, and he was probably curled up in bed with her right now, making love and...

No. She blocked the thought. The last thing she needed in her life was a mental image of Tom being naked with someone who wasn't her.

It wasn't just the holiday or Tom's body she missed. It was still everything. His laugh, his voice, his touch. And it was made all the harder by the fact that she saw him every single day at work. They were friends. They genuinely were. But that didn't mean she wouldn't give anything for things to be different.

Things with Ned were going well, but he wasn't Tom. She just hoped this was like a seesaw – at some point the balance shifted and the ache of losing one person was superseded by growing feelings for someone else.

She gave herself a mental shake. Enough of this. Self-pity and moping weren't in her nature. Time to stop wallowing and start enjoying the day. Later she was having lunch with her family. But right now she had a wildly attractive man lying next to her and it was time to appreciate that. Her hand hadn't even made it to Ned's gorgeous tight buttocks when she heard her front door opening and closing, followed by, 'It's me. If you're doing something indecent, stop it right now because it'll scar me for life if I see it.'

Zoe immediately slipped several notches up the happiness scale at the sound of her sister's voice. Clambering out of bed, she pulled her black silk robe from the back of the door and wandered into the kitchen.

'There should be some kind of punishment for looking that good in the morning,' Yvie commented, through a disapproving purse of the lips. 'I wake up looking like someone has rearranged my face and set off some kind of explosion in my hair during the night.'

Zoe hugged her, laughing. 'No, you don't. You're permanently gorgeous.' She pulled back. 'Hey, what's with the scrubs? I thought you had today off? Do NOT leave me with Marina and Verity. I don't have the emotional reserves to survive a whole afternoon of judgement.'

Yvie flipped open a clear carton containing a 'tear and share' cinnamon roll and broke a chunk off. 'I hear ya, sista. I'm eating my feelings and it's not even ten o'clock.' She returned to Zoe's question. 'And I'll be there, but I just have to nip into work for a few hours first. They called to say they're short-staffed and need help. I'll be at the hotel for the kick-off at two, so you just have to get through pre-lunch small talk and you'll be fine.'

The last words were shouted over the noise of Zoe's Dolce Gusto machine as it delivered a large cup of fuel. She handed it to Yvie, then brewed another for herself.

'Anyway, I just wanted to drop these off, because I'll be coming straight from the hospital and don't trust myself not to crack them open to get me through the shift,' she said, pointing to a large box of Easter eggs on the counter top. Every year, they took it in turn to buy an egg for everyone in the family and this year the task had fallen to Yvie.

She took a large swig of her latte and then laid it down on the black granite worktop.

'Right, I'd better be going. I'll see you lat—' The word drifted off, as Yvie's eyes swivelled to land on Ned, who was walking into the room wearing just a pair of white Calvin Klein's.

Zoe watched in astonishment as her sister visibly squirmed with embarrassment.

'Jesus, what's up with you? You're a woman that gives people bed baths!' Zoe teased her.

'I'm only unflappable with the over-seventy age group,' Yvie quipped, recovering. 'Anyway, better go.' She grabbed another chunk of cake for the road. 'Hi, Ned,' she murmured as she passed him.

Zoe padded behind her, across the gloss oak floor towards the door. 'Listen, just one thing. Any idea why Verity is being completely weird with me just now? It's like she's permanently pissed off with me and I've no idea what I've done.'

'Nope,' Yvie replied, but it was way too quick and Zoe could have spotted the fib with her eyes shut.

'Yvie?' she asked, in a sing-song, I-know-you're-lying tone.

'I'm saying nothing. Sort it out yourself.'

'So there is something!' Zoe said, triumphantly.

Eyes wide, Yvie popped another chunk of cinnamon roll in her mouth to deter further speech, gave Zoe a wave and bolted out of the door.

Back in the kitchen, Ned came up behind her and wrapped his arms around her shoulders. 'What was all that about?' Each word was punctuated by kisses that worked their way along the line of her shoulder.

'I'm trying to get Yvie to spill why Verity is pissed off with me. There's definitely something going on. Is she okay with you in school? Has she said anything?'

His hair, already going in sixteen different directions, flopped over his forehead as he shook his head. 'Not a thing. But then, she was never exactly chatty.'

Zoe twisted around so that she was facing him, chest to chest. 'This is very true. But given that you have the emotional perception of, say, what's left of that cinnamon roll, do you think you'd have noticed if she was off with you?'

Ned lifted her up so she was sitting on the worktop, narrowly missing squashing said cinnamon roll. 'Fair point and the answer is probably no, I wouldn't have noticed. The only thing that was strange though was...' He paused, and Zoe could almost see the cogs of his brain turning. 'She told me a whole load of nonsense about the type of guys you'd been with in the past.'

That got Zoe's attention. 'Like what?'

'Well, she said that you only went for guys who were loaded, who flew first class, drove flash cars. She said that was the kind of stuff that you needed. Weird. Didn't you say the guy before Tom was a...'

'Plumber,' she confirmed, almost absent-mindedly as she focussed on the real issue here. What the hell was going on with Verity? Why would she say stuff like that? They'd had their squabbles over the years, but surely sabotaging relationships took things to a whole new level? This didn't make sense at all.

Only the delicious feeling of Ned's hands wandering up inside her robe made her lose her train of thought.

'Can I distract you with meaningless sex instead of discussing this further?' he asked.

In the choice between pondering over a problem or enjoying the moment, there was no contest. She'd worry about the Verity issue later. Right now, she would return her boyfriend's kisses and succumb to the absolutely blissful feelings that his hands were delivering. 'Absolutely. You should definitely play to your strengths.'

For the next hour, all thoughts of Verity and Tom were banished by the kind of Sunday morning encounter that burns off calories while naked. It was followed up with a bath for two, and then an hour spent reluctantly getting ready to face the world. At exactly two o'clock, with Ned now carrying the large box of Easter eggs, they walked through the sliding doors of the Kemp Hotel.

The Kemp Hotel Group was Zoe's favourite client. A chain of five luxury hotels in Glasgow, Manchester, Edinburgh, Aberdeen and – randomly – Ibiza, owned by Roger Kemp, a lifelong hotelier who had learned his craft in the elite corridors of London's Dorchester and Savoy, and the George V in Paris. Working class Glaswegian by birth, Roger had returned to his home city at the age of thirty and in the last ten years had built up a chain of hotels that were technologically advanced, hip, trendy and uber-cool – all brand messages that were enhanced on TV, radio and in the press, by his marketing team at The B Agency.

Roger Kemp knew his business inside out and personified his brand, right down to Felice, the French model he'd married in Paris on the same day she'd walked for Chanel. Zoe tried not to be jealous of her figure, her bank balance or her shoe collection, mainly because, despite an overflowing vat of blessings, Felice always looked bloody miserable.

Talking of which… The lift in front of them pinged open and Roger and Felice alighted, almost bumping in to Zoe and Ned.

Roger's reaction was instant. 'Ah, you're a sight for sore eyes,' he proclaimed, kissing her on each cheek, Felice standing behind him maintaining her customary expression of aloof disdain. Zoe had tried with her in the beginning but gave up after frosty response number 453. Roger, on the other hand, was on typically chipper form. 'Good to see you're frequenting my establishment. My marketing company charges a fortune, so I need the money,' he teased, then switched his attention. 'Good to see you too, Ned,' he said, with a warm, friendly nod, given that Ned's box of eggs prohibited a handshake. Zoe had learned that it was one of Roger's tricks of the trade. He always remembered a name and greeted everyone as if he was delighted to see them, even if – as with Ned – he'd only met them once before, for five minutes.

'I'd love to stay and chat, but my family are waiting and I'm not billing you for this meeting, so there's no point dragging it out,' Zoe said, with mock sincerity.

'And that's the kind of attitude that makes me glad you're on my side,' Roger bantered back, his amusement obvious. Felice, stunning in a white dress with a red and green belt that announced it was Gucci, stifled a yawn.

They bade their goodbyes, and Ned followed her into the open lift. 'Lucky I'm a secure kinda guy or I'd get worried about how much he likes you.'

Zoe reached up and kissed him on the lips. 'Much as I'm secretly touched by your jealousy, don't be crazy. Have you seen his wife? It would be like trading in his Porsche for a... a...'

'Ford Fiesta?' he asked, citing his own car.

'I was gonna say a bike,' Zoe countered with a giggle as the lift doors opened on the fifteenth floor. The View restaurant did exactly what the title suggested – offered a 180 degree vista of Glasgow. The first thing that caught her eye were the dark skies, visible through the floor-to-ceiling windows directly in from of them. The second was her family, already seated at a table in the far corner of the restaurant. A roll call wasn't necessary. Of course, Marina and her brood, Verity and their Mum and Derek would already be there. Punctuality was an obsession with that lot.

Ned said his hellos to everyone, even making the furrow between Marina's brows ease off for a second. In the light, it was obvious that Marina had lost weight. A new diet? A step-up on the fitness regime? Or something else? Whatever it was, it wasn't making her relax at all. Much as her tailored white jacket and shiny black bob gave the impression of someone who had it all under control, she still had a frown that had become an almost permanent fixture for about the last decade. Zoe genuinely worried that her sister needed either more fun in her life or more anti-furrow Botox.

Yvie wasn't there yet, probably held up in the ward as usual.

But there was Verity. Wearing a cream polo-neck jumper, her red hair loose and hanging in waves around her shoulders, she was striking as always. Although, it didn't escape Zoe's notice that her sister had strategically placed herself between Marina and their mum, so that there was no risk of her being beside Zoe. Meaningless? Zoe's gut told her it wasn't. But then, that gut had also told her that she'd be with Tom until the end of time, so it wasn't exactly reliable.

Her sister clearly had a problem with her and she wasn't leaving here today until she found out what it was.

13

Acting nonchalant around Zoe and Ned individually had become a practised art, but it was a sucker punch to the gut to see them walking into the restaurant all smiley bloody faces and swingy hands. How dare her sister swan around, flaunting her relationship to the whole family? She'd only met the guy in December and she was already acting like they were love's young dream.

This was the first time Verity was going to be in their company for a full day and there had been a giant-sized knot in her stomach since she woke at 5 a.m. that morning. Even cleaning her flat, her car and going on a five mile run hadn't eased it. Now that knot had worked its way up to a seething twist of disdain and loathing that was constricting her throat, making it difficult to even look at her sister.

The problem was that some messed-up part of the universe had taken over, and since Christmas, what had previously been a gargantuan crush on Ned Merton had turned into something much stronger. Despite the fact that he clearly wasn't interested, she thought about him as soon as she woke up in the morning. Last thing at night. And pretty much all day too.

Still, could be worse. She could be stuck between Marina and her mother at a family lunch, one side of her oozing irritation, the other mistaking her for some kind of marriage counselling service. For the last ten minutes, she'd been getting a blow-by-blow account of the latest instalment in her mother's never-ending relationship woes.

'The thing is, darling,' Marge wittered, her blue-mascaraed lashes trembling with emotion, 'you only get one life. And as I said to my ashtanga instructor this morning – by the way, the pelvic strength that gives you would have you cracking walnuts with your thighs...' She paused, thinking. 'Where was I? Oh yes, that's right. I was saying to my ashtanga instructor, Nigel, why should I stay when I'm not being valued for my true self? And Nigel told me I was quite right, too.'

Verity had an urge to bang her head repeatedly off the table until the blood in her ears drowned her mum out. More than that, a tiny seed of resentment began to swell, as it always did. This selfishness was what her dad had to deal with while they were married. This was the kind of thing that ground him down day after day. If only they'd had a happier marriage, maybe he'd have stayed, the divorce wouldn't have happened and then everything that came afterwards could have been avoided.

Self-preservation immediately kicked in and forced her brain to shut down that whole train of thought. Her dad had left them and his memory lived in a place that Verity didn't ever want to revisit.

Tuning back into the excruciating present moment and conversation with her mother was the only option.

'Where is Derek today?' she asked.

Marge flicked her hand dismissively, making the sleeve of her rainbow-hued kaftan droop dangerously close to the butter dish. 'Hospital. Varicose veins. He went in on Friday and he'll be there until Monday. I've told him I'll bring him some profiteroles on my way home. Which reminds me, have you thought any more about getting your eggs frozen? You know, darling, the monthly count will be dropping like a stone at your age.'

On second thoughts, even sitting between Zoe and Ned, joined at the wrist by pink fluffy handcuffs would be less painful than this. There was a time when her mother's wackiness had been more amusing than infuriating, but that moment was long gone. Marge had morphed from mildly neglectful hippie, to completely self-obsessed, to self-proclaimed feminist voice, to kaftan militant, and Verity had found every transition excruciating. What she'd give for a normal mum who baked cookies and didn't discuss her recent vaginal tightening over lunch.

To the relief of her reproductive organs, Zoe and Ned's arrival distracted Marge and she was no longer sitting waiting expectantly for an answer. A split second of relief was immediately countered by... Oh, no. Oh, dear God, no. Ned had pulled out the chair directly across from her and Zoe had plonked herself down next to him. If there was one thing worse than sitting next to Zoe, it was sitting facing her while she shot her megawatt smile at the boyfriend she'd stolen. This was hell. With butter knives that could be used as weapons. Verity surreptitiously slipped her hands under her legs in case she was tempted to take The View's loveliest silverware to Zoe's new Mulberry Bayswater.

Thank God for Marina, who emitted an exasperated sigh,

followed by, 'Anyone heard from Yvie? I hope she's not going to be late. We have to be home by four so that Oscar can practise his clarinet and Annabelle can work on her new routine. We haven't got all day to hang around here.'

'And happy Easter to you too, Marina,' Zoe teased, making the rest of the family laugh. 'Good to see you're taking a relaxed approach to the weekend.'

Verity took a small sliver of satisfaction in the fact that Marina shot Zoe a dagger stare.

Verity was still grinning when she realised that Ned was speaking to her and her entire being went into her practised state of normality-when-dealing-with-sister-dating-traitorous-object-of-affection. Calm. Nonchalant. Act normal.

'Hey, you look great! Glad to be away from the grind for a couple of weeks?' he asked her, slipping straight into teacher talk.

Calm. Nonchalant. Act normal. 'Absolutely. What about you? Any exciting plans?'

Like, say, finishing things with your girlfriend because she's completely wrong for you?

'Don't think so. This one can't get any time off work...' he playfully nudged Zoe's shoulder.

But I'm off. And that's why we would be perfect together. We have the same job, the same holidays, the same schedule, so much in common.

'So I guess I'll just relax and catch up on some reading or do a bit of decorating in my flat.'

Did I mention I have great taste? My home is lovely. I'd be happy to help.

'What about you?' he asked.

Okay, truth or no truth.

The truth was that she had nothing planned other than a

juice cleanse, a daily five mile run, a gym workout and a box set of *Poldark*. But that made her seem completely pathetic, so she went for... for... shit, what could she say? A flyer she'd spotted in the hotel reception came into her mind.

'Erm yeah, I've actually signed up for a week's rock climbing course.'

What? Seriously, what the hell was that? How STUPID could she be?

'Really?' Hang on, he seemed unduly enthused by this. 'I've been wanting to do one of those for ages. Will you ping me the details? I might join you. I mean, if you don't mind. I don't want to cramp your style.'

Calm. Nonchalant. Act normal... even though your head is ABOUT TO EXPLODE.

'Of course.' There was suddenly nothing more important than getting to reception to retrieve a flyer with all the details of that course. And yes, for the purposes of this turn of events, she was going to ignore the slight issues that she was terrified of heights, didn't even like climbing a ladder and had absolutely no desire to do anything that involved her feet leaving the ground.

Flustered, she started to rise from the table. Surely that flyer would still be there. She could just nip down, pick it up and quickly study all the details.

'Excuse me, I'm just nipping to the ladies'.'

'Oh, I'll come with you.'

Verity paused, mid-rise. Dammit. If there was one thing she wanted less than to climb a bloody wall, it was to have the opportunity for a cosy chat with her sister, who would no doubt regale her with cute stories about Ned. Urgh. She'd rather dangle from a thirty foot wall for a week.

Powerless to escape, Verity headed to the toilets, the click of Zoe's heels right behind her.

After lingering in a cubicle for an appropriate time, flushing the loo and heading to the basins to wash her hands, she began to relax. Almost free. Just a quick handwash and...

'V, can I ask you something?' Zoe said breezily.

At least a question was better than some cute little anecdote about Ned and something sweet he'd done for her.

'Sure.'

'Is there a reason that you told Ned that I only went for wealthy guys who could keep me in diamond knickers?'

Verity froze. Rabbit in headlights. Yes, she'd said that, but she hadn't thought for a moment that it would ever get back to Zoe. She'd said it to put him off, to make him see that they were wrong for each other and give up the chase.

Now Zoe was looking at her with a questioning gaze that was somewhere between confusion and a challenge and she was going to have to come up with something really quickly here.

'I did that to help you out.'

A pause, and she could see Zoe was attempting to digest this.

'Help me out how?'

'Look,' Verity began, thinking fast on her stilettoes. 'It was back in January and you were trying to brush him off. Remember? You didn't want to see him. And he kept asking about you...'

'Why didn't you tell me that?'

Think, think, think...

'Because you'd just broken up with Tom and you had enough on your plate! The last thing I wanted to do was give you another problem to solve. You said you weren't ready to be with someone else, I thought you meant it...'

'I did mean it.'

'Exactly! That's why I told Ned that to make him back off and give you space.'

Zoe's expression was changing now, morphing into some kind of understanding and acceptance. Jackpot.

Verity began to gain confidence as she found her stride with the lie.

'I thought I was doing you a favour, to be honest.'

'By making me sound like a superficial cow?' Zoe's words were piercing but they were delivered with an overtone of amusement, so Verity knew she was pulling this off.

'Have you seen how you react to a five star hotel and expensive handbags?'

Zoe feigned offence, then shrugged and laughed. 'True. I may very well have an inner superficial cow, but that's supposed to be between us.'

Back on solid ground, Verity switched on the gold tap to wash her hands in the marble basin and risked taking the joke to another level. 'It was either that or I told him that you had a sexually transmitted disease. It was a close call.'

Zoe's laughter exploded, almost making her drop the lipstick that she held poised and ready to apply. 'In that case, let me thank you for just making me seem mildly despicable instead.'

Verity took a sheet of paper towel from the automatic dispenser. 'You're welcome. Call on me any time you require someone to talk crap about you.'

Zoe was still laughing as she spritzed some perfume on her wrists. Verity fixed her red waves over one shoulder and breathed a sigh of relief, until...

'V, you are okay with me seeing Ned, aren't you?' The giggles were gone now, replaced with something that sounded more serious, a genuine concern.

'Of course, why wouldn't I be?' she blustered.

Zoe was watching her reflection in the mirror carefully. 'Just because, well, you work with him. I know he is a friend. I don't want you to feel uncomfortable, or that I somehow hijacked one of your mates.'

Which was exactly what she had done.

'Don't be moronic. I think it's... really lovely that you're seeing each other. You make a great couple.' Verity waited to see if the Gods of Utter Bollocks would send down a bolt of lightning to strike her down. Nope, nothing. She carried on, 'I'm happy for you. It's good that you've got someone after... you know... Tom.'

A flinch of satisfaction as a shadow of hurt crossed Zoe's face, before she shrugged off the feeling. That was Zoe. Resilient as always. Knock her down and she bounced like a fricking rubber ball.

'Yeah, that one stung for a while. Men, eh?' Again Zoe shrugged off the dip in the mood. 'Anyway, fuck it.'

'Don't swear,' Verity chided.

Zoe paid her no attention, as she carried on, 'We only live once, so there's no point moping. I'm glad you're okay with everything. I definitely got a sense that you were being a bit off with me and I was worried.'

'Not at all! I've just been a bit tired, that's all. We're fine, I promise. I'm really happy for you.' There was just a tiny twinge of guilt when Zoe leaned in and squeezed her tight.

They picked up their bags and moved towards the door, Verity plotting a new excuse to go down for the flyer.

'I'll be two minutes,' she told Zoe as they left the loos.

'Some of the girls at work asked me to pick up a leaflet about the hotel's spa days. I'm just going to nip down to reception and grab one while I remember.'

Zoe's lack of reaction showed she'd bought the story.

'Yeah, no worries. By the way, I heard you and Ned talking about that climbing course. Are you okay if he tags along with you? I'm worried he'll be bored without me next week.'

Verity could feel the flames of fury rising up her neck. It was one thing Ned saying he wanted to come with her, but Zoe acting like she was some kind of consolation prize made her seethe yet again. What was she? Zoe's stunt double? Someone to keep her boyfriend amused while he waited for the person he really cared about to come home from work every night? Damn, she had a bloody cheek!

But she said none of that. Instead, she smiled and took her sister's hand as they walked towards the door. Sod it, she would pick up the leaflet on the way out.

'Of course I'm fine with that. I'll keep him busy, don't worry.'

14

Yvie gently placed the package down on top of the nursing station like it was unstable plutonium and could explode at any moment. She stood back, took a bow, making the corners of Kay's mouth twitch as she attempted to replicate the gravity of the situation.

In hallowed tones she announced. 'One extra-large dinosaur Easter egg, unbroken and uneaten. Please arrange my badge of honour as soon as possible.'

'I'll get Chester on it straight after he's bitten off the first chunk. Although, he'll love this so much he might just stare at it until summer,' Kay told her, before suddenly jumping up, leaning over and giving Yvie a tight squeeze. 'Thank you so much. I can't tell you how much I appreciate how good you are to him.'

Yvie returned the hug but shrugged off the praise, noticing the red rings of tiredness under Kay's eyes. Single parenting with little help, while working every extra shift to bolster her wages, was definitely taking a toll. The least Yvie could do was try to pitch in and take a bit of the pressure off.

'Don't be daft. That's what aunties are for. Wait to see if you're quite so grateful when I'm his go-to person for sneaking him into nightclubs when he's sixteen.' She disentangled herself. 'Right, enough of the mushy stuff. What's happening here today and what do you need me to get started with? Oh, and I need to be away by 1.30 p.m. or Marina will most likely storm the building because my lateness is disrupting her schedule.'

Kay raised one eyebrow. 'You know, I'm absolutely convinced that she has no genetic link to you.'

'Me too,' Yvie agreed, with mock seriousness. 'There's no way I can be related to someone with that level of self-assurance and those organisational skills. Scientists should study us. We're an aberration.'

Kay paused for a second and Yvie knew exactly what she was going to say before it came out of her mouth. 'And is... Zoe going? With Ned?'

A red rash of mortification began to crawl up Yvie's neck, but before she could answer, she was saved by the... chicken.

'Dear God, what is that?' she gasped, as an apparition slowly came down the corridor towards her.

It was huge. It was yellow. It moved. It was... pushing a mop bucket.

'Is that Jean in a chicken costume?'

Kay nodded with complete nonchalance, as if the ward cleaner showing up to work in a chicken outfit was absolutely nothing out of the ordinary. 'Yup. She's going straight to an Easter party for her 231 grandkids, so she thought she'd come dressed and ready.'

'Of course she did,' Yvie said, deadpan. Jean had been the head cleaner on the ward since before any of them worked there, and they all adored the very bones of her.

Although the grandchildren tally was slightly exaggerated, they'd celebrated with her when yet another one of her brood added to their numbers. They were at seven children, twenty-one grandchildren and nineteen great-grandchildren so far. Jean was concerned that if they had many more, they wouldn't all fit in the fifty seater coach they hired for day trips.

'All right, my love?' Big Bird asked with a wink as she glided past them with the mop bucket.

'In case you're in any doubt, I bloody love you, Jean,' Yvie replied, giggling, earning a shake of yellow tail feathers in return.

'Okay, where were we?' Kay said, focusing back on the clipboard. To Yvie's relief, Kay didn't repeat the question about Zoe and Ned, and instead switched back to work stuff. 'Oh yep. Another one of your favourites is back in. Had a fall yesterday. Nothing serious, but we're keeping her for a couple of days for observation.'

'Really? Who?'

'Look behind you.'

Yvie turned, peered through the window into Room 1, a one bed unit that they used to assess new arrivals, and immediately bolted straight for the door. Sitting up in her bed, wearing pyjamas that pronounced she was, '50% woman, 50% angel, 100% adorable,' Babs hooted with laughter at the sight of her.

'Babs! Oh, it's lovely to see you. I mean, I'm obviously sorry about your fall, but if it's any consolation you're looking smashing.'

They both knew it wasn't true. Babs had a furious bruise on one side of her cheek and a bandage around her head, its shape indicating that she had a large pad attached to the back of her skull. Her spirits and her sense of humour did, however, appear unscathed.

'Aye, I was missing you, so I just did a wee bit of impromptu gymnastics to get me back in to see you all for a couple of days.'

Yvie reached over and squeezed her hand, careful not to disturb the IV drip attached to her arm. 'Well, we'll take good care of you, I promise.'

'I believe that's the standard we aspire to for all our patients, Nurse Danton?' Yvie felt her teeth grind together at the facetious tone deployed by Dr Seth Bloody McGonigle, arrogant twat, as he came through the door.

'Of course it is,' she answered with sugary sweetness. 'Thank you for reminding me.'

Babs, however, was not singing off the same song sheet. 'Well, someone has his boxers in a twist this morning, doesn't he?' she teased.

Dr McGonigle froze as Yvie tightened her lips as much as possible, determined to prevent herself from laughing or chirping in on the conversation. Either option would no doubt lead straight to a summons from Human Resources.

To make it worse, Babs wasn't finished. 'Did someone steal the blueberries out of yer muffin, buttercup?'

As Yvie turned to see his reaction, she felt Babs' hand tighten on hers. Dr McGonigle's surprise was written all over his face. Then several things happened at once. Babs' hand suddenly went limp and she emitted a strange, low, moaning sound. Dr McGonigle's expression immediately changed to one of confusion, as Yvie whipped her head round, saw that Babs' head had slumped to the side and she'd lost consciousness. Alarms sounded from the heart-rate monitor that was connected to her finger, indicating that Babs had no pulse. A light flashed above her bed. Her jaw slipped to one side as her face sagged, her body no longer breathing.

'Babs!' Yvie immediately sprang into action, flattening the bed, checking the stats, then calling for a crash cart while instinctively running through CRP drills and then starting compressions to Babs' heart. 'Come on, Babs. Come on,' she begged with every push.

Kay came running in, pushing the cart. Dr McGonigle immediately ripped open Babs' pyjama top, then placed the electrode pads in position, one near her right shoulder and the other beneath the lower left side of her chest. 'Clear,' he said forcefully.

Yvie lifted her hands, all of them on automatic now, their training dictating their actions. But that didn't stop Yvie's heart from shredding with every second that passed, every moment that Babs lay there unresponsive.

There was a commotion at the door as the emergency cardio team, specialists activated by pagers that responded to code blues everywhere in the hospital, stormed into the room. Seth McGonigle didn't even glance at them as he spat out a swift but comprehensive rundown of the situation. 'Mrs Barbara Welsh, admitted last night to A&E, transferred to this ward for observation, head injury, scanned at midnight, no issues on CT...'

On he went, as the defibrillator gave another shock to Babs' heart. No change. Still flatline.

The crash team joined in the efforts. Injecting, massaging, reshocking.

Yvie stood back, let them work, her eyes never leaving Babs' face.

She was gone. She could see it. And, twenty minutes later, the lead medic on the crash team acknowledged it too.

Time of death. 11.05 a.m.

One of the other nurses, a seasoned professional from the heart ward, stepped closer to Babs and reached for the electrode nearest to her.

Yvie put her hand out and stopped her. 'I'd like to do it,' she said quietly.

The other nurse recognised her feelings immediately, like some subliminal code was passed between them. This was more than just a patient. This was personal.

As the team left, Yvie kept her glance averted, unwilling to share the tears that were pooling in her lower lids. Not the kind of reaction that would be expected of an impartial nurse, someone who'd seen death many times in her career in geriatrics. But sometimes... sometimes it was just more than losing a patient. Babs had been in and out the ward many times over the years and she was so much more than a number.

'I'll go and call the family,' Kay said softly. 'You sure you've got this? I can do it.'

Yvie shook her head, her gaze still on Babs' face, settled now into an expression that looked almost peaceful.

'No, I want to,' Yvie murmured. 'But thanks.'

Key left the stillness of the room.

'I'm sorry.' The sound of Seth McGonigle's voice made Yvie start. She hadn't realised he was still there, standing by the door.

No words would come, but she thanked him with a nod.

A sudden thought. This was so Babs – going out while delivering top-grade cheek to someone in a position of authority. A tear fell now as Seth McGonigle left and Yvie closed the curtains, to give Babs privacy. The family would be notified. They might want to come in to see her. It was Yvie's job to make Babs and the scene around her look as peaceful as possible.

She began her work, clearing up the room, removing every trace of the chaos that had torn through there. Order restored, she changed Babs into the fresh pyjamas that Kay had brought in and left on the end of the bed, before letting Yvie know that Babs' daughter was on her way. Finally, she removed the bandage on her head, cleaned the wounds and the hair around it, then gently rested Babs back on the pillow, before taking a paddle brush from the top of the bedside table and brushing her silver hair the way she liked it, the same way she'd done every day for months during Babs' previous stay.

The falling tears didn't make a sound as they landed on the clean new crisp white sheet. 'Go easy, Babs. We'll miss you,' she whispered, stroking her face and then squeezing her hand one more time.

By the time Babs' heartbroken daughter, Pat, arrived, her mum looked serene, with even the bruising on her cheek paling so that, in the dim morning light, it was now barely visible.

There was no mistaking that this was Babs' daughter. In her fifties, she had the same ruddy cheeks, the same silver, curly hair and the same cackle of a laugh that had once filled the corridors of this hospital. Today, there was no laughter.

'Oh, Yvie, I can't believe it. All those months she was in here... I thought we were in the clear.' Standing at the end of the bed, Pat's voice was muffled through the hand that was clasped to her mouth. 'She's always been so bloody tough.'

Instinctively, Yvie wrapped her arms around her. Even through the thick wool of her winter coat, Yvie could feel her trembling. 'I know, Pat. I'm so sorry. She was one of a kind, she really was.'

Pat pulled a tissue from her pocket and dabbed at her eyes.

'I'll leave you alone for a little while. Kay and I will be just outside at the nursing station if you need us.'

She was almost out of the door when Pat replied. 'Thanks, Yvie. For everything. You were her favourite, you know. She never stopped going on about how lovely you are. And my mother wasn't a woman to give out compliments easily,' she added with a rueful smile.

'It was my pleasure, Pat. I'm so glad I got to meet her and spend time with her.'

Every word was meant.

Kay glanced up from the desk as Yvie approached and her expression immediately softened. 'You okay?'

'Just going to take this lot to the laundry, then wash up.'

'It's almost one o'clock, love. Just you head off. Are you sure you're okay?'

Yvie nodded. There was nothing she needed more than to get out of there.

'Thanks, Kay. If you need me to come back in later, just give me a call.'

Kay came round to the front of the desk and hugged her. 'I won't. But I will call to see how you're doing. Love you.'

'Love you, too.' The words came from somewhere inside her inner core of exhaustion, but, right then, she felt... nothing. Numb. Blank.

In the empty staffroom, Yvie tried to lift the kettle and realised that her hands were shaking so much she could barely move it. A memory. A throwback to many years before. She clenched her eyes shut and rested her head against the cold white gloss of the upper kitchen units. It was coming back. The numbness was changing to something else entirely. She could feel it. Her breathing was accelerating, the tremors were moving from her hands, to her arms, to her shoulders, spreading through the channels of her nervous system. Her chest tightened, as if a tank was rolling on top of it, squeezing her heart, trying to force it to stop, but it kept fighting, each beat throwing a punch through the bones of her rib cage. The adrenaline took her legs now and they gave way, making her slump to the floor, gasping for breaths that wouldn't come, sweat oozing from every pore. Eyes squeezed tight shut, she battled to stop the panic rising, using every tool she'd learned and taught to others. Like a drowning soul, she fought to breathe, to get control, to make it subside.

It could have been seconds later or it could have been minutes, but just when it felt like it would end her, the waves eased back, allowing her to rise to the surface for just long enough to fill her lungs, before going down again, then back up, then again, quicker each time, more breath, her chest easing just enough to reclaim her life.

When it finally ended, only anxiety remained. She didn't understand. Her adolescence had been crippled by the panic attacks that had started after the worst time of her life. They'd finally subsided after a few years, with the help of counselling, and now they had suddenly gone from being a horrendous memory to present tense.

Gradually, she pulled herself up, drank a glass of water, regained her equilibrium while checking her breathing, regulating it, steadying herself. A cup of tea. A seat. A few minutes of silence. Then, slowly, almost robotically, she dragged herself into the shower, where she scrubbed until physical pain replaced the void that had been there before.

Outdoor clothes on, bag, boots. Out of the room. Down in the lift. Into a taxi, clear thoughts finally returning.

Why?

Why now?

She'd lost patients before and been sad about their passing. True, Babs was someone she was particularly fond of and she'd died in the middle of a conversation with her, but why had that sparked a panic attack again after all these years? Or was there more to it? Did she just have too much on her mind? Had she let herself become emotionally drained and depleted her mental health reserves? She had no answers. Only questions and anxieties.

A buzz on her phone. Marina.

Can you make sure you're here by 2 p.m.? We don't have all day to wait. Things to do.

Then another. Her mother.

Thinking I'll come home with you after lunch. Need someone to chat to about Derek. Can you pick up something nice for dinner?

Then another. Zoe.

Hey pumpkin, hope it's an easy day at work. Are you on your way? I need some moral support here. And bring a blowtorch to defrost Verity. Ned could do with you being here too – he's outnumbered by people he doesn't know. Love you xx

She wasn't sure if it was the demands, the pressure, or the mention of Ned Merton, but her ribs began to contract inwards yet again, as her throat clenched, and her breaths came faster. She closed her eyes. *Breathe. Just breathe. You've got this.*

Way too soon, the taxi was pulling up outside the hotel. The driver got an Easter bonus as she passed him a twenty quid note, too frazzled and anxious to wait for the change.

In the lobby, she kept her head down, trying desperately to pull herself together. *Calm. Be calm. Be steady.*

By the time the lift doors opened on the highest floor, she was on top of it again.

Okay, she could do this. She could get through a lunch with her family and then head home and she'd find some excuse to put off her mum. Zoe would take her. She wouldn't mind. Actually, she probably would, but Yvie knew she'd do it if she asked her.

As the glass doors to the restaurant opened, they were hard to miss. 'Yaaaay,' went up a rising cheer at the sight of her, mainly from her mum, Oscar, Zoe and Ned. Marina's pinched faced relaxed for a second, which was the closest to jubilation that she got these days.

It took every ounce of strength in her body to slap on a beaming smile and greet everyone with some rapid-fire kiss blowing.

'Happy Easter, you lovely lot!' she proclaimed, forcing herself to sound as exuberant and enthusiastic as she always did.

That was her. Good old Yvie. Always happy. Never a down day. It's what was expected.

Zoe had saved her a seat next to her, on the other side from Ned, and she slipped into it. After a moment, her sister eyed her quizzically. 'Are you okay?' she asked, whispering so no one else at the table could overhear.

'Absolutely fine,' Yvie shot back, with what she hoped was a realistic smile. 'Never better.'

Zoe seemed convinced, so Yvie carried on, deciding to distract herself in the very best way she knew how.

'Right, who's got a menu? I'm famished.'

15

At last, Yvie had graced them with her presence! Just as well she was only five minutes late – any more than that and Marina would have insisted they start without her. Did none of these people have schedules? Things to do? She didn't need anyone to answer that. Of course they didn't – not on a Sunday, with a holiday the next day. Well, it wasn't a holiday for her, Graham or the kids. He'd no doubt disappear into his office later, leaving her to work with Oscar for his grade five clarinet exam on Tuesday. Then, she'd promised to video Annabelle going through her latest routine. The Scottish Contemporary Dance Championships were just around the corner, so there was no time for a day off. If she was placed in the top three in her category, it would definitely make the instructors at the academy realise what a talent she was.

Beside her, Graham was discussing wine choices with the waitress.

'Yes, but is it full-bodied? I do find that Rioja can some-times lack a bit of depth.'

Her hackles began to rise. Could he not just order a bottle of bloody wine? Did he have to go through this whole godforsaken performance every time they went out? This was the guy who'd rebelled against his private-school background and drank cheap cider in dive bars with her during their first year at uni. Of course, his little mutiny didn't last long. By year three, he was in the wine club and vice president of the Fine Dining Society, eating foie gras with his old chums in wood-panelled Edinburgh members' clubs.

'I'll have a Bloody Mary,' she interjected, gratified to see a flash of confusion cross his earnest brow. Christ, he was insufferable sometimes.

Or was he?

Had he changed, or had she?

Once upon a time, she'd adored him. He'd been such a catch, her wealthy, ambitious man. Of course, his mother had been outraged by Marina's pregnancy and demanded that she terminate it. Instead, she'd terminated her plans for the future. She'd been six months pregnant when she'd graduated with a first in international business management – a degree that had been utterly worthless for the last twelve years as a stay-at-home mother and wife.

'Yes, well, perhaps we'll try the Cabernet,' he declared, mighty chuffed with himself as he snapped the wine list shut and handed it back to the waitress.

When had his habits, his mannerisms, the way he cleared his fricking throat before he spoke – when had that all started to irritate the life out of her?

He rewarded himself for his brilliance by putting his hand on her knee. It was all Marina could do not to slap it away, only distracted at the last minute by the buzz of her phone in her handbag.

Fuck.

Everyone who would perhaps text her on a Sunday was right here around this table. Of course, it could be a harmless notification from the bank. Or a thank you from a charity for her monthly donation. Or maybe even a shopping service saying her delivery was on the way.

But it wasn't. She knew it. She could feel it radiating from the depths of her vintage Gucci Positano tote, trying its damnedest to permeate the shell of her family, of her life. Worse, it was like a magnet, forcing her to acknowledge it. It was the car crash you didn't want to look at but yet your eyes were transfixed. Or the scab that you absolutely did not want to pick.

Pulling her bag onto her knee, she delved inside, making sure the tote was angled away from Graham so that there was no chance of him spotting the message on the screen when she found it. She needn't have worried. He was too busy discussing the merits of his new F-Pace Jag with Oscar on the other side of him, next to Annabelle, who was in rapt conversation with her Aunt Zoe and Aunt Yvie about something Jennifer Lopez said on some dance show. She really needed to monitor her viewing more closely.

The iPhone was in her hand now, screen tipped towards her as she strained to see the message without removing it completely from her bag. Sender? It said Edinburgh Hotel. That was all. It was the name she'd saved his number under after the first time he'd texted her, the day after their hook-up. She'd immediately replied, asking him not to contact her again. It didn't take a genius to work out that he must have looked at her reservation record to get her mobile number. But what was she going to do? Report him? *To Whom It May Concern, I had sex with one of your employees and now he's texting me. Please give him refresher training on the extent of his customer service duties, then ask him to delete my number. Sincerely, Married Guest With Plenty To Lose.*

Er, no.

It had been mortifying enough that she'd had to ask Yvie to get her the morning-after pill, but she just couldn't risk getting it herself in case Graham ever found out. It had been hard enough to swallow it past the lump of fear in her throat. Her sister had obliged and swore not to mention it ever again. Unfortunately, the barman didn't feel the same.

Since that first text, there had been another two or three, all casual, all firing right to the heart of the part of her that would kill to protect the family and the life that she had built.

That should be it. Full stop. End of story. Yet... there was a thrill that lived somewhere deep inside her, one that she'd suppressed for as long as she could remember, that was ignited and flamed like a Bunsen burner at the thought of that night. Right now, with Graham smacking his lips and making a complete fricking show of tasting the wine, the feeling was intoxicating, it was bliss, it was...

'Marina, are you okay?' Zoe asked.

Marina's head whipped around like a whirligig in a high wind.

'Yes, of course. Why wouldn't I be?'

Defensive. That wasn't good. Calm down. Move along people. Nothing to see here.

'You just look a bit flushed. Is it too warm in here?' Zoe asked, genuinely concerned.

Thankfully, a new arrival to the table took the heat off her. Quite literally.

'Did I hear someone uttering a complaint in my restaurant?' Roger Kemp asked, his bombastic grin as endearing as ever. Marina had met him a few times when she'd been here with Zoe. It was impossible not to enjoy his energy. He was one of those guys that filled the room and made everyone in it feel completely at ease. Or at least, as much at ease as Marina ever felt. Especially when her family was around.

Text forgotten, phone dropped back into the depths of her bag, she slipped her tote back down on to the floor, while Zoe beamed at him.

'Too hot?' he asked Marina, a playfulness in his voice.

Shit, bugger. Was she really that flushed? And if so, was she too young to blame the menopause? Anything rather than admit that it was down to a reminder of a random hookup that was utterly sublime but could quite easily ruin her life.

Practised smile on, her voice controlled and as close as she could muster to matching his playfulness.

'Not at all. It's perfect in here, as always,' she fired back smoothly. Roger Kemp was one of those people she liked to keep on side as you just never knew when he'd come in handy for staging a private party or getting a dinner reservation at the last minute. It wouldn't harm Graham's profile to be seen as a friend of Roger's. Unlike, say, news that his wife was out picking up random men in bars.

The thought made her shudder.

'Marina, I definitely think you're coming down with something. You're shivering now,' her mother exclaimed.

Jesus, could she not have a minute's bloody peace to have a private emotional reaction to the memory of one of the best and worst things she'd ever done?

A once in a lifetime blip. Something that would never happen again. Absolutely not. No way.

'Anyway, glad I caught you, ladies, because I have a proposition,' Roger was saying now.

'Oh dear. That sounds ominous,' Zoe teased him. 'Will it end with us in debt or jail?'

Roger's laugh filled the room again, other diners turning to see what was going on. 'God, I hope so. Think of the publicity.'

Zoe grinned at him, and for a second Marina had the thought that her sister was far more suited to this charismatic force of nature than she was to Ned. There was nothing wrong with Ned, and there was absolutely no getting away from the fact that he was undeniably handsome with a body that was toned, fit, and incredibly sexy...

She stopped herself. Jesus, her hormones were doing somersaults here. Maybe this was the start of the menopause after all. This had to end. No more obscene thoughts, no more letting her guard down, and definitely no more one night stands. She just had to keep herself busy and concentrate on her family – that way she would never have the opportunity or the time to get up to anything untoward.

'Go on then, proposition us,' Zoe joked.

'Well, I've had an idea that I'd like to put to my marketing guru,' he began, with a wink at Zoe, 'and I thought you lot might be able to help. We've decided to do a push on spa weekends to the hotel in Ibiza. You know, capture groups of girlfriends celebrating special birthdays or having a last blast with a bride before the wedding. Or maybe just a well-deserved rest from work and responsibilities at home.'

Marina began to zone out. Obviously, he wanted them to tell all their friends about this. Fine. She could spread the word amongst the other dance mums, dropping in the fact that Roger Kemp was a personal friend.

'But I want real people to be the face of it. I think it's

important to show chemistry in a campaign and tell the story behind the pictures.'

Marina noticed that Yvie and Verity were leaning forward to listen, as Zoe laughed.

'Good strategy. You've clearly been learning from your marketing guru. I think she sounds fabulous,' she said, returning a cheeky wink that made Roger Kemp's grin even wider.

The whole table was captivated now. Even Graham had stopped sniffing his bloody wine.

'Oh, she is,' Roger agreed, making Zoe laugh and take a mock bow.

Was it Marina's imagination or did an irritated frown just cross Ned's face?

Back to Roger. 'So, I realised that the perfect people to kick off the campaign would be four gorgeous sisters. How would you ladies fancy an all-expenses paid weekend at my hotel in Ibiza? All you would have to do is allow us to take a few photos, give us some quotes and blog about it on the hotel website. Did I mention it's a five star resort and you'll be pampered day and night?'

Suddenly, Marina was paying attention again. A free holiday in a five star paradise sounded great... but she had commitments here. Duties to fulfill. Even as she was thinking it, she knew that wasn't the reason that she couldn't go. She'd had one taste of freedom in the last decade and look what had happened. A twenty-something barman thought they were Romeo and fricking Juliet. It was such a bad idea. There was just no way she could do it. She no longer trusted herself not to act like a hormonal teenager on their first Club 18–30 holiday.

'Oh, dear God, if I didn't already love you because your

restaurant serves this cake, I definitely love you now,' Yvie said, with her fork standing straight up in a slice of red velvet sponge that was so large it could be used as a doorstop.

'Obviously I couldn't possibly refuse my favourite client,' Zoe chuckled. 'So I'm definitely a sure thing.' That made Roger grin and Ned frown again. Oh, there was definitely some kind of weird tensions going on there.

But back to the current tension of her own.

Verity wouldn't agree, Marina was sure of it. There was no way she'd want to spend a weekend with Zoe right now…

'As long as it's in the school holidays, I'm in,' Verity said. Bloody Judas.

Roger Kemp was unperturbed. 'We can make that work. How about the first weekend in July? Glasgow schools have broken for the summer by then, haven't they?'

Verity's face lit up – not a sight that any of them were accustomed to. 'Yes, we break up at the end of June. Guess that means I'm going,' she declared gleefully.

They now all turned to stare expectantly at Marina. Last woman standing. Last obstacle in the plan. Well, she'd never buckled to peer pressure and she wasn't going to start now. She didn't have time to go jetting off. She was a wife and a mother. She'd had her fun that one night, but it was in the past. It was time to make a mature decision and accept her life exactly as it was.

Wasn't it?

Those were all the things she was thinking.

However, the part of her that didn't listen to reason, the same one that got her into trouble just a few months before, had different ideas.

Graham almost choked on his Cabernet as she paused, contemplated, decided, then announced the verdict. 'I think I can make it work too.'

16

Zoe tried to get in the bedroom door, but as usual Verity had locked it. Instead, she settled for banging it so loudly, half the street probably heard.

'Verity! You are a flipping nightmare. Open the sodding door,' she demanded, really, really wanting to use much stronger language but aware that her voice would travel downstairs and she'd be in trouble with Dad for swearing.

Eventually, Verity opened the door just a few inches and peered through. 'I thought you were at work?'

Zoe's Saturday job was the highlight of her week. She'd told a small fib and added a year and a half to her age to get it, but hopefully she wouldn't get caught out. Serving meals and clearing tables at the café was hard work – and she REALLY hated cleaning the toilets – but when she got her five pounds at the end of the day, it was all worth it. 'I was – I just got home. And stop locking the door, it's my room too!'

Verity clearly couldn't care less about her objection and they both knew that she'd still lock the door every day, because she said it was the only way she could get peace and quiet. That's what happened when three sisters shared a room. Marina was the lucky one. Her room might be the size of a cupboard, but at least it was all hers.

Verity sighed impatiently. 'Well? What is it? And why do you have to make so much noise?' she sneered.

'Why do you have to be such a secretive cow?' Zoe shot back. It was a question that she'd asked many times, so she didn't really expect an enlightening answer, which was just as well, because she didn't get one.

'Shut up and beat it,' Verity spat back, as she attempted to close the door. Again, not a surprise. Even on her last birthday, Verity had celebrated turning thirteen by going on a shopping trip to Glasgow with Mum. She hadn't wanted a party or a dinner, and she'd warned them not to do the whole cake thing because she claimed it was 'pathetic'. Zoe didn't get it. What was the point of having a birthday if you didn't enjoy it and eat cake? When she'd turned eleven last year, she'd had thirty friends in the house and Dad had managed to borrow a karaoke machine and they'd had the best time ever singing Spice Girls and Take That and Backstreet Boys songs. Even Verity had joined in, and she might even have cracked a smile. Moody boot that she was.

Zoe knew how to handle her though. She shot her foot into the crack in the door, stopping Verity from closing it, even if it would leave a mark on her Reebok trainer.

'Dad sent me up to get you. We're having a family meeting downstairs.'

Verity rolled her eyes. 'Urgh, what is it now?'

Zoe shrugged. 'No idea, but he doesn't look happy.'

'Just for a change,' Verity mumbled, sarcasm dripping.

Zoe opened her mouth to argue then closed it again. Verity had a point. Mum and Dad's arguments had been terrible over the last year or so. The pattern was always the same. Dad would be in a brilliant mood for ages, playing games and dancing with them and full of ideas for all the things they could do. They'd plan holidays and day trips and they'd turn up *Top Of The Pops* and dance to Kula Shaker in the living room. And then it would all change and Mum and Dad would be arguing and Mum would storm out and Dad would be really quiet and pissed off. In fact, since Christmas they'd barely spoken at all and Dad had been... She struggled to find the best word to describe it. Sad. That was it. Even Yvie couldn't cheer him up, no matter how much she tried.

Hopefully, whatever this family meeting was about would be something that would make things a bit better around here.

'Come on, let's get it over with. I think they're going to tell us that we're booking next year's holiday. I want to go to Benidorm. Everyone is always saying how brilliant it is.'

With stroppy reluctance, Verity conceded defeat and followed Zoe downstairs. Mum and Dad were already sitting at the kitchen table next to Yvie, who was tucking into the carrot cake Zoe had brought her from the café. It was her little sister's very favourite, so she brought her a slice home every week. Over at the kitchen side of the room, Marina was opening a can of peas, while keeping an eye on the potatoes that were simmering on the stove.

'Marina, put those down for now, love, and come sit over here,' their dad said.

'But, Dad, I—'

'For God's sake, Marina, can you just do as we ask for once?' Mum snapped.

Zoe waited for Marina to lose it and fight back. And she'd be right to. Mum was always out and Dad had been acting really weird lately, so they were all pitching in to help with stuff. Marina was cooking and shopping for everything they needed. Zoe was cleaning and working and making sure Yvie was okay. Even Verity had agreed to do the ironing, and she'd stand in the kitchen for ages on a Sunday night, her Walkman headphones on, getting all their uniforms ready for school.

Zoe was kind of wishing she had headphones on now as she waited for Marina to argue, but, to her surprise, Marina just put the can down, came over to the table and sat in the last free chair.

'Right then,' Mum said, her eyes darting to Dad, as if she was waiting for him to say something.

Dad was staring at the table, and only when he lifted his eyes could they see that they were a bit watery.

Zoe felt her skin prickle as she realised this was nothing to do with Benidorm. Her gaze darted to her sisters' faces. Yvie was happily tucking into her cake, completely unaware that anything was wrong, but Marina and Verity were having different reactions. Marina's jaw was set and her frown was pulling her eyebrows down, while Verity had that glazed expression she adopted when she was switched off because she didn't want to be somewhere.

Zoe wanted more than anything to go back to work and escape whatever it was that was causing such a tense, awful atmosphere.

She steadied herself. It couldn't be that bad, could it? Dad's sigh, and the way he took a deep breath before he spoke, told her otherwise. 'Girls, there's no easy way to say this and I'm so, so sorry. I'd give anything not to be doing this to you.'

Oh God. In that instant, Zoe knew, just absolutely knew, what was about to happen.

'You know that Mum and I love you all so much and we are heartbroken to tell you this...'

It was bad. Really, really bad.

'But we haven't been getting on for a long time now...'

Don't say it. Please don't say it.

There was a loud sniff and Zoe realised that her mum was crying.

'We've...' Dad paused, as if he was swallowing back a sob. 'We've decided to get a divorce.'

17

ZOE – IBIZA WEEKEND

'I've just realised that this is the first time we've been apart for more than a day since we made this thing official,' Zoe murmured, from the depths of Ned's goodbye hug. She could smell his aftershave and shampoo – something citrus, with a faint hint of coconut – and it made her want to just crawl back into bed with him.

His voice was still early-morning husky. 'You mean since you stopped playing hard to get and finally decided I was too much of a good thing to pass up?'

Another sniff of the tangy stuff. 'Mmmm. That's exactly what I meant. Obviously, I hadn't got a whiff of that shampoo back then, or I would have been a sure thing from the start.'

'In the name of God, will you two cut it out so we can get a move on?' Verity snapped, in what Zoe recognised as her very best teacher voice: firm, calm, but with a hint of warning and a commanding edge of 'just do as you're bloody told'.

'Oooh, who needs another morning nap then?' Zoe teased her, making no move to disentangle herself from Ned's arms. The flight wasn't for another hour and Marina and Yvie weren't even here yet. The ward was short-staffed again, so Yvie had pulled a double shift, finishing at 6 a.m. and Marina was collecting her at the hospital so she could make her way straight to the airport for the 8 a.m. flight. Zoe had no idea how she did it. Her younger sister impressed the life out of her every single day.

The airport terminal was getting busy though, and they should probably start making their way up to their planned meeting place at the entrance to security on the second floor. Reluctantly, she released herself from Ned's cocoon, just in time to see Yvie and Marina tearing through the glass doors and storming towards them. Like Zoe, Marina was wearing skinny jeans and a tailored jacket, but while Zoe had accessorised with Adidas trainers, Marina was striding on Gucci loafers. Yvie, on the other hand, was in flared palazzo pants, a white vest top and a kaleidoscopic kaftan that reached the floor.

Zoe watched as Verity's eyes widened (white pencil trousers, navy wedges and a fine knit powder blue tank top) and her mouth opened to speak.

Yvie spotted it too, and when she reached them, she immediately put her hand up to stop whatever comment was about to come out of Verity's mouth. 'No, I didn't bloody borrow this from a dreamer called Joseph. Marina's already given me the sneer of "Oh fuck what are you wearing?" so you can save it.'

Verity closed her mouth again, while Zoe threw her arms around her younger sister, laughing. 'Just you do you, my darling. You look freaking spectacular,' she told her honestly. 'Stuff what the grown-ups think.'

Yvie smooched her on the cheek and returned the squeeze, before pinging the waistband of her own trousers.

'Thanks, luvly. I had to go with an elasticated waist. Don't want to take someone's eye out when the button shoots off my jeans after too much paella.'

Zoe didn't get a chance to reassure her that she looked fabulous again because Marina was on the warpath, her voice as sharp as her jet-black razor-edged bob.

'Come on, let's go. Chop, chop,' the sister boss barked at them, as if Marina and Yvie weren't the ones who were late.

The others charged on, while Zoe gave Ned one more kiss goodbye, thinking, to her surprise, that she'd genuinely miss him. Somewhere over the last few months, the seesaw of devastation had moved, and the pain of losing Tom had been balanced out by her growing feelings for Ned. At least, she hoped that was the case. She hadn't quite worked out how much of her feelings for this man were from the heart, and how much came from a determination to pick herself up, get over Tom and move on. Wallowing in painful situations had never been her way. Shut down the hurt, rebalance, make a plan, move on, depend only on yourself and sort it out. Hadn't she learned way too young that it was the only way to deal with a breaking heart?

That said, Ned was definitely making it easy for her. He was funny, cute, sweet and...

'I love you,' he whispered.

... And he loved her?

Zoe froze, glad the others were now storming on ahead, out of earshot. 'Did you just say you loved me?'

His beaming grin was the cutest thing she'd seen in a long time.

'I think I did.'

'And you didn't consider saying that at some point while

we were naked so that I could suitably reward you?' she joked, her grin matching his now.

He loved her. This felt... She paused to consider it. This felt absolutely intoxicatingly lovely.

The terminal was now so busy that people were giving them irritated glances as they were forced to detour around the smiling couple. 'We'll discuss this further when I return, Mr Merton.'

One more long, heated kiss, before he released her with a very sexy murmur of, 'I like the sound of that.'

'Me too. But I really, really have to go.'

It took a massive surge of determination to tear herself away, pick her bag up from the floor and run after the others. She caught them just as they were going through security. If the flight was fuelled by the energy created by Verity's incessant eye rolls of disapproval, they'd make it to Ibiza in record time. Through security, they burst into a jog and made it to the gate, just in time to board the flight. Last in the queue, they finally staggered on, slightly breathless, and slumped into the seats booked by the Kemp Group. Row One. Two on the left, and two on the right.

Marina and Verity were sitting together on the right, so Zoe slipped in beside Yvie, who immediately engaged in flight preparation mode, retrieving an eye mask from her toiletry bag and pulling it on to her forehead. Thick fluffy socks went on next, followed by a rub of her hands with almond cream from a tiny sampler bottle, a slather of moisturiser and then she plumped up her head pillow and slid it behind her neck. 'Kay bought me this travel kit and I think I can pull it off,' she jested, stretching back in the seat. 'I could so get used to this. Remind me to look for all future opportunities to milk your job for luxury freebies.'

'Milk away. But next month's campaigns are dog biscuits and toilet rolls, so you might want to just enjoy this one while it lasts,' Zoe said, as the plane left the ground.

They were ten minutes in when the cabin crew passed with the drinks trolley.

'Courtesy of Roger's credit card,' Zoe said, passing Yvie a glass of champagne, served by an exceptionally handsome member of the cabin crew.

'God, this sucks,' Yvie groaned, with a twinkle in her eye and a new posh inflection in her voice. 'I mean, I don't usually have my first champagne until after 10 a.m.'

Giggling, Zoe raised her glass. 'Cheers, gorgeous ladies. Here's to a drama-free, fun, relaxing, utterly brilliant weekend with my three faves who came from the same womb.'

Verity nearly spluttered her bubbles. 'You really need to work on your toasting speeches.'

'What time do we land and how long will it take to get to the hotel?' Marina asked, her phone in hand, clearly ready to fire the information off to whomever she thought needed to be aware of her every move.

Zoe rhymed off the information while trying to muffle a sigh. This had been Marina's way for almost as long as she could remember. It was like she'd stepped in to be the mother in the family after Dad left them and their mum had neither the skills nor the inclination to put her own life aside to parent her children.

A drop of sadness at the memory of their early life infected Zoe's mood and she pushed it away. Blocked it out. Refused to let it permeate her first-class bubble. This weekend was about enjoyment, about bonding, about reconnecting with the three women she loved most in the world, despite their massive personality differences. Maybe Verity would even lighten up and realise there was more to life than work, exercise and alphabetising her book collection. Perhaps Marina would relax and forget about whatever it was that was giving her face that pinched expression. And maybe Yvie Josephina and her Technicolour Dreamcoat would take the opportunity to have a well-earned break from dedicating her whole life to the NHS and do something for herself for a change.

Zoe caught the drinks trolley on the way back and ordered four more glasses of bubbly. Handsome cabin crew seemed happy to oblige.

'I'm pretty sure champagne isn't supposed to be on my diet,' Yvie announced. 'For the purposes of this weekend, I want you all to humour me and tell me that all liquids are calorie free.'

Zoe kicked off her trainers, pulled her feet up under her and settled in as if she was in her living room. 'It is. I checked. It's just like water. Cheers, gorgeous,'

Yvie grinned as she raised her glass and returned the toast. After taking a sip, she then pulled a copy of *Vogue* out of her bag. 'I've never read this in my life, but I wanted to look like I belonged on this trip,' she hissed, conspiratorially.

'Me too,' Zoe replied. 'So I've brought Brad Pitt. He's in my suitcase.'

Their tipsy giggles drew daggers of disapproval from Marina, but Zoe couldn't care less. They needed this. They all did. How long had it been since they'd all laughed together? And, on a personal level, how long had it been since she'd taken a weekend off work? Since she'd felt sun on her face and sand beneath her feet?

Damn. The familiar feeling began to tingle somewhere in

her gut. She put her head on Yvie's shoulder and exhaled, waiting for the comparison to come. It was a factor of heartbreak that no one had warned her about – every time you do something out of the ordinary, a little masochistic shit of a brain department throws up a comparison to the last time you did it with the person you were in love with.

So... here she was, on a flight heading for a weekend in Ibiza. Last time she was on this same route, she was back in economy. On the scale of comparison, the first class section definitely won.

Last time, she was exhausted because she'd worked two days straight on a pitch that they hadn't even landed. This time, she'd taken the previous day off so she'd have time to get organised and in the holiday spirit. Another win.

Last time she was with Tom...

Thud. Pain. Loss. Huge loss. Despite her absolute determination that she was getting over him and moving on, the lurch of longing almost curdled the Moet in her stomach. It was like a tsunami of hurt, crashing through every barrier she'd spent the last few months building.

Block it out. Push it down. Breathe through it.

Something in her body language or the rhythm of her breath prompted Yvie to drop her magazine and whisper, 'Are you okay?'

Zoe lifted her head from her sister's shoulder, but she swallowed her words. This wasn't the moment to admit how much she still missed him. Ninety-nine per cent of the time, she didn't even admit it to herself, so there was no way she was going to vocalise it here and now, in an airplane full of strangers who could overhear. Not even in front of her sisters. This was to be an upbeat, positive weekend, and she refused to spend it moping or bringing up pointless regrets and tales of woe. How pathetic would that be?

Yvie, eye mask on her forehead, glass of champagne in hand, was still staring at her with curiosity, waiting for an answer.

The only thing to do was bluff it out.

'Yes, of course. I'm great.'

Yvie wasn't buying it. 'And yet your eyes are all shiny, like the time you broke three toes falling off your platforms at that Spice Girls gig.'

'I wasn't crying because of the pain,' Zoe sneered, going right into the same argument they'd had a hundred times about that night. 'It was because I split the arse of my Scary Spice catsuit. Who knew that stretchy Lycra had its limitations?'

Yvie smiled, but Zoe could see she wasn't convinced. She was going to have to give her more, but there was no way she was raining on their first class parade with a shower of misery and heartbreak over losing Tom.

It would have to be something else.

'I'm just feeling a bit emotional. In a good way,' she lied hastily.

Yvie's questioning gaze was just a few inches from hers. 'Because...?'

Because... because... oh, sod it. It was the only thing she could think of that would get her out of this moment without bringing everyone down. 'Because Ned just told me that he's in love with me.'

Zoe waited for the scream. The 'wow!' The shriek of excitement from a sister who celebrated every little milestone for all of them. This was the kind of news that would usually have Yvie summoning a brass band and ordering up bunting.

Instead, all that came was a subdued, 'Oh.' The champagne breakfast was clearly making Yvie act in a sophisticated and classy manner. 'And how do you feel about this? Do you feel the same?' she went on, and there was a definite undertone of caution in her voice.

That must be it, Zoe decided. Her sister was just concerned and looking out for her because she didn't want her to get hurt again. Maybe she would have been better just telling her the true reason behind her emotional wobble and keeping schtum about the love stuff.

But she was in too deep.

She realised she hadn't answered the question. Rabbit, headlights. Did she?

'Does she feel the same about what?' came a voice from the other side of the aisle.

Shit, Verity must have overheard the tail end of the conversation. Now the whole cabin was about to be updated on the developments in her love life. She was going to need another glass of fizz for this.

'Ned told Zoe he's in love with her,' Yvie informed her, in a stage whisper that could probably be heard by people on the toilet at the back end of plane.

'Well, congratulations. Glad to hear things are progressing,' Verity said, before her gaze returned to her book.

Verity's reaction fired several questions to the front of Zoe's mind.

Should she have said anything?

Perhaps she should have worked out how she felt about it before sharing the news?

And, was she imagining it, or had Verity's words been uttered through gritted teeth?

18

Thud. Thud. Thud. Thud. Thud.

Verity tried to make it stop.

Thud. Thud. Thud. Thud. Thud.

Nope, it was still there.

Not even the sound of her feet hitting the treadmill could drown out the sound of Yvie's voice in her head – *Ned told Zoe he's in love with her.*

This was her third session in the gym since they'd arrived at the hotel yesterday. She'd checked in, dumped her case in the room she was sharing with Marina, pulled her workout gear out of her backpack and come straight here to burn off her fury. Even the sight of the gym and its spectacular range of top-class equipment, with stunning views over Playa D'en Bossa beach, hadn't defused her tension, although she had to admit that Roger Kemp knew how to design a hotel. It was opulent luxury, from the modern chandelier in the reception area, to the rich minimalism of the bedrooms, to the Balinese influences of the spa.

Yet none of these things were making her feel any better.

Today alone, she was on mile ten. Her knees hurt, there were blisters on her feet, her hamstrings were on fire and she welcomed every single feeling because at least the pain was a distraction. She'd been so sure that Zoe and Ned's romance was waning. After all, didn't he spend more time with her than he did with Zoe?

It had started with the climbing course. He'd come along as promised and Verity wasn't sure what had shocked her most – the fact that he had turned up or that she'd actually enjoyed it. By the second day, she'd scaled the highest wall in a respectable time, beating Ned on almost every climb.

'You are whipping my ass,' he'd admitted good-naturedly after the third day. 'I think this is going to have to be an ongoing battle.'

Given that he was standing there in his vest top and shorts, his biceps and triceps gleaming with sweat, Verity had been unable to think of a single objection to that suggestion.

Since then, it had been their thing. They headed there a couple of times a week after work, and at least once every weekend. It wasn't tough for either of them to find the time. Verity just switched some of her gym workouts for the climbing centre and Ned came along when Zoe was working late or at weekends – which, let's face it, was pretty much all of the time. What was the point of having a guy like that if you were never going to make time for him?

In Verity's mind, it was all perfectly straightforward. Ned would realise that he wasn't a priority for Zoe. He'd call it a day. Verity would continue to spend time with him and, after a respectable gap – say, six months or so – their friendship would develop into something more. Zoe wouldn't care because by that time she'd either have moved on to someone else or she'd have won some kind of award for workaholic of the year and she wouldn't even notice that Verity and Ned had become an item.

There it was. Simple.

And then he had to go and throw a hand grenade into her plans by telling Zoe that he loved her.

It just didn't make sense. None of it. How could he love Zoe when she always made it clear he was number two in the priority list after her work? How could he love her when the connection with Verity was so strong? He must feel it too. And...

Thud. Thud. Thud. Thud. Her feet went even faster as a horrifying new thought came to the party. Was Zoe some deluded fool who thought she was in love with him too? No. She couldn't be. It was only five minutes since she split from Tom and he was supposed to be the love of her life.

Her train of thought was interrupted by the two young women who had stopped beside the treadmill next to her, huddling over one of their phones, looking at something that was causing dramatic gasps of astonishment. Verity had to clench her jaws shut to stop herself pointing out that this was a gym, not a coffee shop that you hung out in to chat to friends. There was nothing more annoying than people who showed up at the gym in their designer gear and treated it like it was some kind of social occasion. If she wasn't so far into her run, she'd change treadmills, but right now her psyche couldn't handle seeing the time, distance and calories burned going back to zero.

'I mean, like, what the fuck?' one of them, the taller of the two with swishy blonde hair, a caramel tan, perfect skin and an air of cloying overconfidence, was exclaiming in an accent that was pure upper-class Chelsea.

'Yeah, right? What. The. Actual. Fuck?' the other one, same accent but swishy brown hair this time, retorted with exaggerated shock. 'Like, seriously. He's been seeing Araminta for months! She'll be, like, so furious.'

With that, and another synchronised swish of their hair, they finally climbed on to the adjacent treadmills and set them to a slow walk. The one on the direct left propped her phone on the dashboard so she could continue to peruse it while kidding herself that she was actually working out. Not at that speed. It would take three weeks to work off a digestive biscuit.

Verity hadn't meant to look, but it was unavoidable. She could see photos on the screen. Random faces that changed every few minutes when Swishy swiped the screen. It took a moment for her to realise it was some kind of dating site. Not Tinder though. She'd recognise that one from the time she'd signed up to check if Ned was on it. Of course, he wasn't there. She hadn't really believed that he would be – surely there was no way a guy as attractive and decent as him was into trawling for cheap thrills on a dating app? She'd deleted it, her faith in him restored.

The girls were still giggling over the phone so Verity peered at the screen again, trying to make out the name of the site. It was called... She squinted to see it clearer. Your Next Date.

Nope, never heard of it. But then that wasn't really a surprise given that she wouldn't go on a blind date if she was paid a million pounds and armed with a SWAT team and a large vat of antibacterial disinfectant.

Her legs were aching now, the two girls next to her were

SHARI LOW

irritating her with their accents and their inability to form a coherent sentence or one that didn't include the word 'like' used in an entirely incorrect context. With a furious thump, she punched the stop button and jumped off, eliciting aloof gazes from Pinky and Perky.

Grabbing the spray disinfectant from a nearby table, she methodically cleaned every inch of the machine, only feeling a slight de-escalation of her stress levels as she did so. Her mind was elsewhere, thoughts filtering, processing, changing, a possibility building, until she had absolutely no way of doing anything else until she'd checked it out.

Maybe she was coming at this from the wrong angle. Instead of questioning Zoe's feelings, perhaps she should shine a light on Ned's. Was he really in love with her sister? Her earlier question resurfaced in her mind. Could he really be into easy pick ups and online hook-ups? She'd heard rumours over the years that he was... what did they call him in the staffroom? 'A bit of a player'. But she was sure that was just bitchy gossip. Nope, she dismissed the notion for a second time. Ned was a decent guy. Didn't the fact that he'd never once come on to her or made an inappropriate suggestion or comment in all the years he'd known her prove that?

But... it wouldn't hurt to double check, would it?

Decision made, she finished cleaning the treadmill and tossed the towel in the large basket by the reception desk, then pulled open the glass doors that led to a deserted outdoor yoga terrace. Marina had joined the morning class at dawn, but Verity had opted for a hard cardio sweat instead. This wasn't a weekend for peace and tranquility and no amount of attempting to connect with her inner serenity was going to calm her all-consuming irritation and bubbling fury.

Out on the terrace, she squinted against the sun as she

tried to focus on the screen of her phone. No use. She moved to a shaded corner and both the screen visibility and the wi-fi signal improved. Okay. Take a breath.

Her fingers trembled slightly as she clicked on to her apps, then downloaded Your Next Date.

Come on. Come on. How long did it take for a simple bloody... Ping.

Damn. It was asking her to set up a profile. There was no way she was using her own details this time, so she put her imagination to work. Veronica. From Glasgow. A hairdresser. Voluptuous. Great sense of humour. Open to love, fun and brief encounters. The photograph was a random one, taken off Google. But, sticking to the theory that the best lies were the ones that most closely resembled the truth, she chose one of a woman a few years younger than her but with a very similar look – athletic, long red hair, green eyes.

Another few clicks and her profile was complete. Okay, how to search? She completed the 'ideal match' parameters using Ned's details. Male, 35–40. Location: Glasgow. Interests: Sport. Fitness. Enter.

There were pages and pages of men who met the criteria and Verity quickly scrolled through them, heart thudding. Be there. Be there. Not that she was sure why she wanted that to be the case, but information was leverage and if he was on here it meant that he wasn't really in love with her sister. She didn't probe into the possibilities of what would happen if he were in fact cheating. She didn't question herself as to whether she'd still want him if his infidelity then caused him and Zoe to split up. Nope, none of that factored in yet, so there was no point delving into the more unpalatable depths of her – or his – scruples. That problem could wait. Right now, she was still scrolling, still scrolling...

Nope, nothing. He wasn't there.

Verity let the cool of the travertine stone on the walls bring her temperature down another notch. This was good news, wasn't it? She should care enough for her sister to be delighted for her that her boyfriend wasn't a duplicitous scumbag.

She let that thought sit for a moment. Of course she loved Zoe, but this was so much more complicated than that. There was history. Barriers. Fundamental differences in the way they saw things. And, yes, if she was honest, maybe a lot of that was rooted in the past. They'd handled their dad leaving in very different ways. Zoe had used it to fuel and motivate herself, whereas it had forced Verity to shut down, to stop trusting, retreat into herself. For Verity, there would always be the resentment that was locked away when they were teenagers.

Verity shook that one off. This weekend was stressful enough without going there. Focus on the present and the future, not the past.

Another thought. Should she just tell Zoe how she felt? That idea was closed down by her self-esteem before it even grabbed hold. Never. There could only be two outcomes to that scenario. Zoe would stay with Ned and they'd be forever awkward in Verity's company. Or she'd end their relationship, and if Ned really was in love with Zoe, then he'd resent Verity until the end of time. No, their fling had to end organically. Or at least in a way that didn't appear to have any connection whatsoever to the woman sitting on a terrace in Ibiza looking nothing like a voluptuous hairdresser from Glasgow who was up for brief encounters.

She was so busy contemplating the options that she

hadn't realised her thumb was still scrolling up and down until something jarred in her vision.

Hang on – what was that? Swipe back. The photo was years old, taken when his hair was long and pulled back in a ponytail. The only reason she recognised it was because he'd shown it to her when they were surrounded by man-bunned hipsters at the climbing centre. How they'd chuckled over it. She wasn't chuckling now.

He'd used his full name too. Edward. Again, another little nugget of info that she'd picked up over all the time they'd spent together in the last few months.

Yep, there you are, long-haired Edward Merton. There you bloody are.

Had he been there the whole time he was dating Zoe? And what, exactly, was she supposed to do with this information? She'd expected to feel pleased, but now that she'd found it, it set off a riot of inner conflict and her mind was whirring through the possible actions, outcomes and consequences. She could go directly to Zoe, but that could lead to her sister shooting the messenger and she wasn't sure Zoe wouldn't be suspicious of her motives. She could show it to Marina or Yvie, but again, it could come back on her. And even if she went with either of those options, there were many ways he could potentially explain it away. He could say it was made by someone else pretending to be him. He could claim it was ancient history and he'd joined up before he'd met Zoe and then promptly forgot about it. Hell, he could even say it was some kind of school experiment to demonstrate the dangers of these sites to his twelve year olds. That one would have a line of parents at the headmaster's office within the day, but still...

No, there was only one way to make absolutely,

completely, sure it was him, it was active and he was up to no good. If Ned Merton was cheating on her sister, she needed concrete evidence and she'd only get that if she had some kind of direct online contact with him.

Verity took a deep breath. And swiped right.

19

YVIE – IBIZA WEEKEND

'Are those two away exercising again?' Yvie asked, with an eye roll of exasperation that necessitated taking her gaze off the bowl of olives that was strategically balanced in the dip of her cleavage. She picked one, tossed it in the air and caught it perfectly in her mouth, without so much as a slight tremor of the bowl.

On the sunlounger beside her, Zoe put down her Kindle. 'Verity is at the gym, but Marina is over there, sitting in the shade at the bar.' She watched Yvie imbibe another small round fruit, before going on, 'You know, that should be a certified talent. Or maybe a sport in the Olympics. Yvie Danton, gold medallist in oral olive catching.'

'I'd be too busy defending my medal in Wotsit consumption to dilute my athletic prowess into another field,' Yvie deadpanned back.

A couple getting romantic on a nearby sunlounger gave them a disapproving glare, as Zoe's chuckles disturbed their blissful ambience.

'Ssssh, you're upsetting Posh and Becks over there,' Yvie

hissed, only half joking. The couple did indeed bear a passing resemblance to the celebrity couple in their younger years. The woman was in her early twenties, exceptionally slender, with cheekbones that could double as speed bumps, while he had clearly been imprisoned in either a gym or a tanning booth for the last decade, given that he appeared to be concealing several watermelons under skin that was a gleaming shade of San Tropez Ultra Tan.

'Is it still body shaming if I direct it at myself?' she wondered out loud. 'Only, I'm pretty sure that her waist has a smaller circumference than my thigh. I need you to ambush me and dump my body at the doors of the nearest Slimming World class on Monday night.'

This time it was Zoe's turn for a disapproving eye roll. 'Yvie, will you stop. You're gorgeous the way you are. And anyway, she'll look completely haggard by the time she's forty if she keeps up that sunbathing.'

Yvie appreciated the support but pulled her leopard print sarong down just a little to make sure that nothing above the knees was visible. Of course, she should embrace her body and not give a damn what anyone thought. And she didn't, really. Sometimes. Occasionally. She could go through spells of not giving a toss. But the big problem wasn't other folks' judgement, it was what she thought of herself. Almost twenty years of yo-yo weight gain and loss, and she knew what other people had yet to suss out. Her weight depended on so many things – her sleep patterns, her time management – both of which were currently wrecked by the amount of extra shifts she was pulling. Most of all, though, it was an indicator of how she was feeling inside, and the fact that she'd gained two stones since Christmas was confirmation – not that she needed it – that she was struggling with issues that ran deeper than her fondness for a biscuit.

Even without her basic training in psychology, it was very obvious that it was rooted in childhood. Just flicking though family pictures proved it. Age nine – family photos showed a normal, slim child. Age ten – family photos showed she was still in proportion. Age eleven – family photos, now minus Dad, and Yvie was showing definite weight gain. Age thirteen – in the pics is a child who was severely overweight and already on a pattern of yo-yo dieting, interspersed with bouts of comfort eating that blew the diet out of the water.

She wasn't that pained teenager any more though. She'd conquered her weight demons before, losing three or four stones many times over the years. The problem was keeping the bastard demons away. Especially when hers seemed to live in her fridge, her freezer and her kitchen cupboards. She could fix it this time, though, she was sure of it. She just needed to get a grip. Get back in control. It was nothing that a good talking to herself, a bit of perspective, some internal reassurance, a bit of self-care and a large vat of willpower wouldn't sort. In the meantime, she'd lie here in this luxury paradise, feeling completely self-conscious and promising herself that by this time next year, she'd be back here five stones lighter and wearing a lime thong bikini to show off her buns of steel and biceps like tennis balls.

'I'm worried about her, you know,' she heard herself saying, not even realising that her brain had switched from paying attention to her own woes over to her concern for someone else.

'Who?' Zoe asked, her Kindle now discarded beside her. She was also wearing leopard print, but unlike Yvie's, it was in the shape of a size twelve swimsuit that clung to her every curve and with the carefree confidence of someone who had never had to worry about her weight in her life. Zoe was one of those freaks who ate like a horse and never gained a pound. If Yvie didn't love her so much, she'd avoid her at all times.

'Verity. Have you noticed that she's become a little more... uptight than usual? And that's the third time she's been in the gym and we've barely been here for twenty-four hours.'

A faint line between Zoe's brows became deeper as she thought about it. 'I hadn't, but now that you mention it... Bugger, why didn't I notice? It's just been so long since the last time.' Her words trailed off, neither of them wanting to say it.

In college, Verity had become compulsive about exercise, to the stage that it had become almost unhealthy. Thankfully, a guidance counsellor had noticed it and addressed it, giving Verity the tools to understand that she was using exercise as a way to manage her stress. Oh, the irony, Yvie realised. One sister using a treadmill as an emotional crutch, the other using Greggs, a third one so controlled she let in no light for happiness.

For a while, Yvie had wondered if it could be anything to do with Verity's ancient crush on Ned. She'd even dragged her to Gino's for dinner a couple of months before. They'd made it to the tiramisu before Yvie had felt Verity was relaxed enough to broach the subject.

'Hon, can I ask you something?'

Verity looked thoroughly distracted as she pushed her tiramisu around her plate, so Yvie ploughed on. 'You know how you were pissed off when you called me that night Zoe started seeing Ned...'

Verity's response had been so sharp, it had taken her aback. 'You haven't told her that, have you?' she'd snapped.

Yvie knew she had to go gently. Of all of them, Verity was the most likely to bolt under pressure – Yvie empathised, Marina took charge, Zoe made a plan and worked through it, Verity shut down. It was the way it had always been.

'No, of course not. You know I'd never repeat what you tell me. But I just wondered whether or not it was still bugging you?' Even as she was saying it, her conscience was snapping its fingers in her direction and muttering something about hypocrisy. But Yvie's feelings surrounding Zoe's boyfriend weren't important here. What mattered was whether Verity was having a having a hard time dealing with it.

'No, of course not,' Verity had insisted. 'It never really did, to be honest.'

Yvie had vaguely remembered reading something about when people used the phrase, 'To be honest,' it often meant they were being, well, *dishonest*. It was hard to tell in this case; Verity had always been the toughest one of them all when it came to sharing her feelings.

'Really?' she'd probed. 'It's just that even before that happened, I thought that maybe you had feelings for Ned? More than friendship?'

'No!' Verity had blurted, but her body language, her horrified expression, her defensive reaction, told Yvie, without a shadow of doubt, that she'd been right. And her heart sank, because now the truth about what happened on the night she'd gone out with Ned Merton could absolutely, definitely, hurt two of her sisters.

Verity, trying to recover from the outburst, had blustered while pushing her tiramisu around a bit more. 'I mean, sure, at the beginning, I won't deny, I was a bit irritated because I didn't want my sister dating one of my work colleagues in case it got awkward, but it was nothing to do with me having feelings for him.'

Verity's face had flushed bright red and Yvie knew her sister was rewriting history here. The problem had been Verity's major crush on Ned Merton, nothing to do with some kind of potential family/professional conflict. However, for the sake of keeping Verity away from her tendency to be intolerant and defensive, she let it lie.

'... But it's absolutely fine. I'm happy for them. I really am.'

Yvie wasn't convinced, but as she began to argue, she'd felt the familiar quickening of her heart and a massive rush of anxiety coursing through her. She'd immediately cleared her mind and began to deliberately slow her breathing, silently talking to herself the whole time. *You've got this. You're fine. This is just biology. You can handle it.* Thankfully, Verity was too busy staring at her plate to notice. The panic was just beginning to subside when Carlo had arrived with refills for their Chardonnay and by the time his relentlessly entertaining presence had left them again, her internal anxiety and tension over their conversation had dissipated.

Yvie had resolved to keep an eye on her sister. Unfortunately, that wasn't strictly possible on this trip because Verity had spent the whole time in the bloody gym. Either she was trying to outrun her feelings or she was in training for a marathon.

Back in the present, Yvie realised that Zoe was still mulling over the discussion they were having about Verity. Damn, she probably shouldn't have said anything. Wasn't this supposed to be a weekend of fun and sisterly bonding?

She was about to do the sensible thing and brush off the subject of Verity altogether when her phone rang. She'd kept it on standby in case Kay or her mum needed her.

She was right with the first one. Kay's smiley face filled the FaceTime screen. Bugger. She didn't have headphones with her and FaceTime calls were on speaker – this was going to tip Posh and Becks over the edge. She shrugged an apology to them as she answered.

'Hey, ma darling, how are you?'

'Stressed, Overworked. And celibate. So all normal,' Kay replied with a giggle, before her eyes narrowed. 'Mother of God, are you at a pool?'

Yvie turned the phone and then panned 180 degrees so that Kay could absorb the wonder of her surroundings.

Zoe gave a wave as the camera passed her. 'Hi, Kay!'

'Hey, Zoe, I'd say something nice, but I'm hating you every bit as much as I'm hating your sister right now. Jealousy is a terrible affliction. Are those statues in the back there, or real people?'

Zoe tried to angle her body so that her voice wouldn't carry. 'That's Posh and Becks reinvented – not statues.'

'Then I'm glad my West of Scotland pale blue complexion is here and under a thick jumper – I couldn't handle the pressure of lying next to that.'

Yvie wanted to express empathy with that view, but Kay was already wittering on.

'Anyway, I just called to see yer face because I'm missing it,' she began.

'Aw, I'm missing you, too. Wish you were here. This sister thing is over-rated.'

That earned her a playful slap from Zoe.

'That's why I'm glad I'm an only child,' Kay added with a

wink. 'And the other reason I called was to give you high-grade gossip.'

'Kay! How many times have I told you not to spread gossip? It's unbecoming and reflects badly on you as a person and a professional.'

One of Kay's eyebrows raised in scepticism. 'So you don't want to hear it then?'

Yvie cracked, unable to hold the joke any longer. 'Of course I bloody do. Where is it on the scale? Above or below the Head of Dermatology shagging the porter in the cleaning cupboard?'

'Above. And she was just checking his skin for moles. It was a very thorough investigation.'

Zoe and Yvie's laughter was turning heads all around the pool now. They noticed and shushed themselves.

'Okay,' Yvie whispered. 'Fire away.'

Kay held a pause for a second or two to heighten suspense, before blurting, 'Seth McGonigle and his missus have split. She's gone off to Doctors Without Borders for a year.'

'No way!'

'Way!' Kay shot back, the exchange mimicking many discussions with her six year old, Chester.

'Wow. I bow to your mastery in the gossip stakes,' Yvie went on. 'How did you find this out?'

'Ward night out last night at Gino's for Jean's birthday. She invited him as a token gesture and nearly fainted when he actually came. Carlo kept topping up the wine glasses – he was asking for you by the way – and after the fifth or sixth empty bottle, McGonigle cracked and dished the whole story.'

Yvie had little time for the great Dr McGonigle, but still,

that was rough on anyone and he had showed her a glimmer of humanity when Babs died, which had definitely softened her feelings towards him. 'Is he okay?'

Kay thought about that for a moment. 'Actually, he seemed fine. But then, I've seen more emotion from my fridge freezer than that man, so it was hard to tell. Is it wrong that I'm starting to view him as intriguing and mysterious?'

'As opposed to a moody git with the personality of a plant?'

'Yeah, well, I like plants. Anyway, I need to go – I start in five minutes and the entire staff was at the party last night, so I've no idea what I'm going to face on the ward. Jean could be doing the Macarena up and down the corridor with her mop bucket for all I know. Come home soon, doll. We miss you.'

'I miss you too!' Yvie replied, too late, as the screen went black.

She put her head back on the lounger. Seth McGonigle. Wow. She hadn't seen that coming.

Beside her, Zoe cleared her throat and Yvie turned to see an expression of expectation. 'Seth McGonigle? Well?' she asked, words loaded with teasing curiosity and a hint of innuendo.

Yvie batted away the implications in her words. 'Eh, no. Number one, he's very serious, borderline rude. Number two, he's a consultant. Number three, he's a tad self-important. And number four, even if there were no other obstacles, he's that kind of Grey's Anatomy, leading man, way out of my league, kind of guy. Urgh,' she shuddered.

'Yvie! No one is out of your league! Seth McGinty...'

'McGonigle...'

'Seth McGonigle,' Zoe tried again, 'would be bloody lucky to have you!'

Yvie was about to counter that glib claim when Verity appeared, still in her workout gear, looking about as far away from someone who was having a relaxing weekend as it was possible to be. Yvie resolved to try to speak to her again, but not in front of anyone else.

As if she'd been sent a subliminal message, Zoe climbed off the sunlounger. 'I'm just going to say hi to Marina and get us some more drinks. Do you want anything, Ver?'

Verity shook her head. 'No, I'm good, thanks.'

Once Zoe was gone, Verity sat down on the edge of her sunlounger and began to unlace her trainers. 'I'm just going to pop upstairs for a shower. What time are we getting our photos taken?'

Yvie felt her heart speed up at the very mention of the pics. She hadn't thought that through when she'd been enthusiastic about the freebie weekend. Photos. With three perfectly formed and toned sisters. She was going to have to offer the photographer all her worldly goods in exchange for some serious photoshopping.

'I'm not sure, but it's definitely this afternoon. Why don't you stay here and have a drink with us before you go up for your shower?' Yvie suggested, hoping Verity didn't pick up on any ulterior motive.

Verity didn't answer, but she didn't move to leave either.

This might be her only chance, Yvie decided. 'Hon, you are okay about Zoe and Ned, aren't you? Only, you looked a bit shocked on the plane.'

Verity's expression immediately went straight to annoyed. 'I told you ages ago, I'm fine. Why would I care? It isn't as if I have any kind of feelings for the guy. I. Absolutely. Couldn't. Care. Less. So will you stop...'

She was interrupted by the ping of her phone on the

sunlounger beside her, and two heads swivelled as their eyes automatically went to the screen. Yvie could have been mistaken, but she was almost positive she saw a notification there that included the word 'Your Next Date'.

Holy Jesus. Well, there was a turn she hadn't seen coming. Verity on Your Next Date? No way. And yet...

'Verity, is there something you want to tell me?' she teased, gesturing to the phone, a playful grin across her face.

'Yes, there is.'

Yvie almost clapped her hands with glee. Finally! Verity was going to open up, to share...

'How about you mind your own business?' she said archly, before standing up and storming off.

Yvie sighed, leaned back, despaired, picked up her bowl of olives, tossed a little globe of happiness up in the air, opened her mouth, watched it as it fell towards her...

As it bounced off her chin, she wondered if it was a telling omen that she missed.

20

Marina's thumbs fired across the keypad of her phone, her laser focus adding extra pressure to each contact between her digits and the screen. Already today, she'd checked on Annabelle after her contemporary class and made sure that her friend, Cindy's mum, – for the purposes of the favour, Marina was overlooking her disdain for the over-competitive Geraldine – would pick her up to take her to her Sunday ballet session. It was an extra session laid on for the more gifted dancers in the group.

After that, she'd answered eleven – yes, ELEVEN – emails from Graham, about everything from the kids' schedules for the day and the following morning (despite the fact that she'd sent them to him and his secretary, and she'd printed them off and stuck them to the fridge), to their plans for the dinner party she was arranging for his new clients the following weekend, to questions about how to use the washing machine.

And then, finally, she'd emailed Oscar his updated plan for the following week, so that he could spend the rest of the weekend preparing for his activities and studies before school, during school and after school. It was a tough schedule of sport, academics and music practice, but it would give him great time management skills when she eventually handed over the organisational reins.

Only when all that was done, did she sit back and take another sip of her margarita and exhale. This weekend was supposed to have been a relaxing break, but actually, the opposite was true. How could she relax when she had so much going on at home that she needed to keep an eye on? What was she doing here?

By the time they'd arrived on Friday and had food and a tour of the hotel, a couple of hours by the pool, and then dinner in the evening, the day was just about over. On Saturday, Verity had spent most of the day in the gym, while Yvie and Zoe lounged by the pool again. She'd joined them, but after ten minutes, thoughts of home had made her too agitated to sit still, so she'd taken her phone off to the bar and parked herself there to keep in touch with everyone and stay on top of her emails. She was glad when it was time to take the promo photos, because, if nothing else, they were a distraction from running through incessant lists in her mind and making sure everything was ticked off.

Roger had asked that the photos be informal and natural, so there had been little in the way of set-up. Just a quick hair and make-up session, then they'd slipped into the white outfits that the shoot stylist had brought and got to work. The whole process had taken about two hours, which was as much as she could stand because the poor photographer had to continually ask Verity to smile and Yvie to stop hiding behind the others. Eventually, after pics in the restaurant, at the side of the pool, in the spa, and on the beach, the photographer had bustled off, no doubt to photoshop the crap out of the four of them to make them look like a merry band of classy, chic travellers.

After the shoot, they'd had dinner on the beach, but it wasn't a late one because she had yoga this morning. At least she was sharing with Verity, who'd had an early night too. When Zoe and Yvie finally surfaced today, they'd revealed that they'd been in the hotel bar until 4 a.m. The thought threw up a memory of the last time Marina was in a hotel bar, and her face flushed.

'You've definitely caught the sun,' Yvie had told her, noticing her ruddy complexion. 'No idea how, when you've been sitting in the shade all weekend.'

Marina chose not to enlighten her. Instead, she'd headed over to the pool bar for the second day in a row, to spend a leisurely Sunday wondering if there was anything she'd forgotten to do. The early flight tomorrow morning couldn't come quick enough.

'Have you moved since yesterday or are you stuck to the chair?' The warmth in the man's voice made her lift her head. Yves. Forty. French. Married. Did something in finance. Perfect English. Here on a golf trip with his buddies from work. They'd chatted for an hour or so the day before, sometimes in French, sometimes in English, when her language skills fell short of his.

'I'm stuck to the chair. Emergency services are taking a while to get here,' she told him and was rewarded with his crinkly eyes as he smiled. Graham could take note. Here was a man who took care of himself, and who still knew how to communicate with a woman. Yves looked her in the eye, listened to what she said, showed an interest and didn't want anything from her. And yes, she knew what a fucking cliché that was, yet she couldn't ignore it. Nor could she ignore the waves of attraction she felt for him. Enough. Bring the conversation to a close. Behave.

'May I...?' he gestured to the empty seat across from her. 'Only until the emergency services get here, of course.'

Say no. No. Definitely no.

'Sure.' Goddamn it.

He joined her for a drink, that turned into two, then three. Her sisters all popped over to see her at one point or another, but she made no move to make them a permanent addition to the table. The truth? She was enjoying his company way too much. This was nothing like the barman from that night she preferred not to think about. This was different. This was... cerebral. He was wise. Experienced in life. Well-travelled. They were on the same intellectual level.

It was with genuine reluctance that she eventually dragged herself away when Yvie wandered over to say it was time to get dressed for dinner. Tonight they were eating in the hotel's main restaurant again, a gastronomic wonder that served an exquisite fusion of Thai, Japanese and Spanish food. It had been delightful the night before, but Marina would still have swapped it for a toastie and a couple more hours of conversation with the first man who'd properly listened to her in as long as she could remember. That's what happened after four – no, five, margaritas.

'Perhaps I will see you again before you leave?' Yves asked, and right then, something connected between them, a subliminal message, a question asked and answered when Marina shook her head.

'I'm sorry, but unfortunately we have plans for tonight. It was good to meet you, Yves,' she said with absolute honesty as she rose from the table.

He leaned over and took her hand, kissing it, before letting go. Usually Marina hated overfamiliarity, but this was something different altogether. She could still feel his touch moments after his lips had left her skin.

It took every ounce of willpower she possessed to refrain from looking back to check if he was watching her as she walked away.

In her room, she showered and changed, then donned a plain white shift dress for dinner. The sleeveless cut showed off her tennis and Pilates toned arms. The hem stopped just above the knee, flashing the legs that had barely changed since she was in her twenties. All the years of excellent nutrition and dedicated exercise had paid off, so much so that she even allowed herself a small dessert after dinner. Yep, she was living on the edge.

For the second night in a row, Verity was the first to excuse herself. 'I'm going to head to bed. I fancy an early night,' she told them and Marina made a mental note to drop in on her during the week. There was clearly something going on with her. She'd spent the whole weekend in the gym and she never went anywhere without her phone stuck to her hand. It wasn't as if she had kids who'd be calling, or her school would need to get in touch with her. Marina had asked her a couple of times if something was wrong, but Verity had brushed her off. Maybe on home territory she'd open up a bit more. Of all of them, Marina was the only one that Verity ever confided in. Hadn't she told her at Christmas – actually it was more of a hint than a revelation – that she had a thing for Ned? Marina had wondered if that would cause problems when Zoe started seeing him, but Verity had assured her a few weeks later that it was nothing, she was absolutely over it and couldn't care less. She had no reason to lie so Marina believed her. So what was bothering her this weekend? It was strange that she was now keeping something to herself.

She thought about going upstairs with Verity, who was pushing her chair back from the table to make her escape now, but before she could say anything to the others, she spotted Yves and his friends through the glass wall of the hotel, making their way to the bar.

'Shall we have a nightcap in the bar since it's our last night?'

Already on her feet, Verity shot her daggers, and then declined, claiming she could feel a migraine coming on. Zoe and Yvie hopped right on board.

'I told you that underneath all that terrifying efficiency there was a party animal waiting to come out,' Yvie joked, nudging Zoe to play along, which of course, she did.

'Mmmm, I'm not sure. You get the party poppers and I'll start the conga and we'll see how long she lasts.'

Marina pursed her lips and ignored them, determined not to admit she was actually amused. She was happy to be the butt of the joke if it got her into the bar. Of course, once there, she acted surprised when Yves came up behind her as she ordered drinks.

'Mon Cherie. So we were to meet again after all.' Okay, so it was slightly corny, but tell that to the tingles that had begun to make her stomach flip. Ignoring the barman's offer to take her drinks to the table, she delivered Yvie and Zoe's gin and tonics, then came back for her own.

If Yvie and Zoe minded that she spent the next half an hour talking to Yves at the bar, they didn't say anything. They did, however, have plenty of complaints when she went over to their table afterwards to tell them she was tired and going to bed.

'Oh, come on, stay out with us! How often do we get to do this?' Zoe asked.

'You haven't even been to the nightclub yet,' Yvie wailed. 'Come with us. Every dance burns off eighty-five calories – a hundred and fifty if it's anything by Beyonce.'

'Tempting, but I'll pass,' Marina told them, with just a tiny shred of regret. Zoe was right. They should do this more. She'd forgotten what being an independent grown-up felt like, but she was slowly beginning to remember. And much as more time with her sisters would undoubtedly be enjoyable, she was more tempted by another option.

Slipping her bag under her arm, she made her way to the lift and pressed the button for the fourth floor. When the doors opened, she turned left and walked towards her room. And kept walking.

If anyone was manning the corridor's CCTV cameras, they'd see Mr Yves Roche make his way to his suite at the end of the long passageway. They'd see a woman in a white dress with a sharp, black bob, walk a few feet behind him. Then they'd see him hold the door so that she could follow him into his room. If there was sound, they might even hear the thud of his door, as they slammed against it the minute it was closed, lips already on lips, clothes already being discarded. A couple of hours later, they'd see the same woman leave the suite and make her way to her own room, several doors along, creeping in so as not to wake her sleeping roommate. The next morning, they'd see not even a glimmer of regret on her face as she walked jauntily down the corridor, pulling her trolley case behind her, accompanied by her sister.

In the lobby, the rest of their party joined them, the other two wearing dark glasses despite the fact that the early-morning sun didn't reach into the hotel.

'What the hell happened to you two?' Marina demanded, as soon as she saw them.

Yvie groaned as she shook her head. 'What happens in... where are we?'

'Ibiza,' Zoe replied.

'What happens in Ibiza, stays in Ibiza,' Yvie mumbled.

Christ, the state of them. They were a total embarrassment.

All thoughts of the night before locked away, Marina immediately snapped into organisation mode, summoning the car, checking out, counting bags and making sure everyone had passports, purses, et cetera. This stuff was second nature to her. She watched over them, barked orders at them and kept them in one piece all the way to Glasgow airport. When the flight landed at 11 a.m., she had her car keys out and ready to take them the rest of the way home.

Home. Stomach clenched at the thought. The last few days had proved to her that she associated home with slog, with stress, with constant demands on her time, and yet she wasn't sure how she could change it even if she wanted to. It was the life she had built for herself and her family and every bloody bit of it depended on her. It was so far removed from last night and from that night in Edinburgh. For those illicit hours, she was just Marina, and she'd loved every minute of both encounters, but they couldn't happen again. It was reckless. Stupid.

Verity had been sound asleep when she'd got back to the room the night before, and she was so wrapped up in whatever was going on with her, that this morning she didn't even ask what time Marina had got in, but it could have played out very differently.

If Zoe and Yvie hadn't been so hungover today, they could have questioned what time she left them last night and Verity might have been awake and could have realised she'd been AWOL for a couple of hours.

She was dicing with danger. Risking her cosy existence. It had to stop. No more.

They were on the way through the terminal when her phone buzzed.

She assumed it was Graham, asking her to pick up something on the way home, so she was surprised when she heard a woman's voice telling her she was calling from Weirbridge Primary School. That was where Verity worked. Did she have the wrong sister?

'Ms Danton...' That didn't help. Marina's one token act to retain her independence when she married Graham was to keep her maiden name.

'I'm Clara Roberts, head of the summer fair committee.'

'Oh.' Maybe the right sister after all. Marina had helped them fundraise over the last few years as a favour to Verity.

'Yes, how can I help you?'

'Ms Danton, this is a bit of an unusual call. I'm sure you'll understand that it's important for complete transparency that all the prizes at the annual fair are properly dealt with, especially with this year's fair taking place next month.'

'Yes, of course.'

'I'm afraid we've discovered that one of the prizes was never claimed. We feel it's only right that we rectify this, and also that we attain some promotional photographs of the winner that can be used when we offer the same prize this year.'

'And how can I help with this?'

She didn't have time for this right now. She needed to be home, recalibrating back to wife and mother mode, while reinforcing the message to herself that no matter how good they felt, these random hook-ups had to stop. Had. To. Stop.

'Well, I'm afraid it was your prize, Ms Danton. You won a five star dinner with one of our teachers, Mr Merton. We'd like to organise a night that would suit you both to meet. Are you perhaps free next Thursday?'

Marina stopped, closed her eyes. She'd forgotten all about it, cared even less. But there were two choices here. Another night listening to Graham snoring by 10 p.m., or a swanky meal in some upmarket restaurant with Zoe's boyfriend.

As if some cosmic force had taken charge, she heard her own voice saying, 'Yes, that will be fine.'

21

Only a couple of minutes have passed since Roger's call revealing the name on the credit card, but it feels like about a week and a half.

Verity is now staring at me like she could quite happily take the cocktail stirrer from her pink drink and stab me through the heart. Of course, she is the obvious suspect. She'd worked with Ned for years before I came on the scene and, if I'm being brutally honest with myself, on some level, even back then, I knew she had a thing for him. It's absolutely on me that I chose to take her at her word after she told me she had no interest in him. I should have delved deeper. But then, she's so damn infuriating sometimes, that I chose not to.

I take another swig of the pink anti-acid cocktail, buying time before I respond to their confused expressions.

Sister love. It's a complicated thing.

Take Marina, for example.

She has stepped over so many lines in the last year that I sometimes feel like I don't know her at all.

But really, is there even a question in my mind that she would step over the most dangerous line of all?

22

ZOE – ON HER BIRTHDAY

'Ah, I hate slumming it on my birthday,' Zoe whistled, as she slipped into a sumptuous silver velvet dining chair in one of the most luxurious private dining rooms she'd ever seen. Located between The View restaurant and the private corridor that led to Roger Kemp's penthouse on the top floor of the Kemp Glasgow, the corner room was decorated in subtle greys, silvers, cream and crystal, with strategically placed mirrors reflecting the natural light from two walls of floor to ceiling windows. Even the September clouds didn't spoil the view. The most exquisite aspect of the room, though, was the solid wall of fragrant white and pink roses that spanned one corner to another, opposite the window. She knew the flower wall had probably been ordered for a wedding last weekend and Roger had just had it moved here for their dinner tonight, but that just emphasised his thoughtfulness.

'You know, I could just put a blow-up mattress in here and live here forever,' she said, blown away as ever by the room's perfection.

'Yeah, but you might get in the way of the staff serving the soup,' Tom pointed out. Yep, Tom, her former boyfriend, the man who'd broken her heart less than a year ago, was by her side.

'Let me get this straight,' Ned had questioned her when she'd told him about the plans for today. 'So, your favourite client has invited us for lunch on your birthday at his fuck-off posh hotel...'

Zoe had nodded. 'Correct.'

'With his wife, who is completely stuck-up and doesn't give anyone the time of day.'

'Indeed.'

'And he's also invited your ex-boyfriend...'

'He's also invited my friend and business partner,' Zoe had corrected him. 'The fact that Tom and I were once a couple is irrelevant.' For the purposes of this debate, she had overlooked the uncomfortable truth that nothing about her relationship with Tom had been filed in her emotional database as 'irrelevant'.

'And his partner is coming too.'

'Yeah, Chrissie. She's lovely,' Zoe had confirmed. That part was true. Much to her utter disdain, she'd immediately seen why Tom's love for Chrissie was a once in a lifetime deal. She was warm, funny, gorgeous, and they'd liked each other on sight. At least a new friend in the equation was a small consolation for losing the love of her life.

Ned, meanwhile, was still ruminating over the guest list. 'I think I'm washing my hair that day,' he'd said, making Zoe cackle with laughter as she'd pushed her arms around his waist and stretched up to kiss him.

'Nope, you're coming because you love me,' she'd told him.

'And you love me right back?' he'd asked. He was playing now too, but there was a sliver of a point in his comment. Since he'd said the L word, she'd reciprocated, but it still wasn't second nature to her. It had become a standing joke that he always said it first. She really had to make an effort on that, especially as, like now, he'd do anything for her.

That's why, he'd put on his best suit today, a stunning Tom Ford charcoal two-piece Zoe had bought him for his birthday a couple of months ago from a Glasgow menswear boutique called CAMDEN. And that's why he was sitting across the round table from her, with Chrissie on one side and Felice on the other. Zoe, meanwhile, was between Tom and Roger and trying not to allow her mind to be swayed by the subtle aroma of Tom's aftershave. It was Creed Original Vetiver, and she knew this because it was the first present she'd ever bought him. He'd loved it so much, it became the only aftershave he ever wore. The minute she walked into a room, she knew if he'd been there and she was absolutely sure that there would come a time when the scent wouldn't automatically bring on a twinge of sadness. She was over him. She definitely was. It just seemed that her nose had yet to get the message.

The lunch was simple but delicious. Roger had asked what her favourite dishes were and had his chef make them. She could have requested the finest fillet of beef, the most expensive truffles, or something that wouldn't look out of place on the final of *MasterChef*, but no. She'd chosen her genuine faves. It was probably a comedown for a Michelin Star chef to make chicken nachos with spicy salsa, creamy guacamole and a side of Cajun fries, followed by caramel apple pie and toffee ice cream, but he didn't complain.

This was the perfect day and she was touched that Roger

had suggested it and then made it so entertaining with his hilariously indiscreet anecdotes of the goings-on he'd witnessed in his hotels over the years. Although, clearly Felice had heard them all before because she sat there with a thoroughly bored expression. Zoe had a flashback to something her dad used to say if any of them sported a glum demeanor. 'The wind will change and your face will stay like that,' he'd tell them, laughing as he tickled them to make them smile again.

Roger might want to brush up on his tickling skills to crack this one's unamused pout. They were definitely one of those couples that didn't seem, on the outside, to gel. Tom and Chrissie, on the other hand, had happiness and compatibility oozing out of them. Urgh.

'I hate that I like you,' Zoe had told her on their third or fourth meeting.

Chrissie had nodded dolefully. 'I know. It really sucks that I like you too.'

Since then, they'd become friends despite their mutual connection of having been in love with the same man. They had lunch every few weeks, they went to their weekly spin class together and Zoe was a regular at the shop Chrissie worked in, Sun Sea Ski – next door to the menswear place where she'd bought Tom's suit – when she was stocking up for any trips or holidays. She and Tom were also invited to Zoe's family party at Gino's later that evening.

So, unorthodox as it was, this was the perfect setting and guests for her lunch. Even Ned seemed to be relaxing and enjoying himself, although he wasn't having much luck cracking Felice's straight face either.

Zoe was, in fact, enjoying herself so much that she almost missed the significance of the comment.

'I meant to say, my secretary said you rang this morning. Were you calling to offer me a discount on your exorbitant fees?' Roger asked Tom, laughing.

Strange. It was generally Zoe who was the point of contact between the agency and Roger. Tom only sat in on major negotiations and pitches.

'No, I... it's... I...'

Oh shit, Tom was blustering and he suddenly shot an awkward glance in her direction. Someone switched off the light on Zoe's happy glow. Something was afoot and if she didn't know about it, then it could only mean that either she was getting fired and Tom was letting their biggest client know, or...

'Have you set a date for the wedding?' she blurted, ripping off the Band-Aid, and knowing instinctively that she was right. It was the only thing Tom would possibly be uncomfortable discussing in front of her. And, of course, it made sense that the wedding would be in the hotel that had the reputation for staging the best parties in the city. Fuck. She prayed she was wrong. *Fire me. Go on. It'll hurt less.*

Tom was looking at her incredulously now. 'How did you know that?'

'Psychic!' She covered up the blow to the solar plexus with the widest smile she could muster, aware that Ned was now studying her face carefully, no doubt searching for any sign that she was upset by this. And the Oscar for Best performance by a Jilted Girlfriend goes to...

'Congratulations! I'm really happy for you!' she chirped, blowing Chrissie a kiss across the table, hoping she wasn't coming over as too gushy. Thankfully, if she was, no one seemed to notice. Not even Ned, who was giving Chrissie a kiss on the cheek and reaching over to shake Tom's hand.

'When's the big day, then?' Zoe asked, because it was the natural thing to do – if the happy couple concerned weren't your ex and his new fiancé.

'Och, we'll talk about it later,' Tom batted back. 'Today's your birthday. It should be all about you,' he teased.

'Every day is all about me. I welcome a bit of variety,' she drolled back, making everyone laugh. See. This was what she had with Tom. That easy conversation and exactly the same sense of humour, most of it built on self-deprecation, laughter and mutual sarcasm. But she had that with Ned too. Or at least, as close as it could be after only nine months or so together.

Chrissie took up the challenge. 'It's July first next year. Plenty of time to get organised.'

'Organisation of weddings is my speciality, just saying,' Zoe said breezily, the offer implicit. Dear God, what was she doing? Was she really so keen to avoid appearing upset by this that she was offering to help the love of her life plan his wedding to someone else? Her inner self thudded her head against a metaphorical flower wall.

'I'll take you up on that,' Chrissie promised her.

Great. Smashing. Thud.

'Don't you think weddings are so... past tense?' Felice waved her hand dismissively as she spoke, stunning the table into silence.

Roger was the first to recover. 'I bloody hope not. I'd lose a fortune,' he said, covering the second uncomfortable moment of the day perfectly.

Zoe actually felt a pang of sympathy for this good-looking, charismatic, ultra-successful, wealthy pillar of the community whose only problems in life were probably what to buy next and where to park his jet ski. Either Felice was a first-class bitch or they were having problems and this was her way of getting a dig in at him. Either way, what a cow. A very beautiful, Dior-wearing cow.

Roger, meanwhile, had moved on and was already checking something on his phone. 'Yep, we can do that here. I was a bit concerned you were going to say May.'

'Why?' Zoe asked, welcoming the change of subject.

Roger beamed. 'Actually, I was going to talk to you about that on a day that wasn't all about you,' he bantered with a cheeky grin.

'Yeah, well, these two...' she gestured to Tom and Chrissie, 'have already stolen the limelight, so fire away.'

He really did have gorgeous teeth, she noticed, as he laughed.

'Okay, so after almost two years of negotiations, we finalised a deal to take over a Vegas hotel,' he announced, his excitement irrepressible. 'We launch next May. I'll be working with an agency over there on publicity, but I need you to liaise with them on branding and on UK publicity. Oh, and I plan to do a Richard Branson and fly over a jet full of guests for the launch. Zoe, the stuff we did with your sisters in Ibiza was brilliant. Do you think they'd be up for a trip further afield? I know Verity's job might be a problem, but I'm pretty sure the schools have a long weekend break in May and I think it's the same one.'

Zoe was catching on to some of Roger's enthusiasm, especially as she could hear Yvie screaming 'A freebie to Vegas? Yaaassssss!' in her head.

'I'll check with her, but I think I can safely say that if that's the case, they'd all be open to it.' She could check with them tonight at her party. That would be sure to get them all in the mood to celebrate.

'Great,' Roger beamed. 'And you too, of course, Ned. You definitely need to get in on the act this time. Like I said, I'm sure it coincides with the school long weekend in May.'

It was Ned's turn to look delighted. He winked at Zoe. 'I could get used to your birthdays if they're all like this.'

'They are,' she promised. 'Next year, Roger is buying me a private jet and a gold mine.'

Okay, time to leave while they were on a high, and before she said anything stupid or emotionally revealing. The Vegas weekend was only adding a light relief to the stabbing pain of Tom and Chrissie's announcement. She could do this. She only had to keep up this front of nonchalance for a few more minutes.

She took her napkin off her lap and placed it on the table. 'Roger, this was amazing and I can't thank you enough. I've had a wonderful time, but all good things...'

She swallowed back 'have to end with your ex-boyfriend setting a date for his wedding.'

Almost there. Almost.

'My pleasure,' Roger replied. 'You know, I don't say it enough – and I'll deny having said this when it comes time to negotiate our next contract – but you guys are great and I've really enjoyed working with you.'

Zoe felt a flush of pride. She was about to say the feeling was mutual, when Roger went on.

'And, Tom, you know, if you need a best man, I'm free,' he joked.

There was a hesitation, another flicker of the eyes, a pause so pregnant it required stirrups. Jesus, what now?

'Actually, that was something else I was going to talk about some other time,' Tom said, staring right at her.

Words were tumbling in Zoe's head. Spit it out. Let's get out of here.

'Go on then, spill. Are you going to ask Dex?' she said, mentioning their office manager. Tom and Dex, the head of their art department had been friends for years.

'Eh, no. Actually, Zoe... would it be too weird if I asked you to be my best man?'

23

Verity checked her appearance in the full-length mirror on the back of her bedroom door, then fumbled to pull the hem of her dress down an inch or so. The dress was tight, short and red, a violent contrast to her fiery auburn hair. Yvie had been with her when they'd chosen it and she had no idea how she'd let herself be talked into it.

'For God's sake,' Yvie had gasped, exasperated, when Verity had resisted. 'All that running has given you the best legs I've ever seen. If I looked like that, I'd spend every day in hot pants, twerking up and down the street.'

Verity was fairly sure she wasn't kidding.

Yvie was on a roll. 'However, I don't. So I'm going to wear something that covers my cellulite and you're going to wear that dress because it makes you look like a goddess. And then I'll have to stand between you and Zoe to get our pics taken and you'll look like bookends because she'll have on a dress exactly like that one too.'

That had almost sold her. Yvie was right. This was exactly what Zoe would wear.

Verity had stared at her reflection in House of Fraser's changing rooms for another moment. She never wore anything like this. Always played it safe. Conservative. She hadn't owned anything that stopped above the knee since she was a teenager and even then, it was only the skirt she was forced to wear for netball. She wasn't sure why. Lack of confidence? A desire to stay in the background? Give other people nothing to talk about?

A twinge in her gut told her she'd landed on the answer. She could still remember the whispers after her dad left. Eyes that went the other way when she or her sisters entered the room. Marina lifted her chin even higher, Zoe threw back her shoulders in a challenge and Yvie would smile as if she was offering an apology for something that wasn't their fault. But Verity would just shut down and seethe, stay out of the way, silently hate the gossips and anyone who judged them. She was self-aware enough to realise that not much had changed.

Still playing it safe, blending into the background.

Well, maybe it was time that she shook things up a little.

And she had to concede that Your Next Date had something to do with this more adventurous attitude. Verity had no idea how 'Veronica from Glasgow' actually dressed, but she sure got a load of interest.

The thing would ping at all hours of the day and night. Some were just notifications of matches, others were potential dates, trying to strike up a conversation and the others... well, let's just say at least half of them were looking for more than hand holding and a night at the cinema watching the latest Avengers movie.

She should have been disgusted. Turned off. But somehow she had found it fascinating. It was exposure to a world that she didn't even know existed, with real people (or almost real in her case) who were putting themselves out there, flirting, hooking up, chatting and even, in a couple of instances, sending pictures of their privates. She always blocked those ones.

Bizarrely, though, it had become like a new hobby and given her food for thought. Maybe she was too guarded. Too closed off. Ned clearly adored Zoe, who was the most forthright, ballsy, sociable party animal out there. Maybe Verity should take a leaf out of her book. She'd bought the dress. She was wearing the dress. This was her Zoe outfit.

And at least this new boost of adventure meant she was getting something out of the dating app, because the plan to hook Ned hadn't worked. She wasn't entirely sure if she felt relief or disappointment that he hadn't responded to her swipe. So much for that idea.

The beeping horn of the taxi broke through her thoughts. Too late to change now. Instead, she grabbed her bag and walked to the door as gracefully as she could in shoes that made her five inches taller.

As always, she was one of the first to arrive, but at least Zoe was here on time too, greeting her guests at the door of Gino's restaurant. Thankfully, Ned wasn't at her side, gushing over her sister and piling on even more attention to an already ridiculous event. Yet another difference between her and Zoe. Her sister loved to celebrate her birthday. She'd thrown a party every year for as long as she could remember. Verity, on the other hand, preferred a dinner with just her sisters and Mum, and even then, only if they forced her.

'Happy birthday,' she said, thrusting a gift bag towards her sister. It was one of those Diptyque candles that Zoe liked. Way overpriced, in Verity's opinion, but at least it solved the problem of what to buy her every year.

'Thank you and...' She looked Verity up and down and shrieked with delight as she gestured to Verity's outfit. 'Oh, my God, we're like twins!' She wasn't wrong. Zoe was in a short, pink dress that clung to all her curves and was almost exactly the same style as Verity's. Zoe's gaze had gone downwards now. 'Well, hello Verity's legs, pleased to meet you after all these years,' she chuckled, giving her a tight hug. 'Yvie told me you'd bought this, but we had a ten pound bet that you'd change your mind and take it back.'

'I hope you lost your money.'

'I did, but it was worth it. You look fricking sensational!'

Another hug, but this time Verity took the opportunity to scan the room, searching for... There he was. He caught her eye and started walking towards them, eyebrows raised in surprise.

'Well, the kids in your class wouldn't recognise Miss Danton tonight,' Ned told her, before giving her a hug and then a kiss on each cheek.

Verity felt her face flushing and fought to control it. Mission accomplished. He'd looked at her differently. Maybe she should channel her Your Next Date alter ego more often. A pang of something close to remorse. Maybe, she chided herself, she should get a grip and stop caring what her sister's boyfriend thought of her. It wasn't as if she was trying to take him from Zoe. More that... hell, she just hoped their relationship would die a natural death and he'd realise it was Verity he was meant to be with all along.

'Hello!' Zoe cried, greeting the next arrivals, her attention on them now.

'Come on, I'll get you a drink,' Ned told Verity, holding his hand out. She took it and followed him, praying desperately that she wouldn't go crashing down off those heels and break an ankle.

'What would you like?' he asked her at the bar.

'Vodka tonic,' she replied, with absolutely no idea where that came from. She was usually a wine drinker – Zoe was the only one of them who drank vodka.

Ned bought the drinks, then handed hers over. 'You really do look amazing,' he told her and she could see he meant it. If she'd realised that all she had to do to get his attention was wear a short dress, high heels and go for the glam look, she'd have done it at the start, seduced him before he met Zoe and saved herself months of heartache.

'Thank you. You don't look so bad yourself.' It wasn't an empty compliment. She'd always thought that he bore a distinct resemblance to a younger Ben Affleck, but that had never been truer than tonight. It was a rough guess, but she'd place him somewhere between *Armageddon* and *Jersey Girl*. She clearly had to stop watching movies and get out more.

'We had an interesting day today,' Ned began, and Verity's heart clenched when she realised that he was about to tell her something about Zoe. So much for small talk and perhaps even a conversation that didn't involve her sister. Did he even see that she existed or was she just an extension of Zoe, someone to bounce problems off and talk things through? Veronica from Glasgow wouldn't stand for this kind of crap.

Right now, though, Verity didn't see that she had a choice. If there was a positive here, at least he felt close enough to her to make her his confidante.

Play along. Listen. Learn what's going on.

'Really? What happened? Weren't you having lunch at the Kemp?'

'Yeah. With Roger and Felice, and Tom and Chrissie.'

'I can see why it was interesting,' Verity admitted, but she couldn't resist twisting the discomfort level up just a notch or two. 'Tom's lovely. I really admire how those two have managed to adjust their relationship and revert back to being just friends. I don't think I could do it. If I was that in love with someone, I couldn't just snap my fingers and make that disappear.'

The frown that made his eyebrows narrow told her that she'd scored a direct hit. Bingo. He paused for a moment, obviously thinking through what he was going to say next.

'Look, can I ask you something and swear you'll give me an honest answer?'

This was absolutely not a promise that she would keep. 'Of course you can.'

'Do you think there's still something between them? I just get this... feeling. Nothing I can put my finger on. She works late with him almost every night. They work weekends together when they have a job on. And she talks to him more than she talks to anyone else – me included.'

Verity took a sip of her drink while she contemplated her answer. Middle of the road. Non-committal. 'That's only natural though, isn't it? They're business partners, they've worked together for years and they were friends from the start. They're a huge part of each other's lives and I think they always will be.'

It was definitely wrong that it felt good when that one caused another frown of consternation.

Ned sighed, running his fingers through his Ben Affleck hair. 'I don't get it. He asked her to be his "best man" today. I mean, what kind of stunt is that? So stupid.'

'Absolutely,' Verity replied, feigning horror. 'Why would he do that? And why would she agree?'

'Fucked if I know. Anyway, please don't share this with her – I just wanted to get your thoughts. There's a shorthand between them, a connection that I don't think we have yet.'

'Maybe that just takes time though.' Sympathetic. Caring. Not believing that for a second. She clenched the straw between her teeth, going for unconsciously sexy. She had no idea if she was pulling it off, given that she'd never aimed for 'unconsciously sexy' in her life. Not that he was noticing. He was still banging on about bloody Zoe.

'You could be right. But sometimes I wonder if there's a part of her that's still in love with him. And if there is, then maybe this isn't going to work out.'

He was raising the possibility of it not working out and what she said next could influence that. Rock. Hard place. If she assured him that Zoe was over Tom, then they would dally off into the sunset together. If she said she thought there was still something there, it could break them up, but the risk of that strategy backfiring was huge. Hadn't her last comments to Ned, when she implied Zoe was shallow, come back to bite her? He'd never asked her why she'd fudged the truth about Zoe's ex-boyfriends. Zoe must have explained it in a way that he'd decided to accept it and move on, no hard feelings.

Indecision made her suck on her straw even harder. He didn't even notice. This was the kind of inner conflict that made her want to turn around, walk out, go home, pull on her trainers and run. She needed to feel her heart beating on the inside, needed to sweat out all the indecision and tension.

She wanted him. With every breath of a body that was wrapped in a bright red minidress, she absolutely wanted him. But if it was going to happen, she saw now that it couldn't be because she lied.

However, that didn't mean she was going to make it easy for him.

'You know what, Ned, I can't give you an answer. The only person who really knows whether or not she's still in love with Tom is Zoe. So I think you're going to have to ask her yourself.'

24

YVIE – ON ZOE'S BIRTHDAY

'Shouldn't you be gone by now?' Kay bustled past her with an armful of charts and then thumped them down on the nursing station desk. 'Tonight's backlog,' she added, popping a pen into the top pocket of her scrubs. 'I'd beg you to take them off my plate and set fire to them, but if we both lose our jobs, we'll never shop in Krispy Kreme again.'

Yvie feigned a shudder. 'And that's a life that I don't want to think about.'

'What kind of a life is that?' asked a voice behind her.

Bloody hell! Why was he always sneaking up on her? Did Seth McGonigle just prowl the corridors, waiting for moments when she was talking about something completely stupid and then choose that second to inject himself into the conversation?

'A life without doughnuts,' she said, as if it was the most natural thing in the world.

He had no answer, just blinked, shrugged and waited for the moment to pass before he could get back to the subject of work. 'Can someone check on Mr Price in an hour – I've topped up his pain meds, but I just want to make sure that they ease his discomfort. And I'm going to operate on Mrs Spector's ankle first thing, so can we make sure she's nil by mouth after midnight?'

'Aye aye, captain, we will indeed,' Kay assured him. 'Or rather, I can. Cinderella here is off to a ball.'

Yvie felt an inexplicable urge to explain herself. 'Not a ball exactly. Just a restaurant in the Merchant city... it's my sister's birthday party.'

He lingered and for a horrible moment Yvie wondered if he was waiting for her to invite him. Surely not. He was a consultant. She wasn't just going to blatantly ask him out, even if she wanted to – which she definitely didn't.

'I think he was waiting for you to invite him,' Kay whispered after he eventually headed off.

'Shut up!' Yvie shot back as if it was the most ridiculous thing she'd ever heard, despite having exactly the same thought. She then leaned forward conspiratorially. 'But it did seem like that, right?'

The corners of Kay's mouth were rising. 'It sure did. Would you? He's been away from his missus now for a few months. He must be prime dating material. I would totally ask him out.'

'Well, why don't you then?'

'Because someone like that isn't going to be interested in a skint single mum who works all the hours God sends.'

'Well, he doesn't know what he's missing. He'd be lucky to have you and I reckon you might even put a smile on that moody face.'

'That's not all I'd do,' Kay added, laughing. 'It's been so long since I had sex, I might just skip the date and go straight to the tickly bit.'

Yvie pursed her lips, feigning outrage. 'Sister Gorman, I feel your salacious comments about a male member of our team are highly unprofessional and I'm considering reporting you to HR first thing in the morning.'

Kay feigned repentance. 'I'm terribly sorry, Nurse Danton, and you're absolutely right. Can I buy your silence with the offer of a bottle of Prosecco and a chicken curry on Saturday night?'

'Throw in prawn crackers and it's forgotten,' Yvie told her, giggling, before blowing her a kiss and taking off.

Yvie counted the steps until the inevitable happened. Ten. Fifteen. Twenty. Twenty-five. Her stomach began to clench. Thirty. Sweat pores opened and she could feel her temperature rising. Forty. Almost at the door now and... Yep... there was the tremble of her hand as she pushed it open.

It was difficult to say when it had become a regular occurrence. Maybe just after the Ibiza trip? Around early summer? She'd hoped the panic attacks were isolated horrors, but that's when the everyday general anxiety had flared too. So many times she'd thought about telling Kay, then changed her mind. Her friend relied on her both in and out of work and she was already stretched to capacity dealing with a busy ward and bringing up Chester on her own – the last thing Yvie wanted to do was to give her another problem to deal with, another thing to worry about. It was so much easier to pretend, to smile, to make jokes and then to walk away and let the darkness consume her.

In the staff changing room, she put her head against the cold metal of the lockers, and took deep breaths. There was no escaping the irony. Every day, she helped people overcome their fears, their anxieties, and in some cases, cope with fairly significant mental health issues and yet here she was, taking her own advice on how best to deal with the physical symptoms but ignoring the most important healing step of all: talk to someone.

Breathe. Just breathe. She said it over and over again, and just when she was beginning to think she wasn't going to be able to stop it escalating to a full-scale panic attack, she felt her heart begin to slow, the tremors start to subside. Breathe. Just breathe.

Only when she was sure it was over did she get changed into the outfit she'd brought for the party. Black trousers. A black vest top. A long red glittery chiffon cover-up that reached her ankles. It wasn't exactly sexy, but lump coverage was what mattered here. The anxiety had contributed to a few more pounds and she was at her heaviest weight ever. She heard a voice in her head saying that the diet was starting the next day and then another, more realistic part of her brain telling the first voice to shut the hell up.

She had this. She could do it. Deep breath. Smile. Let's go.

Opening the door of the changing area, she took a strong step forward... right into the finely toned chest of Seth McGonigle. 'Shit! Sorry! I didn't see you!'

He shrugged and – oh, flipping miracle – smiled. 'That's okay. I didn't see you either.'

Awkward pause. 'Right, well, I'd better go. I'll erm...'

'You look really nice. Am I allowed to say that? I never know with all the rules about what's appropriate now.'

She chose not to mention that Kay's comments about him earlier definitely didn't fit into the category of 'appropriate'.

'I, erm... Yes. Sure. Thank you. I'll see you later. Have a good night.'

Face burning, she took off, practically jogging to the lifts. At this rate, her feet would be shredded by the time she got there. Luckily, a taxi was in the rank at the entrance to the hospital, so she jumped in it and gave him the address of Gino's.

Fifteen minutes of chat about *Britain's Got Talent*, *Strictly Come Dancing*, the political divides of the country and the state of Scottish football later (he had cast-iron plans to improve them all), she was deposited at the door. Okay, she could do this. She was going to have a fantastic night. She would dance. Eat. Drink. Laugh. And be absolutely normal. Smile on. Let's go.

Gino was the first to spot her. 'Yvie! Ah, my favourite! You just made an old man very happy.'

Zoe immediately appeared behind him. 'Don't listen to him – he told me I was his favourite. I think he's playing us off against each other. Just as well we both love you, Gino.'

Gino threw his arms up in delight, almost taking out a whole tray of drinks being carried by a passing waiter. 'Ah, you're only human,' he bellowed, before walking away, a booming cackle emitting from his considerable girth as he went.

'I would actually fight you for him,' Zoe said, deadpan.

'Stilettos at dawn,' Yvie giggled, before opening her arms wide. 'Happy birthday, sis.'

The warmth of Zoe's hug had a peculiar effect on her, making her eyes fill with tears. That was a first. Shit, what was going on? Where was all this emotion coming from? It was like all her senses were heightened and she was flailing from one dramatic reaction to another. She swallowed the lump that had become lodged in her windpipe.

'Did you see the Ibiza photos? I thought they were fabulous!'

The lump got bigger, so all Yvie could manage was a stuttered lie. 'Yeah, they're... erm... great.' The pics of their trip had gone up on the Kemp Hotels website a few days ago and Zoe had sent them all the link. Yvie had clicked on it, hoped, prayed – and then been absolutely devastated by what she saw. Three gorgeous, slim, happy women and then there was their fat companion. 'You do not look fat, you look curvy and glorious and fricking spectacular,' Kay had told her, but Yvie refused to see it. She'd closed the link. Deleted it. And fought with all her might against an urge to cheer herself up with something delicious. Instead, she'd started a diet again the next morning and then berated herself when it failed on day two, after a twelve hour shift left her reaching for a Mars bar.

Zoe leaned in, so her mouth was almost at Yvie's ear. 'I'm so glad you're here. Not just because I love you – although I do – but for God's sake can you talk to Mum? She's been sitting over at the buffet with a face like a wet weekend since she got here.'

No! This isn't my job. I'm here to dance and eat and drink and take a night off from taking care of the rest of the world! Her reply – yet another dramatic reaction – screamed in her mind, but thankfully the fecking lump that was still in her throat stopped the words from coming out. Instead, the only thing that got by it was a murmured, 'Sure,' before Zoe was distracted by the arrival of Tom and Chrissie.

Yvie hugged them both. She'd always loved Tom. He was exactly the kind of guy Zoe should have ended up with. Ned? She felt her heart begin to speed again. *Don't think about it. Don't think about it. Don't think...*

'Sorry, have to go. Apparently, I'm on mother duty tonight. Not sure why I drew the short straw,' she added, with a pointed glare at Zoe but her tone making it clear she was teasing.

'Because you're the closest thing we've got to Oprah,' Zoe replied. 'You're like the fourth emergency service for this family. Police. Fire. Ambulance. Yvie.'

'You forgot Haagen-Dazs. They're my fifth.'

The others laughed and Yvie bowed out, scanning the room for Marge. To the left, she spotted Carlo, serving a table in the far corner of the room but still managing to give her a wave and a smile when their gaze met.

Scan right. Yep, there Mum was, over by the buffet, resplendent in... Holy fuck. A white top and trousers and a floor length red chiffon glittery cover-up. Yvie felt something inside her die. She'd turned up to an event wearing the same outfit as her mother, aged fifty-four. And it was red. With glitter. People were going to think they were some kind of mother/daughter cabaret act. Bollocks. Bollocks.

'Hi, Mum,' she used every ounce of strength to greet her breezily, giving her a warm hug, too. 'You look lovely.'

'So do... Oh my, we're wearing the same outfit!'

Yes we are, Mother. She didn't state the obvious out loud. Even worse than the matching styles was the fact that Yvie's was a size 20/22 and Marge's looked like it was in the 8/10 category.

'I must be so trendy these days. You know, Nigel, my ashtanga teacher, was just saying that the reason I look so good is because I embrace youth and take such an interest in today's styles and fashions. He sees me, Yvie, you know? He actually sees who I am.'

Shoot me. Shoot me now.

'I see you too, Mum,' Yvie countered, popping a chunk of bruschetta from the buffet into her mouth.

'Oh, I know, dear,' Marge said, in a tone that suggested she absolutely didn't. 'You girls are all just so busy though.'

Well, hello passive-aggressive dig. It was all Yvie could do to stop her jaw dropping. She spoke to her mother every single day, listened to her, encouraged her, tried to make her feel loved. And yet, she was apparently 'too busy'. Yvie bit back her rising irritation and looked for a way out. Over at the bar, she could see Verity deep in conversation with Ned. There was a twosome she'd do anything to avoid. But wow, she looked incredible in that dress. Marina? Another scan of the room. Nope, she wasn't here yet. Hell must have frozen over. Marina had never been late for anything in her life.

Her mum was still speaking. 'I don't think Derek has ever truly understood me. As soon as his varicose veins have healed, I'm going to leave him, Yvie. I know I've said it before, and I know I've left him and gone back on more than one occasion, but I mean it this time. This chapter of my life should be about self-care and putting myself first...'

Yvie couldn't stand it. She actually couldn't bear to listen to another moment of the same moans, the same self-centered twaddle she'd been listening to for years. Decades! Right here, right now, for reasons she didn't even understand, she felt like it was going to make her head explode, blasting grey matter all over Gino's beautiful cream walls. She glanced around, searching for an escape, only for her eyes to fall on Ned. As his gaze caught hers, he winked and she felt the tightening coil of pressure inside her snap.

'Mum, I'll be back in a second, I just need to nip to the ladies'.'

Marge stopped, and there was no disguising her sneer of irritation.

Yvie ignored it, turned, darted around the corner and...

'Woah, there,' Carlo said, spinning on his heels and flattening against the wall so that she wouldn't send him flying.

'Sorry, Carlo, I...'

The feeling of suffocation gripped her throat and she knew she had to get out of there. 'Is there a back door? I'm not... not... feeling well and I just need a bit of fresh air.'

Carlo immediately switched to concern as he registered her rapid breaths, her flushed face, her shaking hands. He quickly opened a door behind him and steered her through the kitchen and out of the back door. Outside, in the alley, he pulled over a crate and gestured to her to sit.

'Can I get you a glass of water?'

Yvie could feel the burning embarrassment rise, the redness creep up her neck and face, the suffocation tightening her chest even more. She didn't want to explain, didn't want to discuss it, she just wanted to get out of there.

'I'm fine, thanks. I'm just going to grab a taxi and get home. Just a migraine.'

'Are you sure?' He didn't look convinced. 'Let me drive you...'

'Carlo, you have a restaurant full of people in there. I'm fine. Honestly. I'll text my sisters and let them know. Thanks...'

With that she took off, striding to the end of the alley. She was a few steps in when she realised Carlo was running at her side.

'At least let me make sure... Taxi!' he shouted, spotting an empty one just as they reached the main road. This area of Glasgow was busy and teeming with cabs at this time of night.

The taxi screeched to a halt and Carlo opened the door for her. 'Are you sure you don't want me to get your family? They'll want to come with you, to take care of you.'

It took every ounce of strength she had to act somewhere

near normal. 'Absolutely not! I don't want to spoil the party. Thanks, Carlo. It's just a migraine. I'll be fine after a lie down, I promise.'

She closed the door, gave the driver her address and clutched on to the handle as he did a U-turn and headed in the direction of her home, her own words echoing in her ears. 'I'll be fine,' she'd said.

They weren't even out of the street when the tears began to stream down her face.

She wasn't fine.

She was so very far from fine.

Right now, she wasn't sure she'd ever feel fine again.

25

MARINA – ON ZOE'S BIRTHDAY

'Dear God, woman, have you met your end in there?' Graham moaned from the other side of the bathroom door.

Christ Almighty. There were five other bathrooms in this house and yet he didn't want to have to walk approximately twenty feet to use the next closest one.

'I'm waxing a delicate area! It takes time!' she shouted back, knowing that would send him bustling off. There was nothing like the mere thought of any form of treatment that could possibly stray near her vagina to make him run for the hills. It was a bloody miracle they had two children. Had he always been this uptight? When had the slick, go-getting, impressive guy she'd married turned into his father? Marina stopped the thought right there, before it led her to wonder when she'd become so fucking rigid and controlling that she'd turned into his mother.

She'd just done what she needed to do and look how everyone else in this family was succeeding because of it. Graham was making more money than ever, because she made sure she supported him, his clients and his ambitions.

Annabelle had been offered a place at the dance academy and was doing great, travelling to Edinburgh, with Marina ferrying her there at the crack of dawn on a Monday morning and then collecting her and bringing her home on a Friday evening. Oscar's grades were hitting straight A's and he'd made the first teams in rugby and hockey. Every one of them was winning and she just had to make sure she continued to provide the help and the push that they needed to sustain it.

So why was she sitting on the edge of the bath, dressed for a party that she should have left for an hour ago, absolutely dreading going? Why did Zoe have to make such a bloody fuss of her birthday every year anyway? It was only another day. Honestly, that level of self-indulgence was just ridiculous.

Right. Let's go. Time to move. She just had to stand up, fix her lippy... And yet she wasn't moving.

On the granite top of the double sink vanity unit, her phone buzzed. Marina reached over and tilted it so she could read the screen.

Are you at the party yet? Sorry, I have a splitting migraine and had to go home but didn't want to spoil the fun so didn't disturb Zoe. Can you let her know please? Have a great night. Love you, Yxxx.

Brilliant. Just bloody brilliant. She wasn't even going to have Yvie there to distract her.

Now she definitely had to go. One sister missing might have been acceptable, but not two.

She clipped on her earrings, straightened her dress (Celine, black, off the shoulder, knee length, body-con, accessorised with strappy Jimmy Choo sandals), shoulders back, and slipped into organisation mode. Within ten minutes, she had Annabelle and Oscar pass inspection, ended Graham's hunt for his cufflinks (in his flipping cufflink box where they always were) and shooed them all into the taxi that she, of course, had summoned. She was glad when Graham sat in the front, leaving her to get in the back with the kids. They both immediately pulled out their phones and she knew that would be them lost to her for the rest of the journey.

In one way, that was a plus, because it meant she didn't have to fake cheeriness. But on the flipside? It gave her way too much time to contemplate why she was dreading tonight so much.

Ned Merton.

Marina closed her eyes, glad of the darkness, and tilted her head so that it was resting against the window of the taxi.

Six weeks on from the date night for that school fundraising committee and she could still remember every detail. After her initial rash agreement, she'd backtracked furiously, realising how absurd it was. She didn't have time for this. She was busy. Couldn't someone else do it? All her objections to it had been refuted by the chief fundraiser, a woman who could match Marina toe to toe in the stubborn stakes. For the sake of transparency and credibility, they needed to ensure it went ahead, she said. They needed photos so they could advertise it as a prize again this year, she said. Mr Merton was a very popular teacher, so it always raised plenty of money in the raffle, she said.

Marina had realised she wasn't getting out of it.

'Why wouldn't you want to go anyway?' Zoe had asked her, finding the whole thing hilarious. 'My boyfriend is lovely. I'll vouch for him.'

Zoe's attitude had mollified her. And after all, it was a night out in a fabulous restaurant with no-one to organise, fetch, carry or check on. Besides, that woman at the school wasn't going to give up. Time to surrender.

'Okay, but I'll only do it if you come along. Feels weird otherwise.'

'Deal,' Zoe had assured her.

That's why she'd turned up at Ned's suggested restaurant (The View in the Kemp Hotel, of course – Zoe had got them a freebie for the school funds from Roger) at seven o'clock on a Thursday night, resolving to give this an hour of her time and then bail out and leave Zoe and Ned to it.

The photographer sent by the school (Alfie Paton, age ten, accompanied by his dad, sporting the camera he got for Christmas) spent a good half an hour taking snaps of them pretending to drink, pretending to eat sumptuous appetisers, with Marina pretending she wasn't wondering where the hell Zoe was. The photography team had just left, after announcing that they had enough footage and Alfie had to get home because it was nearly his bedtime, when the text came in to both Marina and Ned at the same time.

So sorry, you two lovelies – won't make it tonight – something's come up at work and I need to pull an all-nighter. You two go ahead and have fun! Love you both xxxx

Ned had visibly deflated. 'Surprise, surprise,' he'd said, but his smile was hiding nothing and the edge of irritation in his voice was loud and clear. 'She's got a big pitch tomorrow, so it's not a shock really. I've been staying at my own place all week to let her get on with it.'

Marina, meanwhile, had felt a raging exasperation. What the hell was Zoe playing at? Didn't she see how completely inconsiderate this was?

'Look, it's fine,' Marina had said, trying not to sound as snappy as she felt. 'The school has their pictures, so all's well. I've got a million things at home I could be doing, so we can just call it a night.'

She was so sure that he'd want to bail out, that she hadn't even considered that he would offer an alternative, so she was surprised when he'd said, 'Me too. But, to be honest, it would probably involve beans on toast and crap telly, so if you want to stay here and eat Roger Kemp's finest food, I'm up for that.'

Marina had thought about it for a second or two. As offers went, it wasn't the worst one – a fabulous meal, in a gorgeous restaurant and a chance to spend a couple of hours in the company of a man that didn't seem to think she was only there to facilitate his every bloody breath.

'Sure,' she'd said, lacking conviction, but then immediately following it with a more assertive, 'Why not!'

'Great,' Ned had replied, raising his glass again.

Marina was suddenly aware of how they must look to the other diners in the restaurant. She'd dressed for the occasion, in a navy dress she'd bought for one of Graham's company dinners – conservative neckline, stopping just above the knee but skimming her body like a glove so that it was demure yet sexy. Ned matched the look. He was in a beautifully cut suit, his wide smile perfect, his eyes full of mischief. She could absolutely see what Zoe saw in this man. And why Verity had such a crush on him before Zoe nabbed him. She'd asked Verity a few times since then how she felt about him and she swore she was completely past it and couldn't care less. Now, being in his company like this, Marina wasn't so sure. If she were single and a few years younger, she'd be attracted to him too.

For the sake of the photos, and because they'd been

waiting for Zoe, they'd just asked for starters. Ned called the waiter over and explained that no one else would be joining them now and asked to see the menus again so they could order main courses. As soon as that was done, and they were alone again, he opened with, 'So, tell me about you. What should I know about Marina... actually, I don't even know your surname.'

Marina took a sip of her wine. 'It's still Danton. I didn't change it when I got married. Thought I was too much of a feminist to be defined my husband's name.'

Her cheeks had burned with the irony of that statement. She hadn't wanted to take his name, yet she'd somehow gone on to surrender her whole life to him and their children.

'I like that,' he'd said, leaning forward, as if he was genuinely interested. 'It wouldn't surprise me in the least if Zoe did the same. I don't think I've ever met someone who depends on people less than she does. She's like some kind of laser-focussed force of nature. And a complete workaholic. I think I spend more time with Verity than I do with Zoe. Not that I'm complaining... she's worth the wait.'

The lurch of jealousy was so strong, it took Marina a moment to process it. It wasn't jealousy that Zoe had this man, it was jealousy that he spoke about her with such obvious admiration. When was the last time Graham had said that she mattered? That he noticed what she did?

'But, anyway, back to you. Zoe said you went to uni. What did you study?'

That had started a conversation that didn't stop, except for a few moments when their main courses were being delivered, or their wine glasses topped up, or they were asking for another bottle. And very little of it was about Zoe, or Verity, or anything other than the two people sitting at the table.

The moon was high in the sky outside the floor-to-ceiling windows by the time they'd finished their coffees (Irish, potent and thick with cream).

Marina had had a thought that made her smile without even realising she was doing it.

'What are you grinning at?' Ned had asked her, amused.

At the beginning of the evening, almost two bottles of wine ago, she'd have been embarrassed to say, but sod it. 'I was thinking that we were pretending to enjoy ourselves in the photos earlier, but I've genuinely had a lovely time.'

The neck of his shirt was open now and it was obvious he was completely relaxed, his long fingers slowly twirling round the spoon from his coffee. 'Me too. I can't believe the time has passed so quickly. Feels like it's too soon to call it a night.'

His stare was locked on her now, the reflection of the candle on the table making his jaw look even sharper, his teeth even whiter, eyes even darker. Dangerous, even.

Marina wasn't sure how to respond to that. Reality check. This was her sister's boyfriend. He was being friendly. Getting to know his girlfriend's family. This was a school raffle prize, for crying out loud. And yet...

Was it her imagination or was he looking at her in a way that wasn't covered by any of those categories?

'There's bound to be a nightclub open somewhere,' he'd suggested, still slowly, expertly, twirling that damn spoon.

That was the moment – choose quit or go. Call it a night or take another step towards something she wasn't sure she understood. What the hell was wrong with her? This wasn't some stranger in a bar, or some French tourist that she would never see again. This was Ned. Verity's friend. Zoe's boyfriend. And she wasn't even completely sure what was happening here. Was he coming on to her? Or had those hook-ups with the other guys turned her into some sex-crazed idiot who now thought every passing bloke wanted a wild night of passion with her? She had absolutely no idea what he was thinking. But hell, she definitely knew what her own body had in mind.

All she wanted to do was...

'Mum! Mum, wake up, we're here,' Oscar demanded.

Marina's eyes flew open, heart racing with that insane but very real fear that someone could have known what she was thinking. The complete disinterest on Oscar and Annabelle's faces told her differently. They were too busy trying to get a few more seconds on their phones before they had to put them away. In the front, Graham was handing over twenty quid for an eighteen pound fare and telling the driver to keep the change.

They climbed out, Marina straightening her dress once again, then patting her hair to make sure her bob was still perfectly in place.

'Shall we?' Graham said, gesturing to the entrance of Gino's.

Marina had to bite back a sarcastic retort. Why did everything he did and said bug her now? It was like some floodgate had opened and all the minor irritants that she'd let slide for years now made her teeth grind.

As soon as they opened the door, Zoe's open arms greeted her. 'Yay, you made it!' she cheered, hugging her niece and nephew, then working up to the adults. She'd just let Marina go, when Ned appeared from the corridor to the cloakroom beside them.

'Well, hello,' he exclaimed, grin beaming as always. He

shook Graham's hand, then high-fived the kids, then, finally, stepped forward, arms open to hug Marina.

If anyone noticed that she stiffened slightly, they didn't say.

That night at the Kemp, she'd refused Ned's offer to go on to a club because she had no idea if it was an innocent suggestion or something more. She still didn't know.

Was it a harmless bit of fun? After all, he spent loads of time with Verity too. Maybe he was just one of those guys who was comfortable in female company and who had lots of friends of the opposite sex.

Or maybe her radar wasn't off, and he really had been hinting at something more.

'It's really good to see you,' he said, when his mouth was so close to her ear she could feel his breath on her cheek.

That night, she'd refused him. She'd said no. She'd gone home and she'd lain next to a husband who hadn't made her feel desired in years. But Graham wasn't the issue here.

It was Ned Merton.

That night, she'd done the right thing, but she found herself so attracted to him that she wasn't sure she trusted herself to do the same in the future.

26

THE GIRLS – SEPTEMBER 1999

'He must not be in,' Marina said, as they knocked for the fifth time and still got no response.

'But he knew we were coming,' Yvie said, the hurt making her voice tremble.

Zoe threw her arm around their younger sister. 'Maybe something important came up at work. Or maybe... maybe he just forgot. It happens. I completely forgot two orders of egg and chips yesterday at the café, and I got a right bollocking.'

Verity knew Zoe was just trying to stop Yvie worrying. She was the most likely of all of them to fret about the others and they all hated to see her upset. Except, obviously, Dad, who wasn't here waiting to spend the day with them as they'd arranged. Totally thoughtless of him and Verity just didn't understand it.

'Let's go home and phone him,' Marina suggested. 'Or maybe Mum has heard from him and has a message for us.'

'Mum's out with Gregor today. They were going shopping for a new car. Mum says she wants a BMW,' Yvie said.

Verity had to clamp her mouth shut to stop herself making a bitchy comment. Mum had been seeing Gregor for about four months now and he'd already moved in with them. It wasn't that they disliked him, because he was nice enough, but it was just that, well, sometimes it seemed like their dad had just been written out of their lives. Like he'd never happened. It was just Mum, Gregor and the girls, one big happy family, and Dad didn't even get a look-in. And Verity really hated that.

'It would be a lot easier if we had one of those mobile phones,' Zoe said. 'I'm saving up for one, but it's going to take me years unless someone leaves me a mahoosive tip! Right, let's go. We can come back later when we know what's going on.'

Verity stayed quiet, but she'd already decided not to go along with Zoe's plan. This was the third time Dad hadn't been here when they'd come to visit, so it wasn't a complete shock, but still, something didn't feel right. She wasn't going to say that to the other three here though. Zoe would just tell her she was crazy and everything was fine, Marina would get all bossy and Yvie would only worry and get upset.

'You three go on and I'll catch up. I just want to nip to the bookshop and see if they've got a book I was looking for.'

'Which one?' Zoe asked.

Shit. She couldn't think, so she went on the offensive. 'Does it really matter?' she answered with a withering stare. There. That would get rid of them.

With a couple of eye rolls, her sisters headed off down the street in the direction of home, while she started to walk slowly the other way. When she saw over her shoulder that they were out of sight, she doubled back to Dad's flat.

He'd moved there about six months ago, not long after

their parents had announced they were getting divorced. It was a ground floor flat in a tenement building about a mile away from their house. At first, they'd visited him a couple of nights a week and every Sunday, but that had dwindled as the months passed and he told them he was working later at nights. Now they just came on a Sunday, and even then he wasn't always there.

Verity didn't understand it. None of them did. Dad had always been the fun one in their family, but now he was so different most of the time. Sad. The older three sisters had talked about it and decided it must be because of the divorce. He was lonely. He missed them. No wonder he wasn't on top of the world any more.

They were just all hoping it would get better over time.

She'd read in loads of books about couples who split up and became friends again after a while, so maybe that would happen here. Or maybe, Yvie's night-time prayers would be answered and they'd get back together. Although, every time Verity heard Yvie say that, she told her not to be so stupid – what was the point of getting her hopes up? Of course, Marina and Zoe thought she was terrible for slating Yvie's dream, but she didn't care.

It wasn't that she disliked her sisters – although she knew that's what they thought. It was just that there was always noise and chaos and they were always there, while she preferred to be on her own so she could read or study. Dad had always said she was so smart she could be a teacher and she liked that idea. He looked so proud when he said it and she knew it would make him so happy. Besides, how cool would it be to help people learn stuff? And not just because she could boss others around for a change.

Back at the flat, she thudded on the door again, just in case Dad was in a deep sleep. Still no answer.

She bit her bottom lip while she decided what to do. He didn't ever open the front windows because they were directly on to the street, but maybe...

Taking a chance, she headed through the close to the back court, a concrete area with drying lines and sheds with overflowing bins that smelled. It made her stomach churn a bit, so she tried not to breathe in. Turning left, she tried to peer in the window to her dad's bedroom, but no luck – the curtains were closed. That's when she noticed a tiny gap at the bottom of one of the windows where it hadn't been closed properly.

Using all her strength, she pushed it up just far enough that she could pull over an old milk crate from the bin shed and stand on it, then climb in.

Actually, 'climb' was a bit of an overstatement. She forcefully launched herself forward in a dive that took her through the curtains, and she landed with a thud on the carpet.

The first thing she noticed in the dark room was the smell. It was like nothing she had experienced before. It was sweet and sour at the same time, like the room hadn't had any fresh air for a long time. Deciding to rectify that, she pulled the curtains open.

That's when she saw him. Her dad was lying on the bed, with his clothes still on, although his T-shirt was all dishevelled and there were stains all over it.

A cold horror spread through her as a terrifying thought popped into her head. Was he dead?

Just as she was about to stick her head out of the window and scream for help, he moved, grunted.

Oh, thank God. 'Dad?' she said, tentatively.

No reply. Just another grunt.

In a split second though, her relief turned to anger. He'd been there all along, while they were outside banging the door. Could he not even have got up for them? Set his alarm? It was almost noon. Why was he still sleeping? He'd never let them stay in bed until that time.

'Dad!' she repeated, louder and more forceful this time. 'Dad, wake up!'

She said it again. And again. Shaking him the final time until he finally opened his eyes. The weirdest thing happened. For a moment, it was as if he didn't recognise her, and then she saw confusion, then something else. Irritation, maybe?

'How did you get in?' he asked sharply.

That took her aback a bit. Mum was the one who could be harsh with her words, not Dad. But still, he was the one who'd messed up here and he had no right to take it out on her.

'I climbed in the window. I was worried. I mean, what are you doing? We were outside banging the door for ages and you didn't answer...'

'Verity, I'm not feeling very well today.'

Oh. He was sick. Her anger immediately dissipated as she realised he couldn't help it and she felt a wave of guilt for being angry with him.

'Do you want me to make you something to eat? A cup of tea?' It wasn't just Marina who could do this stuff – she could take care of people when she wanted to.

'No. I think it would be best if you just went home,' he said in an unfamiliar, dead tone.

'But why?' she challenged him, anger rising again now.

Why did he want her to go? He was her dad. Didn't he want to see her? Didn't he care?

'Verity, just go. I'll phone you later when I've sorted myself out.'

She sighed, confused, agitated. 'No. Look, I'll help you clean up and then I'll make you lunch and...'

'Verity, just go!' he bellowed, more loudly than she'd ever heard him shout. 'Just do what you're bloody told for once in your life and go home.'

The shock was like getting punched in the face. He'd never shouted at her. He'd never been unkind. This was her dad. He loved her. He was her favourite person, the only one who really understood her and didn't mind that she was a bit weird, a bookworm who liked her own company. 'Just be you, darling,' he'd tell her. 'That's all you need to be.'

He wasn't saying that now.

'Get out!' he shouted again, even louder, making Verity's whole body shake and her legs feel like they were going to give way beneath her.

Fear, confusion and panic consumed her.

She could have stayed and fought with him, but she didn't. She turned around, sped down the hall, out of the front door and she ran. She ran really, really fast, until her thudding heart was due to the exertion and not just the absolute terror of what had just happened.

She didn't stop until she was home, upstairs, and back in her room. Alone. Absolutely terrified about what had just happened.

And even more scared when she wondered what would happen next.

27

ZOE – LAST CHRISTMAS AT MARINA'S HOME

'Don't you think it's crazy how much life can change in a year?' Zoe said, popping a mini mince pie in her mouth, her hand moving quickly to avoid Marina smacking it with a spoon.

Yvie was the first to take her up on the question, the two large green baubles on the bosom area of her red jumper rising and falling with every gesticulation as she spoke. 'You think? Let's see... last Christmas, I was single, knackered, I'd just finished a double shift and came straight here after no sleep, I was several stones overweight and vowing that "By this time next year, I'll have Jennifer Lopez's arse."' She stopped for breath. And a mini mince pie, her favourite kind, with the raisins inside and the icing on top. 'This year, however, I'm single, knackered, I've just finished a double shift and come straight here after no sleep, I'm several stones overweight and, ah, about ten minutes ago I announced that by this time next year I'll have Beyonce's arse. So yeah, I'm totally changing things up. Pass me a bit of that yule log before I start to weep.'

Zoe did as she was asked, once again avoiding Marina's tendencies towards violence with a spoon. As always, Michael Bublé was crooning in the background, and Zoe definitely couldn't remember him ever singing any Christmas song that included four sisters and an assault charge.

'I don't think my life's changed at all,' Verity added, with a vehemence that was so excessive, Zoe glanced at her to check she was okay. What was rattling her cage tonight? She'd been tense and brittle since she arrived. Not that that was anything new – she'd been tense and brittle for years, although it had got even worse over the last twelve months – but Zoe was hoping that Verity would find a bit of Christmas cheer at some point in the day. Maybe she was just knackered, Zoe decided. She'd seen how chaotic it had been for Ned over the last few weeks of term. There had been Christmas concerts, the school winter fair, trips to carol services, classrooms to decorate, hyper children to calm down and five nativity plays over three days. At one point she had found him up at 3 a.m. making shepherds' costumes out of her spare room sheets. She'd been so impressed by his dedication that she'd forgiven him for destroying her bedlinen.

'Mmmm, my life is definitely different now,' Marina concluded, raising her head from the Scotch Broth she was stirring on the stove. 'I'm going straight to the Scotch Broth and not wasting time with sushi that will end up in the bin,' she looked pointedly at Verity, who refused to take the bait and apologise for last year's Sushi-gate.

'It does smell incredible,' Zoe offered, melting as another whiff from the stove assaulted her nostrils. Despite all the bickering, the dramas, the differences, the presence of Graham's bitchy mother, and whatever nugget of infuriation her own mother would bring, Marina's house at Christmas was one of her favourite days of the year. The work Marina put into it was evident, from the décor, to the meal, to the gifts, all in size order under the tree. Perfectionism was alive and well in this house. But it was more than all that. Their relationships might not be perfect, and God knows, Marina and Verity were hard work sometimes, but it was the one day of the year that they were all together and made an effort.

'Dad would have loved this.' The thought caught her off guard, especially when she realised that she'd said it out loud, causing a pause in the conversation as they all contemplated that for a moment.

'He'd already be lining up the Pictionary, Monopoly and planning songs for the singalong later,' Yvie said, her face lighting up at the memory, piercing the sadness that had descended on the room.

Zoe joined her on the reminiscence train, bursting into the chorus of 'Hi, Ho, Silver Lining', with Yvie joining in on the next line and Marina and Verity adding the 'Now Baby' at the end.

They were still laughing, Zoe and Yvie wiping tears of amusement and emotion from their eyes, when Marge burst in, looking flustered. 'Marina dear, Nigel is having a lovely time chatting to your father-in-law, but he's asked me to check if this wine is organic?'

'It certainly is,' Marina assured her confidently.

It was enough to have their mother bustling back into the living room armed with good news and reassurance.

'Is it organic?' Zoe asked, surprised.

'Absolutely no idea,' Marina retorted, still stirring, a brilliantly wicked gleam in her eye.

Zoe and Yvie were still laughing when Verity quipped, 'There's something that's changed since last year. Daddy number four on the way, a yoga bendy replacement for poor old Derek.'

It hadn't been much of a surprise to them when their mother finally left Derek just after Zoe's birthday party back in September. It had, however, been a bit of a shock when she'd invited them all for lunch a couple of weeks later and they'd turned up to find that Nigel, the ashtanga teacher, was there, and Marge was introducing him as her new lover. Even the thought of Marge using the word 'lover' still made Zoe shudder.

'I've heard that 'poor old Derek' cashed in his pension and went running off to Puerto Banus on his varicose vein-free legs, so I wouldn't feel too badly for him,' Zoe added. She'd heard that from Tom, who ran into Derek at Glasgow Airport, just as he was making his bid for freedom. 'He said if Marge wants to chase him for his money, she's going to have to find him first, because there was no way that "snidey, bendy little fucker" was going to see a penny of it. He was referring to Nigel there. Apparently, Derek thinks he's been after Mum for ages.'

Marina rested the spoon for a second. 'Yeah, well, Derek had a lucky escape, if you ask me. She's getting more insufferable with every year that passes. Pass me some more wine, will you, V?'

'Marina! It's Christmas! Don't be so horrible,' Yvie reprimanded her.

Marina shrugged, clearly caring not a jot that Yvie objected. 'But it's true.'

'Yeah, well, nobody is perfect.'

Zoe kept her mouth clamped shut, knowing better than to go anywhere near this discussion. They all harboured deep feelings for both of their parents and they all made it their mission to keep those feelings to themselves. Zoe wasn't sure when it had been agreed, or how it had happened, but there was an unspoken understanding, had been since they were teenagers, that nothing good could come of talking about their mum or dad, or what had happened to them back then or since. Although, Zoe wasn't quite sure it was healthy to keep it bottled inside either.

But that was for another day. Right now, she had to get the conversation back on to much lighter ground. 'Right, I'm changing the subject because this won't end well.' Nobody argued. 'Soooo,' she continued, 'going back to what I was saying – and not to make it all about me – but my life has changed hugely. This time last year, I was in pieces over Tom...'

'Do I remember you saying he'd set a date for his wedding? You know, the one that's not to you?' Verity barbed, but the fact that the corners of her mouth were twitching told Zoe she was just trying to get a rise out of her.

'Are you trying to make me cry, Ver?' she asked, voice full of sass, 'Because, I swear to God, if you do, I'll blow my nose on your sleeve.'

Verity suddenly looked uncomfortable as she rubbed the arm of a glorious deep red sweater dress that Zoe was fairly sure was cashmere. Her sister had really upped her wardrobe game in the last few months. If she didn't know better, Zoe would suspect Verity had a secret man somewhere that she was trying to impress. Compared to Yvie and Verity, she was positively plain in a white merino wool polo neck and red tartan straight leg trousers. Ned had been making jokes about Rupert The Bear since she'd bought them.

'Back to me,' Zoe said, making it clear she was taking the piss and she hadn't turned into a complete narcissist. 'As I was saying, before I was so rudely interrupted, this time last year I was in pieces over Tom, and I honestly thought I'd lost the love of my life.'

Yvie budged up closer to her and slung one arm around her, giving her a squeeze. 'He was a fool to let you go.'

Zoe shook her head. 'Nah, he wasn't really. He's so happy with Chrissie and they have their boy together and they've made their family complete. I love them.'

Which was all true, she reflected, with a twinge of sadness. Maybe there was a tiny part of her that still wished it had been different, but...

'If Tom and I had stayed together we'd just have worked day and night until the end of time. It's good that we've both met people with different lives. It stops us living and breathing work 24/7.'

Which was also true. Mostly.

'Anyway,' she went on, making sure she sounded strong and cheery, 'the point is, I felt completely crap when I was here last year and I had no idea what was going to happen or if I'd ever feel normal again and now I... well, I do. And I don't usually stop and think deep and meaningful things about life, but I know that I owe you three a thank you.'

'Jesus, this is like Gwyneth Paltrow's Oscars speech. If you start crying, I swear I'm leaving,' Verity said, eyes rolling. All of which made Zoe laugh because she wouldn't have expected anything different.

'Just for that, I'm starting with you, V. Thank you so much for hanging out with Ned while I've been working so much. I love that you do that for me and sometimes I think that if he wasn't kept busy with all that stuff you two do together, then I'm not sure he wouldn't have got pissed off with me and taken off with someone else.'

Zoe watched as Verity visibly squirmed, as expected. She'd always been hopeless at accepting appreciation and having heartfelt moments.

'You're welcome,' Verity shrugged, face flushed.

'And, Marina, thanks for always organising our family stuff and for being a brilliant hostess, because if it was left to me or Yvie, we'd be eating pizza for Christmas dinner and Quality Street for dessert.'

'You just described my favourite meal,' Yvie interjected.

Zoe hadn't finished with Marina though. 'Oh, and thanks for doing that whole thing for the school fundraiser. Ned said you had a great night.'

'Yeah, we did,' Marina agreed, stirring a little faster now.

'I'm feeling nauseous,' Verity deadpanned. 'Is your bucket of gratitude empty yet?'

Once again, Zoe ignored her. 'And, Yvie, thanks for always listening when I was being pathetic. Which I know was a lot. And thanks for feeding me, making me laugh and joining me in drinking so much on our trip this year that I think I've probably drowned a considerable number of my brain cells.'

'All part of the service,' Yvie said warmly, although Zoe didn't miss the flicker of a frown that crossed her brow. Nope, it couldn't have been. Maybe it was just a twinge of discomfort – Yvie had been complaining since she arrived that her bra was too tight. Or maybe it was another migraine. They must be really severe for Yvie to have left her birthday party early, and she'd cancelled on her a few times since because of the headaches too. Zoe made a mental note to ask her about them later and insist she get checked out. The irony wasn't lost on her that Yvie was a nurse, yet she was the least likely of them all to take care of herself.

'And all that being said,' Zoe went on, 'I've got something

amazing to tell you. Something that will involve a short trip and will absolutely shock the knickers off you...'

'Oh. My. God.' Yvie exclaimed, cutting Zoe off before she could blurt out her news.

'What?' Zoe didn't understand – how could Yvie already know about the Vegas trip?

'You're getting married?' Yvie gasped.

Zoe didn't even get the words out to answer her, because right at that moment, Verity fainted and went crashing to the floor.

28

Verity wasn't sure if her head or her pride hurt more. She'd come to, to the sound of a panicked interrogation.

'Verity? Christ on a bike, VERITY! Are you okay? ARE YOU OKAY?' And that was from Yvie, a trained medical expert. No wonder the NHS was in crisis.

'Verity!' Her mother's voice now. 'Nigel is a yoga professional. Shall I get him?' she heard Marge say to the others.

'Only if you want her to do the downward dog before she stands up,' she heard Marina retort drily.

For a moment Verity was tempted to play dead and hope they all gave up, but she couldn't stand the thought of her new cashmere dress spending another minute on the floor, even though she was pretty sure Marina would have demanded that her long-suffering cleaner scrub the tiled surface to operating theatre standards.

There was a chorus of relief when she opened her eyes and then began to gradually, gently, push herself up.

Zoe pulled a chair across from the kitchen table and Yvie

and Marina helped lift her up on to it. Another moment of lost dignity.

'I got the fright of my life there,' her mother wittered. 'I walk in just as my daughter falls to the floor. I think I'll need to meditate for a few minutes just to re-centre my chakras. That kind of stress is terribly ageing.'

With great wisdom, Marina stepped in before Verity blurted out something that could never be taken back.

'Do you know what would help, Mum? Could you go and cajole everyone into the dining room and let them know that dinner will be served shortly? And ask Graham to refill the drinks. Here...' She thrust a basket of bread rolls into Marge's hands. 'You can get them started with this and I'll bring the soup in a couple of minutes.'

Verity could see that Marge was contemplating putting up an argument, but she took one look at Marina's face and decided not to even try. It would take more than determination and the back-up of Nigel, the yoga guru, to challenge Marina when she wanted something done.

Not for the first time, Verity was thankful that Marina automatically stepped in to take charge. Now, she was getting the first-aid kit from the kitchen cupboard, and she handed it over to Yvie, who opened it and surveyed the contents.

'Holy crap, Marina – next time we run out of supplies, I know where to come. We could operate a field hospital with this lot.'

Verity felt the irritation rising again. 'I'm fine,' she insisted. 'I just got a bit hot. Must be this dress. I'll go and throw some cold water on my face and I'll be fine.'

'You'll just sit there and do what Yvie tells you,' Zoe countered, handing her a glass of water. Apparently everyone in the room now thought they had some kind of authority over her.

It was three against one and she knew her odds of victory were slim, so she just shut up and let Yvie get on with it. First, she pulled a digital thermometer out of the huge first-aid box and took Verity's temperature.

'Slightly raised, but nothing dramatic,' she said, more to herself than anyone else.

Next, she took out a battery-operated blood pressure monitor and held it up, looking at Marina questioningly.

'Really?'

'I bought it for Graham,' Marina explained. 'He has a stressful job. High level of heart attacks in his field, so I was just being cautious. I check it once a month.'

Even for Marina, that was dramatic, Verity decided. But then, she was hardly one to talk, given that she'd just been sprawled on the floor in need of smelling salts. Although, she was 100 per cent certain this was nothing to do with job stress.

A few squeezes of a handpump and many beeps later, Yvie read the digital screen. 'Okay, so your pulse is normal, but your blood pressure is a bit low. I'm not sure that's what's caused this, though.'

Only because Verity raised her eyes at that moment did she notice that a silent glance passed between Yvie and Zoe, then extended to Marina.

'Okay, what's going on? You three look like you're about to stage an intervention. What is it now?'

Verity knew she was coming over as a tad aggressive, but it was exceedingly tiresome seeing them make a drama out of nothing. Why couldn't she have had brothers? You know, blokes who were great company but didn't want to know every fricking nuance of her emotional and personal life. And yes, for the purposes of that analogy, she was over-looking the fact that she was not on the moral high ground here and, on top of that, her sisters were actually doing a pretty decent job of caring about her. Just like they'd done when they'd asked her at various points over the last year whether she still had feelings for Ned. Of course, she'd denied it. Swatted away their concern. Refuted the very idea of it. Although, fainting at the suggestion of Zoe and Ned getting married probably wasn't going to help her denials. She appreciated that they cared, but still, they were way too much sometimes and this was one of those instances in which they had to butt out of her business.

It seemed Marina hadn't got that memo.

'Right, I'm going to say it because these two will beat about the bush and we'll all be fainting from bloody hunger if we don't eat soon. So. We're worried about you. You're exer-cising too much and it almost seems like it's becoming a bit obsessive again.'

Verity's jaw dropped. So it wasn't concern that she still harboured feelings for Ned. It was worry that an old issue was resurfacing. Well, she wasn't having it. 'Don't be ridicu-lous. You're shaming me for trying to be as healthy as I can possibly be?' Even as she tried to brazen it out though, she felt a sinking sensation in her stomach. She knew exactly what they were talking about. It had even crossed her own mind, but she'd squashed the thought, unwilling to face it.

'Come on, V,' Zoe began, and Verity couldn't bear the sympathy in her voice. She didn't need pity from anyone, especially the sister who had inadvertently caused all this. Yet, she was still speaking.

'You know what happened after Dad...'

It was a small mercy that she chose not to finish the sentence. Verity didn't actually think she could take it. It would be too much. She'd crack. She was already feeling vulnerable, so the last thing she needed was for the most painful thing that had ever happened to her to be brought up and for her to fall apart on Christmas Day in Marina's kitchen, while Michael Bublé sang 'Santa Claus Is Coming To Town'.

This time it was Zoe who hadn't got the memo, because she was still trying to make her point. 'It was exactly like this, V. All those months afterwards, years even, you were running too much, not eating enough. It's just what you do when you're under pressure. We're not trying to shame you; we're just worried about you.'

If her blood pressure was low a minute ago, it was definitely on the rise now. How dare they bring this up? How dare they?

'This has got nothing to do with that!' she chided them. 'Absolutely nothing. If you must know, I've been feeling so much better since I upped my exercise...'

'We're now straying into an area of which I have no personal experience,' Yvie interjected, and Verity almost softened, realising that Yvie was trying to lighten the mood. However, she was too irritated to back down.

'As I was saying, I feel so much better. I'm thinking of maybe competing in some way and I just wanted to push myself a little and see how I got on.' None of that was true, but it was all she could come up with on the spot.

'Okay,' Marina said. 'You heard her. Everything is fine. Let's move on.'

'Are you sure, Verity?' Zoe didn't give up easily.

'She's already explained it, Zoe. What else does she need

to tell you? Let it go. And if you dare start singing that song, I'll thump you,' Marina said, impatience ripping out of her. Verity knew Marina would be getting anxious about their Christmas Day running behind schedule.

Yvie was in front of her again, repeating Zoe's question. 'Are you sure you're okay?'

Verity tried the conciliatory approach, adding an overtone of exasperation for effect. 'I am. Don't you think you know me well enough that if I were having problems you'd see it? Don't you think you'd know if I was cracking under pressure or buckling under the strain of some big problem?'

A change came over Yvie's face right then – as if she'd decided to drop it, to stop delving, to take her usual approach and fall back on humour to get them past a sticky situation.

Yvie shrugged. 'You could be living a double life as a high-class escort for all we know. It's always the quiet ones.'

Verity decided not to even dignify that with an answer.

'Look, I really do feel fine, but thanks,' she said firmly. 'Now, I'm going to get up because I really need to go to the loo – and, no, I don't need any of you to come with me. Is anyone planning on trying to stop me?'

No one spoke, so she took that as a no.

'Excellent,' she said, in her best school teacher voice. 'Then I'll be back in a minute. Marina, you might want to serve that soup before your mother-in-law starts some kind of mutiny.'

With that, and as strong a posture and walk as she could manage, Verity picked up her handbag and headed to Marina's downstairs loo.

Inside, she locked the door and plonked herself on top of the seat lid. All she wanted was five minutes to herself to recalibrate and calm down. She had no idea what happened out there. Yvie had said something about Zoe and Ned getting married and then she'd crashed. They were getting married? Surely bloody not?

She closed her eyes, unwilling to even think about it, but knowing she had to, because if they were going to announce it, she had to have a game face prepared.

The thought actually made her heart hurt and she wasn't ready to go back in there yet.

Reaching into her bag, she pulled out her phone and made a note to herself to call a doctor on the first day the surgery was open after Christmas, and make an appointment to see about the fainting. The truth was, it wasn't the first time she'd been dizzy lately. Much as she hated to admit it, maybe she was overdoing things as they'd said – exercising way too much and not eating or sleeping enough.

She flicked through her home screens, found the notes app and... That's when she saw the tiny little square on the Your Next Date icon that told her she had a new message. She had no idea how long it had been there. She'd switched off the alerts because it was going all day long in her desk at school, so the only way to see if someone had contacted her – or should she say, *Veronica* – was to actually view the app. She'd also stuck it on page three of her home screen, in between her electricity supplier and her notes app, so no one was likely to spot it if they glanced at her phone. Now, curiosity got the better of her. Besides, what else was she going to do for the next five minutes? Sit downstairs and watch Zoe and Ned make big sodding lovey eyes at each other over the table?

See who is interested in you, demanded the notification. No doubt it was yet another married guy who just fancied a fling on the side. Or someone looking for a late-night booty call. It really was time she took Veronica from Glasgow off this app and shut the whole thing down. It was getting ridiculous, and more than that, it had been entirely pointless. But again, what else was she going to do for the next couple of minutes? May as well have a look.

Back to the screen. *Okay, go on, tell me what weirdo has the hots for me now.*

She pressed the notification.

And there it was.

One new match.

Edward Merton.

29

'I do like your jumper dear. Very... unusual.' Graham's mother was the master at giving a compliment, while her tone made it absolutely clear she thought the opposite.

Yvie cast her eyes downwards, aware that her attire was ludicrous. Two huge green glittery baubles strategically applied on to a bright red sweatshirt, so that one was over each boob. It had seemed like a hilarious idea when she and Kay had spotted it in the new boutique in the High Street a few weeks before, but they had clearly overlooked the fact that lunchtime Prosecco had been imbibed before the shopping trip. This morning, she'd been in such a rush and knackered after a night shift at the hospital that she hadn't given it much thought. Now she looked at Zoe, with her gorgeous white sweater, at Verity, who looked spectacular in a divine red dress, and Marina, in a stunning emerald jumpsuit, and she realised she was the joke. The comedy act. She felt a wave of absolute crapness drag her down. She was drowning.

'Well, I like it, Auntie Yvie!' Annabelle assured her.

'Thank you, my love,' Yvie said, reaching over to the seat next to her to kiss Annabelle on the cheek. 'That's all that matters to me. Oscar?'

'Yeah...'

'Oscar, don't say "yeah",' Marina chided him. 'It's 'yes'.'

Oscar took another stab at it and Yvie felt bad for getting him into trouble. Marina really needed to chill out sometimes.

'Yes. You look, like, super cool.' He let that one trail away and Yvie thought Marina was going to have a hissy fit. She shot her nephew a wink. They had their moments, but they were great kids, these two, and she loved them dearly.

And she was fairly sure they didn't give a crap about what she wore or how she looked.

However, right now, that wasn't making her feel any better.

She knew things had to change. The weight. The stress. Just always being knackered. But she felt like she couldn't even get her head above water for long enough to breathe, let alone pull herself out of this cycle of anxiety, indulgence, regret, fear, panic and exhaustion.

So, instead, she forced her face into a smile. 'Thank you! It was either this design or one with two elves engaged in activities that I'm not sure are appropriate for a family dinner,' she joked, setting Annabelle and Oscar off on gales of giggles and breaking the tension around the table.

She had no idea what was going on today. Verity had barely said a word since she did the full-scale faint in the kitchen, Marina was sitting at one end of the table with a face that was completely devoid of festive joy, her mother was trying to overcompensate for the weird atmosphere by being ridiculously jolly and attentive to Nigel, the yoga guru, who, in turn, was calling her Cupcake and had just suggested that they spend Boxing Day doing a colon cleanse. If Marina didn't punch him by the end of the night, it would be a Christmas miracle.

In fact, given that Graham and his parents never exactly radiated excitement, and the kids were probably just dying to get away from the table so that they could go and Snapchat their pals, the only people in this whole gathering who were radiating the joy of the season were Zoe and Ned. And she was pretty sure she wasn't the only one who noticed that right now Ned had his arm slung protectively around the back of Zoe's chair and was using his thumb to gently stroke the back of her neck.

The burst of anxiety came from nowhere, starting in her gut, rising, spreading, making her nerve endings shoot to the surface of her skin. Oh God, no. Not now. Please don't do this. Her legs began to tingle, ignoring her pleas. She knew the only way to have a chance of stopping this was to get up and get out of there for a few minutes, to head it off before it escalated into something that there would be no hiding.

'I'm just going to grab my phone from the kitchen – just realised I told the ward I'd keep it on in case they need me.'

'I'll get it for you,' Marina offered, beginning to rise from her chair.

Yvie bolted up even faster, nudging the table and causing all the glasses to rattle. Thankfully nothing spilled, but she felt her heart rate shoot up a few more notches. 'No, no, it's fine. I'll be two seconds.'

'These young ones and their phones,' her mother interjected, and for once Yvie was oh so grateful for Marge's need to have a condescending opinion on everything. 'Nigel is always saying that one day we'll discover the radiation from them has been destroying all our brains. He won't have one in the house, will you, my pumpkin?' On top of the increasing panic, Marge's sickly, adoring tone was causing Yvie to experience the urge to roll her eyes and vomit. And she'd thought her mildly inappropriate glittery chest balls were going to be her biggest problem today.

In the kitchen, she went straight to the sink by the window, leaning on it with both hands, staring into Marina's perfect, picture book garden to give herself something to focus on.

Come on. You've got this. Just breathe. You're fine. You're fine. You're fine.

Her body finally responded, her beating heart slowing, the pressure inside her chest subsiding, her shaking hands becoming still. She had it. She was fine. She could do this. She could breathe.

'Are you okay?'

She hadn't even heard him come in behind her, but now, just by sliding her eyes to the side, she could see Ned standing there, a few feet away, closing the door behind him.

'Just feeling a bit dizzy,' she managed to say in a semi-normal voice. 'Happens sometimes when I've come off a night shift. Just lack of sleep.'

He nodded, then walked towards her, put the empty wine bottle he was carrying down on the worktop next to her, and leaned forward so he could see her face.

'Can I get you anything?'

There was concern in his voice, and Yvie couldn't help wonder if it was fake. Actually, she'd been wondering for a long, long time if everything about Ned Merton was fake. Her pulse quickened again and she fought to control it.

He was standing right next to her now, leaning back

against the quartz worktop so that he was facing the opposite way to her, into the centre of the room. 'Can I ask you something?'

'Can I stop you?' she shot back, knowing what was coming and fairly sure any objections she had wouldn't make a damn bit of difference.

She was right.

He just carried on speaking. 'You've never said anything to Zoe about what happened that night I went out with you and your friend. And, don't get me wrong, I'm really glad you haven't. But I just wanted to know why – and whether this is something that's going to come up and blindside me at some point. Should I be worried?'

Should *he* be worried? Should *he* be *fucking* worried? The voice in her head was getting louder with every word. That was the crux of it. He didn't care about what happened. All he cared about was himself, his own preservation, keeping his dirty little secret, in case it came up and made Zoe think differently about him. He couldn't stand the thought that it could cause a problem in his perfect relationship.

She replayed the question in her mind. Why hadn't she told Zoe?

It was complicated and there wasn't just one straightforward reason.

To start with, that careers day at school, and what happened afterwards, was long before Zoe even met Ned Merton.

Immediately after it happened, Verity's reaction had convinced Yvie that her sister had feelings for Ned so she'd been too wary, too worried about hurting Verity to reveal the truth, to disclose what had gone on with Ned and his games. What kind of sister did that make her? Okay, so she and

Verity weren't as close, but still, she should have been upfront with her. She hadn't been. And the truth was, it was because she couldn't stand delivering bad news, hated to make people unhappy, and if that meant protecting Verity from the truth, then that's what she would do. So she'd stayed quiet, hoped that Verity's thing for Ned would wane, because it was very, very clear that he wasn't interested in her. Yvie just didn't want to be the one to break that to her.

And then...

How could she possibly have predicted that Ned and Zoe would get together? And, of course, yes, she should have told Zoe what had happened, but so much time had passed, and if it all came out, then Verity would want to know why she'd been kept in the dark and... Fuck, it was just a complete shitshow and she couldn't win no matter what she did. So she'd done nothing. Buried her head. Tried to forget about it. Ignored it. Hoped it would all go away. Prayed that Zoe would see sense, realise he was a rebound guy and dump him. Hoped that Verity would want nothing to do with him because he was her sister's cast-off. Made wish after wish that Ned Merton would be out of the picture for good and she'd never have to see his face again.

She should be so bloody lucky. Didn't the truth always come out eventually? Didn't secrets – even from the distant past – always get found out?

The memory of their encounter that night had been torturing her for a long time, and now this prick, this absolute arrogant, duplicitous, two-faced prick, was wondering whether his own actions were going to 'come up and blindside' him?

Violence in every form was abhorrent to her, but right now Yvie wanted to slap his face until it bled.

'No, I haven't told her, and it's too complicated to tell you why. But you can probably boil it all down to the fact that I'm a coward.' She hated herself. She really did. 'Don't you think it might be something that you should share with your girl-friend?' she challenged him, but she saw immediately that her words were wasted when he shrugged.

'No point, is there? We've all got pasts. I don't see the point of dragging it all up. Zoe and me, well, we've got a good thing going now. A really good thing. There's no way I'm letting something inconsequential spoil it. Especially a sister with a grudge to bear. We can't have that, can we? It's not my fault that all of you Danton sisters can't seem to get enough of me.'

The crash when the empty wine bottle hit the floor stunned them both, and it was only when she jumped back and felt the glass sear her foot that Yvie realised she had been the one who had swiped it from the worktop.

Rage was an unfamiliar emotion for her – that had always been more in Verity and Marina's personalities – but right now she was furious. Insanely, violently, completely fucking furious.

'Whoa!' he mumbled, jumping back, staring at her as if she was crazy. 'What the fuck did you do that for?'

Yvie stepped towards him. 'You are a dick,' she hissed in his face. 'And my sister deserves so much better than you. If you fucking dare hurt her, I swear to God I will harm you. Do you understand me?'

Yvie couldn't believe this was coming out of her mouth. She wasn't the one who challenged people, she wasn't the one who made threats or forced confrontations. Her whole life had been about keeping the peace, making everyone happy, smoothing over troubled waters. But Ned Merton...

Argh! Ned Merton, and the way he had played with other people's feelings, was sending her over the edge.

He didn't get a chance to answer her question. A creak signalled the opening of the kitchen door and Yvie turned to see Verity standing in the doorway, taking in the scene before her. Ned. Yvie. A broken wine bottle. Blood seeping from her foot. Yvie had no idea that she was even hurt, her pain receptors overwhelmed by the adrenaline that was consuming her.

'What the hell happened?' Verity gasped, rushing forward.

This was Yvie's moment. If she chose to, she could blurt it all out, reveal the truth to Verity, then get Zoe in here too and blast the secret out and watch Ned Merton face what he'd done. She could do it. And yes, it would hurt them, but surely it was better to know the truth and understand exactly who a person was?

This was it. Tell. Or don't. Hurt her sisters for the greater good, even if they would think less of her. Or don't. Wipe that smug look of victory off Ned Merton's face. Or don't.

She tried to rapidly run every option and consequence through her mind, guessing at outcomes, and all the while her eyes were locked with his, a vile sneer on his face, as if he was almost daring her to say something.

Verity didn't even notice, too busy grabbing a tea towel from the worktop and diving to the floor to wrap it around Yvie's foot.

'Bloody hell, it looks like a crime scene in here. Sit down. You're bleeding all over Marina's travertine floor. She'll go apeshit if she sees this.'

Yvie let herself be guided to a chair, then Verity pulled over another one – the same one Verity had sat in after she'd fainted earlier – and propped Yvie's leg up on it with a towel underneath to protect the wood.

Ned, meanwhile, had jumped into action, soaking a huge wad of paper towels and then handing the sodden lump to Verity to press against Yvie's foot. It was all she could do not to kick him in the face with it. Behind Verity, he was gazing at her, almost daring her to do it.

'Let's try to get this cleaned up before anyone comes in. The last thing we need tonight is any more drama. Marina's already stressed out of her head, the kids are getting edgy, I fainted, and the whole night is in danger of being chalked up as yet another Danton Christmas disaster. Honestly, why can't we just have a drama free Christmas for once in our lives? And how did this even happen?' she asked again.

Ok, last chance. Tell Verity. Go on. Get it out.

'I must have... must have...' Yvie tried to get her brain to work in rational thoughts. What had happened to her? Ned Merton had happened. But now Verity's words were echoing in her head.

'The whole night is in danger of being chalked up as yet another Danton Christmas disaster. Honestly, why can't we just have a drama free Christmas for once in our lives?'

She couldn't add to this family's heartache. Couldn't cause a scene. Couldn't explode a bombshell into their Christmas celebrations. They'd had enough of those to last a lifetime.

Instead, she blustered, 'I accidentally knocked an empty bottle over and stood on a piece of the broken glass.'

Verity nodded. 'That's Marina's fault for making us all take our shoes off the minute we walk in the door.'

When Verity finally pulled the towels back, Yvie bent her knee and brought her foot up to survey the damage. It was mostly superficial cuts. Nothing serious. No major damage done.

She just wished she could say the same for the rest of her life.

Maybe there would be a time when she would have the courage to tell everyone the truth. But it wouldn't be tonight.

30

'You have got to be kidding me,' Marina blurted, her mouth wide with horror as she saw the oozing puddle of red liquid on her travertine tiles. 'Tell me that's the raspberry sauce I'd left out for the ice cream? Actually, don't tell me that because I'll never get it out of the bloody floor.'

Marina was very aware that it didn't reflect well on her that her first instinct here had been concern for the tiles rather than her sister, who was looking exceptionally pale, with one leg up on a chair and the other with... Bugger, was that her new Cath Kidston towels that were wrapped around her foot? They were limited edition!

Seriously, this day could not get any worse. She'd woken before dawn, Graham's snoring rousing her from her sleep way earlier than she had planned, and she'd lain there for a while, listening to him, wondering how much longer she could take this life, here, with him. Actually, that wasn't quite true. The reality was that she didn't have an option, despite her growing realisation that this marriage wasn't working, wasn't giving her what she needed on any level.

She felt unappreciated, unfulfilled, and yes, pretty unloved. On the physical side, they hadn't had sex for weeks. Months maybe. At least, not with each other. Marina flushed as she pushed down the memories of her dalliances. There had been a couple more since Ibiza. Different hotels each time. Different men. She could barely remember their faces, but she remembered exactly how they made her feel.

If Graham noticed their sexual drought, then he certainly wasn't saying anything. He was too consumed by work, too wrapped up in his life outside the house, that their interactions when they were alone had become almost completely perfunctory.

Did you manage to collect the dry cleaning?

Oh, David was saying that they're looking at skiing the first weekend in February next year. Can you give Samantha a call and suggest meeting them there?

That bloody light is flashing on my dashboard again. Can you get it booked in for a service?

But as for her? She couldn't remember the last time he'd touched her, spoken to her properly, the way... She squeezed her eyes shut as the thought set her brain on fire. The way that Ned Merton had talked to her. Like he cared. Like he wanted to hear what she had to say. For a minute back on that night they'd had dinner, she'd even thought that he was interested in her sexually. She'd felt something, a moment. Now, she knew it was all a figment of her imagination. Of course, he didn't. She'd just had her head turned by the attention. They'd met many times since then and he'd never been anything but friendly and warm. What did it say about her and her marriage that she was so starved of genuine affection she was actually imagining her sister's boyfriend may have been attracted to her?

Christ, even thinking that through, she could hear how pathetic it sounded, how needy she was becoming.

That didn't mean it wasn't her reality though.

And the kids... well, they couldn't care less about anything that didn't come from their phones. It wasn't their fault, of course. They'd turned thirteen a few months ago and they were just being teenagers and she adored them with every fibre of her being.

This morning, she'd pushed herself up in bed, deciding that none of that mattered right now though. What mattered was that she created a wonderful Christmas.

All day, she'd bit her tongue as she cooked, she cleaned, she passed around gifts. She saw the kids' faces light up when they opened their iPads, then turn to frowns when she'd tried to give them a hug afterwards. She'd watched Graham laugh with delight when he opened his gift – a letter detailing the agenda for a golfing trip to Marbella that she'd spent weeks planning for him and his chums. And she tried not to show her disappointment when she opened hers – a cashmere cardigan that he'd probably sent his secretary to buy in her lunch hour. She'd been hinting for weeks about a Chanel scarf, but, of course, he hadn't heard her. He never did.

Holding back her feelings, on she'd toiled, making the house look spectacular, the food and wine divine for her family. And what happened?

Later, she'd feigned delight when she opened the annual cookbook from her mother-in-law, who'd shot thinly veiled barbs and jibes at her all day, Graham was too busy playing the jolly host to notice, the kids moaned every time they were asked to put down their gadgets, Verity bloody fainted in the kitchen, her mother turned up with Nigel, who may be the most boring man on God's green earth, Zoe went on some touchy-feely gratitude rant, which was easy for her when she was living the perfect life with a man who actually cared about her, and now? Now, her best fucking Cath Kidston towels were being used as a tourniquet!

And, as she'd mused right at the start of this damn groundhog Christmas Day, she didn't have an option and she had to suck it up because – and this was the biggest bloody bitch of all – she knew the damage that breaking up a marriage caused and she wasn't going to see that happen to her family. No way. Not now. It wasn't happening here. Not on her watch. Merry fucking Christmas.

'What happened?' she gasped, still staring at the blood-fest in the kitchen, still unable to work it out.

It was Verity who finally enlightened her. 'Yvie was just being her usual clumsy self, knocked an empty wine bottle off the worktop and then stood on a piece of glass. The cut doesn't look deep though.'

'It's nothing,' Yvie stressed. 'I just need to keep it elevated for a few minutes and it'll be fine.'

Marina felt her rage, already simmering, begin to threaten to boil over. It wasn't fine. Her Cath Kidston towels were definitely not fine.

'And you?' she fired at Ned, probably unduly harshly, but she couldn't work out why he was in here in the first place.

He put his hands up as if in surrender. 'Nothing to do with me,' he said, grinning. 'I was just in the wrong place at the wrong time.'

Her gaze spun as Yvie emitted a weird strangled sound.

'What?' Marina demanded. 'I thought you said it was okay?'

'Just a... shooting pain,' Yvie said, through gritted teeth.

'Holy crap, what happened in here?' Zoe joined the party, striding into the kitchen, her hand flying to her mouth as she spotted the state of Yvie and rushed immediately to her side. 'Honey, are you okay? What can I do? What do you need?'

It didn't escape Marina's notice that that was the reaction she should probably have had. Some things just came easier to others.

'I'm fine. I really am. I'm just going to call a cab and get home, so I can bathe this. I'm knackered too. I really just want my bed.'

'Don't be daft, you're not phoning a taxi on Christmas night, you'll never get one, and if you do, it'll cost a fortune. Ned and I will take you home.'

'No!' It came in stereo, as both Yvie and Verity blurted it out at exactly the same moment.

Verity was the first to follow it up. 'I'll take her. I've only had one glass of wine because I was planning to drive home anyway.'

'Honestly, I'm happy to do it,' Zoe offered.

The valve on the pressure cooker of Marina's head could withstand the force no longer. It shot off, allowing the contents of her brain to explode.

'You will fucking not!'

The heads of the four other people in the room – her sisters and Ned – spun towards Marina, shock written all over their faces and she knew it was because her words had come out as some kind of low, malevolent growl. But she was just getting started and she was completely incapable of holding back the oncoming tirade.

'Do you really think you can all just piss off and leave me here with a mother-in-law who fucking hates me, a husband who barely knows I exist and OUR MOTHER? Our bloody mother and her fricking boyfriend, a snivelling little shit, who has sat there and judged us all day?'

So much for her general rule of not using profanity in the house.

Right now, however, that was the least of her worries. Her mouth was still barking out thoughts without having put them through any form of filter.

'Why do you think you can do this to me every year? I work so bloody hard to make this day perfect and then you three come in...' She made eye contact with each of her sisters in turn, skirting past Ned because as far as she could see, he was just a bystander in all this. 'And you bring all your self-bloody-centred dramas and woes and you turn what should be a perfect day into a complete... complete... CLUS-TERFUCK every time. Verity, I don't know what was going on with you this morning, but whatever it is you really need to get it sorted out. And, Yvie, when are you going to get a grip and find some balance with your work so that you're not permanently exhausted and you can actually get a life? And, Zoe, we're happy for you, we really are, but your relentless fricking optimism is starting to get right on my tits. And meantime, none of you notice, YOU DON'T NOTICE,' she repeated to make sure that they didn't miss the point, 'that all I'm trying to do is make everything perfect for everyone and nothing, NOTHING,' she echoed again, 'is fucking perfect for me! You three are the most selfish bitches I've ever encoun-tered in my life.'

Silence. Complete, utter, tense, awkward silence. In her peripheral vision, she could see that Ned's gaze was fixed on the floor, but her sisters were all just staring at her, word-lessly, with wide eyes and dropped jaws. Marina knew why. The Danton family didn't do confrontation. They didn't do honesty. They spent all their time tolerating problems, smoothing them over and hiding the cracks.

No more. She wasn't doing it. Although, a massive boulder of regret was already forming in her gut and about to detonate in her chest. She shouldn't have picked today for this. It was too... fragile. Too sore. Too close to the heart.

'Marina, I'm sorry.' Zoe was the first to speak, and Marina could hear genuine regret among the shock and confusion. 'You're right. Although, we do appreciate that you do this for us every year, but I guess we don't show it because we're all... distracted. Maybe it's easier to focus on ourselves than on the day and all the crap stuff it throws up for us.'

Something dropped in Marina's mind and she immediately saw what Zoe was saying. She was surprised she hadn't considered that before. It wasn't an excuse, but it was the start of a tangible explanation, and it brought Marina's fury down just enough to make her stop shouting at everyone.

'If I'm relentlessly optimistic,' Zoe went on, not letting Marina off the hook on that one, 'it's because I don't like the alternative.'

Another chink of understanding.

Verity wasn't quite so conciliatory. 'You're not the only one going through things,' she said, her tone close to sulky and petulant. 'At least you've got something. A husband. A family. Your life isn't so bad, so maybe you want to think about that instead of feeling so sorry for yourself that you think it gives you permission to speak to us like that. You're not in charge of us, Marina. You never have been. You just thought you were.'

The mercury on Marina's ire scale began to rise again as she faced Verity down. How dare she?

'I think what Verity is trying to say is that none of us gives enough thought to the others,' Yvie jumped in, the peacemaker as always, and Marina had a flashback to the little girl, always trying to make everyone happy, always scared in case something else was going to go wrong, when the truth was that the worst had already happened.

'You don't have to explain me, Yvie,' Verity spat.

'I know I don't, but I also know that in your heart, you're a really good person and you wouldn't want to hurt anyone,' Yvie persisted, her skin devoid of all colour, wearing the physical and emotional pain of what was happening here all over her face.

'Wouldn't I?' Verity challenged her.

'Enough!' Zoe again, stepping in to nudge things back on course.

Marina was still standing against the wall, arms folded, feeling a huge balloon deflating inside her. How long had it been since she'd lost her temper like that? Ten years? Twenty? They'd just pressed her buttons... No, that wasn't true. *Life* had just pressed her buttons and she'd snapped. And now that the pressure cooker had been taken off the boil, the fury had subsided and left room for remorse to begin to creep in. Zoe had a point. And poor Yvie was sitting there with blood oozing from her foot. No-one was skipping through daisies here.

'Look, I'm sorry,' she heard herself saying. 'I'm just... going through something. I don't even know what it is, but I shouldn't have taken it out on you.' The next shock of the day was the single tear that was running down her cheek. She never cried. This wasn't her at all. 'But I meant it when I said that I didn't want you all to go.' She suddenly realised that she couldn't think of anything lonelier that being here, in this kitchen, after they'd gone tonight.

'It's fine, we'll stay,' Zoe said, her eyes flicking to Ned, who nodded. He hadn't said a word during the entire fight. Clearly a man who knew not to get in the middle of a family when tensions were high.

'I will too,' Verity said grudgingly. 'But only if you promise to stop being a bitch.'

'Yvie?' Zoe asked. 'If we dress your foot from Marina's mighty first-aid kit and then prop you up on the couch, do you think you can stay?'

Marina didn't even have to wait for the answer. Yvie would always try to take the path that made the people she loved happy.

'You may have to fill me with wine and Quality Street,' Yvie countered. 'And let me win at Pictionary. I think those are reasonable demands.'

Trust Yvie to try to lighten the mood. Marina's remorse was now being joined with a sliver of shame. She shouldn't have exploded, and she shouldn't have said those things.

A flashback to another kitchen filled her head. The four of them. Teenagers. Home-made Christmas decorations draped around them. All of them stunned, shocked, tears on some faces. 'We just have to stick together,' she heard her younger voice saying. 'Always,' Zoe had added. 'Deal?' Yvie and Verity had nodded with sad, heartbroken determination. 'Deal.'

Maybe they all needed a reminder of that.

Marina sighed. 'I was just thinking about that day... when we all said we had to stick together. We still do.'

'You're right,' Zoe agreed.

'I think we all need to cut each other some slack,' Yvie offered. 'And maybe spend more time together. I feel like we've become a bit disconnected. Maybe we need to take care of each other a little more.'

Marina wasn't going to argue with that.

'Shit, I forgot!' Zoe blurted. 'Yvie, you're right. I started to tell you earlier, before Verity fainted and I got distracted. I've got news for you all. Actually, I've known for ages, but I wanted to keep it as a special Christmas surprise.'

Marina closed her eyes. What now? What fucking bomb-shell was Zoe going to hit them with now? Getting married? Pregnant? Won the lottery? Bought a fricking puppy?

It turned out it was none of the above. Zoe's face beamed as she revealed her news. 'Roger has invited us all to Vegas for the opening of his new hotel. So... erm... yay. Who's up for a family trip?'

31

Marina is the first to laugh at the absurdity of it all. 'This is the craziest thing to happen to us since last Christmas when I lost the plot and...' she pauses, then goes on, 'Actually, nope, there have been crazier things than that this year. They should make a reality show with us. It would need an explanatory subtitle though. Keeping Up With The Dantons, the Family Who Never Knows What The Fuck Is Going On.'

Verity tuts. 'Marina, do you really need to...'

'Swear?' Marina retorts, taking a large gulp of her pink cocktail. 'Yes, I fucking do. It's the new me. I've decided it's liberating.'

It is official. My family is coming undone. Marina, the grown up who rarely uses vulgar language or indulges in excessive alcohol, is swearing and knocking back the booze. She's had a nightmare of a year, I think. Been forced to reassess her life and make some changes. There was so much going on that we didn't even know about and, to be honest, I was pretty bloody shocked when we found out how she was feeling.

Meanwhile, when Verity isn't working, running, or making cocktails with tinned fruit, she is in a permanent state of irritation. I worry about her. Sometimes I think she's a bit broken. I just don't know how badly.

I glance over at Yvie, trying to catch her eye. We've always had a telepathy thing going on. Not today, though. She's said nothing since she tried to encourage us to heal our wounds by eating Jean the Cleaner's lasagne.

We are unravelling at the seams and my one month marriage is just a part of it. However, I disagree with Marina's suggestion of a reality show, because no one would believe it.

A choking noise makes my head snap up, and I realise that it's Yvie. At first, I think that I'm going to have to step in with the Heimlich, but she manages to clear her throat just in time, before she starts turning blue.

'Yvie! Don't do that to me! My nerves are frayed enough without any near-death experiences today.'

I mean what I say, but my mind immediately goes back to Roger's message. It just doesn't make sense. How could one of our credit cards be used to pay for the room in which my husband shagged someone else? It's just incomprehensible. Completely baffling.

When I'd asked which one of them had slept with my husband, it was just a reaction to Roger's revelation, but I don't believe for a second that any of my sisters would do that to me or anyone else.

I would know. Wouldn't I?

'Erm...' Yvie is trying to speak. Probably wants a glass of water.

I begin to get to my feet, careful not to stand on any of the wedding presents that are still strewn around the floor.

'I'll get you a drink that doesn't contain alcohol,' I tell her. 'I'll be two secs.'

'No. Don't go,' she says, stopping me in my tracks and making me wobble so that I almost take an extra step that is perilously close to the soup tureen Marina's mother-in-law sent over – which did, of course, accompany the obligatory cookbook – *101 Quick and Easy Soups*. Shoot me now.

Yvie's eyes fill and I can see she's shaking now, and her breaths are coming heavy and fast.

'Yvie,' I tell her calmly. 'Don't panic. You're okay. Whatever it is, we can sort it.'

She shakes her head. 'I don't think we can.'

I can't quite comprehend what she's saying.

'I've got something to tell you. I planned to tell you after Vegas, but then...' she doesn't finish that sentence. Instead she wails, 'You're going to hate me.'

'Of course I won't...'

She cuts me dead. 'You will. But before I tell you, I just want to say I'm so, so sorry and if I could go back in time, I'd do it all differently.'

'Do what differently?' I ask, still grasping for understanding.

'Everything,' she says. 'But I'll start with the credit card. I think you'll find that was mine.'

32

'What do you think?' Roger Kemp asked, as they surveyed the sight in front of them.

Zoe's gaze went from one side of the panoramic view to the other. They were on the roof of the Kemp, Vegas, a spectacular building on the strip, that had the mountains on one side, the neon lights of the city on the other, and was close enough for the guests to get a spectacular view of the Bellagio Fountains from the viewing deck they were standing on now. That would be enough of a selling point, but the hotel's unique feature was right in front of them, in the shape of a platform that stretched from the roof out into the sky, six hundred feet above the scorching earth. On it, was a podium for the marriage celebrant, and space for the happy couple and two witnesses.

It had been Roger's brainchild. The Leap. The perfect wedding venue for thrill seekers and adrenaline junkies. The idea was that the couple got married on the edge of the platform, hundreds of feet in the air, with just glass beneath their feet, and then after they said 'I do', they could leap from the platform wearing harnesses and abseil down the building. It was completely terrifying but utterly unforgettable.

The first wedding was taking place in ten minutes, and representatives from the world's travel press already had their cameras and their iPads out, furiously taking notes and ready to film it. The actual event had been planned and organised by the hotel's own marketing department, but Zoe had engaged her own film crew too and they were waiting, set up in the best viewing spot. This footage would form an integral part of the marketing campaign for the hotel in the UK, and Zoe wanted it filmed to her own direction.

The hotel team had chosen 6 p.m. because the sun was low in the sky, and the temperature had dropped to make it bearable enough to cover an outdoor event. The last thing Roger wanted was sweaty, sunburnt, pissed-off writers saying anything negative about such a spectacular stunt. Although, even in just a white shirt and cream dress trousers, Zoe was already feeling uncomfortably hot.

Roger grinned. 'Is the metaphor too much?'

'What the whole "marriage is a leap of faith" thing? No. I think it's wonderfully romantic actually,' Zoe replied, realising, to her surprise, that it was absolutely true. She'd never really thought about getting hitched before. Well, only once. And only for five minutes when she and Tom had walked past a beautiful old church in the West End of Glasgow and she had a sudden mental picture of the two of them running down the steps, her in a white dress, him in a kilt, both of them laughing as he picked her up, spun her around...

She blocked the thought. So much for that. About two weeks later, he'd broken her heart and now Chrissie would be the one running down the steps with him.

'I'm just going to go find out where the happy couple are,'

Roger said as he stepped away to speak to the head of his hotel marketing team.

Shoddy work, Zoe decided. Although, of course, she'd never say that. But if she were running the event, she'd have made absolutely sure that everyone who needed to be here was present and correct long before the owner and the press arrived.

'Fancy it?' Ned asked, coming up behind her and slipping his arms around her waist. She'd noticed he often got a bit territorial around Roger. It was sweet. Endearing. As long as it didn't escalate into some weird jealousy thing. Not that it would – if he had some troubling psycho streak, she was pretty sure she'd have sussed it by now. And anyway, he was looking so incredibly handsome in his loose fitting white linen shirt and navy blue chino shorts that she was only capable of positive thoughts when it came to Ned Merton.

'Fancy what?' she asked, remembering his question.

He gestured to the platform. 'Dropping off there after you've tied the knot?'

Zoe didn't even need to think about it. 'Oh, dear God, no. I'm more of a beach in Bali kind of chick. Verity would be more the abseiling down a building kind of girl.'

Ned's gaze flicked around him.

'Where are your sisters? I thought they'd be here by now?'

Zoe shook her head. 'No room. We had to turn press away, so there definitely wasn't space for civvie bystanders. They only let Felice in because she doesn't take up much room,' she gestured with her head to the corner of the terrace, where Roger's model wife was wearing a characteristically bored expression but looking incredible in a red, Bardot-style dress and huge dark glasses.

'Nope, she certainly doesn't.'

Zoe thought she detected an overtone of appreciation in his comment and gave him a swift but playful dig in the ribs. 'Hey! Eyes off the supermodel,' she ordered, laughing. Who was the jealous one now? Back to the conversation... 'Anyway, the girls were all meeting at six and they were going for cocktails and then for dinner. I said we'd catch them tomorrow and spend the whole day together. Thought we could have a night on our own tonight since we'll be with them for the rest of the weekend. And I also thought we could have a romantic dinner in the restaurant here – just the two of us. If we ever get done, that is.'

They'd arrived early that morning and her sisters were determined to banish any hint of jet lag and party into the night, stopping at some of Vegas's landmarks on the way. Naturally, Marina had made a list and organised it all. Zoe was glad for them. Christmas Day at Marina's had been a corker, and not in a good way, but strangely it had perhaps been the kind of explosion they needed to clear the air and make them all a little more tolerant of each other. They were four strong characters, but sometimes they forgot they had to be gentle with each other too.

As that thought dawned, she realised that she wished they were here to see this. Maybe they could go catch up with them later, after all, and she could tell them all about it. If they ever got this show on the road.

Her eyes sought out Roger, and when she spotted him, she could see it wasn't good news. For a man who didn't often get flustered, his face was a picture of exasperation.

She watched as he gesticulated to the person he was talking to, then walked purposefully back towards her, shaking his head.

'What's up?' she asked, concerned. Roger wasn't just a

client, he was a friend and something was clearly sending him off the deep end – metaphorically, given they were standing on top of a building.

'The couple haven't turned up. Bloody unbelievable. We've got the world's travel press here to cover the first wedding and there isn't a bloody wedding to see. How the hell can our people here be so incompetent? How? How does something like this even happen?'

Zoe knew better than to vocalise her earlier thought that this wouldn't have happened if the event had been on her watch. This wasn't a time for unhelpful smugness or self-promotion. 'What are you going to do?'

'I've got no bloody idea. You?'

This wasn't good. This really wasn't good. It was so important that the launch went off perfectly because mud stuck. If something like this damaged the image of the property on opening night, it could have far-reaching consequences for the hotel and, most importantly, for Roger. All it took was one person to write a scathing piece – and some people loved to make a name for themselves by stirring up trouble – and a ball of negativity could start to roll, gathering more fodder as it went. It would be a PR and image disaster.

'We could do it.'

At first Zoe thought it came from Roger, but then she realised that the voice came from the other side. Roger was already striding off to talk to his hotel manager, no doubt trying to come up with a back-up plan. It was Ned who had spoken and now she wasn't entirely sure what he was talking about. 'What?'

'We could do it,' Ned was beaming with the most mischievous grin as he repeated it.

'We could do what?' she asked, needing to make sure she was picking this up correctly.

'Get married.'

Yup, that's what she'd thought he meant. Wow. 'You want to marry me?' she asked, feeling incredibly stupid, like she was still having problems translating some foreign language.

Ned was full-on laughing now. 'Of course I do!'

'You mean fake it, for the launch?' This wasn't computing and quite frankly she had other things to worry about right now, like finding Roger and the bride and... Oh.

Ned slipped his arms around her waist and pulled her to him. 'I mean do it here, for the launch. I love you, Zoe Danton, and I'd be absolutely thrilled if you'd just hurry up and say that you'll marry me and then jump off a building with me.'

Great big cackles of laughter were coming from her now too. He was bonkers. Crazy. But... oh, she'd be lying if she didn't admit that there was something wildly exciting and romantic about this. The spontaneous marriage bit. Not so much the hurling herself off a building. Did she want to marry Ned? Maybe she actually did. Hadn't he picked her up after Tom had broken her heart and restored her faith in love and relationships? They'd had a brilliant time together and he was gorgeous, he was funny, he was romantic and kind and he understood her workaholic tendencies, but more importantly he loved her. And she loved him back. And right now she couldn't think of one good reason not to do this. Again, apart from the abseiling bit. But then, what a story they'd have to tell the grandchildren!

'Okay!' she blurted, completely shell-shocked that she was actually saying it.

'Okay?'

'Okay!'

'Yassssss!' he yelled, punching the air.

The journos around them began to take notice and she was pretty sure that some of them thought this was all part of the script for the launch. If only they knew.

'Roger!' Zoe shouted him back over. 'We're going to do it. Ned and I – we'll be your couple and get married.'

He seemed to think it was a joke. 'Look, I appreciate how far you'll go in the line of duty and all that, but even I wouldn't ask you to do this.'

'You're not asking us,' Ned fired back. 'We're doing it because we want to get married and, well... this isn't exactly what I'd planned...'

He's been planning it, Zoe realised, and the thought made her laugh even more.

'... But it makes some story and I can't think of a better way to do it. Although, we'll have to go to the courthouse and make it official tomorrow, because you can't actually marry properly without a licence. I've eh, been looking into it,' he added, and Zoe wasn't sure if his face was flushing due to bashfulness, excitement or the heat.

It didn't matter. What counted was that he really had researched it. He really had been thinking about how they'd get married. This was incredible.

'Are you sure, Zoe?' Roger was asking her now.

'Yes! But I just need to go and find my sisters because... Bugger, it's after six! They were going out for a drink. I've no idea where they even are. I could call them, but...' She glanced around again. The journos were hot, they were getting impatient, many of them were staring at her expectantly now, wondering what was going on. Even Felice was staring at her with undisguised impatience. Although, that was how she looked most of the time.

'Sod it, let's go. Let's just do it now.'

'Zoe, I think...' Roger began, and she could hear from his tone that he was about to argue. She had no time for it.

'Roger Kemp, move your fine self out of my way so that I can go and get married to the man I love, please.'

Defeated, but incredulous too, Roger took a step back and summoned his PR manager, who immediately went into recovery mode, sorting out the celebrant, the witnesses and the ceremony.

'Have you abseiled before?' he asked.

Zoe almost choked. She'd been attempting not to think about that minor detail. 'Yes, but not from this bloody high.'

'Babe, if you're too scared we can forget it. Do it tomorrow somewhere on land.'

Zoe thought about it for about a second and a half. 'Sod it, let's go.'

And that's how, at approximately 7 p.m. on a sweltering night in Vegas, Zoe Danton, wearing multiple safety harnesses, took several steps on to and along a precipice so high it almost gave her a nose bleed, holding hands with the man who'd proposed only moments before.

'Do you, Zoe...' the celebrant checked his notes. '... Danton, take Edward...' checked again, 'Merton, to be your lawfully wedded husband?'

'I do.' Oh God, she was doing this. She was really doing this. Marina would kick her arse for not letting her organise it.

'And do you, Edward...' a pause while his memory kicked in. 'Merton, take Zoe Danton to be your lawfully wedded wife?'

'I do.'

'Then, by the power invested in me by the state of Nevada, I hereby pronounce you man and wife. You may kiss your bride.'

Ned leaned towards her, kissed her, while cheers went up and dozens of camera flashes went off all around them.

They took another small step forward, turned around so they were facing the building, then reached out and took each other's hands, barely cognisant of the men who were adjusting their harnesses for the next step in proceedings.

Out of the corner of her eye, Zoe saw her bloke gesture to the one attending to Ned. 'Good to go when you're ready,' her guy told her.

Three.

Two.

One.

Zoe closed her eyes, and sent up a message to the person she realised she wished was there more than any other.

'Watch me fly, Dad,' she whispered.

Then, to cheers and screams of delight from the crowd, she leaned backwards and took the biggest leap of faith she'd ever taken.

She just hoped she would find a soft place to land.

33

No matter how many times she looked at it, it was still there and the words didn't change.

Hey Veronica. Fancy meeting up for a drink sometime? Or more? No strings attached, just a bit of fun. I promise you'll enjoy it.

Yep, still the same. Veronica from Glasgow's Your Next Date profile had lain dormant for months with just the notifications from strangers she had no interest in contacting. At Christmas, when she'd got the notification that Ned had swiped right on her profile making them a match, she'd sent him a message, trying to instigate a conversation, testing his fidelity and curious to see how far she could take it, but there had been no reply. That is, until two days ago, when this offer of a drink had come through. She checked it yet again. Yes, it was still there, and no, she still didn't know what she was going to do with it.

Things had changed. Most importantly, her feelings for Ned Merton had become something different.

She wasn't sure if all the running had finally cleared her mind, or if it was the support of her doctor, a lovely woman she'd gone to see after she fainted at Christmas. 'I just need some iron, or something,' Verity had said brusquely. A lesser doctor would just have handed over a prescription, but this one took the time to understand exactly what was going on. When Verity finally gave her the bullet points – her family background, her previous history of obsessive exercise, her current emotional state, her romantic quandary, the doctor had exhaled deeply. 'That's a whole lot you have on your plate there.'

That was all it took. A stranger that she could unload to. Someone who listened. The opportunity to be vulnerable. It was a small step, but it caused a bigger shift. The doctor had suggested Cognitive Behavioural Therapy – CBT, she called it – and after researching it for hours, putting it off for days, and then going to see a therapist once a week for the last month, Verity found that she was letting go. Uncoiling the strains. Looking at things through a new lens. Finding new ways to cope with the compulsions that made her run.

When it came to Ned, her feelings were changing too. He'd stopped being the first thing she thought about in the morning and the last thing at night. She'd stopped imagining what he would feel like to touch, how he'd propose to her, what their children would look like. Perhaps it was the blow out with her sisters, maybe it was a gradual realisation that, no matter what, there was now no future in which she and Ned could reasonably be together. He'd been with Zoe too long. He was hers. And, no matter who saw him first, he'd always be thought of as Zoe's ex.

They still spent time together, still hung out, went climbing, had a drink after work, but she was aware enough to realise that another reason for the shift in her feelings was blatantly obvious – he was still on dating apps and she thought so much less of him because of it.

She'd thought about telling Zoe, but still, she had no credible story to give to her. What would she say?

Would she tell her that she'd got a notification from some dating app that Ned wanted to match with a fictional woman called Veronica, so she'd sent him a message and he hadn't replied? It wasn't enough. He could just claim it was an old profile he'd forgotten about and that the notification of a match had been a blip in their system.

He could, that is, until this latest message came through.

Every hour of the last two days, she'd thought about going over to Zoe's flat to tell her, but she'd backed out every time. How could she do that to her right before their trip to Vegas, a jaunt Zoe had been beyond excited about for months? The Kemp Group was so important to her and the last thing she needed was some kind of personal distraction that could derail everything she'd worked so hard for. So Verity had kept her mouth shut, resolved to tell her when they got back to Glasgow. It could wait another couple of days. She'd waited this long – what harm would another forty-eight hours do?

The phone over by her bedside rang and Verity threw herself across the gorgeous, plush, quilted satin of the duvet cover to reach it. Roger Kemp had once again designed a spectacular hotel. This place was gorgeous. Sumptuous. Absolute luxury. And she may never be able to afford it on a teacher's wages, so she was going to take advantage of every single moment of this trip. She'd already been down to the gym just after they arrived and did five miles in front of a floor-to-ceiling window, with mesmerising views over the desert to the mountains. She'd cut her running to three times a week now, and it was no longer an obsessive challenge. Now, it left her calm. Centred. Although, her serenity was about to be interrupted by Marina barking in her ear.

'Have you seen Yvie? She's not answering her phone.'

'Hi, Marina, lovely to hear from you, how are you this fine evening?' she chirped, sarcasm oozing.

'Urgh, sometimes I really wish I had brothers.'

'Hang on, isn't your room opposite mine and yet you're phoning me instead of knocking on my door?' The hotel was still in the 'soft opening' phase and not yet operating to even half capacity, so Roger had given them all separate rooms, with Verity and Yvie's adjoining, and Marina's directly across the corridor.

'I'm multitasking,' Marina explained. 'I'm talking to you while having text conversations with Graham, Annabelle and Oscar. Honestly, I go away for one bloody day and Oscar has forgotten to go to his Mandarin tutor, Annabelle has had a meltdown about her solo in this week's dance competition and Graham, a man with a master's degree, is having trouble microwaving soup. I bloody despair, I really do. Anyway, have you seen Yvie or do I need to notify emergency services?'

'No, but hang on...'

Verity placed the phone handset on the bed, got up, went to the solid walnut door on the wall next to her, opened it and entered Yvie's room. Her grin was automatic, as she immediately sussed the issue. Twangs of country music were belting out from the bathroom door, overlaid with Yvie's voice singing in a manner that she was fairly sure Dolly Parton had never envisaged when she wrote the song.

'Jolene, Jolene, Jolene...'

Verity opened the bathroom door.

'Jol— Bloody hell you scared the crap out of me there!'

Verity struggled to keep a straight face. There was Yvie, wearing a shower cap, in a bath so full of bubbles, it looked like a foam party.

'Don't say it,' Yvie warned. 'I may have slightly overdone the bubble bath.'

'Really? I didn't notice. Anyway, Boss Sister is on the phone and she wanted me to check that you're still alive.'

'Please report back that I am indeed. I'll be ready in ten minutes. God, you look hideous, has anyone told you that before?'

Verity actually laughed, knowing full well that Yvie was joking. Another shift that had escalated over the last few months, was that – inspired by the bold red dress at Zoe's birthday party the previous year, and the way it made her feel – she'd decided to fully overhaul her style. Gone were the sensible clothes and the conservative outfits. Tonight, she was wearing a silver, chain-mail minidress with spaghetti straps and heels so high she was close to six feet tall in them. She'd seen the look in a magazine and ordered each individual item from the stores' websites. The first time she tried it on to show her sisters, she thought she'd never have the nerve to wear it again, but Zoe had demanded that she brought it here and wore it. Maybe that was the sister thing that she never quite got before. The acceptance of support and encouragement. Her walls weren't down, but she'd definitely taken out a couple of bricks.

Back in bubble central, Yvie was pinging her shower cap and having a dilemma. 'I can't decide whether to wear a glittery floor length kaftan or a glittery floor length kaftan.'

Verity pretended to think about it. 'I think you should go for a glittery floor length kaftan.'

'Great idea!' Yvie concurred, grinning.

Sometimes Verity wondered if Yvie would ever come to terms with how she felt about her body. It seemed to be an ever-swinging pendulum between embracing her curves and a desperation to lose them. If only Yvie would accept the reality that she was beautiful either way.

'Right, we're leaving as soon as you're ready, so hurry up.'

'Yes, mam,' Yvie replied, before rejoining Dolly. 'Jolene, Jolene, Jolene, Jolee-ee-een.'

Back in her own room, Verity picked the landline up again. 'She's in the bath and she'll be ready in ten minutes. We'll bang on your door when we're ready.'

Marina sighed. 'Okay, but hurry up – we've got a schedule to keep to.'

Of course they did. Marina had run through their plans for almost every one of their sixty or so hours here on the plane. And yes, they all knew it was a ridiculously long way to come for such a short time, but they didn't care. They were going to catch a show, have a lesson at the poker tables, lunch at the Venetian, a visit to the Palazzo, cocktails overlooking the Bellagio fountains, an open-top bus tour and a quick spin around the mall. And anything else they could find time for. But right now? Dinner and drinks, perhaps even a club later. If only Zoe was with them tonight, it would be perfect, but of course she had other plans for the evening – the launch and then a romantic dinner with Ned.

Verity checked her watch. Ten minutes and counting. Enough time for a drink from the minibar. She padded over, poured a large glass of Chardonnay from a half-bottle and lay back on the bed.

The thought of Zoe's romantic dinner with Ned made her

ponder on her own feelings. If she could have Ned Merton lying here next to her right now, would she want him?

She took her time with it, had to be sure. It was a relief when the answer finally came. No. She wouldn't. She really wouldn't.

But another thought barged its way in too. She didn't want Zoe lying next to him either. Not because she was jealous, because she really didn't believe she was any more, but because Zoe didn't deserve a duplicitous, unscrupulous, potentially unfaithful boyfriend like him. If he'd contacted Veronica, how many others had he messaged? How many hook-ups had he had? How many times had he lied to her sister? Verity didn't know the answer, but she was pretty sure that it wasn't zero.

Another thought, a new one, a blast of reality that made her squirm. Zoe didn't deserve a sister like Verity either. They'd never been close – their childhood had probably seen to that – but over the last year, with the trip to Ibiza and then especially since the Christmas blow out, Zoe had really made an effort to bring them together. More than that, Zoe had trusted her, thanked her even, for hanging out with Ned and all that time Verity had actually, she could see now, been behaving like a first-class bitch. The only defence that she had was that she'd isolated herself for years – and it didn't take a psychologist to work out why – and somehow gone to a place in her head where other people didn't matter. Now she was beginning to understand that they did. And no-one mattered more than her sisters.

She had to tell Zoe the truth about Ned – she just had to work out where and when to do it. Zoe had the launch of the wedding venue at the hotel tonight, but they were all spending the day together tomorrow. Maybe she could get

Zoe on her own for a drink and tell her everything, show her the app, the message, reveal all that she knew and – the most important bit – ask Zoe to forgive her for her behaviour.

The door from the adjoining room flew open and Yvie burst in, resplendent in her glittery floor length kaftan. 'Right, you gorgeous woman,' she hollered, 'Take me out on the town and show me a good time and remember, what happens in Vegas stays in Vegas. So when Kay asks you if I bought shares in Dunkin' Donuts, you deny everything.'

They mattered, she thought again. Yvie mattered, Marina mattered, Zoe mattered. She had to know for sure that they'd have a chance to have that conversation tomorrow.

'Agreed. Listen, I just need to use the loo first. I'll meet you over in Marina's room in two minutes.'

'Oh God. You're going to leave me over there with her when we're...' she checked her watch. 'Four minutes behind schedule. My nerves will be shredded in two. Right,' she took a deep breath, 'I'm going in. Wish me well and if I don't make it, you can have this kaftan. You might want to use it as a tent one day.'

Off she went, shuffling on her silver wedges to Marina's room. As soon as the door was closed, Verity picked up her phone, took a deep breath and called Zoe's number to arrange to meet before breakfast in the morning. Just the two of them and a large dose of honesty.

It was time she started being the sister that Zoe deserved...

And that meant telling her everything.

34

'I think she's flirting,' Yvie whispered. At least that's what she thought she was saying. She'd had a few cocktails, and then a few more, and she wasn't sure that her tongue was still adhering to instructions.

'Who's flirting?' Verity asked haughtily. She didn't get drunk very often, but when she did, she always went super-posh. Yvie wondered if her sister realised that she'd started the night as middle-class Glaswegian and ended it sounding like she was seventh in line to the throne.

'Marina!' Yvie exclaimed. 'Look, she's flirting. She's been flirting all night. That's the third dance she's had with that bloke.'

Eyes switching to the dance floor, Yvie was gratified when Verity saw what she was talking about and nodded in agreement. 'Definitely flirting,' she confirmed solemnly.

'I knew it!' Yvie insisted triumphantly. She might have indulged in a few alcoholic beverages, but sober or drunk, she was fairly sure that when Marina's arse was grinding up and down on some guy's pelvic area, that could safely be construed as flirting. The thought set her off on a fit of the giggles.

'What? What are you laughing at now?' Verity demanded, before taking a generous suck on the straw that was inserted into her Cosmopolitan.

'I'm imagining Marina doing that with Graham, and his mother trying to separate them with one of her bloody cook-books. Block that penis with 101 Ways To Cook Chicken.'

That set them both off this time and Yvie could actually feel the tears of laughter running down her face. She was going to pay for this in the morning, but right now she didn't care. This was the first time in a long, long while that she'd actually felt like anything approaching normal. The stresses and strains of her world were under control. She couldn't go in if the ward called her. She'd spoken to Kay a little while ago and everything was fine. Her mother was now so busy doing whatever she did with Nigel – that thought made her shudder – that she didn't call her with a long rant of woes every night. As for her sisters, Verity actually seemed to be relaxing and enjoying herself for once, and Marina was doing something that may require a surgical procedure to reverse, but at least she looked happy.

If only Zoe were here, it would be perfect, but Yvie understood that her sister had to work tonight. At least she'd see her tomorrow and they could hang out all day. It didn't detract from the fact that right now, nothing was wrong. She wasn't worried about anything. She'd even drunk enough cocktails to make her feel less hideous in this horrendous glittery kaftan. It had been necessary to put Dolly on full blast when she was in the bath because she was trying to take her mind off her dread that she was, once again, going out with her gorgeous, slim, stunning, sexily dressed sisters, while she was looking like something that could house a family of four for a week in the Lake District. With glitter.

Sod it. Diet tomorrow. Right now, she wasn't going to let it spoil her night, or her weekend for that matter. They were here, in an incredible nightclub, in one of the most fabulous new hotels in the world, and she was loving everything, from the cocktails that floated on a tray of dried ice, to the glitz and glamour of the surroundings, to the party atmosphere.

She was bending over her straw, when she heard the sexiest American voice, one that sounded like it came from the Deep South and knew how to lasso a moving object. 'Excuse me, mam, would you like to dance?'

'Oh, I'd love...' she raised her head, and that's when she realised that the voice had been directed at Verity. The shame burned her cheeks, but the only saving grace was that it seemed the music had been too loud for Woody The Cowboy to hear her mistakenly accept his invitation. The only other saving grace was that the seventh in line to the throne didn't want to dance, so she brushed him off with a royal rejection. Off he trotted, dejected.

All at once, Yvie felt her spirits drop like a stone as tears sprang to her bottom lids. Blinking them back furiously, she tried to talk herself back on to an even keel. Come on. Who cares? He was just some random bloke. And who wouldn't want to dance with Verity – she was bloody gorgeous.

'I've been a complete cow, you know,' Verity blurted.

What was her royal highness on about now?

Yvie took a deep breath, told herself again to pull it together and leant towards her sister. 'You've always been a complete cow,' she joked, trying to lift this party back to the happy place it had been just minutes before, when the only problem was whether or not Marina may accidently impale herself on a stranger's crotch.

'No, Yvie, I mean it. I've... Okay, I'm going to tell you because I need to tell someone and you've always been the best listener of us all.'

Even in her intoxicated state, Yvie recognised this as an official medical condition called Drunken Confessional Syndrome. Actually, it was only official according to her and Kay, but countless times over the years in their professional and personal lives, they'd encountered perfectly rational people, who drank their body weight in alcohol and had a sudden and unassailable urge to confess every dark act they'd ever committed.

'Okay, shoot. I won't judge you. At least, I say I won't, but I definitely will – I'll just hide it well,' Yvie chirped, still trying not to take this seriously.

Verity swayed a little on her stool, then blurted, 'I tried to take Ned from Zoe. I loved him, Yvie. I really did. Or at least, I thought I did.'

Yvie felt her stomach begin to twist with dread. The one subject she really couldn't talk about was Ned Merton. It was bad enough that he'd tagged along on this trip. She'd made a conscious plan to do everything she could to avoid him for the next two days. And, well, forever. However, she couldn't ignore what her distraught sister was saying about him right now.

'You loved him?' This was news. Sure, she knew that Verity had a thing for him way back as far as that careers fair at their school – that was why Yvie had never confessed what actually happened that night. She also been pretty sure that attraction was still there when he started seeing Zoe, but Yvie hadn't realised that it was so much more than that, especially since Verity insisted that she was over it. Or maybe, it had just suited Yvie to believe that. She had absolutely no idea though, that Verity was actually in love with him. 'Oh, V, I'm so sorry. I didn't know.'

'Don't feel sorry for me, I don't deserve it!' Princess Verity commanded forcefully. 'I tried everything, Yvie. I told him lies about Zoe, I hung out with him all the time, hoping that he'd realise he wanted me instead. I even took up rock climbing so it would look like we had loads in common. I flirted shamelessly, practically threw myself at him, and I was desperate for him to take me up on it, no matter what the consequences would have been. I was shit to Zoe, shit to everyone actually. I'm so sorry. I was probably shit to you too. I'm horrible, I really am.'

The knot in Yvie's stomach tightened just a little bit more as she floundered over what to say. Hadn't they all made mistakes? Hadn't they all done something stupid? Hadn't she made her own mistakes where Ned Merton was concerned?

She put her hand over her drunk sister's arm and squeezed it. Verity would have forgotten this whole conversation in the morning, so there was no point getting too deep and meaningful, and besides, for her own sake, she really had to get off the subject of Ned Merton.

'Look, none of that matters now, Ver. The only important thing is that you and Zoe are okay. And whatever you did, it obviously didn't have any effect on Zoe's happiness, so you're in the clear. Forget about it. Move on.'

With stunning insight, especially given her blood alcohol level, she realised that she had basically just told Verity everything she wanted someone to say to her. *It didn't have any effect. You're in the clear. Forget about it. Move on.*

'I can't move on,' Verity wailed. 'Because I know something about him that will devastate Zoe.'

One sentence. Just one sentence that immediately set off explosions inside her. Was it about her? Had Verity found out about that night? Adrenaline started to pump once again, heart began to race, hands began to shake...

'What is it, Verity? What do you know?'

'I can't tell you,' Verity countered. 'Oh shit, look. Marina's coming back. Promise me you won't say anything. Promise!'

It was all Yvie could do to get the words out. 'I promise,' she murmured.

Marina was beside them now, her face flushed, her sleek bob pushed back and uncharacteristically messy after all the exertion. 'Ladies, I think I'm going to call it a night, I'm exhausted.'

'No wonder, after all that activity. I reckon that was at least 800 calories burnt off an hour up there,' Verity retorted and Yvie wondered if she was forcing herself to act normal or if she'd already forgotten the conversation that they'd just had.

I know something about him that will devastate Zoe.

Yvie had to know what it was, had to find out if it was the same thing that had been eating away at her for as long as Ned Merton had been in their lives. But she knew she wasn't going to find out here.

'Me too. I think jet lag is getting the better of me,' she said, deliberately acting breezy. Marina could spot a drama with her eyes shut, so they had to act innocent and get out of here before she sussed something was afoot and deployed her killer interrogation skills.

Verity reluctantly climbed off her bar stool. 'Can I bring my drink? It's not even half done and it's delicious.'

'Why does she sound like she's off *Downton Abbey*?' Marina asked, puzzled.

'Don't ask. Just walk on the other side of her in case she makes a bid for another cocktail.'

It took them fifteen excruciating minutes to get to their rooms on the thirty-fifth floor, mainly because Verity pushed every button and then giggled the whole way up. This was a whole different Verity that Yvie wasn't sure she'd ever seen before. She was a bit of a train wreck, but she liked her a lot.

When they finally got to their corridor, Marina kissed them goodnight and opened her door directly across from theirs, while Yvie steered Verity into her own room. Her sister flopped down on the bed, remarkably managing not to spill a single drop of her cocktail.

Yvie wasn't sure she was going to have much success, but the sickening feeling in her gut told her she had to try.

'Verity, what did you mean when you said you knew something about Ned?'

Verity's head shot round to meet her gaze, as if she was shocked that Yvie knew anything. 'Nothing. I shouldn't have said anything. Forget it.'

'But, Verity, if it's something bad, we need to talk about whether we should tell Zoe.'

'Exactly!' Verity wailed, pushing her body up so she was leaning on her elbows. 'I tried to tell her. I called her earlier, but she didn't answer. I need to tell her, Yvie.'

'Tell her what?'

'That... that... Ned tried to pick me up on Your Next Date! Well, not me, exactly. A woman I made up to try to see if he'd start up a conversation with her. And he did. I know how twisted this all sounds.' All Yvie cared about was that the secret didn't involve her. Verity didn't know. Thank God, she didn't know.

'Listen, darling, don't worry about it. Just get some sleep and we can talk about it again in the morning. We'll sort it out.'

Yvie wasn't sure that was true, but anything to get away. Verity seemed to be sobering up a little now – Yvie just hoped that she wouldn't sober up enough to notice that every part of her was shaking, partly from anxiety, partly from relief, partly because her heart was pounding and her blood thundering in her ears. The feeling of suffocation was beginning to wrap its way around her. She needed to get out of there and back to her own room.

She left Verity trying valiantly to take her stilettos off and went through the connecting door into her own room, closing it behind her.

She didn't even make it to the bed before her legs buckled and the fear consumed her, full on, straight to the height of the worst panic attack she'd ever had. She pulled at the neck of the kaftan, knowing logically that it wasn't choking her but feeling the opposite. She gasped for breath but couldn't make her lungs work. She felt a weight on her chest and she knew... this couldn't be a panic attack, it had to be worse. It was a full-scale heart attack and she was going to die, right here, on the floor of this hotel.

A sound. The adjoining door opening. 'Yvie, do you think I should go find Zoe now and tell her that... Yvie! What the hell...?' Verity rushed towards her, fell to the floor beside her. 'Oh God, Yvie what's wrong? What's happened? What should I do?'

Yvie didn't have enough breath to answer, still gasping like a fish out of water, desperately flailing on the floor.

Verity panicked, stood up, dashed out into the corridor, kicking a bin into the doorway so the door wouldn't shut behind her, then started banging on Marina's door. 'Marina! Marina! Wake up! I need help! It's Yvie. I need you to open your door! Hurry up! Marina!'

A noise.

A door opening.

A pause.

Then Verity's voice again.

'Who the hell is he?'

35

MARINA – LAS VEGAS, ONE MONTH AGO

Marina knew when she was caught. It was like finding the kids with their phones under their pillows or the time she saw Oscar in the amusement arcade in town when he should have been in double physics. Caught. No feasible excuse. Hands up.

But right now, she had no time to think about the consequences of that because Verity was screaming about Yvie and, through the open door across from her, she could see her youngest sister lying on the floor. Fuck.

Pulling the hotel robe around her, she charged across the corridor, no idea what was going on. Was she choking? Some kind of allergic reaction? Had her drink been spiked? God knows, she'd warned them about... Fuck it, she'd find out the facts later.

She practically skidded down to her knees, lifted Yvie's head, pushed back the sodding hair from her face. 'Yvie! Yvie!'

He sister was staring at her, wide-eyed, breathless, struggling so hard to say something...

'I'm having... having...'

Marina suddenly realised what was going on. This had happened at the tennis club a couple of years ago to her mixed doubles partner, a stockbroker who had just lost a fortune in some crash and who slid to the ground at the side of the court. At first, they'd thought it was his heart, but they'd learned later it was a horrific panic attack.

Another memory... Yvie, about thirteen, struggling to breathe and their mother coaching her, telling her to slow down, that the doctor was coming.

'Don't speak, just breathe!' Marina ordered. 'Come on, Yvie, just breathe. I've got you. Breathe with me, darling, come on. Breathe with me.'

Marina just kept repeating it, repeating it, repeating it, while Yvie gasped, sweated, trembled, and just when Marina was questioning whether she'd got it right, and was about to yell at Verity to call an ambulance, she felt a shift, a slowing in Yvie's frantic spasms for breath.

'That's it! That's it, Yvie. Breathe, darling. Try to slow it down. You're doing it. I've got you.' She said it over and over again, for what seemed like an age but was probably only a few tortuous, excruciating minutes, until Yvie finally regained control, flopping with exhaustion against her.

'Verity, get some water,' she ordered calmly, and when she returned with it, Marina helped Yvie's shaking hands hold it to her mouth.

Eventually, when she was ready, Verity helped to pull her up to a sitting position on the floor, and Marina sat beside Yvie with her arm around her, Verity in front of her, holding her hands.

'I'm... I'm sorry...' Yvie began, but Marina gently shushed her.

'Don't you dare be sorry. But you have to tell us what's going on, Yvie. Is this the first time...?'

Marina felt a crushing weight of devastation as Yvie shook her head. How could she not have known this? Why didn't she notice that something was wrong? Yvie was always so bright and cheery, the happy one, the warm, cuddly, dependable support who was there for everyone else. How was it even possible that none of them had seen this?

After a few moments, Yvie found the strength to speak. 'It's been happening for a while. Maybe six months or so.'

'Why didn't you say anything?' Verity gasped and Marina realised that the drunk woman in the lift had quite literally been shocked sober.

Yvie shrugged. 'You're all dealing with your own stuff and I thought... I thought I could handle it. I'm a fricking nurse!'

'Oh, for God's sake, how could you be so bloody stupid?' Marina snapped, then immediately reeled as she realised what she'd just done. 'Oh shit, I'm sorry, Yvie. It's just... it's just that...' How could she explain it? It's just that she was so terrified of the ground being pulled from beneath her feet, that she felt she had to control every single thing in everyone's lives, because that was the only way she knew it would be okay.

'You're scared,' Yvie whispered, understanding, getting it.

Of course she would, Marina thought ruefully. She nodded, her arms going around Yvie, pulling her head down on to her shoulder, stroking her hair. 'Oh, baby,' Marina murmured, all her anger gone now. Yvie was right. All that irritation and rage... it all came from some deep, dark, petrified place inside her.

And now she needed to understand what was dragging her little sister down too.

'Do you know why it's happening? Surely it's not...' Why couldn't they say it? Why could none of them say the words? Why had they all spent twenty years ignoring the biggest thing that had ever happened to them?

'No. It's... I think it's been a lot of things. I've just not been feeling myself for ages, and I haven't been honest about it. I just put a face on, pretended I was fine, but everything has been eating away at me. Meanwhile, I'm eating everything in sight. I've put on so much weight...'

Marina opened her mouth to speak and Yvie knew she was going to say something to refute that.

'Don't say I haven't, because it's true. I don't usually mind being heavy, but lately, when I'm around you lot, I've been feeling so self-conscious about it. And I'm tired, Marina. I don't sleep, I don't take care of myself, I just do what everyone needs me to do and I don't... I don't know what I need to do for myself any more. It's like I'm scared and anxious all day long, and then it just takes one thing, one extra worry or fear, to tip me over and then... and then this happens.'

Marina got it. All of it. Except one crucial bit.

'But why tonight? What happened to trigger this tonight? We all had a great time, didn't we?'

'Some more than most,' Verity interjected, with a pointed glare at her.

Shit. The guy. Her sister had seen the bloke in her room. Marina shut the thought down. That was unimportant right now.

'Yes, we did, but... Look, I'm going to tell you because I have to and all I can say is I'm sorry and beg you to try to understand.'

'Of course we will,' Verity reassured her, but Marina could see by Yvie's expression that she wasn't convinced.

'Ned,' Yvie blurted.

Marina didn't understand. 'What about him?'

'Oh God.' Verity this time. Her voice low now, full of dread and disbelief. 'You're in love with him too?' she asked Yvie.

Questions were ricocheting around in Marina's brain now, firing off the inside of her head. 'What are you talking about, Verity? What do you mean 'in love with him too'? Am I the only one who has no fucking clue what is going on here?'

Verity straightened up, inhaled, blurted, 'I told Yvie tonight that... Oh, sod it... I tried to take Ned from Zoe. I know, don't say it! I've been a complete bitch and I'm so sorry and it's a long story that I'll tell you in a minute, but first I need to know what this has to do with what happened here tonight. Did I do this? Was it because of what I did? Oh God, Yvie, tell me it's not. Are you in love with him?' she asked again.

'It's not because of you and no I'm not,' Yvie rushed to reassure her. 'But it's a long story...'

'We've got time,' Marina said, suddenly thinking that she'd left a stranger in her room, he'd probably ransacked the place by now, stolen her money and her passport and was back downstairs spending her cash on cocaine and hookers. She didn't even feel the need to go and check. Later. One problem at a time and this one was way more important.

'Remember a couple of years ago, I came into your school,' she was looking at Verity, 'to give a talk on a career as a nurse.'

'I remember that,' Verity said. 'Kay was with you too. The kids loved it.'

'They preferred the delivery guy from Just Eat,' Yvie chided her, with a very faint smile for the first time since they'd got here. 'Anyway, after it, Ned and Kay and I, we went out for a drink because she had a babysitter and we wanted to make the most of it – you said you couldn't come because you had some parents' meeting but you called me the next day and you weren't pleased with me for going. I brushed it off, said it wasn't much of a night, that nothing happened and we all went home early.'

Marina watched as Verity racked her brain, then latched on to the memory. 'That's right. I had a family conference for one of my kids. You said you were home for nine.'

'I lied. We went out, and we had dinner, and then we drank too much, and we ended up in a club, at two o'clock in the morning.'

'In your nurses' uniforms?' Marina asked, always needing to understand the full facts.

'Yes. Everyone thought we were stripograms. Anyway, Kay went to the loo and...'

Marina had a sinking feeling of dread as she watched Yvie pause and inhale, clearly trying to summon the courage to go on.

After a moment she found her voice again. 'Ned and I were dancing and then we were in a corner and then he was telling me how attracted he was to me and I thought...' Yvie closed her eyes, obviously replaying it all in her mind. 'I thought I'd got lucky. So, so lucky. He was gorgeous, and funny, and he was flirting with me and saying all these things he wanted to do to me. Me!'

Marina felt a piece of her heart chip off. How could her gorgeous, incredible sister think so little of herself that she was so grateful that Ned Merton took an interest in her? And no, the irony that she'd had a similar reaction to his attention didn't escape her.

Verity looked stricken now, struck speechless for once.

Marina leaned over and lifted her jaw so that her mouth closed.

'Go on.'

'He suggested that we all go back to his place, and I agreed and I was so thrilled, so excited. We got there and he told me there were drinks in the fridge, so I went to the loo to fix myself up a bit, then went into the kitchen to get the drinks, and then, when I got back to the living room, he and Kay were gone. I thought it was some kind of stupid prank, but then I opened the bedroom door and... they were in bed. Naked. Having sex.'

'Oh, Jesus.' Marina's words. 'What did you do?'

'Nothing. I just got out of there. Went home. Cried.'

'And you never told...' Verity began, but Yvie cut her off.

'I never told anyone. I didn't tell Kay – she still has no idea he was coming on to me while she was in the toilets at the club. She'd never have done anything with him if she'd known.'

'But she had sex with him while you were in the flat!' Verity gasped, incredulous.

Yvie nodded. 'I know. But you don't understand. She was as thrilled as me that she'd met someone. We don't get out much,' Yvie admitted, with a rueful smile, before going on, 'She thought it meant something. Or at least, she did until he kicked her out of bed the next morning and she never heard from him again. She called him a couple of times, but he blocked her.'

Marina could feel her rage rising again. 'What a bastard.'

'He is.'

'Why didn't you tell me all this at the time?' Verity asked, still clearly shocked and stunned.

'Because you worked with him and he was your friend and you liked him. And when you called the next morning you were annoyed as that's when I sussed out that you might have feelings for him so I just bottled out. I was embarrassed, mostly. I didn't want you to know how pathetic I was, so I just shut up and tried to forget about it. Kay did too. And then he got together with Zoe, and I thought he was a rebound guy and she'd dump him and then... she didn't. But by then it was too late to say what had happened because I should have told you long before then. I'd dug a hole with my silence. I just kept hoping it would all go away. Carried on. Acted like it had never happened. I blocked it all out. We're good at that, aren't we?'

Another chip of Marina's heart broke off. Yvie wasn't wrong. They'd all learned to block out pain far too young.

Verity was still connecting the dots. 'You know, I'd heard so many rumours that he was a player and I chose to ignore them. Deep down, I think I knew they were true. I guess we're also good at lying to ourselves.'

Yvie nodded sadly. 'Worse, I even forced myself to be civil to him when we were all together, so that none of you, especially Zoe, would notice anything was wrong. I actually thought... I thought he'd forgotten all about it. Been too drunk to remember or something. I only realised a couple of months ago that he remembered it all, at your house at Christmas.'

'When you cut your foot?' Marina tried to put the pieces together.

'Yeah, I swiped the wine bottle off the worktop because he was being a dick to me. He warned me not to tell Zoe. Or any of you. Fuck, what a mess. I'm so sorry I let you down.'

'You didn't let anyone down,' Verity spat. 'He did.'

'You mean that? You're not going to come into my room later and suffocate me in my sleep?'

Verity shrugged, 'Maybe. But only because I want that kaftan.'

That's when, just because the night couldn't get any more surreal, Verity began to laugh, then Yvie, then... Oh, fuck it, Marina was laughing too. This was a mess, an absolute roaring debacle, but they were all okay. It could be sorted. It could be fixed. No permanent damage done.

'I'm going to have his balls for this,' Marina promised, wiping away tears of their collective hysteria. She meant it. There was no way that fucker was going to do this to her sister. Zoe would want to know too and she'd feel the same, Marina was sure of it.

'Eh, can we talk about the balls that are in your room first?' Yvie asked, eyebrows raised. 'I know it's none of our business, but since we're sharing...'

Marina closed her eyes, thought about it. Like Yvie and Verity, she'd been keeping everything to herself, internalising her feelings, her unhappiness. Maybe it was time to end that.

'Hang on, I'll need coffee for this,' she said, clambering up and reaching for the bedside phone to call room service.

'And a cinnamon bagel! I think I need my comfort food,' Yvie added.

Marina ordered cappuccinos and bagels for all of them, then pulled three pillows off the bed, slid back down on to the floor, slipping one of the pillows under her buttocks and giving the others to her sisters.

'The guy in my room – this wasn't the first time,' she began, then watched as their eyes widened with surprise.

'Seriously? I have no idea who you are right now,' Verity whistled.

'Me neither,' Marina admitted.

'Hang on, hang on – go back to the start. You've been doing this the whole time you've been married?'

'No!' Marina countered. 'The first time was about a year ago. I was in Edinburgh in a hotel bar and there was a barman and he was... interested. And before you say anything, V, I know how weak and pathetic that sounds.'

'Don't worry. I think we've already established that weak and pathetic may be a family trait,' Yvie offered.

'Maybe,' Marina went on. 'It just felt so good. Graham and I, well, I don't think there's been anything there for a long time.'

Yvie's eyebrows went even higher. 'Really? But you always seem so... sorted.'

'I guess we are. We're a good team. We know how to work together, but that's only one side of it. I'm not saying it's just his fault, because it isn't. He switched off and became more and more enmeshed in his work, in his life, status, his network of friends, and I did my job, which was to build this perfect life, perfect family, make us all succeed. But somewhere along the way we lost sight of each other. Forgot to be in love any more.'

'And you didn't think about leaving him?'

Marina had been staring at the floor, hoping she could hide the discomfort on her face, but Verity's question made her head whip up. 'And give the kids a life like ours?'

They had to know what that meant. Insecurity. Instability. Fending for themselves. A complete lack of emotional support that damaged them all in so many different ways.

'But you're not like Mum and Graham isn't like Dad,' Yvie pointed out softly.

'I know, but still... I want them to know that they're safe. I want them to trust us, trust that their lives will always be okay, that nothing will change, nothing bad will happen. I push them, sometimes too hard, I know, but I'm always right there when they need me. I can't even contemplate an alternative to that.'

She could see that they had questions, objections even, but only Yvie spoke, and it wasn't to argue.

'But what about you? Who's been there for you?'

Marina smiled. 'You, mostly. When I call you most nights to have a moan and a rant, that's me just wanting someone to listen. I love you for doing that. I know I've been a pain in the arse to you.'

'You haven't,' Yvie had the grace to argue. 'But me listening isn't enough. You have to have more than that.'

How come the youngest of the sisters was the one with the most insight, Marina wondered. And yet, all this time she was unravelling too.

'I do. And that's how it began. I told myself that the first one would be a one-off, but it wasn't. There was Ibiza...'

'Oh, my God, you shagged that French guy you kept talking to?' Verity was gobsmacked.

'And there were others.' She wasn't going to get specific and she absolutely wasn't going to tell them that she had even found herself attracted to Ned. Yvie didn't need to hear his name again right now.

'Anytime I got the opportunity,' she shrugged shamefully, hearing how sordid it sounded. 'I'd make excuses to stay over in Edinburgh after I dropped Annabelle off at school, or the night before I picked her up, and I'd go to the hotel bar – a different one each time – and just sit there. It didn't always end in sex though. Sometimes it happened, sometimes it didn't. I know it doesn't make sense, but the only way I can explain it is that I just wanted to feel something. All day every day, I went through the motions for everyone else, I was mum, I was wife, and I just wanted someone to notice that I was more than that. I just wanted to feel like me. Like I said, it wasn't the sex that even mattered – although, if I'm honest, that gave me a thrill and became completely intoxicating. Sometimes it was just talking to someone, the contact, the feeling of freedom that I was with someone who didn't need anything from me.'

Yvie sighed. 'Christ, we're shite sisters. We should have been able to do that for you, to give you that.'

'How could you, when I didn't tell you it was missing?'

'We should have seen it, though.' Verity went on, 'You've just always been so organised, so capable and you seemed so together. I thought you were the strongest of us all.'

'I don't think I am,' Marina said, meaning it. 'I think I just learned really young that I had to make it look that way. I know now that I have to make some decisions though. I need to fix this. Fix everything. Fix my life. And not because I need it to be perfect. Just because I need to be happy.'

'We'll help you,' Yvie promised and Marina smiled. She absolutely felt that they would. Right now she felt a closeness to both these women that she wasn't sure she'd ever felt before.

'And I'll help you too,' she said to Yvie. 'I remembered earlier that this happened before...'

Yvie nodded. 'A few times when I was growing up. The first one was right after Dad...' She didn't finish. 'Mum was at her wits' end, but back then the doctor just said I'd grow out of it and I guess in a way he was right. The last one before now was when I was thirteen or fourteen. I think they've just started again because I reached a low point and my anxiety flared. You know, I'm clearly the worst nurse – I couldn't even formulate a plan to help myself.'

'Actually, I think I can help you a little,' Verity offered. 'I've been seeing a therapist...'

Marina almost fainted and she could see Yvie's surprise too. Verity. The most insular, private woman she'd ever met was seeing a therapist.

'... Because you lot were right – God, I hate saying that. I was getting that compulsive way again, obsessively running and fixating on things. I think the whole Ned thing was part of that too. I'm not looking for sympathy or using that as an excuse though, because the honest truth is that it was my choice to behave like that and I knew it was wrong, but I still did it. Anyway, I've been doing CBT and it's really helped me. I could put you in touch with my therapist, if you want to give it a try?'

Yvie nodded. 'I do. I'm really proud of you for getting help with it, V. But I have to say, I couldn't be any more shocked if you told me you were picking up random guys for sex.' She said that with a teasing grin in Marina's direction, making her laugh again. Only Yvie could take your sorest spot and soothe it into something funny.

There was a knock at the door, and Marina got up to answer it. The room service waiter pushed in a trolley, wedging the door open with it and then lifted the individual items from the top, placing them on the table in the corner of the room. While he did so, Marina spotted the guy she'd been with earlier leaving her room. He must have waited to see if she'd come back, then given up and got dressed. He managed an embarrassed wave, then disappeared down the corridor.

The sisters fell silent while the waiter worked, pausing their conversation until he'd left.

Marina handed them each their coffee, then placed a plate heaped with bagels on the floor between them.

Yvie lifted one from the top. 'You know, tonight has been a bit of a nightmare, but weirdly I feel so much better because everything is out in the open.'

Marina picked up the next one. 'Not everything. You know we have to tell Zoe all of it. And I know it's the guy she's in love with, but when she understands who he is that will change. She'll be as pissed off as we are.'

'You're right,' Yvie said, 'She needs to know. As soon as we get home, we have to tell her so she can get shot of him.'

Verity's nodding head indicated that she agreed too. Although, the fact that she was reaching for a bagel and she hadn't eaten a carb in the last decade, did suggest she was finding it emotionally difficult. 'I was planning on speaking to her tomorrow,' she said, staring at the buttery treat in her hand, 'but it's probably best to do it at home so she can process it without him around.'

Marina was about to concur, when there was a pinging noise, actually a double ping, one nearby, one further away.

'That's the group chat,' Verity said. 'Zoe must have sent us a message. My phone is through there,' she gestured through the adjoining door to her room. 'But here...' she reached over to the handbag on the floor where Yvie had dropped it, pulled out her phone and tossed it to her.

Marina watched as Yvie read the screen, then choked, spluttered, gasped. At first, she thought another panic attack was kicking off, but no.

Yvie turned the screen to face them.

'Zoe?' Marina asked. She wasn't wearing her glasses, so she couldn't make it out.

'Yep.' Yvie's voice was strangled, as if she couldn't get the words out, but she kept trying. 'Her text says that a few hours ago, she got married to Ned.'

36

Yvie had been staring out of the window for the last hour, her breath misting up the Santa they'd drawn on the glass with spray snow a couple of weeks ago. Where was he? He'd said he'd be round first thing this morning and it was almost lunchtime now.

'Yvie, come on, how about a game of Pictionary? Or Scrabble?' Marina suggested, but Yvie shook her head. She knew her sister was just trying to distract her.

'Not without Dad.' She'd said the same yesterday, the first Christmas Day they hadn't played board games because, like now, it just wouldn't feel right without him. None of this felt right. The house was still all decorated, the leftover turkey was in the fridge, her Quality Street tin was half full, and yet nothing was the same as all the other years when Dad was still here.

'We've got to make new traditions,' Mum had explained, when she broke the news over dinner a few weeks ago. Gregor was sitting in Dad's old chair at the dining table. That still made Yvie sad. 'Your Dad and I have had a chat and we're going to alternate Christmas Day from now on.'

Yvie was pretty sure what 'alternate' meant – she might only be ten but she wasn't daft. Still, she wasn't sure exactly what would be happening.

Zoe had got in there with the question first. 'So how will that work then?'

Her mum had taken a bite of her steak pie before she answered. 'Well, this year, you'll have Christmas here with me and Gregor, and Dad will come and pick you all up on Boxing Day and you can take whatever things you want to over to his house – like your games and stuff. Then next year, you'll go to Dad's flat on Christmas morning and spend Boxing Day here.'

'But why can't we just all be together?' Yvie had blurted. 'Why can't Dad come here too? He's okay with Gregor, he told me that and he wouldn't lie.'

'Because it's not fair to Gregor,' Mum had insisted. 'Or me, for that matter. We want to cherish these first Christmases together as a couple.'

'I suppose what's fair for us doesn't come into it?' Marina had asked from the kitchen, where she was scooping Angel Delight into bowls.

Mum had ignored her. That was it settled then. It hadn't been mentioned again, not even yesterday, apart from when Dad called them in the morning to wish them a Merry Christmas. He'd sounded sad, Yvie thought, and she'd wanted to run all the way to his house to give him a hug and tell him she loved him. Of course, Mum wouldn't let her.

Now, he was hours late and Mum was getting more annoyed as the day went on.

'Do you think he's okay?'

'Of course he is,' Mum answered, getting up from the chair and heading towards the kitchen. Yvie guessed that she was going to phone their dad again and ask him why he wasn't here yet. She'd been calling every hour but said it was just ringing out.

'It's all your fault anyway,' Verity muttered in her mum's direction. 'If you'd just let him come around yesterday, then this wouldn't have happened.'

It wasn't often that Yvie agreed with one of Verity's nasty comments, but this time she did.

The afternoon passed and by four o'clock it was getting dark and Yvie knew he wasn't coming. The realisation and the worry about why he wasn't there made her feel sick in her stomach. Marina and Zoe had even got so annoyed that they'd ignored Mum's orders and sneaked out of the back door and ran over to his house, but there had been no answer.

So Yvie sat. Saying silent prayers that he would be okay, the way the teacher always told them to do in school.

Dear God, I promise that I'll be really good and I'll make my own bed and I won't make anyone upset or cross with me if you will just please make my dad be fine.

It was after 8 o'clock when she thought God had been listening, because the doorbell finally rang.

'Dad!' she yelped, jumping off the chair and dashing into the hall so that she was first to reach the door. She swung it open. 'Where have you been?'

Her question trailed off as she saw that it wasn't Dad. Standing outside were two police officers, a man and a woman, both of them with very serious faces.

'Hi,' the policewoman said. She had a friendly voice, but Yvie could tell she wasn't happy. 'Is your mum in?'

Yvie had that horrible sick feeling again.

'Is this about my dad? Is he okay?' the words were tumbling out, and she could feel the tears rushing to her eyes and starting to overflow.

Two arms went around her shoulders. 'Yvie, come back here,' Marina coaxed her gently.

'No!' Yvie yelled. 'Not until they tell me what's happened to Dad.' She was sobbing now, so hard she could barely speak.

Marina pulled her right back. 'Come in,' she told the officers, who then stepped into the hallway, just as Verity and Zoe came down the stairs to see what all the fuss was about. Both of them immediately looked worried, which made Yvie cry even harder.

'Sorry, I was in the kitchen.' Another voice in the packed hall. Her mum. Who hadn't been in the kitchen at all – she'd been sitting outside the back door, huddled under a blanket with Gregor, while he had a cigarette. 'Yvie, stop that crying. Can I help you, officers?'

'Mrs Danton?' The policeman this time.

'Yes.'

The policeman glanced around at all the girls before he spoke again.

'I wonder if there's somewhere we can go in private? We'd like to talk to you about your husband, William Danton.'

Her mum didn't correct them, even though she'd had a party a couple of weeks ago to celebrate her divorce being final.

Yvie felt Marina's arms go tightly around her in a protective hug, and then she saw Zoe and Verity's tears begin to fall too. She knew then that God hadn't been listening to her prayers at all.

The wedding venue was exquisite, the music was divine, and the wall of flowers behind the celebrant was utterly breathtaking. Zoe felt the tears pool in her eyes as she stood at the front of the aisle next to the man she loved. The man she used to love.

She'd been thinking about this moment for the last month and now it was here. The last time she was at a wedding, it was her own. Now, Tom was getting married and it couldn't be more different from two people standing on top of a roof and taking a leap of faith.

Once upon a time, she'd thought she might be his bride, but here she was, his best man, wearing a perfectly tailored, pale blue, trouser suit that matched the dresses worn by the four bridesmaids who were walking down the aisle towards them, the strains of a string quartet playing Barbara Streisand's 'Evergreen' in the background.

Behind them came Chrissie, utterly divine in a satin alabaster, forties style dress, with a shawl neck and a gentle flare to the floor, on the arm of Ben, the son she and Tom had made together when they were teenagers. Although the two of them had lost touch before Chrissie found out she was pregnant and Tom hadn't found out about Ben until he was almost a teenager himself, if Tom had bumped into him in the street, he would have known this boy was his son. He was Tom's double.

As Zoe watched Chrissie come towards them, the biggest smile lighting up her gorgeous face, she spotted her family – Marina with Graham, Yvie with Kay as her plus-one, Verity flying solo, next to her mum and Nigel – a few rows from the back of the function suite, grinning as wedding guests do. They'd all known Tom for the best part of ten years and loved him as Zoe's friend and colleague, then as her boyfriend, and she knew they'd love him still as Chrissie's husband.

As Chrissie reached the end of the aisle, Ben shook his dad's hand, then took his place in the front row, giving Zoe a moment to step forward and hug her. 'I'm so happy for you both.'

Chrissie kissed her. 'Thank you for everything, Zoe. We love you.'

For a moment, Zoe wondered what she was thanking her for. For letting Tom go? For accepting Chrissie as a friend? For making this work for all of them? The truth, she knew, was that no thanks were required, because Tom and Chrissie were simply meant to be together and no matter what obstacles were put in their way, they would have been overcome. Zoe had let him go and accepted it because there was no choice. It was their destiny, not hers.

Tom followed suit, kissing Zoe's other cheek. 'Thank you,' he whispered, before he took his bride's hand and they turned to face the celebrant who would declare them man and wife.

As Zoe stepped back, her eye caught her husband's, sitting at the end of the same row as her sisters and her mum. No smile there. His jaw jutted forward and if he was radiating anything, it was irritation. She wondered if he too was thinking how different this was from their wedding. And if he was, did he resent it? Was it making him regret what they'd done?

The sound of the celebrant's voice faded into the background, as Zoe closed her eyes, went back there to that moment at the top of the Kemp Vegas and watched herself step over the edge. 'Watch me fly, Dad,' she'd whispered.

She'd felt the sudden drop, then the thud as their feet hit the side of the building. Step by step, they'd worked their way down, and by the time they'd reached the ground, the thrill was coursing through her, her senses heightened by the danger.

Ned had unclipped his harness, climbed out of it, thrown his arms around her. He'd kissed her. 'Happy Wedding Day,' he'd said, beaming, clearly thrilled and excited.

And she'd felt... nothing.

'I think we need to get you a ring, Mrs Merton,' he'd declared, taking her hand, gesturing to her to look upwards, where dozens of people were looking over the balcony, explosions of light – fireworks and camera flashes – everywhere.

They'd done it. She'd got married. She should be the happiest woman in the world. So why did she have a feeling of absolutely certainty that at some point before stepping off that building she'd lost her senses? Or maybe she'd found them on the way down? It had to be the shock, she'd told herself. She loved Ned. They were meant for each other. This was going to be great. Even if she had to fake it for a moment until her feelings caught up.

Pushing her doubts aside, she'd summoned up some playful enthusiasm. 'Ooh, buying me jewellery. I think I like married life already.'

Back in the hotel, they'd gone straight to the mezzanine floor, a glorious glass gallery above the main gambling area – a sea of roulette wheels, card tables and slot machines – that housed the hotel's stores. As always, Roger had secured the most prestigious brands for his hotel. Dior. Gucci. Bvlgari. Tiffany. They were all there, in one long line of opulence and indulgence, all ready and waiting to help those lucky Sin City casino winners spend their profits.

She'd never been the type of girl to plan or imagine her wedding, but the ring was a different story. She'd seen it in a magazine years ago and it had stuck. A simple platinum band from Bvlgari, set with pavé diamonds all the way around. Perfection. And yet now it didn't seem right. She'd steered him into Tiffany and convinced him – and herself – that she just wanted a plain silver band. Why? What was suddenly making this whole thing jar with her?

With the blue box in a bag, and a shiny new addition to the third finger of her left hand, they'd headed back out. 'Let's go and find my sisters,' she'd said, knowing as she suggested it that it was exactly what she needed. They would be thrilled for her, celebrate her happiness, make some of this – any of it – feel great and they'd take away the growing unease that was sitting in the bottom of her gut.

Ned had wrapped his arms around her. 'Let's not. Let's go back upstairs and celebrate, just you,' he'd kissed her, 'me,' another kiss, 'and a bottle of champagne.'

He was right. Wasn't that what any bride would want to do? Of course it was!

She'd raced to the lift with him, they'd soared back

upwards to the floor below the one she'd abseiled off less than an hour ago, and they'd opened the bottle of champagne that Roger had already sent to their room.

They'd made love for hours, he'd said all the right things, she'd said them back, while he gently rubbed the ring on her finger. Only when he'd finally fallen asleep, did she send a text to her sisters' group chat.

OMG! Guess what happened a few hours ago? We got married!!!! Let's celebrate tomorrow! Love you, from ZOE MERTON!!!!!

They wouldn't know that the tears were choking her as she pressed send.

But that could be normal, right? How many times had she read about the anticlimax couples felt after their wedding day? And hadn't hers been a tad more unusual and bizarre than most? It was only natural that she would have mixed emotions, mixed feelings.

When no texts came back from her sisters, she'd switched her phone off, she'd snuggled into her new husband and she'd gone to sleep.

The next morning, she'd woken to the sound of the room phone ringing and picked it up to hear Roger's gregarious greeting. 'Hey, how's married life?'

'Eh, quite uneventful so far. You know, apart from the throwing myself off a building bit. If you ever consider sacking us as your marketing agency, I want you to think about that moment and remember I almost propelled my internal organs out of my body for you.'

'That might be the sweetest thing anyone's ever said to me.'

'Really? Then Felice really needs to work on her chat.'

A pause. Shit. She wondered for a moment if she'd gone too far. Jesting about a client's wife probably wasn't the done thing. But hey. Abseiling. Six hundred feet above earth. A near-death experience. That trumped a cheeky remark. Besides, it was true.

'Anyway, I'm calling because the world's press wants to talk to you.'

'Why?'

'Haven't you checked your phone? This whole thing has gone viral and your lovely face is plastered all over the internet. Although, you're screaming for your life, so it might not show you in the most flattering light. Anyway, I need you to get up, get moving and bring your husband along because this is going to run and it's going to give the hotel so much publicity I might have to give you shares.'

As always, Zoe's mind went to the professional angle. Yasssss! This was the kind of thing that launched a new project into the stratosphere. Excitement started to build. Bookings would soar. More excitement. Roger would commission The B Agency to do more work. More excitement. Other corporations would see what was happening here and it would bring in new clients. So much fricking excitement! This could take the agency to a whole new level.

'I'll take my reward in free holidays to your hotels for life – as often as I want and my sisters get to come with me,' she'd demanded, only half joking. Only after she said it did she realise that she should probably have mentioned that her husband was part of the deal too. This married lark was going to take a minute to get used to.

'Done! 'Now could you please get yourself down here and get started?'

'I'm on my way!' she'd jumped up, giving Ned a quick shake.

'Hey, wife,' he'd murmured sleepily, slipping almost immediately into sexy. 'Come back to bed and...'

'I can't, babe. I've got a work thing downstairs and you need to come too. I'll make it up to you later.'

She'd ignored his objections and went into the bathroom – wall-to-wall book-matched Carrera marble and the kind of room that would be featured in interior design magazines.

She had one foot in the shower when her mobile rang. With her dry hand, she flicked it on to speaker. Marina. And her sister was obviously on the warpath, because she went straight to the point. 'Did I imagine it last night or did you send us a text saying you'd got married?'

'I did!' she'd exclaimed, thinking that she'd need to postpone any celebrations until after they'd made sure that every element of this was capitalised on. They had to strike while the publicity iron was hot.

'What the fuck were you thinking?'

Okay, so not the reaction she'd expected – congratulations would have been a good start – but thinking about it now, she knew Marina would be furious that she hadn't been allowed to organise everything. She really was going to have to get her control freakery sorted out. Zoe's hackles had immediately shot to the upright position.

'Look, Marina, I don't have time for this right now. I know it's a bit of a shock, but I'm happy. Go give someone else a bollocking because the last time I checked, you weren't my mother.'

She wasn't sure which one of them hung up first. She just knew that she had to get to work, and when she did... wow, it was incredible. The next two days were a whirlwind of podcasts, photo shoots, videos, interviews and, God love him, Ned went along with it all. She barely saw her sisters again until the flight home, and even then, they were pretty subdued and slept most of the way while she wrote up features, made lists, drafted emails to press outlets in China, Russia, Japan – all the huge markets that would adore this kind of stunt.

It was the biggest success of her career and she'd been riding it ever since – it had been a workfest since the moment she landed and Tom met them at the airport, threw his arms around her. 'You are sen-fecking-sational!' he'd laughed. 'Our phones haven't stopped ringing.'

That was four weeks ago. Since then, her sisters had called. She'd fobbed them off because she had to work. Wedding gifts had been delivered. She hadn't sent thank-you notes yet because she had to work. Ned had fully moved in and then almost immediately suggested they start looking for a place together. She told him they'd do it soon – but right now she had to work. He'd tried to talk her into going on holiday and she'd agreed, as long as it was after work calmed down. And so it had gone on, right up until this morning, when she pulled on her suit for her ex-boyfriend's wedding. Ironically, throughout it all, she'd had to put her own marriage on the back burner. She wondered if she should have minded that more? Plenty of time for her and Ned later, she told herself. In the publicity world, it was all about catching a wave and for the last month she'd been busy riding it for the sake of Roger's hotel and her own agency.

Now, standing there at the end of the aisle, with nothing to distract her other than the sound of the choir singing 'Saving All My Love For You' while Tom and Chrissie signed the register to confirm their union, a thought came into her head and meandered around, weaving its way through the chaos and demanding peace and tranquility so that it could finally be heard.

The way Tom looked at Chrissie. The way Chrissie looked at Tom. There was no leap of faith there, only certainty.

Shouldn't that be the way she felt when she looked at Ned? And yet, here she was, standing at the end of the aisle, trying to hide the fact that her heart was actually crumbling inside her.

She had to find a way to put it back together again.

He was standing over by the bar on his own, a bottle of beer in his hand, when she spotted him. It could have been a shot from a magazine – the handsome guy, in the bar of a luxury hotel, gazing out through the floor-to-ceiling windows at the city skyline. For a moment Verity thought about ignoring him. She hadn't planned to confront him tonight but now, seeing him looking so smug, she felt her fury rise. She had too much to say and this might be the only chance she got to say it, while everyone else was busy mingling.

She brushed down some invisible crease on her black and cream shift dress – an indulgence from Joseph, but it was a special occasion and she'd chipped in with Marina to buy it because it would fit them both – and with her gin and tonic in one hand and her phone in the other hand, she strode over.

Ned spotted her coming, and he opened his arms to greet her, kissing her on each cheek as always. 'Hey! I was beginning to think you were avoiding me.'

That wasn't a surprise. For the last month, she'd stayed

out of the staffroom at school, dashed off immediately at the end of the day, and refused his texts inviting her to go climbing with him. The sisters had postponed their plans to speak to Zoe because she'd been so busy that they hadn't been able to tie her down to meet with them. Suddenly, Verity decided to come at it from a different angle. If she couldn't share the truth with Zoe, then maybe it was time for some honesty with Mr Merton.

'I was,' she said simply, but she couldn't help the faint smile on her lips. He probably thought it meant that she was joking. She wasn't. It was actually down to the fact that she relished the prospect of what was about to come.

'I don't think I've congratulated you yet on your wedding.' It could have been the light, but she was sure that a shadow passed across his face. Maybe all wasn't quite so wonderful in the land of marital bliss. The thought cheered her and spurred her on – not because she wanted Zoe to be unhappy, but because her sister deserved so much more than this farce of a marriage.

'Eh, actually, no one has. I've said to Zoe that we need to have some kind of celebration over here too. I feel like she missed out on having the whole wedding experience because it was so spur of the moment and so far away. I want her to have that. She deserves it.'

See, this was what he did. He came over as a nice, decent, thoughtful guy. Why was that? Why didn't he have 'Not To Be Trusted' stamped on his forehead just to make it easier for unsuspecting women to spot?

'I've missed you,' he said, changing the subject. 'We haven't been to the climbing centre all month and Zoe has been working day and night. I texted you a few times.'

He did this too. Made you feel special. Wanted. Like he cared about you.

She took a sip of her gin and tonic. 'I know, I'm sorry. I've been really busy too. I joined one of those dating apps. Your Next Date.'

A flinch. She saw it, although she didn't know if he even realised that he did it.

'Really? That's great. I'm glad. You deserve to meet someone nice.'

She wanted to take her drink and slowly pour it over his head.

'It's definitely been interesting. You'll never believe who I saw on there.'

I dare you, she thought. *Go on. At least have the balls to admit it.*

'Who?' Nope, he was a coward to the end, but he was staring straight at her, and for the first time, she thought she saw disdain there. Well, welcome to the party, the real Mr Merton.

'You,' she said simply.

He feigned confusion, then realisation. The kids in the nativity play – even the ones who dropped the baby Jesus – had better acting skills than this chump.

'Oh, my God, is that still there? That's from ages ago.' He went for good-natured incredulity and statement of innocence. 'That's from... oooh, maybe four or five years ago. I had no idea it was still in there.'

'Yeah, the picture looked a few years old.'

'Exactly!' he exclaimed, a little too desperately. 'That's hilarious. I must remember to take it down tomorrow. I don't think Zoe would see the funny side.'

He signalled to the barman for another beer. Either he'd

suddenly developed a raging thirst, or he was desperately looking for distractions that would buy him time to think.

'Gin and tonic?' he asked her. That bought him even more time – enough to come up with the idea to navigate out of deep waters by switching the subject to her.

'So, tell me, any matches? There must be, if it's kept you busy for a month.'

'A couple of interesting ones, but to be honest I find it all a bit off-putting. I'm pretty sure half the guys on there – women too, probably – are already in relationships and just looking for a bit on the side.'

'Maybe,' he concurred, but there was a renewed wariness there. 'What makes you think that?'

'Because someone I know decided to test the theory. Put up a false profile and swiped right on a guy she knew was in a relationship.'

Again, it was probably subconscious but also so telling that he was now pulling at his tie and opening the top button of his shirt. It was tempting to just blurt it all out, but no. *Make him sweat, Verity. Make him sweat.*

'Wow. That's pretty sneaky.'

He was throwing back his beer now. Must be the heat in here.

'And did she get anything from it?'

She could see that he didn't want to ask but couldn't help it. This was like seeing a car crash in the distance and not being able to look away when you reached it.

'You'll never believe it, but she did.' She feigned astonishment, milked the pause, drew it out. 'She swiped right on her sister's boyfriend.'

Was it her imagination or did he visibly deflate?

'And guess what happened?' she went on.

He didn't say anything for a long time. It was like the bit in every episode of *Line Of Duty*, where the person under interrogation has to decide whether to chuck in the towel and confess or keep winging it in the hope that all the evidence was circumstantial.

Another swig from his bottle of Bud, his grimace suggesting it wasn't enough to get rid of the bitter taste in his mouth. 'I've no idea.'

'Well, wait 'til I tell you. It took ages, months actually, but eventually he sent her a message suggesting they meet up. When was that now?' She pretended to rack her brain. 'Mmmm. Must have been about a month ago. Yeah, because it was just before we went to Vegas and my sister got married there. To you. Actually, you might recognise the name that was used on Your Next Date. Veronica. From Glasgow.'

The towel came flying over the ring. Ding ding.

Several seconds passed and Verity could feel the tension rising. Whatever he had to say, she was ready for it.

He tried to shrug it off, play it down. 'Okay, so what? It was just a bit of stupidity. You know that was before we got married.'

'Yeah, but you'd been together for over a year.' Gloves off. Her tone lowered to a menacing hiss of contained rage that she wasn't sure she'd ever heard coming out of her mouth before. 'How dare you do that to her? What gives you the right to think you can treat her like that?'

'It was nothing,' he shot back, going on the offensive now. 'Nothing. I didn't even follow it up. It doesn't matter.' His voice was rising and his face was getting closer to hers. 'Are you going to tell her? Are you going to wreck your sister's happiness and for what? One harmless message?'

'It's not harmless.'

'Of course it was! She is out every night of the week, working until all hours, weekends too. I just got a bit bored, that's all. I wouldn't have gone through with it.'

'Wouldn't you? Because according to the staffroom gossip, you've shagged half the teachers in the school.' For a minute she was tempted to throw in what he'd done with Yvie and Kay, but she knew Yvie wouldn't want that. That was her sister's situation to handle how she chose.

'Not after I met Zoe.'

'I'm not sure that's true.' She wasn't. But it didn't matter.

'You've completely got the wrong end of the stick. I was just bored. Wanted a chat. It meant nothing.'

Ah, the old 'it meant nothing' chestnut.

She pulled her phone out of her clutch bag and read the message on her screen shot.

'Hey Veronica. Fancy meeting up for a drink sometime? Or more? No strings attached, just a bit of fun. I promise you'll enjoy it.'

'You fucking bitch.' Gloves tossed out of the ring, first punch thrown.

Verity lifted her chin, determined to show he didn't intimidate her. 'You think?'

The most attractive man in the room got ugly real quick.

'You're doing this because I didn't fuck you. You couldn't handle the rejection. Do you think I didn't know? Didn't see what you wanted? Even after Zoe and I got together, there you were, hanging around, begging for it. How do you think Zoe would feel about that? So here's what I suggest we do, Verity. You don't mention the message, and I won't mention that you were still there, practically gagging for it, and I could have had you all day long if I'd wanted you.'

The wind was thumped out of her chest, she felt dizzy,

her legs turned to jelly and she just wanted to check out before any more blows were inflicted. It was almost a knockout.

Then he spoke again.

'If it's any consolation, you weren't the only one. Yvie. Marina. Could have had you all if I'd wanted. The full set of Danton sisters.'

Almost a knockout, but not quite. It was like the moment in *Rocky* when he climbed back off the canvas. If the canvas was a very expensive Canadian walnut floor in a luxury hotel. A year ago, she was so disconnected from her sisters that she might not have reacted the way that she did. Not now.

She inhaled. Exhaled. Ding ding.

'Let me tell you something, you spineless prick. If you think you could have any of us, then you're deluded. But if you want to tell Zoe that, then on you go. See if she believes you. Because here's the thing. I'm not going to say anything to her about the message or any of the things you've just said...'

His eyebrows lifted in surprise.

'At least not yet. I'm going to give you the chance to tell her first and you can dress it up any way you want. You're going to do your own dirty work and bail out of this sham of a marriage because my sister deserves so much better than you. But if you don't do it, then I'm telling her everything – my part in it too – because I'd rather lose a sister than have her live her life with a duplicitous prick like you. Oh, and this...' she turned her phone so he could see the flashing red button that showed the phone was recording every word that had been said. 'I'll play it for her too, so she can hear what a scumbag you really are. See you in school, *Edward*.'

And with that, she spun on the Jimmy Choos she'd borrowed from Marina and strutted out of the bar.

39

'Are you crying again? You'll ruin your gorgeous make-up and that would be a travesty.'

Yvie wasn't lying. Kay had pushed the boat out for today. She'd had her hair done so it fell in loose coppery waves, she was wearing false eyelashes so thick they could sweep the floors later, and her frock was a dramatic, one-shouldered, red sheath that clung to her curves in the most flattering way. When they'd chosen it, Kay had put it on her credit card with her eyes squeezed shut because she knew she'd be paying for it forever. It was worth it though. For someone who, like Yvie, spent her whole life in hospital scrubs with no make-up on, it felt great to be glamorous and sexy for a change.

'Jesus, you should have an endorsement deal with Kleenex,' Yvie teased, handing yet another tissue over to her friend, who took it and, instead of blowing her nose, just waved it about as she spoke, staring at Tom and Chrissie the whole time. The couple were on the dance floor again, smooching to 'At Last' by Etta James. They were staring into each other's eyes, no words needing to be said, just so in love that Yvie could see why Kay was weeping.

'It's just that they look so... perfect. Honestly, I'm not bitter that someone else has found love while I'm going to be single until the end of fricking time. I'm happy for them. These are happy tears.'

Yvie knew differently. After a few drinks, Kay sometimes got a bit maudlin, especially at events like this. It was a Catch-22 situation. She'd brought her along as her plus-one for a night of food, drinks and dancing – all of which they'd thoroughly enjoyed, mostly thanks to the table of absolute characters they'd been placed on. As soon as they'd arrived, one of the women, a platinum blonde with a beehive hairdo the size of a small hedge, had stood up and hugged them in turn. 'I'm Chrissie's next-door neighbour, Val,' she'd announced, 'and this is my man, Don. I know he's gorgeous, but don't be getting ideas, because at his age his heart couldn't take it.'

Yvie and Kay had still been laughing when Val had moved aside to introduce the woman behind her.

'And this is my niece...'

'Liv!' Kay exclaimed, with obvious delight.

'Bloody hell, it's a small world,' Yvie had gasped, loving this turn of events. Liv was the charge nurse on the palliative care ward at Glasgow Central and both Kay and Yvie had worked with her at various times in their careers there. That's how, instead of two guests at a table of strangers, Yvie and Kay had immediately been welcomed into Val's fold and, by the time pudding was served (Yvie ate Don's – Val said he wasn't allowed it because of his cholesterol), Yvie and Kay had been made honorary members of Val's family.

And what a hoot they all were. They'd drank far too much, sang, danced their shoes off, and the chat round the table was outrageously funny. There had been a couple of surprises too – especially the bit where Val got Tom's Aunt Flora up to dance and they did a flawless, utterly jaw-dropping jive that could have been straight out of a Gene Kelly movie.

Now though, at the end of the night, the mood had shifted a little. Val was leaning over the back of her seat, talking to Liv and the guests at the table behind them, leaving Yvie trying to console a sobbing Kay, while Tom and Chrissie were still smooching to Etta on the dance floor.

And the other side of the Catch-22 was kicking in. The wedding had been incredible – but for someone looking for love, it was also a reminder of what they didn't have.

'It'll happen for you, pal,' Yvie told her, knowing that it was something that kept Kay awake at night. She and Chester were doing great, but it had always just been the two of them and Kay wanted a future that gave Chester more people to love, a family that had more than just two in it. Three, if they counted Yvie, which they always did and Yvie was so grateful for that. If the last few months had taught her anything it was that you could never have too many people to love. Maybe it was time that she thought about being open to meeting someone too. First though, she knew she had to look after herself a bit more, before she could even think about caring for a partner.

'Do you think?' Kay asked wearily. 'How long has it been? I haven't had sex since... since...' Yvie saw her eyes dart to Zoe, who was over at the other side of the room talking to Roger Kemp and Verity, then move to Ned, who was propping up the bar, swaying as if he'd had one too many beers. 'Urgh, I can't believe I slept with him. How could I have fallen for all his bullshit?'

Yvie didn't say a word. Kay had liked him a lot and been so hurt after he'd ghosted her. Bastard. Tonight, they'd both given him a wide berth, refusing to even glance at him until now. In fact, Yvie had avoided him since Vegas, when the truth about what he'd done had come out. Just a fuckery of timing that it was the same weekend he'd married her sister.

As if he knew that they were talking about him, Ned Merton turned his head, looked their way and smiled. Yvie shuddered. Fuck him. Since they came back from the trip, she had met up with Marina and Verity a few times to discuss what to do about the Ned situation, but they needed to get in a room with Zoe too, and she'd been too busy at work to fit them in. Yvie hadn't told Kay anything about what had happened between the sisters in the hotel room that night – Zoe deserved to know everything first.

'How's the other love's young dream?' Kay asked now, gesturing to Ned and then casting her eyes over to Zoe again. Kay and the rest of the world had seen the video of Zoe and Ned abseiling off the building and it was still being hailed online as one of the most romantic events of the year. If only they knew the truth.

'They seem... fine.'

'Was it just a publicity stunt?' Kay asked. 'It just seemed a bit sudden. And, let's face it, he didn't strike me as the marrying type. He's a serial shagger.'

'To be honest, my love, I've no idea if it was a stunt or real. It's always hard to tell with Zoe.' Non-committal. Vague. But the truth was, this wasn't the time or the place to go into it. She would tell Kay the whole truth about Ned's behaviour and his Your Next Date activities when it was all sorted, one way or another, and it was just the two of them, a bottle of plonk and a large extra-hot pepperoni pizza.

'What's hard to tell with Zoe?' Verity asked with a slight slur as she slipped – a tad wobbly – into the free chair next to them. She'd been up dancing with Dex and the other guys from Zoe's office all night. A year ago, Verity would have sat in the corner, judging everyone and living up to her uptight reputation. Now she'd changed and it was all for the better. Although, right now, her liver might not agree.

'Oh, nothing,' Yvie countered, waving her hand as if it were irrelevant trivia, then switching the subject immediately. 'You having a good time?'

'Yep, but I've been ditched by Mum and Nigel, and Marina and Graham – they all buggered off ages ago – and I have to go home,' she told them. 'It's been great, but it's time to call it a night. I've got a ten mile run with the triathlon team in the morning and I'm going to have a bitch of a hangover.' It was Verity's new thing – she'd joined when she came back from Vegas and was planning to compete in her first Iron Woman by the end of the year. Her level of exercise was still high, but it was controlled now, no longer an obsessive reaction to her emotions or stresses. Yvie had told her she'd bring the Mars bars for the finish line. Joking aside, she was beyond proud of Verity for tackling her issues and in the last couple of weeks, she'd made an effort to do the same. It wasn't easy but she'd been making time to get more sleep, to eat better, to be kinder to herself, and she'd made an appointment to see Verity's therapist. Small steps but her panic attacks had reduced – only one since they'd returned home. She was absolutely positive that sharing her worries and anxieties with her sisters had been the beginning of the healing process.

'I'm ready to call it a night too, I'll come with you.'

'Noooooo,' Kay interrupted them. 'I'm not ready to go

home yet. Chester is away with his wee pal until tomorrow afternoon.'

'I know! But since I've volunteered for the early shift tomorrow morning so that my lovely pal and co-worker Kay Gorman can have a long lie-in, I need to get to my bed.'

'Urgh, you've always got to come back with a great point when I'm being a brat,' Kay pouted. 'I really need to get a new pal.'

'Yeah, well, can you get one that'll do the early shift in future and then I can have a long lie-in too?' Yvie batted back.

'Excuse me, everyone! Can I just have a word...' Miss James had sung her last line and Tom was now on stage with the mike. 'First of all, thank you again to everyone for coming. I thought I couldn't get any happier after I married Chrissie, but you lot have made it even more incredible.'

Yvie's eyes flickered to Zoe, who had stopped speaking to Roger and was now watching Tom, with an inscrutable expression on her face. Yvie's heart went out to her. This kind of stuff would have crushed other people, but Zoe took it all, powered through everything that was tossed her way and did it with such grace that Yvie was in awe of her. Even if she had just married a tit.

When the applause and cheers died down, Tom went on, 'I just want to say that I'm the happiest man in the world tonight and I'm not going to make another speech but my wife and I—' A roaring thunder of cheers made Tom laugh and take a bow. 'My wife and I thank you from the bottom of our hearts and we love you all. In fact, we love you so much that we've persuaded Roger to keep the residents' bar open for as long as you want, so everyone is welcome to stay and carry on partying. Thank you again and have a great night.'

'Yes!' Val exclaimed, across the table. 'Yvie, pet, you're with me on the karaoke.'

'There's a karaoke in the residents' bar?' Yvie asked, surprised that a hotel as upmarket as this had something so rowdy.

Val shook her head and emitted a wicked cackle. 'Nope, but there will be when my Don gets some Tom Jones on the iPhone.'

Yvie's giggle came with a bittersweet groan, and Kay stepped in to explain. 'Val, I want to stay and this bore is going home. I mean, just because she's got to be at work in six hours...' Kay teased. 'She's a total lightweight.'

'Not something I've ever been called before,' Yvie retorted with perfect comedic timing.

'Aw, pet. The NHS should give you lot a medal, they really should. I'm always saying that to our Liv. The work you do... Yer all gems. Yvie, I'm gutted you have to leave – we definitely need to plan another night out. And, Kay, stay with us, lass! We'll take care of you. It looks like there's gonna be quite a crowd, and you never know what might happen. Our Isa met her husband at the party after I married my Don.'

'Yeah, stay, Kay,' Liv, who had just returned to the table with an elaborate cocktail in hand, begged her.

In a split second, Yvie saw the solution that would make everyone happy. There was a small hitch, but it was easily overcome. Val had got sidetracked by a passing guest, so Yvie leaned into towards Kay, ensuring she was the only one who could hear what she was saying. 'Babe, why don't you stay here with Val and Liv – I'm actually totally jealous – and then just get a room in the hotel tonight.'

Kay's face lit up, then immediately fell again. 'Don't be

daft. This place costs a fortune. A night here would keep Chester in trainers for a year.'

Yvie had already thought of that. She slipped her hand into her clutch purse, pulled out her credit card and surreptitiously pressed it into Kay's hand. 'Take it. Please. I'll book you a room downstairs and you pay for it with this. My treat. And tomorrow morning, you sleep late, order room service, go to the spa and enjoy every minute of it. Put all of it on this card too. Call it an extra birthday present.'

Kay stared at her, open mouthed but eyes gleaming. 'But my birthday's not until October.'

'Well, you'd better drag it out then,' Yvie joked, rising from her chair and addressing everyone at the table. 'Right, Kay's going to stay and I'm off. Think of me when you're staggering to your beds at 6 a.m. and I'm already up and on my way to work.'

She almost didn't get the last word out, because Kay stood up, threw her arms around her, muffling her mouth. 'Thank you. I fricking love you.'

'I fricking love you back. Now, behave yourself and don't let this lot get you drunk or arrested.'

'Oh, we can't make promises like that, pet,' Val quipped.

Yvie worked her way round the table, kissing everyone, saying goodbye, making plans to meet up again for a night out, then took Verity's hand and finally tore herself away. The look of sheer joy on Kay's face was worth every penny of the credit card bill that would come her way. At least Roger gave all the sisters a 50 per cent discount after their advertising campaign had been used to launch their Ladies Who Live It Up campaign at his Ibiza hotel.

Scanning the room, she searched for Zoe so that she

could say goodbye, but she'd disappeared. No matter. She'd text her on the way home.

Down in the lobby, they exited the lift to see plenty of people still milling around.

'Give me two minutes – I just need to go book a room for Kay.' Yvie went to reception, explained the situation and the very efficient receptionist assured her she'd arrange it all and leave a key ready for Miss Kay Gorman to collect. Yvie could barely concentrate on what she was saying, too busy trying not to gape at Roger Kemp's size zero wife, who was standing nearby, looking faintly irritated. Wow. There was a woman who'd never cheered herself up with a chicken and sweetcorn pizza.

Booking complete, Yvie made her way back to the lobby sofas, where Verity was waiting. 'Right, my love, come on. Let's grab a taxi.'

'Sounds like a plan,' Verity replied, managing to rise from the black velvet couch gracefully despite the short dress, the high heels and the consumption of several gins.

They'd almost made it to the door, when Yvie glanced to the left and saw a couple sitting there, the woman's face a mask of sadness as she brushed tears away from her cheeks.

Yvie immediately froze, put her arm on Verity's. 'Look.'

'Is that Marina?' Verity whispered. 'I haven't got my glasses on and it's too far.'

'It's Marina,' Yvie confirmed. 'With Graham. And I've no idea what's happening, but it doesn't look good.'

40

MARINA – TOM'S WEDDING

If there was a hell on earth, it was being forced to be at a wedding and celebrate a blissful couple's happy ever after when your own marriage was crumbling to dust, Marina decided. She'd sat through the ceremony. She'd suffered the speeches and the declarations of everlasting devotion. She'd put a happy face on for the other guests at their table. And then she'd practically punched the air with glee when her phone buzzed in her bag and she pulled it out to see Annabelle's name flashing on the screen.

'Excuse me, it's my daughter. I just need to take this.'

'Everything okay, darling?' Graham asked distractedly, liqueur in hand, breaking off the conversation he'd been having for the last two hours with the man next to him, after he'd discovered he was in asset management and they might have some mutual business interests.

Marina had amused herself by talking to Verity, mentally making her to-do list for the week and picturing Tom and Chrissie in twenty years' time, staring at each other over a dinner table with nothing to say. Yes, her bitch award was still on her mantlepiece.

Taking short steps in her forties style, mauve pencil dress, she hurried out of the function suite, pressing the green button on her phone to accept the call as soon as she found a spot quiet enough to have a conversation.

'Hello, sweetheart, how are—'

She stopped, confused. There was a sound on the other end of the phone, but it was indecipherable, a howling noise that took her a few moments to recognise as her daughter sobbing her heart out.

'Annabelle! Annabelle, what's wrong, darling? Are you okay? Annabelle, take a deep breath and try to speak. Oh God, are you hurt? Are you in danger? Annabelle, please...'

A cold terror was making her whole body tremble and her knuckles turn white. This wasn't her daughter. She loved her child, but there was no getting away from the reality that Annabelle's fall back behaviour was bold, demanding, stroppy and disdainful of everything around her. Marina had enough self-awareness to accept that particular apple hadn't fallen far from the tree.

But that stroppy teenager wasn't the person on the other end of the line now. This girl was distraught, hysterical.

'Annabelle!' Sharp this time, harsh even, but she was all out of other options and fear had that effect on her.

A pause in the sobbing, just long enough for Marina to say again, 'Tell me, darling. Whatever it is, we'll sort it. Tell me what's wrong.'

'I... I... I...'

'You what?'

'I... hate it here, Mum. I hate it.'

Marina was dumbstruck. Surely she didn't mean... 'Darling, what do you hate? The dance academy?'

'Y... y... y... yes.'

'But why? I thought you loved it there?'

'I... I... I...'

Marina waited, saying nothing. This didn't make sense. It was Annabelle's dream. She didn't even complain when, like this weekend, she had to stay extra nights because she had competitions.

'I... I've always hated it. I just said that I loved it, but I don't. Mum, I just want to come home. Please let me. Please.'

Marina had been through milder versions of this before when the kids had wanted to give up piano, or tennis, or violin, and each time she'd refused to let them. This was different though. This was desperation, bitter unhappiness, bottled-up feelings boiling over. This was misery.

'Annabelle, stop. Please, darling, calm down. Tell me why. Help me understand.'

For the next fifteen minutes she listened as her daughter told her everything, how she'd realised a while ago that dance wasn't her passion, how she was crumbling with the insecurity that was endemic at the academy, how she hated the classes and the rivalry and jealousies, how she just wanted to have a normal life, with free time and friends.

Marina listened, a sinking feeling of realisation growing with every passing minute. She knew she had to ask the question, but she also feared she already knew the answer.

'But, Annabelle, why have you stayed this long?

'Because it made you happy.'

Crash. Every building block of her maternal existence crumbled to the ground. And as it did, a series of pictures of Annabelle, looking sad at the sidelines when she was waiting to go on stage, of blinking back tears when her teacher was screaming instructions, flashed through her mind. And more. Oscar, his little face frowning as he tried desperately to master a new concerto on his clarinet, or putting his head in his hands when he failed for the fifth time to understand a maths problem and Marina made him try again.

What the hell was she doing?

'Darling, listen to me. Pack your bag. Just bring with you whatever you need. Come home, and we'll talk—'

'Don't try to make me go back, Mum!' Annabelle begged, obviously thinking that Marina was just trying to bring her home for a breather so she could fix her up and send her packing again. Dear God, what had she done to her children? She only wanted them to have the best life and somehow this was where they were. How could that be?

'I won't, Bella,' she promised, using the nickname they'd had until Annabelle turned ten and insisted on being called by her full name. Again, apple, tree.

'You can stay at home for as long as you want, I promise. It will be completely up to you. Let's just figure out how to get you back here tonight.' She'd already had a couple of glasses of champagne so she couldn't drive. She racked her brain, trying to work out the logistics, and realised there was one obvious answer. It would be expensive, but sod it.

'I'll send a taxi for you, darling, it will be there in an hour or so. Will that give you enough time?'

'But what about Miss Branston?' There was a tremor in her voice as she said it.

Marina closed her eyes. 'Don't you worry about Miss Branston, I'll take care of it.'

'Thanks, Mum.'

Marina melted as she heard the relief and the genuine

feeling in those two words. Thanks mum.

'I love you, Bella. And, honey... I've got you. It's all going to be fine.' She meant every word.

'I love you too, Mum. See you soon.'

'Bye, darling. Call me on the way if you need to talk again. I'll keep my phone by my side.'

Call disconnected, Marina switched in to hyper-organisation mode. She dialled the taxi firm Graham's company used and asked them to send a vetted driver from Glasgow to Edinburgh to pick up her daughter, then she called Miss Branston and informed her that there had been a change of plan this weekend and she was bringing Annabelle home. She kept it curt and didn't allow the teacher time to pry. She'd discuss it properly when the time was right. The two calls that were going to return her daughter to her took exactly four minutes. Marina really didn't mess around.

'What's going on?' Graham had left the wedding suite to come and check what was happening, still with his Drambuie in his hand, of course.

'Annabelle is coming home. She's unhappy and I've sent a car for her.'

To his credit, he was immediately concerned. 'Is she okay?'

Marina nodded. 'She'll be fine. She'll be home in a couple of hours, so I just want to make sure we're back before her.'

She stood up, about to walk back into the function suite, when something stopped her. Her daughter had just been brave enough to make a change. Where was Marina's courage?

'Actually, Graham, can we talk? There are some things I need to tell you.'

He didn't hide his surprise. 'What, now?'

'Now,' she said. Again, to his credit, he went along with it and followed her. They found a table in the downstairs bar and she struggled with where to start, before blurting it out, 'I think I need a break.'

A break. She'd been thinking it through since they landed back from Vegas and she knew it was the right thing to do. She wasn't going to tell him about the hook-ups or how strong her hatred of her life had become, how she'd begun to resent that every moment of her day was lived for the people in her family, how she had nothing left. Nothing. Nothing of herself to give because she didn't even know who she was any more.

She didn't say any of that, because the truth was it was all her own fault. She'd surrendered her life. He'd never demanded it or said she couldn't do something else. She'd chosen to live this way and she'd been sucked into some vortex of expectation, where she was so busy trying to make everyone and everything the best it could be, that she'd forgotten that the most important thing was to make sure everyone was happy.

Herself included.

And when she'd realised that happiness was a distant memory, her feelings had turned into resentment – of her life, her husband, and yes, her family too.

It was time for a change. The truth was, she'd always been too afraid to let their perfect little unit change because she didn't want to wreck their family, didn't want the kids to feel how she'd felt after her dad was gone, to have the responsibility of taking care of everyone. She'd spent her whole life in fear that something else would go wrong and it had paralysed her, made her too afraid to make difficult changes in case her family fell apart.

It had taken her a while to realise that wouldn't happen.

The kids' lives wouldn't be like hers, because, as Verity had said, Marina was nothing like her mother.

They would be fine. She'd make sure of it.

But she needed to do it on her own terms.

'Six months,' she told Graham eventually, surprising herself when she realised that tears were running down her face. 'Then we can see how we feel. I know it's a shock and I'm sorry, but I need to find the life I want first before I know if it can be with you.'

She wasn't giving him false hope, but she wasn't ruling out a reconciliation either. She'd loved him once. Maybe, after a bit of time and space, and rebuilding her life again on her own terms, she would discover she still did.

Now that she'd told him what she wanted, she braced herself for objections. They didn't come. She waited for him to say something, anything, but he sat there, staring into space. She was about to give up on him, when he finally spoke.

'The other day, I caught myself wondering what the hell I was doing all this for,' he said, still staring into a void in front of him.

'I know that work has taken over my life. I'm not sure how we got here, but it's where we are and I think I have to work out what I want too.'

Now she was the one shocked into silence. He was unhappy too? How could she not have known that?

He leaned over and put his hand on hers and looked at her in a way that he hadn't done since the kids were small and they were just two twenty-somethings starting off a family and a life together.

'I miss the guy I used to be too. He loved you more than

life, you know.'

Marina nodded sadly. 'I know. The woman I used to be loved him too.' It was true.

It was heartbreaking that the first real conversation they'd had in years was the one in which they were saying goodbye to their marriage and each other.

'I want to leave the house. You can stay there.' She hadn't thought this through, but even as she was saying it, she knew it was what she wanted. What was the point of searching for change if you stayed in the same place? 'The kids and I will move somewhere else, at least for a while.'

She knew he wouldn't argue. Whether he decided to make changes to his life or not, the reality was that right now he worked fourteen hour days and knew nothing of the kids' schedules or needs.

'Okay. I can see them whenever I want?'

'Of course,' she told him, meaning it.

They felt silent again, both of them thinking it through, too stunned to be sure what they still needed to discuss. She had no idea how long they'd been sitting there, when Yvie and Verity appeared at their table.

'Hey,' Yvie said gently, 'Are you two okay?'

Marina swiftly wiped away the tears from her face with the palm of one hand, still holding Graham's with the other.

'We will be,' she said, hoping it was true. 'Yvie, can I ask you something?'

'Sure.'

It had just come into her mind, but as soon as it had, she knew it felt right.

'I know we're always leaning on you, and we promised we wouldn't do that any more. But can the kids and I come and stay with you for a while?'

41

NED – TOM'S WEDDING

Why? Why did it have to be so fucking complicated? Life was too short for this shit.

The wedding was coming to an end now, the lights were up and the last few guests were drifting down to the residents' bar after Tom had announced that it was being kept open for them. Ned Merton wasn't ready for the party to end, especially not after the night he'd had. Who the fuck did that bitch Verity think she was, dishing out ultimatums to him?

He ordered another beer from the free bar, then raised the bottle in a silent cheers to the man who was at the other side of the room, saying goodbye to his wedding guests. May as well spend as much of Tom Butler's money as possible. A tiny revenge, but it made him feel better.

See, Verity had it all wrong. It wasn't him, Ned, who was the problem in the relationship with Zoe. It was Tom sodding Butler. Always there. Right there. Taking Zoe from him, even though he'd dumped her for someone else.

His eyes went to her now, standing across the room, chatting to a group of guests he didn't know.

God, she was beautiful though. And smart. And everything a guy could ever want. He closed his eyes, his mind slipping into his memories. Right from that first moment he saw her in the staffroom, half pissed and desperate to party, he'd known he wanted her.

At first, he'd thought she was a pushover. They'd spent the night together and he'd thought it was a done deal. She was his for as long as he wanted her. But, no. She wasn't like the others. She was the first one who'd toyed with him, brushed him off. So, yeah, he could admit that she'd become something else.

A challenge.

That's how it had been ever since. She'd been there, in a relationship with him, married to him, but always just out of reach. He'd become obsessed with winning, with having her, making her his.

When the wedding opportunity came along in Vegas, he'd known it was his chance to win her, once and for all.

But nothing had changed. Since they'd abseiled off that building, she'd still been the same, still unavailable, too busy, relegating him to second place, third even. Tom Butler. And even that flash bastard, Roger Kemp. They both got more of her attention than he did.

And, as for him, so what if he'd had a bit of fun on a dating app? He wouldn't have been pushed into doing that if the woman who would become his wife had paid him any attention, would he?

'Hey, Mr Merton, how are you doing there?'

He hadn't even seen Zoe sneaking up on him. Now, he watched as her eyes narrowed, the smile on her beautiful face a bit uncertain. Okay, so he'd had a few beers. More than a few. He deserved it.

'I'm fine. Why wouldn't I be?'

She shook her head. 'No reason. You just seem a bit...'

'Pissed?' he spat, finishing it for her.

She laughed. She actually fucking laughed.

'Yeah, well, I was going to go with "tired", but okay. Sorry I haven't seen much of you tonight, babe, it's just been so busy with making sure it all went well and—'

'I don't care.'

Her smile dropped and he watched as her eyelids drooped for a second as if she was weary. What did she have to be weary about? He was the one who'd been treated like crap here.

'Look, I'm not going to argue with you here. I'm sorry if you're annoyed...'

Was she though? Nah, she wasn't sorry. Not in the least. She was placating him, like he was some kind of clueless idiot.

'I'm not. Like I said, I don't care,' he repeated.

'Okay,' she said simply. Calmly. 'I'm going to go home now. I'm tired. Are you coming?'

She didn't even care enough to fight, to complain, to call him out.

Well, fuck it, he didn't need this any more. What was the point? Did he really want to wait around until she snapped her fingers and gave him the respect he deserved? Did he want to find out if she would believe Verity's story or if he could win her over with some bullshit explanations? Did he want to keep trying to have someone who would always put her job first?

Nah. He was in charge of his own life and he'd already wasted too much of it on Zoe Danton. He was done. It was time to give up on the challenge. Her loss.

One day she'd realise she'd messed up, but it would be too late. Serve her right.

It was time to enjoy his life again. Starting right now.

'No, I'm not coming. I'm going to stay here a while longer,' he told her.

Stay. Fight. Argue. Beg me to change my mind.

She didn't.

She turned and walked away.

That said everything he needed to know.

Forget Zoe Danton. He didn't need her.

He could have anyone he wanted.

And tonight he knew who that would be. He'd had his eye on someone else all night, and she'd been on his radar for much longer.

For a man who thrived on a challenge, his next one was coming right up. It was only much, much later that he realised Zoe had walked away with her dignity intact and his credit cards in her handbag.

42

'I'll start with the credit card. I think you'll find that was mine.' Even as Yvie is saying it, my mind can't compute what is going on. 'But it's not what it looks like. It wasn't me. Not this time.'

'What do you mean "this time"?'

'We're going to need another round of cocktails for this,' Verity whistles and disappears into the kitchen, clearly aware of what is about to be said. Does everyone know what's going on except me?

'Ned,' Yvie splutters. And then it comes out. The whole story. The night she'd gone out with my husband, then been devastated when he'd had sex with her friend. The story ends with a woeful sigh. 'And I gave my credit card to Kay on the night of Tom's wedding so she could stay at the hotel.'

'So it was Kay who slept with Ned?' I gasp, shocked.

Yvie immediately shakes her head. 'I really don't think so. I honestly don't believe she did because she'd have told me, I'm sure of it. But since none of your cards were there that night, and mine definitely was, it must have paid for his room. I don't understand any of this, but I'll need to speak to her to find out more. I'm just so sorry that it's happened to you. Don't hate me for telling you all this. Please don't hate me,' she begs.

I fly out of my chair and throw myself on top of her, wrapping my arms around her. 'Of course I don't hate you, you daft bint. I bloody hate him for being an arrogant snake. Jesus, I can't believe I never saw who he was. I honestly can't believe it.'

Actually, that isn't true. I know why I saw none of it. In the week since Tom's wedding, the seven days I've spent here alone, I've done the soul searching that I should have done a year and a half ago when Tom Butler broke my heart. The truth is, I didn't look. I didn't care to see who Ned was, because I'd used him to tape over the pain of losing the man I thought I'd spend my life with and I'd used him to convince myself that I was fine when I really wasn't. Habit of a lifetime.

'What I don't understand is why you didn't say anything about how he'd treated you and Kay? Why didn't you tell me about it?' I ask.

Yvie shrugs and I can see she is mortified.

'In case I found out.' Again, it takes me a minute for my brain to catch up and realise that has come from Verity, who's come back into the room carrying another tray of neon pink filled glasses.

'But why... why would that be a problem?'

Verity sighs. 'She suspected I was in love with him. And she was right.'

Holy. Fuck. The fact that deep down I'd known it all along only makes it worse to hear it being said out loud. Still, I wanted to understand more.

'But I asked you...'

'And I lied,' Verity says.

'Because...?' I probe.

She puts the tray down on the table and distributes the drinks, making me wait for an explanation. That's Verity. Always plays to the beat of her own drum.

'Because I was so angry at you for taking him in the first place.'

For the second time this afternoon, one of my sisters goes on to tell me things about my husband that I didn't know. How she felt about him. The flirting. The fury at my relationship with him. Then – and this takes the wind right out of my sails – setting up a false profile on a dating app to see if he was playing around.

The worst bit? The moment in Verity's recording of their conversation at the wedding, when he admits that he'd played her from the start.

Compared to that, the news of his secret Your Next Date habit doesn't even make a dent.

'I'm sorry,' Verity says, when she's told me it all. 'I really am. All I can say is that I was in a weird place. I think I've been there for a long time.'

For the first time, the room falls silent and I realise that all my sisters are staring at me, waiting for me to speak.

'You all knew this?'

Marina nods her head. 'Not at the start. It all came out in Vegas. The night you got married. When Yvie had her panic attack.'

'You had a panic attack?' I gasp. 'When did they start again?'

'Maybe a year ago now.' It's no consolation that she seems to regret not telling me.

'Bloody hell, Yvie, I'm so sorry. I had no idea. I would have been there for... Hang on, is that why you left my birthday party?'

Yvie nods and I feel like the worst sister that ever lived. I'll make it up to her. I will.

'Is there anything else I should know?' I blurt. 'Marina, is my husband your secret lover on the side or something?'

I know I'm being facetious and ludicrous, but I can't help it.

'No, but she has been picking up strangers for sex,' Verity says casually.

I drop the glass. Neon pink gunk and pineapple is spreading all over my floor and I don't care. I listen. Dumb-founded. Where have I been? Where have we all been? We're family – how could we have lost each other like this?

Yvie, my smiley, caring sister was cracking under the pressure of taking care of everyone but herself.

Verity, aloof and closed, was fighting her own battle, tormented by unhappiness but determined not to let anyone in.

Marina, so in control of the lives of everyone she loves, had an area of her own life that was so out of control.

And me? Head in the sand. Working. Focusing on stuff that didn't really matter so that I didn't need to deal with the pain of what did.

And that's when I see it. I see the person I called on when I needed it most. I see the cause of it all, the reason that we've become the women that we are.

'Watch me fly, Dad.'

We all flew in different directions, all trying to survive from the moment he left us.

The moment he *chose* to leave us.

Will Danton, our father, had been divorced from our

mother for fifteen days when he swallowed a bottle of pills on Boxing Day, 1999, after a long, undiagnosed and untreated battle with depression.

Marina was fourteen. Verity was thirteen. I was twelve and Yvie was ten. And none of us knew that something so awful was blighting his life. Back then, people didn't talk about mental health, let along educate teenagers on the signs and symptoms. Even our mum hadn't realised that he desperately needed medical help, or I really believe she'd have tried. Our mum is many things – she's quirky, and self-centred and she lives life on her own (and Oprah's) terms, but she wouldn't stand by and let someone suffer if she thought they could be helped. She'd have forced him to get treatment, would have supported his recovery, but she simply didn't comprehend the extent of it. For a while afterwards, all of us, except Yvie, blamed Mum at some point or another. The truth was, it wasn't her fault.

We'd learned later from his workmates that Dad had refused to see a doctor even when he knew that he was unwell. He'd eventually been fired from his job on Christmas Eve. He'd spent Christmas Day in the one local bar that was open throughout the festivities. He'd left very drunk at closing time. And then he'd gone home and at some point in the next few hours, he'd taken his own life.

He'd left four girls, who'd built walls that dated back to that very moment in time, who'd formed the personalities they needed to survive the trauma of that kind of loss. Yvie's need to take care of people, especially those she loves. Marina's desire to control every little detail in case something goes wrong, especially at Christmas, the toughest time of all for us. Verity's fearsome ability to shut down and close off when she feels vulnerable. And my determination to be independent and take care of myself.

I understand now that we all became extreme versions of those teenage girls, our personalities defined in that moment of loss, and we've all been fighting our own battles ever since.

Maybe it isn't too late to fight them together.

Last night, I sent them all a message on our group chat, telling them what I'd known for a week, since my husband came home dishevelled, unshaven and shifty the night after Tom's wedding and told me he'd slept with someone else after the reception. Someone you know, he'd sneered, before grabbing a change of clothes, taking his credit cards back out of my handbag and walking out the door. I'd taken a few days to sort it out in my head, to give him time to come back and pack up most of his stuff, grateful beyond measure that we hadn't had time to go to the Vegas courthouse to make the marriage legally binding. I took off my wedding ring, counted my blessings, and then I texted the only three people in the world that I wanted to see.

'My marriage is over,' I said in the message on the group chat. 'Can you come over tomorrow?'

My wedding band and my husband are no longer around, but my sisters are here.

And now they are waiting for some reaction from me, to the things I've learned today, to the fact that they've shared their faults, their weaknesses, their mistakes and their secrets. It's time for me to do the same.

'I love you all, do you know that? The truth is, I've been a pretty crap sister over the last year. I've not been paying attention to what was going on with any of you. I'm so sorry and I don't have any excuses other than I was so consumed with trying to get through losing Tom. Just like I honestly think we've all been trying to deal with losing Dad since it happened. It seemed easier to slip into denial about how much Tom had hurt me, and just try to patch over the pain with Ned and work and nothing much else. I should have been there for you all too. The only consolation is that maybe it needed to happen this way though, because if the last year has taught all of us anything, it's that we will always stick together, just like Marina said back then. I'm so grateful I've got you three beside me. I'm just sorry it took the arrival of Ned Merton in our lives to get us to this point, but I'm so happy we're here.'

It's Yvie's turn to pounce now and she hugs me so tightly she nearly collapses my lung. Marina, calm, controlled, boss sister, follows suit and piles on top of us. Even Verity surrenders, adding to the pile up but doing it slowly so she won't crease her shirt or do herself an injury.

I've never felt so much love. Or gratitude.

'Oh, and for the record, I never believed that any of you would ever sleep with my husband. My *ex-husband*.' I add. 'But if any of you take a notion to, I believe he's newly single and can be contacted on Your Next Date.'

We're still laughing when Verity climbs up and goes to make another round of cocktails.

EPILOGUE

SIX WEEKS LATER – THE FIFTH ANNIVERSARY PARTY OF THE
KEMP IBIZA

The sun is falling in the sky as a gang of us sit on the beach,
the sound of retro nineties hits coming from the speakers in
the bar a few feet behind us. So far, we've had Take That, the
Spice Girls and Robbie Williams. It's like reliving our teenage
years.

'I still can't believe that you thought I'd spent the night
with that tosser, Ned Merton, even for a minute,' Kay says to
the group. 'I mean, fool me once and all that... No offence,
Zoe,' she adds quickly.

'None taken,' I laugh. The credit card payment is still a
mystery because we all know now who was with Kay that
night and it wasn't Ned.

Yvie nudges her best friend playfully, her face bright with
mischief. She is looking so much better already. Having
Marina and the kids at the flat for a couple of weeks until
they found their own place was a very crowded but very
genuine boost for her, especially as Marina immediately
organised a nutrition plan and cooked her healthy meals for
breakfast, packed lunch and dinner. On top of that, she's

already started counselling and she is open to taking meds if she needs them to get the anxiety under control. Carlo is helping and has taken up where Marina left off. When I told him what was going on – she'd insisted it wasn't to be a secret – he'd shown up at her flat with a low-fat, delicious meal from his father's restaurant. Every day for a month now.

Yvie answers for us. 'We didn't really. We knew it had to be a mistake. I mean, you clearly had a much better option.' Yvie nods in the direction of Dr Seth McGonigle, standing over with Tom, Roger, Carlo, Nigel and the rest of the guys at the firepit in the sands. Turns out that early in the morning after Tom's wedding, Kay called him from her suite at the Kemp and asked him to meet her at the hotel for breakfast. It had been bold. Reckless. But neither of them are having any regrets about it. Chester is away for a rare weekend with his dad, so Kay and Seth decided to take up Yvie's invitation to join us here. Seth still makes Yvie talk nonsense, but now that she's got to know him out of work as Kay's boyfriend, she's come to realise that he's just one of those guys who can be perfectly friendly and happy on the inside, but his brain forgets to inform the outside.

'Can't believe you got there first,' Marina whistles, referring to Seth, but we all know she is kidding. She's sworn off men until she's sorted herself out. After two weeks at Yvie's, she found a gorgeous flat for her and the kids. Annabelle is back in the same school as Oscar and their new home is only five minutes away, so they can walk there and back and it's easy for them to get to all their extra activities. If they feel like going, that is. Marina doesn't insist. She's just enjoying the time they have together, especially now that there's less of it, since she's started working as Roger's executive assistant. He says he's fairly terrified of her, but his life has never been more organised. Graham, on the other hand, has cut down his hours to spend more time with the kids and he's met a life coach called Debbie who's determined to address his work/life balance. Marina, Annabelle and Oscar are hoping she'll succeed.

'Don't listen to her, Kay. She wouldn't stand a chance with you around,' Verity tells her with a cheeky wink, as she stretches on her towel, loving the fact that she's teasing Marina. She is so tanned – no surprise given that she's already been here for a fortnight. She had shocked us all when she announced she was taking a year out to teach English over here, and promptly packed in her job and moved a week later, but so far it definitely looks like it's working for her.

'Verity, leave your sister alone and stop teasing her.' That comes from our mother, who has broken off from staring at the third finger on her left hand for as long as it takes to chide Verity. Last night, Nigel slipped down on to one very bendy knee and proposed to her. Now she is sitting, taking in the chat, the atmosphere and the ocean breeze, while staring at her stunning solitaire engagement ring. We're happy for her, but there's no doubt that, even now, we all feel a tiny twinge of wishful thinking that things could have been different. Every one of us would give anything for Dad to be here right now too. Over the last few weeks we've talked endlessly about how much we miss him, how devastating it was that he couldn't get the help he needed. Our dad loved us. There's no world in which he'd have left us if he didn't feel in his mind right there and then that it was his only option. I think maybe now that we are all finally talking things through and dealing with our own feelings and rela-tionships with each other, we have a better understanding of his issues and the place he was in. He'll always be the little piece that's chipped off our hearts. We just need to learn to help each other deal with the moments when that missing chip hurts the most.

'Roger's coming over,' Mum points out, as he crosses the sands towards us. 'Has he told you any more yet?'

'Not since this morning's text,' I reply.

The mystery had rumbled on in the background since that day we'd all congregated at my flat, drinking those awful pink cocktails and eating Jean's surprisingly delicious lasagne. Roger had called later that afternoon to say that there had been a mistake and Yvie's card had been used for two rooms. He didn't quite understand it, but he was going to get to the bottom of it and get back to me. He'd texted me earlier today to say he'd found out the answers. Not that they mattered. Ned Merton was long gone – I'd had no contact with him since that day – and I no longer cared who he'd spent that night, or any night since, with. This morning, Roger had texted to say he had more news. I was intrigued to hear it, but at the same time, I didn't really care. Nothing would make a difference to the outcome.

'Ladies!' Roger greets us, as he reaches us. 'Can I borrow Zoe for a moment?'

'Make it fast because you've got a 5 p.m. meeting in the lounge,' Marina tells him, making him wince and us laugh.

I clamber up, brush the sands off my white skirt and walk with him.

'So... this is awkward,' he says, and I notice that he seems uncomfortable. Not something I've ever seen before. He's usually so confident and sure of himself.

'What's happened?'

'Security have checked all the CCTV and talked to the

staff again. We missed it the first time because they weren't looking for it, but they've discovered that it was Felice.'

I don't understand what he's saying. 'What was?'

'In the room with your husband on the night of Tom's wedding. It's why she left me. Actually, she left because we'd been over for a long time before then, but I guess that must have been the final straw.' It was only a fortnight ago that he'd told Tom and I that Felice had gone and they'd ended their marriage. He hadn't gone into detail, but I'd definitely got the impression it was a relief and there was zero chance of them getting back together.

The shock made my jaw drop for a few speechless seconds, before I checked to see if I'd understood that correctly, 'Felice spent the night with Ned?'

He nods. 'We've pieced together that she was at the hotel reception when Yvie booked the room in Kay's name and explained that she'd given Kay her credit card. The next morning, Felice got a junior in the finance department to charge Ned's room to that card too.'

'Because...?'

Roger sighs wearily, shrugging. For a man who's just discovered his soon-to-be ex-wife has been unfaithful, he doesn't seem too troubled.

'Because she wanted to cover their tracks. If she'd comped the room, asked someone to make it a freebie, she knows I'd have found out about it. She was aware I wanted out and she didn't want to give me any ammunition by getting caught with someone else. Charging it to Yvie's card was an opportune solution that bought her some time. I did more digging today. She's rented a flat in Glasgow. I can't think of any reason she'd have to stay there unless she was seeing someone.'

I'm stunned. 'You think she's with Ned?'

'I do.'

'Wow.'

That strikes me speechless for a second, while so many pieces of a jigsaw slide into place. Ned has always resented Roger. He loves a trophy. And a challenge. Felice would certainly be that. When the shock wears off, I check for stings of pain and realise there are absolutely none. I genuinely don't care.

'It's bizarre. They have absolutely nothing in common.'

'I'm not sure that's true,' he says softly, his expression indecipherable.

'What do you mean?'

'Well, didn't you say that Ned was always jealous of our friendship? Felice was exactly the same. She was convinced I had feelings for you.'

He shrugs apologetically as he says that, and I pause again to take it all in.

'Are you okay?' Roger asks me, and I can hear the concern. 'What are you thinking?'

'I think they deserve each other.'

Roger Kemp, my client, my friend, the man who makes me laugh, challenges me, respects my professional judgement, helps me and the company I work for thrive and – most of all – embraces my dysfunctional family, matches my gaze and smiles, then leans down so that his lips are just inches from mine. Once I get over the surprise, I realise that I like it. A lot.

'Can I ask you something?' he says.

'Anything.'

'Do you think we do too?'

I smile, my heart thuds a little faster, and as I go up on my tiptoes to kiss him, I realise that I know the answer to that.

'Maybe we do.'

I know now what I should have seen before now. Ned was right to have concerns about Roger because there's always been something more than just a professional relationship between us. And I want to find out exactly how much more is there.

Last time, a leap of faith resulted in a one month marriage that's already over. But even so, right here and now, with Roger's lips touching mine, I realise that I want to take another leap.

Dad, hey it's Zoe. I'm about to fly again.

And this time, I don't have a single worry about falling.

ACKNOWLEDGEMENT

Thank you, thank you to my brilliant editor and publisher Caroline Ridding, for her unfailing support, inspiration and encouragement. I never forget how lucky I am to be working with you.

And to Amanda Ridout and Nia Beynon, who – with Caroline – have welcomed me into the Boldwood fold. I'm so excited to see where this next adventure takes us.

To Jade Craddock and Rose Fox, much gratitude for nudging my novels into shape.

To my pals, who supply endless chat, laughs and biscuits, I owe you all cocktails. And caramel wafers.

And to every person who picks up my books, a million thanks for reading. I heart you.

Love,

Shari x

MORE FROM SHARI LOW

We hope you enjoyed reading *My One Month Marriage*. If you did, please leave a review.

If you'd like to gift a copy, this book is also available as a ebook, digital audio download and audiobook CD.

Sign up to Shari Low's mailing list for news, competitions and updates on future books.

http://bit.ly/ShariLowNewsletter

ABOUT THE AUTHOR

Shari Low is the #1 bestselling author of over 20 novels, including *One Day In Winter* and *With Or Without You,* and a collection of parenthood memories called *Because Mummy Said So*. She lives near Glasgow.

Visit Shari's website: www.sharilow.com

Follow Shari on social media:

facebook.com/sharilowbooks

twitter.com/sharilow

instagram.com/sharilowbooks

bookbub.com/authors/shari-low

ABOUT BOLDWOOD BOOKS

Boldwood Books is a fiction publishing company seeking out the best stories from around the world.

Find out more at www.boldwoodbooks.com

Sign up to the Book and Tonic newsletter for news, offers and competitions from Boldwood Books!

http://www.bit.ly/bookandtonic

We'd love to hear from you, follow us on social media:

facebook.com/BookandTonic

twitter.com/BoldwoodBooks

instagram.com/BookandTonic

Made in the USA
Columbia, SC
12 June 2020